"You don't think I'm too tall?" Angela asked.

"With your body fitting mine perfectly like this? I don't think so, baby. You're perfect." Then he lifted her chin and studied her face. How could she ever doubt that she was exquisite? The look in her eyes made his chest constrict. Whoever told her that her height was a problem was a fool. He pressed her closer.

Angela sucked her breath at his arousal. They did fit perfectly, right to the V between her legs, she thought in amazement. "You're the perfect one," she whispered as her hands lifted to his face. Her fingers ran over the planes of his face, his ears and then they came to rest on his lips. She caressed them gently, appreciating his beauty through her fingers.

"I want you so very much, Angela, I ache." Jerry whispered and licked her finger.

Angela gasped at the heat from his mouth. The nerves tingled where his wet tongue had grazed. Then his lips closed on hers.

An imprint Genesis Press Publishing

Genesis Press, Inc.
315 Third Avenue North
Columbus, MS 39701

Copyright© 2003 by Bella McFarland
One Day At A Time

ISBN: 1-58571-099-7
Manufactured in the United States of America

First Edition

Visit us at www.genesis-press.com
or call at 1-888-Indigo-1

One Day At A Time

By
Bella McFarland

Genesis Press, Inc.

Chapter 1

"Why Montana, Angela? Why not go on a Caribbean cruise or visit an island resort?" Nikki asked as she tilted her head to stare at Angela McGee's pensive face.

Angela shrugged. Nikki Taylor was her childhood friend and legal advisor but at times she was so damn nosey. Angela wasn't about to disclose her reasons for going to Montana, not to Nikki anyway. "Hmm-mm, I want to go to a place that's different, a place where I can breathe fresh air and just relax. I doubt that I can do that on a cruise or at a resort. Such places usually have meddlesome people and the last thing I want to do is socialize." Her smile disappeared when her glance shifted to her five-year-old nephew, Reggie.

Reggie was lying on a hospital bed, stiff and silent, his mind locked in some place where no one could reach him. Even with the best experts at his disposal, Reggie had not awakened from the coma caused by the accident that had killed his father and mother— Angela's sister, Savannah. "Oh, Nikki, when I look at him I wish I didn't have to go."

"Don't start on that, Angela. You need a break or you'll make yourself sick," Nikki protested.

"What if he wakes up while I'm gone? What if he gets worse? It has been hard enough for me to see him lying there so still when he was once full of life. But now I have this nightmare that something might happen while I'm gone."

"You've been by his side every day for the last six months, Angela. You've become a recluse, you don't date any more; you even stopped writing music, except for those you compose for him."

Angela shrugged indifferently. She once aspired to become a

professional singer, but circumstances forced her to forget that dream. Well, not exactly circumstances, just her parents and her innate will to please them. One unemployed artist in the family was enough, her parents had said when Savannah had insisted on being a professional painter. And like the dutiful daughter that Angela was, she had pushed aside her personal dream and gone into nursing.

"Things never go as we plan, Nikki. Sav didn't foresee the accident that killed her and Bernard or the traumatic effect it would have on her only child. But it happened. And in her will, she entrusted me with the care of Reggie. Yet here I am leaving him with strangers." Angela's voice shook as she finished the last sentence. She blinked rapidly to stop the sudden rush of tears. It had been a year but she still couldn't deal with her sister's death. Reggie's coma made it hard to let go. Every time Angela saw how still and unreachable her nephew was, she was reminded of those last moments when she'd held her sister in her arms. Angela was a registered nurse but she'd been helpless to save her sister. And now, she couldn't help her nephew either.

But her helplessness was easily transformed to anger at the thought of the person responsible for the entire tragedy getting off lightly and living his life to the fullest just because he was rich and famous. Baseball legend Jerry Tyrell Taylor a.k.a. JT, the marble man, hadn't cared enough to check on the victims of his wife's carelessness—a woman whose state of mind had been entirely his fault.

Even now, a year after the incident, Angela could recall the headline...L. A. ANGELS' PITCHER, JERRY TAYLOR, EXONERATED OF WIFE'S DEATH.

How could he be blameless when bystanders had said otherwise? According to the papers, an eyewitness had seen Carmen Taylor trying to get away from her husband, Jerry, before she drove her Porsche into the highway. Another witness claimed that Carmen had been meeting another man at the time and that Jerry had caught them together. Whatever the outcome of the police investigation, Jerry Taylor bore some responsibility for his wife's untimely death. Wasn't he seen running after her, jumping into her car, and trying to wrestle the wheel from her hands? Hadn't she been busy shouting at him instead of watching where she was going? The justice system may have exonerated him but Angela hadn't. In her book, Jerry Taylor killed her sister, Sav. The fact that he had never bothered to apologize to her family or visited Reggie only made him more guilty in her eyes. And he should be made to pay.

"Hey!"

Angela blinked and turned apologetically toward Nikki. "Sorry."

"Do you know you do that a lot?" Nikki asked.

"Do what?" Angela asked defensively.

"Space out. One minute you are here and the next gone. And the expression on your face is usually very peculiar—a mixture of anger, pain, and regret. There was nothing you could have done for Sav, Angela. And, Reggie...well...he'll come back to us when he's ready. None of this is your fault, you know."

"Don't analyze me, girl. Of course I know it isn't my fault. I just regret not spending enough time with Sav while she was alive," Angela finished wistfully.

"With the demands of those art exhibitions, you're lucky to have seen her at all. But at least you often babysat Reggie while she was gone."

Angela knew that if it weren't for the fact that she ran her Website design business from home and that she had flexible hours at the private hospital where she worked part-time, she would never have been there for her only sister or nephew. "She had so much talent, Nikki. She didn't deserve to die that young."

Nikki nodded. "Wasn't it spooky the way that museum in San Francisco called and offered to exhibit her work? Now her paintings are the in thing for most African American art collectors."

"And worth every dollar they pay." The cheapest of Sav's paintings had been sold for five hundred dollars. She hadn't been gone six months when everyone was talking about owning an original Hanna Vas—Sav signed her name backward on every painting she did. She even used the pseudonym when she exhibited her work. "I just hate how the art world makes money off dead artists, Nikki. I'd rather

One Day at a Time

have her alive and selling her work for pittance than renowned and dead," Angela murmured.

"So would I." Nikki got up and glanced down at Angela. "Now, unless you intend to miss your flight, we better get moving."

Angela nodded then glanced briefly at Reggie. "Do you think they'll take good care of him?"

"Yes, they will, Angela. Look at this place." Nikki spread her arms for emphasis. Reggie had a room in a private hospital and nothing was spared for his comfort. The hospital was only a few blocks from Charles Maitland's mansion—his paternal grandfather. The millionaire car-dealer had even donated funds towards the hospital's new wing so that his grandson would be given the best treatment. "Does this look like a typical hospital room to you? The room is done with Power Ranger paraphernalia—Reggie's favorite TV-series. He's under watch by private nurses—paid for by Maitland. And he has state-of-the-art instruments monitoring his vitals twenty-four-seven. Let's not forget Marjorie Maitland, his larger than life grandmother. She is in here every other day, reading to him. In fact, I'd bet he's had more stories read to him than any five-year-old child under the sun. Everything around here indicates he is cared for. What more proof do you need, huh?"

Nikki was right. Reggie had his grandmother watching over him equally as much as she. "Under Marjorie Maitland's watchful eyes, the nurses wouldn't dare be anything but efficient. If Marjorie weren't here, I would never dream of leaving," Angela said with a satisfied nod.

Nikki smiled. "She's hard to argue with."

"Yeah, she took one look at me a few weeks ago and told me I had to take a vacation. When I tried to protest, she told me she didn't want me falling sick or being sloppy around her only grandson because I'm overworked. The next thing I knew, Maitland was offering me an expensive Caribbean cruise ticket?"

"He did? Why didn't you take his offer?" Nikki asked in exasperation.

Angela smiled at her friend's tone. "Because I don't want to go on a cruise, nosey. Besides, I could pay for my ticket if I wanted one." Angela looked at her watch and got up. "I better tell Reggie bye."

She walked to her nephew's side and touched his hand. "Hey, baby, Aunty Angela here. How are you doing today? I hope much better. You know what? I went for a run in the park this morning and you wouldn't believe what I saw..." Angela spent the next ten minutes sharing her day with Reggie, talking about things she saw and did. By the time she was done, she was tearful again. Taking a deep breath, she stooped low and kissed his brow. "I'll read you a story tomorrow and sing some of your favorite songs." She kissed him and quickly left the room, fighting back the tears. Stopping by the nurses' station, she reminded them once again to play him the tape she had brought. "I'll be sending you one tape a week until I get back, just like we'd discussed."

When the nurse nodded, Angela gestured to Nikki that it was time to leave. Briskly, they walked out of the building.

Nikki was opening the door to her red BMW when she asked Angela, "So, what are in the tapes you'll be sending while on vacation?"

"Stories from books...things I see...songs that used to make him laugh," Angela said defensively.

"Angela!" Nikki protested.

"I don't want him to feel abandoned, Nikki. He's lost so much. And since he can hear when we talk to him, I want to make sure he doesn't think he has lost me, too."

"Oh," Nikki mouthed.

"Yes, 'oh' is the right response, counselor. Do you know that for such a brilliant lawyer, you're so naive about some things?"

"That's why I have you—to remind me to switch off the analytical part of the brain and turn on the emotional center. So, what is the real reason why you refused Maitland's offer? Wouldn't you rather lie on the deck, ignore the other passengers, and just relax? Or better yet, meet some gorgeous hunk to make your vacation interesting?"

Angela's far away look was Nikki's only answer. She hated

One Day at a Time

lying to her best friend but this was one time she would keep her plans to herself. Truth was that Jerry Taylor was the reason Angela was venturing into Montana. If Nikki knew that she had made a deal with the law firm of McQueen, Fischer, and Taylor to be Jerry Taylor's assistant for a month, this best friend would drag her to the nearest cruise ship and captain the boat herself if need be. "Big sky country won hands down."

"But why would you want to go to some God-forsaken, uncivilized farm in Montana and hibernate for weeks?" Nikki asked in amazement.

Angela laughed. According to Nikki, if a place didn't have sky scrapers, it was uncivilized. "I always wanted to see how ranchers lived. Besides, I haven't seen Melissa Taylor for a while. She's convinced me that I'll enjoy visiting Montana." The lie rolled smoothly from her lips but guilt quickly followed. She was shamelessly using Jerry Taylor's sister's name as a cover up. She'd made the acquaintance of the gregarious Melissa Taylor during her last interview with the lawyers, Aaron Taylor and Cyrus McQueen. She just couldn't dare reveal to Nikki her reasons for going to Montana. Nikki might think she'd lost her mind.

"I hope you get some rest. You need someone to pamper you for a while."

"I hear there are some fine brothers out there in Montana. I might even meet that hunk you mentioned," Angela interjected playfully.

"You've got to be kidding! Montana is vast, hot, dusty, filled with stinking cows, and mean horses. The men there need women to pamper them. Don't they pay women to marry men and live out there?"

"Wrong century," Angela said with a laugh.

"Okay! If some tobacco chewing, mucous-spitting, leatherskinned cowboy pampers you, I'll take leave of absence from my practice and join you."

"Deal," Angela said with a twinkle in her eyes.

"You wish." Nikki shook her head in defeat. "So, where did you meet this Melissa? And how come I've never heard of her?"

"She and I were in college together. If you must know, we roomed together for a couple of semesters." *The lies we weave, may the good Lord forgive her.* She knew nothing about Melissa except that she was Jerry Taylor's younger sister. "And you don't know everything about me, Nikki Hudson."

"Puh-lease," Nikki said as she rolled her eyes.

"Get off my business and drive me to the airport, midget."

"Don't push it, giant," Nikki retorted.

Angela grinned. She would miss Nikki and her sassiness. Nikki and Sav were the only ones who ever got away with calling her a giant. Angela was tall. At six feet, she was an oddity among her friends and relatives. As a child, she'd always felt self-conscious about her height. And although she didn't mind being teased by people who loved her, it hadn't always been amusing to be the tallest girl on the block and the butt of everyone's jokes. Even Sav had been much shorter than she, despite being her twin. In her class, Angela had been taller than most of the boys and they had hated it. They had teased her endlessly and shamelessly. But she'd had her sister and Nikki as her champions. They would gang up on anyone stupid enough to call her names. Still, their support didn't stop Angela from being embarrassed and hurt. Not only had she been gangly, she had been reed thin and had despaired of ever developing curves like Nikki or Sav. Then to add insult to injury, she'd developed breasts earlier than most girls her age. The combination of breasts and a tall, skinny body hadn't been attractive. Lord, Angela lost count of the number of times she'd longed to blend into the background and be left alone. It never happened. The comments were hurled at her and they had hurt. She was still a bit wary of people who mentioned her height although now she had curves to go with her it, and combined with her smooth, deep chocolate skin, her heart-shaped face, slanted eyes, and sensuous lips, she was unforgettably beautiful. And although her height remained a point of contention with some men, over the years, she had grown more and more tired of their insecurities and more and more comfortable with herself.

One Day at a Time

Nikki's car followed the hospital's curving driveway, past manicured lawns, and water fountains to the white gate separating it from the rest of San Diego. Soon, they were on the highway heading for the airport.

"So what are you going to do with your clients while you're gone?" Nikki asked.

"Ever heard of a laptop and a cell phone?"

"Ha! Oh, you mean you could access the Internet, eh, between milking the cows and shoveling horse manure?"

"You're so funny," Angela retorted. "But if it will ease your mind, I have everything set. I've finished the contracts that were due this month and have the next month to myself—no deadline or last minute conferences. Khalid can take care of things while I'm gone. If not, he can reach me on my cell phone. But, I'm hoping he won't need to." Between shifts at the hospital, Angela had taken evening classes in graphic design, HTML, Dream Weaver, and Flash. But when she'd playfully designed a website for Nikki for her birthday, Nikki had shown it to her partners at her law firm and the next thing Angela knew, the firm was paying her hundreds of dollars to design for them a one of a kind Website. Nikki's law firm was her first paying client, but the word spread fast and others soon followed. She designed one site for her hospital, then her parents' high school, and before she knew what hit her, her e-mail was jammed with requests for her distinctive websites with their eye-catching graphics. After six months of juggling increasing clientele and her nursing duties, she'd decided to reduce her work load by reducing the number of hours she worked at the hospital.

For the last three years, Angela had developed a routine that made it possible to balance her two jobs. She even had a part-time employee, Khalid Williams, who maintained the sites for her. Because of her flexible hours, she had been able to baby sit Reggie when her sister and Bernard were out of town. And after the accident, when Reggie's condition didn't improve, Angela had told Maitland that she wanted to help. No one was going to do a better job at nursing Reggie than his favorite aunt, she had insisted, and Maitland had agreed.

"Angela! You're spacing out on me again. Did you finish the Sea World contract, too?"

"The check should be in the mail, counselor."

"What about the one for that law firm—McQueen, Fischer and Taylor?"

"Who lit a match under your pants, midget?" Angela asked defensively. Nikki didn't need to know about the law firm and its connection to her sudden interest in Montana. For months, she had been researching Jerry Taylor. While going through old newspaper articles and the Internet, she had learned that Jerry Taylor originally came from Montana and that he had a brother and an uncle who owned a law firm in the San Diego area. After more research on lawyers with the name of Taylor, Angela had found Aaron Taylor listed in the bay area. After contacting a high school friend, Janine Forster, who by luck worked there, she was able to make the first contact. Creating a website was the perfect pretense for meeting Aaron Taylor, whose family resemblance was obvious. She had finally found Jerry's brother. She later learned that the famous Cyrus McQueen was their uncle.

Then one day, while visiting their offices, Angela happened to hear that they were looking for an assistant for a recluse client who lived on a ranch in Montana. Her interest had been aroused. But when Janine told her that the client was actually Jerry Taylor and that it was next to impossible to find the kind of assistant he wanted, Angela knew that she'd hit the jackpot. However, she didn't openly offer her services. She casually mentioned to Janine that she was thinking of taking a vacation for a couple of weeks but hadn't decided on where to go.

The next time Angela saw Janine, the woman had asked her if she'd be interested in vacationing on a ranch. Angela had tentatively indicated she might be persuaded but on the inside, she was elated. At last she was going to get the opportunity to investigate and confront the man who'd put her nephew in a coma and killed her only sister.

Aaron Taylor and Cyrus McQueen took over from Janine.

One Day at a Time

Angela made them work hard at convincing her to vacation in Montana while assisting Jerry with his work. They kept saying he needed someone with her computer skills and how they would appreciate it if she could help them out. Of course, they never openly said that it was Jerry who needed an assistant. They often referred to him as their client. But Angela had known it was Jerry. Janine had told her so. Secondly, Aaron's wife, Sheryl, and his sister, Melissa, had attended her last interview, obviously to check her out before sending her to their brother. And despite her personal feelings toward Jerry Taylor, she'd been impressed by his family's affection and concerns.

In the end, Angela had completed the Website for the law firm and asked for a month to finish her other obligations, before taking them up on their offer. And here she was leaving sooner than she had expected to. Aaron Taylor had called and asked her to go a week early. She neither knew what the big hurry was nor did she care. She had her own agenda and it didn't include showing an interest in Jerry Taylor's affairs.

"Could you tell my parents that I'll get in touch as soon as I've settled in?" Her parents were presently at a teachers' conference and weren't due for another week.

"I'm sure they'll understand, Angela. Besides, your mom has been pushing you to take a break for the last couple of months." Nikki pulled up at the Delta terminal, found a parking space, and walked her friend into the building.

"Yeah, but I was waiting until the last minute before telling them where I was going. Like you, they wouldn't have understood. Mom would have badgered me nonstop about my choice." Nikki laughed knowingly at her comment. Angela ignored her. After checking in her recorder and suitcase, she turned to her friend. "I'm going to miss you, girl."

"Same here. Call me," Nikki commanded as they hugged.

"Yes, ma'am." Angela winked at her before moving toward the metal detector and the security guards. Less than an hour later, she was in the air heading to Helena and Jerry Taylor.

Chapter 2

Jerry Taylor leaned back on his seat as a frown crossed his handsome, brown face. Blunt-tipped fingers moved to his temple to soothe his throbbing head. He switched the telephone to his right ear and murmured something into it. His body shifted as he bit his upper lip in concentration. Anyone who knew him would know that he was restless. Jerry was an outdoor person. He wasn't happy unless he was working alongside his farm hands. The sounds flowing through the window and into his den weren't helping either.

A horse neighed from a corral and the call was answered by another horse a few yards away. A meadowlark made flutelike, gurgling notes as it took off from its nest on the ground. Those nature calls beckoned to him but he knew he couldn't hurry his caller, not Doctor Raul Rojo. The Chilean doctor had saved his sight by performing a daring eye operation and for that, Jerry would be forever grateful. He would control his impatience until the good doctor finished his explanation.

"Keeping my appointment is not the issue, Raul. What would the Californian doctors tell me that can't wait until you get here?" Jerry asked in exasperation.

"Jerry, we need to make sure everything is okay—that your eyes are healing well and that you are not pushing them too fast and too soon. Besides, you need a new prescription for those headaches, *mi amigo*," Raul answered from across the sea, patience in his voice.

In addition to being a genius with lasers, Raul must have telepathic abilities, Jerry thought with a grimace. The headaches hadn't been this bad for a long time. "You know I hate popping pain killers. No more medication, Raul. I can handle it. The sunglasses you recommended are permanently perched on my nose—which, as you can imagine, makes me look ridiculous when I'm indoors. But if I go back to seeing blurry images then I'll call you." Jerry chuckled before adding, "And you know what that would mean?"

"No, I don't believe I do," Raul answered.

"Your ninety percent success rate will be reduced a notch." His comment elicited a chuckle from the Chilean eye specialist. "You're the best in the field, Raul. The doctors here couldn't treat me before, and I don't want them messing with my eyes now. I'll take my chances and await your arrival."

"You're a very stubborn man, Jerry."

"And you are a brilliant doctor, my friend. I'll call you if there are any changes"—there was a pause—"You know something, Raul? You could always bill me for every second I keep you on the phone." An amused chuckle greeted Jerry's comment. He smiled.

"Don't push your luck, *mi amigo*. However, I'll let it pass because you're giving my wife a wonderful gift by paying for our trip. Call me if you need anything, okay?"

"Of course," Jerry replied.

"I have to go. *Muchas gracias,* Jerry."

"That's my call, my friend. See you in a couple of weeks."

Jerry smiled as he hung up the phone. He stretched his lean torso while his eyes shifted around the room. At last, he sighted a pile of files haphazardly placed on one of his desks. They contained all his records—management, insurance, financial, income, and expense records. Beside the files was a computer. He was going to lose some of the records if he didn't have those files computerized, he thought distractedly. Unfortunately, he couldn't afford to turn on the damn machine because of his eyes. At the rate at which his sight was improving, he couldn't dare expose them to the glare from a computer screen.

The smile that had transformed Jerry's face disappeared as memories flooded his mind. Every thought he had always ended with his eyes and why he had to be careful with them.

A year ago, he had lost his sight in the accident that took the lives of his wife, Carmen, and their unborn child and the best doctors in the U.S. gave up on him ever seeing again. One eye specialist after another had prodded him and theorized about his lack of sight until Jerry had been close to losing his sanity. Being a guinea pig wasn't fun and he'd promised to never be subjected to that kind of clinical torture again. So, instead of giving in to his condition, finding a guide dog, and becoming a recluse—a miserable recluse at that—he'd sold his house in California, borrowed a few farm workers from South Creek—his grandfather's ranch—and moved to the house he'd built south of Butte, Montana.

Jerry had always dreamed of following his grandfather Hawk's footsteps and becoming a rancher. That became the focus of his existence until he started seeing blurry images and flashes of color. That was three months ago. Gradually, his eyes became more sensitive to light. Each incident brought a rush of agonizing headaches originating from the back of his eyes and slashing past his temples to the inner recesses of his brain. But consultation with the specialists in California proved fruitless. They had told him to take more pain medication when it happened. Incompetent fools, Jerry had called them before storming out of their offices.

But a few weeks later, one of the nurses from the doctors' offices had called his home and left a number and a name. His physical trainer, Lester Wilson, had copied down the phone number and the name of Dr. Raul Rojo. At Jerry's directives, Lester had researched the doctor through the Internet and made that first call to Chile.

Raul turned out to be a brilliant specialist in the use of lasers to treat damages to the optical nerves and retina. The medical world called him a radical who played God with people's eyes but Jerry hadn't cared. In his opinion, the Chilean's ninety percent success rate had spoken for him. Besides, Jerry had reached a point where he was willing to risk anything to see again. A month after that first call, Dr. Rojo had flown to the United States, all expenses paid by Jerry. After endless tests, the doctor had agreed to operate. Using the facilities of a private hospital in L.A., Raul had performed miracles. And although Jerry's eyes were healing slower than he would have want-

One Day at a Time

ed, he was on his way to regaining the full use of them. However, his experience with the California specialists had made him distrust them, and he wasn't setting foot in their building for an eye exam, not if he could help it.

Jerry sighed and reached for his temples. He started to massage them in circles. Would he ever get rid of these headaches? Headaches and nightmares were the bane of his existence. The nightmares woke him up nearly every night—the ghastly accident, the helplessness he'd felt as the oil tanker ran down his wife's car. Then there was the explosion from the tanker, the blinding light and the fumes, the sting in his eyes, and waking up blind and helpless in the hospital.

What had made Carmen so upset that day? A year later and Jerry still didn't know the answer to that particular question. Had she really been meeting another man as the papers had implied? Could another man be the reason why she had changed drastically during those months before the accident?

Even now, Jerry could clearly remember the events preceding the accident. For one, his fun, loving, and happy wife had turned into a mean, vindictive person with mood swings. She had also started drinking heavily. It wasn't until two days before the accident that he learned of some of her reasons. She had come back from a party, drunk as usual, and boldly told him that she was pregnant. Laughing hollowly, she informed him that she had known it for months but was keeping it from him.

Why? He had asked in shock. Granted, they hadn't been sharing a bedroom for a couple of months, but not telling him that she was pregnant was going too far. What mother could consume alcohol the way she did when she knew she was with child? Didn't she want his child? He had asked. And she had laughed at him. The more he pleaded with her to think of their unborn child and change her habits, the more she had laughed. She didn't care, not about the child she was carrying or his concerns.

Unfortunately, he had to leave for Phoenix for a game the day after Carmen's revelation. Despite Jerry's begging her to accompany

14

him to Phoenix, she had refused, claiming she had appointments she couldn't cancel. So after the game, he had taken a late flight home. He had been determined to find out what was wrong with his wife and to salvage what was left of their marriage. But on his way home from the airport, he had spotted her car outside a restaurant near their house. Worried that she might be too drunk to drive, he had parked his car beside hers and gone in search of her.

He hadn't taken more than a few steps when she came out of the restaurant looking very distraught. He did what any concerned husband would do; he followed her to her car and tried to stop her from driving. But her hysteria level went up a notch as soon as she recognized him. When she jumped into her sports car and started it, he got in, too.

He recalled how she kept repeating that she was sorry and that she didn't mean to do it. His attempts to calm her down were futile. What was she sorry about? Was it for the things she had said before he left for Phoenix? Was it for her drinking? He hadn't known the answers then. But being more concerned with her safety than his, he had reached over and buckled her seat belt while reassuring her that everything would be okay. While he fumbled with his own seatbelt, she'd reversed the car with squealing wheels. After that, things happened quickly.

In her hysterical state, Carmen didn't stop at the stop sign or bother to check the traffic on the highway. Instead, she surged onto the highway at a high speed, and hit another car. Jerry, still unbuckled, was flung aside and ended on the grassy divide between the two highways. The impact of hitting the ground had left him dazed but not for long. Like a scene from a horror movie, he had watched an oil tanker run down Carmen's car, swing out of control and hit the other car, run into a wall, and finally burst into flames.

A shudder ran through Jerry's frame as he recalled the horror and the anguish he had felt as he watched those events. After that, he had welcomed oblivion. It wasn't until later in the hospital that he'd learned the extent of his injuries. But it was weeks later that he was told that the people in the car that Carmen had hit were Hanna Vas, a

One Day at a Time

young African American painter, and her husband.

Could he have prevented the accident? Had he been responsible for the changes in Carmen? Had he been too busy with his ball games and literacy meetings to help his own wife? And who was Carmen meeting on the night of the accident?

Jerry squinted as he looked through the window to the circular arena beside his house. He forced his mind to return to the present and leave the past alone. The past only filled him with confusion and pain. The present was a new beginning for him—new beginnings with horses, a ranch, and people he could trust.

Jerry's grandpa Hawk—half Crow Indian and half Irish—and a no-nonsense man if one ever lived—had instilled in him the love for the land and animals. In fact, part of Jerry's youth was spent on his grandpa's ranch, branding and rounding cows with the ranch hands, breaking new colts, and learning everything there was to learn about horses. So, while his grandpa was a cattleman, Jerry had always dreamed of being a horse breeder. And now, looking at his horses grazing behind the white wooden fence of the pens, paddocks, and pastures, his goal seemed even closer. He was determined to breed the finest race horses this side of the Rockies.

He smothered a curse and stood up, his head pounding in earnest now. He needed to swim or maybe go for a ride to ease the tension. Physical exertion usually made the demons that tormented him rest and brought him a brief peace, he thought as he walked from his den.

A sound got his attention when he started across the foyer. His eye traveled past the curving staircase to the second floor where Sally Briscoe stood, a startled expression on her face. What was she up to? Sally was his former nanny who now took care of his house. Her husband, Winston, was Jerry's foreman.

She was carrying a load of sheets and from the look of things, she was about to enter the guest room beside his bedroom. "What's going on, Sally?" Jerry asked calmly, his hand coming to rest on the stair rail.

She glanced downstairs and smiled uneasily, "Just cleaning, Jerry."

16

She was lying and feeling guilty, too, if the expression on her face was an indicator. And since when did she clean at four o'clock in the afternoon? "Where is Winston? I need the sauna heating system fixed and the light bulbs in my bathroom replaced. We were supposed to be fixing the fence this afternoon, too."

"Oh, he went to Helena to pick up more supplies. He should be back any time now."

He frowned. "Since when do we get our supplies from Helena?" Why would Winston take off without consulting him? With the amount of work that had to be done around the farm, he needed everyone to do his or her share.

"Since you decided that your horses needed better feed. The best for your mares, you said." Sally added with a shrug.

"He should have consulted me," Jerry answered, not that his disagreeable tone made any difference. Sally had known him since he was a child. When his grandfather had told him to take some workers from the main homestead to help him settle in his farm, Eagle's Hill, Winston and Sally had volunteered. The two of them were a team. They never had any children but treated Jerry, his brothers, and sister as their own offspring. Their loyalty, love and devotion to Jerry's family were never in question although he must have tested their love in the last year. Still, they had resiliently put up with his ever-changing moods without complaints. They had treated him like he was the same young man they had known before the accident. And when his operation was successful, they had celebrated with him. In fact, it was their attitude that had made him ride while blind.

Jerry would never forget how Winston had taught him how to tell directions by using sounds, the wind, and the warmth from the sun. Or how he would quiz him on where every item was in the stalls, the tack room, the grooming room, the feed room, in the yard, along their riding paths, and even around Jerry's special pond in the canyon. It had taken him several weeks but Jerry had learned to ride his horse, Thunder, unaided.

Jerry's eyes warmed at the way Sally kept staring at him. It was obvious she wanted to be left alone to finish whatever she was doing.

And with the sunglasses planted on his nose, she couldn't see his amusement as he deliberately delayed her. "I wanted those things fixed today," he said finally. "Thunder also needs to be exercised. Could you tell Mac to saddle her for me, please?" Mac Murdock was one of the young ranch hands.

Sally opened and closed her mouth. Jerry would bet that she wanted to tell him to saddle his own horse as he'd often done the last six months. What was stopping her? She had never curbed her tongue around him before—another indication she was up to something.

"Sorry, Jerry, Mac went with Sly to check on Mystery and Buttercup at Circle K Ranch. I don't think Thunder will wait for him to come back. That mare of your gets quite edgy when not exercised." Sly Nunez was a horse trainer who'd recently joined Jerry's employ while Mystery and Buttercup were two of his broodmares. He was breeding them with a stallion from Circle K Ranch.

If Winston was around, they would have gone to get the mares, Jerry thought in frustration. Then there were bales of hay that were supposed to be picked this morning from his grandfather's farm. Winston must have forgotten about that, too. *Damn it!* He thought angrily. Why had Winston left without checking with him?

Jerry focused his attention on Sally. It wasn't her fault Winston was gone. But she was acting too contrary for him not to wonder what was going on. Who were they trying to sneak in his house now? "Okay, Sally, I'll saddle Thunder. Just remind Winston to fix the heaters as soon as he gets home."

As Sally disappeared into the room, Jerry's mind came up with the possible reasons for preparing the guest room. Aaron's family wasn't due to visit until summer. His younger brother, Tahj, was somewhere in Central America. His sister, Melissa, could never keep a secret—she would have called if she were coming. And his kid brother, Blake, was too busy at school to be visiting in the middle of the semester. Only one reason was plausible. They must be expecting his new assistant.

But why the secrecy? His uncle and brother had been given the task of finding him an assistant. Unfortunately, their tastes didn't seem to coincide with his. Whoever they sent was supposed to help with his correspondence and create a database for his farm records but from their looks, his interfering family was trying to remind him that he was still a man despite his poor sight. All the three assistants they had sent had been unmarried, pretty women with minimum computer skills. Well, none of them had lasted more than two weeks. Most of them couldn't hold a decent conversation without saying what a great baseball player he was or mentioning games they had seen him in. And would he go back to baseball when he got better? They had all acted as if his blindness was only a passing phase, a thing that used to annoy him during those months when he couldn't see a thing.

Jerry shook his head and headed outside. He had told his brother that he didn't want any more female assistants. So, whoever they were sending had better be male and he'd better know a lot about computers.

Jerry stepped outside and groaned. It was hot! The afternoon sunlight hit him like a heat wave from a hot oven. After a few steps, he stopped. It was too scorching to ride hatless, he thought.

He walked back into the air-conditioned house and sighed blissfully at the coolness. Where had he left his hat? The racks in the kitchen and the family room had only Sally's assortments of hats. He checked the den then the dining room. Where was the damn Stetson? He was cursing under his breath as he started up the stairs when the front door opened. He turned.

The sudden change in light intensity bothered Jerry's eyes so much that he closed them. He knew a person was on the doorway but before he could ask who it was, the person spoke.

"Ah, Jerry, I was afraid you would be home."

Winston! "Where in world did you disappear to, Winston? Did you forget that there are things that needed your attention today? The downstairs heater is broken. Someone forgot to store the empty gas tank and left it out there for some thief to come and relieve us of it. What about the northern fence? Did you forget we were to work on it this afternoon? I don't want our neighbor's cattle grazing on my canyon and destroying years of work. The hay bales were supposed to be picked from SC ranch and Mystery was to be transported from Circle K today. I'll have the mare foaling there, and knowing Darden, he'll charge me interest for every second she stays there. But what was I told? You went to get horse feed. What kind of horse feed took you all the way to Helena?" He continued listing the chores that hadn't been accomplished because of the foreman's disappearance.

Jerry's voice reached Angela and she was tempted to run. She took a step closer and peeked behind the foreman who seemed rooted in the doorway. For the second time since her arrival in Eagle's Hill, Angela had to snap her mouth shut before she was caught gawking. First, it was the Tudor house with its majestic entrance, flower beds, ponds, and neatly trimmed lawn that had impressed her. Now it was the owner, Jerry Tyrell Taylor.

The pictures Angela had perused didn't do Jerry justice. The man exuded a masculine aura that reached over and grabbed one's attention. He was impressively tall. Or were the cowboy boots and the tight jeans adding to that impression? The jeans hugged his narrow hips while his strong powerful legs were planted on the floor as if he owned not only this beautiful home, but the whole world as well. His powerful thigh muscles flexed noticeably as he shifted his stance. Angela's eyes moved upward, passing a wide chest in a checkered cotton shirt to his face. Hmm-mm! A strong face, whatever was not hidden by the dark glasses, she thought with detachment. Wide forehead, shortly cropped hair, lean cheeks with high cheekbones, strong jaw line, and a determined chin.

Winston moved forward and his action left Angela feeling unexpectedly vulnerable. Instead of following him into the foyer, she took a step back. Now, she could only see part of the room and the foreman. What was she doing hiding outside? Why was she scared of meeting Jerry? Wasn't this what she'd been looking forward to the last month? Besides, he was just a man, no different from ones she had dealt with before.

"Sorry, boss. I had to run an important errand today," Winston replied.

When Winston spoke without any hint of remorse, Angela dragged her eyes from the cherry plank floors and the gleaming, hand-made banister to look at him in amazement. What was going on here? Why was the foreman so nonchalant when Jerry seemed fit to be tied? In fact, the foreman was grinning toward a doorway in such a way that Angela's eyes followed his glance. A short and heavyset walnut-brown woman was holding a ladle near a doorway, a wide grin on her face. The woman turned and nodded at Angela good-naturedly as if Jerry's anger wasn't something new.

"Why is everybody acting so weird? This has been going on for days—tiptoeing around the house, whispering behind my back, unexplained telephone calls. Just because I don't say anything doesn't mean I don't sense things."

Angela jerked back and frowned. Why was Jerry wearing sunglasses indoors? His uncle had hinted that he wasn't well, and yet she had never seen a more healthy person. Could something be wrong with his eyes? Was that why he stopped playing baseball or why his family didn't want people to know where he was? Could it explain why he had not apologized to her family or come to see Reggie? No, that wasn't possible. He had family members he could have sent on his behalf. He had no excuse.

"I can damn well feel your presence, Sally. Stop lurking near that doorway and say your piece. Not a damn thing has ever stopped you from voicing your opinions."

"Now, now, Jerry, there is no need to swear in every sentence. Your mom would die of shock if she heard you. And don't forget you are not old enough for me to put soap in your mouth." The twinkle in Sally's eyes belied the words coming from her mouth.

Angela smiled at the older woman's words. The idea of putting soap in Jerry's mouth was funny, especially coming from a pint-sized woman he could easily carry with one arm. Angela, on the other hand, would like to do more than that. Like put chains on him and torture him until he went down on his knees and apologized to her, her family, and her nephew for what he'd caused. The thought gave her the courage to step forward and enter the house.

21

One Day at a Time

Jerry didn't bother to answer Sally's outrageous comment. Such was the price he paid for having a housekeeper who had changed his diapers and spanked his naked behind when he was a child.

He turned to Winston and saw a woman hesitate before entering the room. With the light coming from behind her, all he noticed was her height and her long legs. Who was she? "Who did you bring with you, Winston?"

"Who we have here is your new assistant, Jerry. Your uncle and brother found her. All I had to do was to pick her up at the airport and deliver her to the farm."

"My what?" Jerry's voice struck them like a flash of lightening.

Angela stepped forward. "Your new assistant, Angela McGee. Maybe we caught you at a wrong time, Mr. Taylor. I could always go back outside and come in again." She was trying to lighten the mood but the silence that followed was deafening and unnerving.

Jerry's senses reeled. Feeling like someone had gut-punched him, he leaned back in rejection. Carmen's voice! How was that possible? Jerry whipped off his glasses in disbelief. The sudden change in the light intensity made him squint. He allowed them to adjust to the well-lit foyer.

"Are you okay, Mr. Taylor?" Angela asked with concern.

Of course, she wasn't Carmen. Jerry thought dispassionately. His wife was dead, taken by fate a year ago. Who was this woman who talked like Carmen? She had the same husky intonation, a pitch lower than most women, suggestive, and beckoning. It was Carmen's voice that had first drawn him to her—the woman who he'd believed was to be his mate for life. As it shook with emotion, her voice had promised to love and cherish him, and yet later, it had accused him of unfaithfulness and deceit. When they'd talked about children, Carmen's voice had rose with excitement at the possibility, but later it become shrill as she began to resent her pregnancy. Were his ambivalent feelings toward his dead wife making him imagine her voice coming from another woman?

When the continued silence became unbearable, Winston stepped in. "Ms. McGee, Jerry is not usually this unwelcoming but the surprise of..."

"Who are you?" Jerry interrupted with a voice devoid of emotion as he tried to fight the magnetism of her voice.

"Angela McGee. I've been employed on your behalf by the law firm of McQueen, Fischer, and Taylor of San Diego. I have the papers, in case you need to verify it." Angela finished in a pleasant voice when what she really wanted to do was bombard him with endless questions. What happened that day, a year ago? Had he been fighting with his wife? Had he driven her to being careless? Did he know how many lives her actions changed? Her heart was drumming so loud she was sure everyone in the foyer could hear it. *Collect yourself, Angela! Remember Sav.*

"Well, Ms. McGee, you just became unemployed. Good day and good-bye."

"Now, now, Jerry. . ." started Sally.

"Jerry, your uncle said that ..." Winston interrupted.

Jerry stopped both of them with a look. Then speaking with a chilling but calm voice, he said, "I am still the owner if this home, this land, and your employer. I want her gone. I didn't ask for another damn female assistant. I refuse to deal with or waste my time with incompetent women. Winston, take her back to the airport or wherever she came from." Then fixing the foreman with a look that could have shriveled a lesser man, he continued, "Next time you feel the urge to go behind my back and conspire with my uncle, make sure your bags are packed, because you'll be leaving. And that goes for you, too, Sally." He stared them down. Then slowly replacing his glasses, he turned and headed up the stairs, mumbling to himself. "Damn interfering family!"

Chapter 3

Angela was shocked when she realized the arrogant man was firing her and without due cause. She had known he would be egotistical but not this much. Who did he think he was? And what did he have against women assistants? Angela wasn't confrontational by nature but this man just rubbed her the wrong way. She stepped forward, determination overriding her dismay.

"Just a minute, Mr. Taylor," She snapped. "I have a signed contract stating I'm to be your assistant for a month, and in exchange I'm to get room and board. It is very legal and very binding."

"Well, Ms. McGee, I didn't sign the damn document so don't you dare think of binding me to it." Jerry ground out without turning around. He continued up the stairs.

Fire sparkled in Angela's eyes as the insufferable man continued to walk away from her. "Mr. Taylor, Aaron Taylor and Cyrus McQueen acted on your behalf and that makes you responsible." She moderated her tone and tried not to let her temper get the best of her. But damn it, this man was responsible for her family's loss. Sav would still be alive if it weren't for him. But why was she insisting on staying where she wasn't wanted? After all, she was doing the law firm a favor, not the other way round.

Jerry stopped and turned. As he started down the stairs toward her, Angela stiffened. He looked like a graceful, jungle cat stalking a prey. *I will not be intimidated*, Angela vowed as he got closer; and yet, apprehension tightened her gut. Had she gone too far?

As Jerry approached her, a flowery scent teased his senses. Hers! He clenched his teeth as his body started stirring. Of all the times to react to a woman, this was not one of them. Then he made the mistake of looking below her sparkling eyes to her full lips. He swallowed and mentally cursed his uncle and brother, again. "Let me make this clear, Ms McGee. I don't give a damn about what you do, what you think, or what you want because around here my word is the law. But when I said I don't need a female assistant that is exactly what I mean. Now, if you want a paycheck or severance monies, I'll give them to you."

"I don't need your money, Mr. Taylor," Angela interrupted.

"I'll gladly pay you for the month you so badly want to spend here." He continued as if she hadn't spoken. "Just get the hell out of my house!"

Forgotten were Jerry's two employees as Angela lost her temper. "I swear if one foul word comes out of your mouth again, I'll help Ms. Sally clean it with the strongest soap in this house. Just because you are injured does not give you the license to be rude, to order people around, or be irresponsible."

Her words stilled his movements. Where was the pitying expression that had made him fire her predecessors? "Are you implying that I am still blind, Ms. McGee? Is that what my brother and my uncle led you to believe?" His eyes narrowed. "Let me make this clear, there is *absolutely* nothing wrong with my sight!"

"The more reason for you to act with decorum," she replied calmly. He looked the type who would probably die before admitting any weakness.

"Decorum?" Jerry folded his arms across his chest and surveyed her from his position. She may be a tall woman but he still toppled her by at least three inches. And from the look in her eyes, she hated looking up at him. She was probably used to looking down her nose at everyone.

He turned his head sideways and contemplated her. She was beginning to fascinate him and that wasn't a good thing in his book. His previous assistants wouldn't have known the word decorum, let alone use it. But this woman was different. His eyes traveled from her long legs, passed curvaceous hips, tiny waist, to well-sized breasts. Desire flashed through him. He brought it under control with ironclad will. Her eyes still shot sparks at him and added character to an already beautiful face. With her smooth, wide forehead, arrogantly arched eyebrows, and slightly slanted eyes, she was very striking. But the most alluring thing about her face was her mouth. She had naturally pouting lips that intrigued and annoyed the hell out of him.

Jerry straightened his body and glared at her. How dare she preach to him in his own home while reminding him of his sexual abstinence? He was pissed off by the entire situation, and it was her fault he couldn't formulate a decent thought. "So, Uncle C sent me a priggish school ma'am to squeeze money out of me? I don't need lessons in etiquette, Ms. McGee."

"I'm not after squeezing money from you—Mr. J.T., the marble man. Not everyone is motivated by money." A muscle ticked on his cheek. Angela ignored it and waved the contract in front of his face. "I just need you to honor this agreement. In exchange for my services I was promised room and board, nothing more and nothing less."

Her services? The words brought to mind an image of her endless legs wrapped about his flank. On top of that, her soft and alluring scent teased his nose. His eyes narrowed as he reduced his tone an octave. "Oh, now we come to the reason for all this outrage. Could you be having another reason for wanting to be in my house, Ms. McGee?" He was deliberately antagonizing her now.

Jerry's soft and seductively low tone teased Angela's senses. Goosebumps spread throughout her body. "No!" she snapped.

He saw her nose quiver as she inhaled sharply. Ah, she wasn't as calm as she pretended to be. "Are you a fan, baby?"

Angela's eyes narrowed. "Definitely not, I hate baseball."

Jerry tilted his head sideways, again, and smiled—a slow wicked smile that anyone who knew him would know; he was about to be outrageous. "But I'm not baseball, baby. I'm JT, the marble man. Want to see what became of the marble man? Want to warm my bed?"

His voice had gone huskily low. Angela's breath got caught at the picture his words evoked. Her brain sent provocative messages to her body. Her skin tingled in reaction. She didn't want to feel this way, not for this arrogant man. He was her arch enemy, for crying out loud. He might be responsible for her sister's death. Might? When did she start giving him the benefit of doubt? Was her reaction to him making her act like a nitwit?

With Sav's name repeating in her head, Angela let her gaze insolently travel down his body and then back up. Straightening her spine and lifting her chin, she used her most blasé tone to say, "You could hope."

She regretted her words as soon as they left her mouth. Jerry didn't look like a man who could ignore a challenge. Her thoughts were proven right when he imitated her gesture. His head dipped as if his eyes were traveling up and down her body, too. She physically braced herself for a disparaging comment about her height. She'd heard it all. What harm could one more do? She was either too tall, too huge, a giant, giraffe, last of the Amazonians or a Watusi woman-warrior. Let him say his worst. She didn't expect anything better from him, anyway.

Jerry liked what he saw. Maybe he liked it too much becaus heat stole through his body straight to his loins. She was beautiful enough to be a model but she was so curvaceous, the focus would be on her and not the outfits. He wouldn't mind having her model for him in her birthday suit, preferably in his bed. But right now he resented her sudden intrusion into his life and her smug attitude. Who did she think she was? "Don't worry. I like my women sweet-natured. You're an acid-tongued virago."

Angela ground her teeth at the insult. "Good! Because I don't like arrogant, domineering, chauvinistic jocks either. And for your information, not every woman who meets you wants a part of you. All I need is for you to honor this agreement, simple and straight." Her smile hid the fact that she really wanted to kick him on the shin as she shoved the contract under his nose.

Jerry grabbed the offending papers from her hand and without looking at it, pushed it in the back pocket of his pants. His eyes stayed on her. Battle lights were dancing in her eyes. He didn't know why but he was beginning to enjoy their sparring. Maybe that was why he said, "Well Ms. Angela McGee, I will neither honor an agreement I didn't sign, corporate with an assistant I don't want, nor be polite to someone I don't like or know." He then crossed his arms across his chest and challenged her with his stance.

"I'll sue you." No man had ever tried her patience like this man.

"Try me."

There was that arrogant smile on his face, again. "Oh, I forgot, you can afford it. How about this? I'll make just one phone call and poof, your hideaway is no more." Angela's voice rang with satisfaction.

Jerry stiffened. "You wouldn't dare." He growled then took two steps to glare at her. She leaned forward, too, until their faces were just a few inches apart. Her scent filled his nose. This time, he stiffened.

"Try me." She repeated his words smugly. "Wouldn't it be fun to have reporters swarm here like flies and camp outside your door?"

"Ah-m, Ms. McGee..." Sally's voice piped.

"Ms. Angela, please..." Winston said at the same time.

She ignored the servants and zeroed in on the impossible man before her. He might be gorgeous, manly, and dangerous looking but she wasn't easily intimidated. In fact, he was glaring at her as if he'd like nothing better than to grab her and smother her to death. But she'd never run from a challenge before and this man offered her one with every cell in his body.

Ignoring the uneasy feeling settling in her mid-section, she took her time as she gazed around the premises. "Your foyer could comfortably accommodate twenty of them, with room to spare."

Jerry could not believe the nerve of this woman. Just because she was beautiful didn't mean she had to bend people to her will. He was incensed by her attitude. But what irked him most was the smile on her lips. It was triumphant, as if she knew she'd already won and that her stay was guaranteed.

"Winston! I want her gone," Jerry uttered in a chilling voice and turned to walk toward his den. His family was going to hear a mouthful before he was through.

Angela blinked as if awakening from a dream. She closed her eyes in dismay and clenched her teeth. She and her temper, she thought angrily. Why didn't she think before she opened her mouth? So what if his attitude annoyed her? Yes, he was bad tempered but it was his house. It was going to kill her to apologize, but she had no choice. Damn, the man made her so angry.

Angela was about to open her mouth when Winston spoke from behind her. "I'm sorry, Jerry. That's not possible."

Jerry stopped and turned. "What isn't possible?"

"Taking Ms. Angela back—the truck's radiator is busted. I need to fix it."

Jerry slowly walked back. He took in the protective way Winston had positioned himself behind his unwanted guest. Then a glowering Sally followed her husband's example and went to stand beside Ms. McGee. If Jerry wasn't incensed by their defection to the woman's side, he would have found the situation amusing—the tall, young woman being defended by a diminutive housekeeper whom he usually lifted without an effort and an old cowboy with a limp. And from the looks on their faces, they were making their position clear— Ms. McGee wasn't going anywhere. "Let me see if I got this right. My two-year-old Pathfinder has a busted radiator?"

"Unfortunately, yes." The foreman replied.

"The pick-up?" Jerry asked with a raised eyebrow.

"You lent it to your grandfather last week," Winston replied.

"And the cars in the garage?" His face was now expressionless.

Winston winced. "Bad back, I can't fit in those tiny cars. Besides, they're automatic and I'm used to stick shifts."

Jerry almost smiled at the sincere look on the foreman's face. "And Lester is too busy to drive her, I guess."

"He's had a touch of too much sun and is taking it easy, might even be the flu. It's been going around the last couple of weeks." At Jerry's raised eyebrow, Winston continued. "Big Joe and Little Joe are working on the fences, Sly might still be at the Circle K Ranch, and Mac is tending Philly." Winston turned to look at Angela who was listening to the conversation with wide eyes. "Philly is one of

One Day at a Time

Jerry's broodmares. She's due to foal any time now." Finally, Winston turned to look at his wife. "Well, Sally is...she's..."

"Yes?" Jerry prompted blandly.

Sally jumped in with, "I'm trying to fix the stoves. One of the fuses got burnt and now none of the stoves is working. If I'm to fix dinner, I need to work on it."

In other words, there would be no dinner on his table if he forced Ms. McGee to leave. "Is there anything else that I need to know ...I mean, eh, anything that's gotten broken in the last ten minutes that I should be aware of?"

Winston and Sally stared at him calmly. Jerry glanced at Angela who had a twinkle in her eyes. So she found his predicament funny, did she? His most trusted employees just turned against him and she was amused? "Maybe you two have an urge to go visit South Creek Ranch? They might have a few things for you to fix, too." He watched as the two employees started to look uneasy. Of course, he would never send them back to the SC Ranch. It just annoyed him that they were siding with a stranger against him. He turned his eyes on Ms. McGee and saw that the smile had disappeared from her face. He stared hard at her but the woman insolently stared back. Ms. McGee wasn't easily intimidated. Expressionlessly, Jerry murmured, "I need to make a call, excuse me."

"Does that mean Ms. Angela stays?" Sally asked.

Jerry glanced at Sally then at his new assistant. He was tired and his head was pounding. He didn't want to deal with this, not now. "You have a fuse to fix, don't you? Let Ms. McGee worry about whether she stays or not." Jerry replied before disappearing in his den.

Angela felt a hand on her back and turned. Sally was smiling at her while gently directing her away from the foyer. "C'mon, child, you did great. It was time somebody told that boy a thing or two. Ever since the accident, we tend to let him get away with too much. I'm afraid we've spoilt him dreadfully."

That boy—if he was ever a boy—wasn't only dreadfully spoilt, he was arrogant, dictatorial, and a chauvinist. Whoever heard of such open gender discrimination in this day and age? Just what did he have against women assistants? Angela thought angrily. And Sally was right about his getting away with things. Not this time. If he had had anything to do with his wife's accident, she would find out.

"Let's go to the kitchen and get you something hot. You must be tired after your journey." Sally pushed the door. "Would coffee do?"

"Coffee would be nice, thank you." Angela turned and gave Jerry's den one last glance before following the older woman.

The warmth in the kitchen enveloped Angela. Her face though flushed from the confrontation with Jerry welcomed the heat. Slowly she inhaled, liking the mixture of spices and wood wax. Her eyes fell on the half hexagon cherry counter with a green veneer top. Curving from the sink and the cupboards and offering a surface for a group of up to five to sit and eat comfortably, it was a work of art and anyone who loved to cook would appreciate the width and accessibility that it offered. The kitchen boasted a Jenn-Aire grill and two ovens, and at the corner on a dais were a side-by-side commercial size stainless steel refrigerator and freezer. Ladder-back stools with fluffy rusty cushions were placed strategically around the counter. To the right was a comfortable striped brown and burnt-orange couch with two matching chairs facing a TV set. It was on but turned low in volume. The area was carpeted with a rusty colored carpet but the rest of the kitchen was done with checkered beige and brown linoleum. A little beyond the counter and to the left was an oval cherry wood table with six ladder-back chairs around it. The place had handmade cherry cabinets filled with kitchen paraphernalia. She could have a ball in this kitchen—that was, if she stayed.

Sally was laughing while holding her heavy bosom until she caught Angela's expression. "There's no need to look like that, child. Although I think we did go too far this time." She chuckled. "But you've won. Not only that, your presence here is going to bring some very interesting changes. Oh yes, very interesting changes indeed," the housekeeper chuckled.

"Explain to me how I've won, Ms. Sally?" Angela asked just as the backdoor opened and Winston walked in.

One Day at a Time

Sally pulled out a chair for Angela while grinning happily. "Because you're not going anywhere and Jerry knows it. He was just venting his frustrations. C'mon, sit down and I'll get that cup of coffee I promised you. Do you take cream, sugar, or honey?"

"Just cream, ma'am," said Angela.

"Just plain Sally—Winston and I have no time for those mister and missus-stuff."

It was pointless talking to Sally about her misgivings, Angela thought. She'd decided that Angela was staying and nothing was going to change her mind. "Please, I really must insist on talking with Mr. Taylor, again, Sally."

"Then you'll have to wait for, uh, an hour or so." The older woman said while staring out the window.

Angela was bewildered. "But why?"

"Jerry just left. I know he wanted to take Thunder out but I think something else is chasing him from the house now," Sally finished with a chuckle. "Rest, child, and wait for him to come back. Then you can have your talk." The woman patted Angela's shoulder and left the kitchen.

***

Jerry left the house in a hurry, as if the demons were chasing him. Was he running away from *her*? What a crazy thought! He never ran from any situation, let alone a woman. That was right. Angela McGee was just a woman—pig-headed, quick-witted, and beautiful but still just a woman. Her sudden appearance had thrown him off. That was all. He hadn't expected her and she had walked in when he was venting his frustrations on Winston.

How dare she invade his home? And what the hell were his uncle and brother up to? He'd specifically asked for a male assistant and Angela McGee was too much of a woman to be considered male.

He was so consumed by his thoughts that he almost bumped into Sly. "How is Mystery, Sly? Did you bring her back?" He paused long enough to ask.

"She's doing fine. Do you want to see her? I have her in the south west paddock with Philly." Sly nodded toward the paddock.

"I'll check on her before I leave. Did Darden give you the papers, too?" Jerry asked.

"Yes, I have them in the tack room." Sly replied.

Jerry nodded. "Good! I'll put them in her file."

"I think we might have a problem with Ellie—possibly a sand crack." Sly said as he fell in step with him.

Jerry paused and squinted toward the corral where Elegant Ellie was grazing peacefully. He changed directions and walked toward the filly. "You saw a change in her gait?"

"Yes. It is very slight but I noticed it today when I was training her. When she walks, she extends her right foot far forward and then brings the heel down first," the trainer explained.

"Damn, Drew! Not only was he a thief and a drunk, he was also a slob." Drew Hogan was the trainer Jerry had hired while he was blind, a man who could've ruined all his foals and mares had he stayed in Eagle's Hill a day longer. The man was lucky Jerry had caught him sneaking a drink from his basement a couple of weeks back. If the trainer were still around, Jerry would have no problem forcing him to pay for his laziness. He smothered another curse. Sand cracks if left untreated could lead to lameness and he had no intention of raising lame horses. "Damned if he hasn't injured my filly!"

"Don't worry, Jerry. I caught it early and we can fix it. Ellie will be fine. And at the pace she is training, she will be ready for shows in no time."

Jerry nodded. Sly was a man with an impeccable reputation whom Jerry had been lucky to find between jobs. He had only been at Jerry's farm for two weeks but was already respected by the other workers. The Texan knew everything there was to know about horses. He was hard working and very competent—a blessing after Drew. "I should have double checked everything he did. I believed him when he reassured me he'd taken care of the mare."

Jerry walked to where Ellie grazed. He whistled and the eight-month-old filly looked up. Then she moved closer to him. Jerry patted her head and murmured a few endearments before opening the gate and going into the corral. He lifted her leg and examined her toes. "Are you going to work on it today?"

"Yes. But I'll check all four of them. I believe that if Drew didn't bother with one hoof wall then the other three were ignored as well."

Jerry swore again as he left the corral. Ellie was a beautiful, grey, Arabian horse with good pedigree. Jerry couldn't afford to have something happen to her. "Do we have enough toe clips?"

"Yes. We might be running a little low on tetanus antitoxin though, but we have enough for our Ms. Elegant here." Sly answered as they walked from the corral and headed toward the barn.

"Good. I'm taking Thunder out but I'll check with you when I get back. I need to know how bad that crack is."

"Ellie is a sound filly. She'll pull through this," the trainer reassured Jerry before he disappeared into the tack room.

Although a cracked heal was not something to laugh about, Jerry smiled in satisfaction at the trainer's reassuring tone. Sly had only been with him for a short period but it was obvious he'd already realized that Jerry was a perfectionist. For his horses, Jerry expected nothing but the best. He worked hard and expected his ranch hands to follow his example. Everyone in Eagle's Hill was accountable for their actions. However, Jerry still tended to blame himself if anything went wrong. He believed it was his responsibility to confirm that a task was completed according to his instructions. It wasn't a sign that he thought his ranch hands were incompetent. It was just the way he did things. Luckily for him, his workers understood that and respected him enough not be offended.

Jerry was adjusting the saddle on Thunder when Sally hurried toward him, waving a telephone. He looked at it with a frown. "Who is it, Sally?"

"Maya, she insists on talking to you."

Jerry thanked her and took the phone. He spoke into it as he walked his horse out of the corral. "Ma?"

"Hey, baby, I just wanted to make sure that you don't forget about dinner this Sunday."

Maya Taylor, Jerry's mother, had lived in California and New York for over twenty five years but South Creek Ranch in Montana would always be home to her. That was where she was born, where she brought her children every summer for vacation, and where she now resided. A year ago, she had been the main buyer for a prestigious California gallery, then Jerry's accident happened and she decided a big city wasn't her thing anymore. A ruse, if Jerry ever heard one. His mother had wanted to be near him and to watch over him while he recovered from the loss of his family and dealt with his blindness. At fifty-four, she was still robust and beautiful, and in Jerry's opinion, she could still have a whole new life, if she so desired.

Jerry laughed and said, "You know I never forget or miss a meal, Ma."

"And I never miss calling you to remind you. Are you very busy, dear?"

"I'm readying Thunder for a ride, Ma. Is everything okay at SC?"

"Oh yes, couldn't be better. Dad was smart to hire Bill Skywalker, the new foreman. Are you going out alone?" His mother's voice was now laced with concern.

Jerry groaned and patted Thunder's head. The horse was getting restless. "C'mon, Ma, we go through this every time you call. I've been riding alone for months now and haven't come to any harm."

"And I've been a mother for thirty four years and still have a right to worry about my children. I know your eyes are getting better but you shouldn't take chances with them. Take Mac or Winston with you, dear."

"Okay," Jerry agreed.

"Hmm-mm, when you agree so sweetly and so fast like that, I know you're only humoring me. Impossible boy! Ah, have it your way. Run along then but just...just be careful. I love you, baby."

"Me too, Ma," Jerry said with a grin. He shook his head as he handed the phone back to Sally. "She's unbelievable."

One Day at a Time

"She's a mother. It's her job to worry."

Jerry got on his horse and adjusted his sunglasses. "I was hoping she would go back to L.A. now that I'm okay. There is no need for her to hang around the farm just to check on me."

Sally snorted. "You still think she left her job because of your accident? Our Maya got tired of living far away from the farm. Besides, she loves the rodeos, the barrel racings, and the powwows too much to ever want to go back to California. She's happy here. And your grandparents need her more now, especially with your uncle refusing to remarry and take over the farm."

Jerry grinned. He couldn't imagine Uncle Cyrus as a farmer. Uncle C was the consummate urbanite, a man who was more comfortable pushing keys on machines or manipulating people in and out of court. No, his uncle was better suited at bringing criminals to justice than rounding up strays on a cattle ranch.

The smile disappeared from Jerry's face as he remembered his uncle's latest scheme. "Where is Ms. McGee?"

"She's in the kitchen, resting and waiting for you. Poor child, she looks utterly defeated." Sally looked up at Jerry.

Jerry tilted his Stetson and looked toward the canyon. He didn't need to see Sally's chiding expression to know he had been unnecessarily rude to his new assistant. He didn't want to feel guilty either but he did. Damn his family! He had been caught by surprise and he hated surprises. Besides, his reaction to her had thrown him off balance.

Jerry turned and found that Sally hadn't moved an inch. He would apologize and send Angela home first thing tomorrow morning. "I didn't want another female assistant."

"I thought you were more concerned with whether she can organize those records of yours." Sally put her hands on her hips and added, "Don't they put people in jail for refusing to employ women?"

Jerry shook his head at her comment but refused to be drawn into another argument. "Is she any good with computers?"

"Now, you know I don't know computer talk, Jerry. If you want to find out, you'd better ask her yourself. You aren't really going to send her away, are you?"

"That depends, Sally," he replied mysteriously. He smiled and told Sally he'd see her later, then headed toward the canyon—his favorite spot. It was the place where he relaxed and forgot his worries, or like today, a place to think things through.

Jerry rode by the paddock where Philly and Mystery were grazing. He watched Mystery for few minutes as she ate and then nodded in satisfaction. Now that the mare was breeding, he would observe her eating and drinking habits, and her emotional state for any changes.

He moved closer to where Philly was grazing. Philly was one of the two Arabian broodmares that he owned. She had cost a lot of money to acquire but was worth every dollar. She had perfect conformation, was sound, and had a genetic background that any breeder would envy. She was also due in less than a month. Hers would be the first foal to be born at Eagle's Hill.

Jerry had one other Arabian mare—Philly's cousin Wind Dancer; two Thoroughbreds—Mystery and Rameses; two Quarter horses—Buttercup and Taharqa, and one American Saddlebred—Zuri.

Playing baseball and earning top dollar had made it possible for him to buy the best mares and to start on his lifelong dream. Whether the dream became a reality would depend on his will, hard work, and his natural knowledge of horseflesh. But there was no doubt about that last quality. He'd been good with horses since childhood. He could train and calm any colt, pick the best stallion from a herd, or detect any physical defect or emotional problems in a mare. But with the help of Sly and Winston, he would breed and train and if possible, race some of the best horses in the Rocky Mountain region. Oh, yeah, he was determined to make Eagle's Hill profitable. He had no intention of turning it into a money-sucking hole.

Chapter 4

Exactly an hour later, Sally went to tell Angela that Jerry was back in the house. Angela washed her face before leaving the room they had given her. When she reached the top of the stairs, she glanced at the area dividing the left wing from the right wing of the second floor. Jerry had turned the divide into a photo gallery. Instead of going down the stairs, her feet carried her toward the works of art adorning those walls.

There were paintings of various Native American chiefs including Sitting Bull, the famous massacre at Wounded Knee, Buffalo soldiers, Nat Turner, and other African American heroes. Some were original works by various African American artists. Angela recognized a few of them from the pictures she'd seen in art magazines at Sav's house. Reluctantly, she turned and headed downstairs.

Jerry's deep voice pulled her toward the partially opened den door. Her heartbeat increased in tempo and her palms started to sweat. She didn't know whether it was caused by the inevitable confrontation or the nerves snapping and tingling in her body at the thought of being in his presence, again. She could feel the sweat trickle down the small of her back and she suddenly wished that she'd taken time to shower.

Oh, this had to be done, she thought, thoroughly annoyed with herself. *She will apologize and be civil, and not lose her temper.* Wiping her palms on her dress, she lifted her hand to knock. A chuckle followed by laughter came from the room and made her pause. Jerry was on the phone. Angela dropped her hand and waited.

"You can't get out of this one, Uncle C. I specifically asked for a male assistant, not another one of your females." Jerry watched as

Angela peeked into his den and then moved back. "Obviously, my wishes aren't important."

His uncle chuckled. "We just couldn't find a man that looked trustworthy. Count yourself lucky we convinced Ms. McGee to help you out."

"Yeah, I'm on my knees thanking the good Lord." Jerry added sarcastically. A door opened somewhere and he saw Angela's shadow. Why wasn't she coming in? She was shamelessly eavesdropping on his conversation. "Just do me a favor, Uncle C. If this doesn't work out, don't send me any more assistants. I'll find a way to deal with my problems."

His uncle reassured him. "Don't worry, son. This is it. Although Ms. McGee is on loan for only a month, she is the best. Is she nearby? I would like a word with her."

"As soon as she stops eavesdropping on my conversation, I'll let her know you want a word with her." Angela made a sound and Jerry looked up. She appeared in the doorway, looking remorseful for being caught listening behind the door. "You make a habit of listening to private conversations, Ms. McGee?"

Angela flushed. "Only when the door is open and I'm the subject," she replied with a deadpan expression. Jerry smiled, and she visibly relaxed. "Will you forgive me if I humbly apologize?"

He raised an eyebrow. "For eavesdropping?"

"And my earlier insolence," she added.

"On your knees?" He asked hopefully.

She smiled. He was too bold. "Can't—knee problems."

Jerry burst out laughing. "Have a seat, Ms. McGee." Jerry nodded at the chair in front of his desk and went back to talking to his uncle.

When he chuckled, Angela's eyes moved to his lips. She stared hard at them without paying attention to the words emanating from them. He had sensual lips. Angela shifted her body. Why was she thinking about his lips when she was supposed to be looking for proof of his guilt? She needed to show that he was a heartless, spoilt celebrity...a monster who was capable of getting away with murder.

One Day at a Time

What she had observed so far was revealing. He was very arrogant, a mark against him. But he was also handsome and utterly male, a combination that was likely to make her forget her objectives.

She did her best to ignore him. Every time she looked at the man, her focus on the real issue shifted. She didn't want to know or even like him. What she needed was proof of his guilt. She turned her attention to his den as if the room might shade some light on his personality.

It was a very masculine domain, smelling of leather and old books. And despite the presence of two computers on a workstation to her left, it still gave an illusion of agelessness. For one, not much light was coming into the room. To add to its mystery were jungle green and brown wallpaper, brown draperies that looked like they were once monks' robes, shelves of horse-rearing and ranching books and journals, an ebony table, and a black leather chair. The only thing missing was a fireplace and a dog warming itself at the hearth. Reluctantly, she had to admit that the room suited him. It was dark and masculine, just like the man.

She heard Jerry's voice rise sharply from the monotone he had been using and turned to look at him. He was looking her way again, drilling into her as if looking for all her secrets. She shivered. What a contradiction Jerry Taylor was turning out to be. She didn't know which one was the real man. The handsome jock that had loved fast cars and beautiful women or the brooding, angry man she'd met earlier? Or had circumstances forced him to change and accept a life of obscurity in a farm, surrounded by old servants and farm animals?

"Why don't you tell her yourself, Uncle C?" Jerry thrust the phone toward Angela.

Angela reached for it. Their fingers grazed. She did her best to ignore the heat that slashed up her arm at the contact. Instead, she wrapped her palm around the small, black instrument, and asked warily, "How many assistants have they hired before me?"

"Three."

"All of them females?"

"Yes and some of them thought it was okay to go beyond their duties." He started to rub his temple, trying to ease the ache in his head and stop the slashes of light dancing behind his eyes. These attacks tended to occur at weird moments and were rarely welcomed, but to have them now was adding insult to injury.

"What happened?" She asked in a gentler voice. There was a pause in the conversation and from the twist of his mouth, she couldn't tell whether he was irritated or amused by her question.

When did her voice lose that husky, man-bewitching quality that had reminded Jerry so much of Carmen? "Well...eh, nothing...it's not important!"

"Did they try to compromise you?"

Jerry's lips curled in amusement. In his book, women got compromised not men. "You really do have a way with words, don't you?"

Angela shrugged before speaking on the phone. "McGee here."

"Ah, Ms. McGee, this is Cyrus McQueen. May I call you Angela?" When she said it was okay, Jerry's uncle continued. "I guess by now you know that you weren't expected. I'm sorry about that. Jerry had requested a male assistant but we couldn't find him any. We were despairing when you showed up to fix our website. Immediately after meeting you, I thought you were the type of a person he needed. Unfortunately, I knew being an assistant was way beneath your capabilities and so I didn't dare ask. But when my secretary mentioned that you were thinking of taking a vacation, we thought it wouldn't hurt to convince you to take it in Montana while helping my nephew out. I promise you, the farm is the best place for a vacation. Have you had a chance to look around? You'll find that my nephew has a beautiful home with all the amenities of a five-star hotel. The pool is usually heated if you like swimming and the horses are very agreeable, in case you fancy a ride. Have you met Sally yet? She makes the most mouth watering steak in the entire state."

Angela almost smiled at the salesman's pitch and cajoling tone Cyrus was using. The man knew he had been wrong and was only trying to save face. "No, I haven't looked around but I've met Sally. However, that does not absolve you from what you did, Mr.

One Day at a Time

McQueen."

"Please, call me Cyrus. I can imagine how you feel and I ask for forgiveness and understanding. You've met my nephew. He's not a very accommodating young man. And I was acting out of love and concern for his well-being"

Jerry was worse than being unaccommodating, thought Angela but she made no comment. She waited to see what McQueen was going to come up with next.

"My nephew needs someone to take care of his records. He has good ranch hands but none of them can work with computers. He is going to lose most of his records if you don't help him out, Angela. Please, we're already interviewing and we might find a replacement soon. Could you stay for the next couple of weeks or until we find someone new?" Cyrus asked hopefully.

Angela rolled her eyes in exasperation until she saw Jerry's expression. He'd tried to hide it but she still caught the pain lurking in the depth of his eyes. Also, the constant rubbing of his temple gave him away. The man was in pain and she would bet that her sudden appearance didn't help, either. "I don't know if that's a good idea, Mr. McQueen. What you've done is put both Mr. Taylor and me in a very uncomfortable position. I don't appreciate being yelled at and made to feel unwelcome when I was guaranteed otherwise. Why didn't you just tell me the truth? I would have understood. As for your nephew, I'm sure he doesn't need the added stress of dealing with an unwanted guest—a female one at that. And seriously, who can blame him for being wary of another female assistant? His experience with them has been less than satisfactory."

Jerry leaned back on his leather chair and watched the sparks in Angela's eyes as she took on his uncle. Somehow it made him feel better that she understood his misgivings and outburst. The voice that had been a soft purr was now filled with steel as she told off one of the best criminal lawyers on the west coast. Jerry's family liked to push people around too much but as usual, his brother wasn't in his office and his uncle was getting the blunt of Angela's displeasure. Uncle C was his mother's younger brother. When Jerry's dad—a San

Diego police officer—died in the line of duty, Uncle C had helped with their upbringing, and helped his only sister to raise her children. He was strict but loving, and he definitely never spoilt any of them. He neither pushed them into doing things they didn't want to do nor tried to make them into carbon copies of himself. Aaron's decision to become a lawyer and later to join his law firm was his own decision, not Uncle C's. Jerry played professional baseball only after getting a degree in agricultural engineering. Each of his siblings had chosen their own careers, too. Tahj, Jerry's immediate follower, used to be with the FBI but now ran a private detective agency, Melissa was a reporter, and Blake—the baby of the family—was at UCLA taking premed classes while kicking ass on the basketball court.

Jerry forced his thoughts away from his family and focused them on Angela. What was it about her that fascinated him? He'd known his share of beautiful women so her looks wasn't the issue. Was it the way she confidently faced him? Or was it the strength he saw in her? Would she stand by her man through bad times? Or would she be easily swayed by others' opinions? She looked like the type who could take on anyone if her beliefs were questioned or someone she cared about was under attack.

Jerry jerked up when he realized what he was doing. Damn! He was comparing Angela McGee with his wife, Carmen.

Angela looked up to find Jerry's eyes on her. He was frowning so furiously that she turned away. She forced herself to respond to what was being said to her across the wire. "Oh really, Mr. McQueen...don't you think it is his decision whether I go or stay? I understand your reasons and I hope you understand mine."

"We can't force you to fulfill the terms of the contract, Angela. You're doing us a favor and we appreciate that. So, I'm asking you to find it in your heart to be generous, to see my nephew as a person in need of help. Please, have a little compassion and help him with his work."

How could they insinuate that Jerry was helpless and to be pitied? Angela looked at the virile man seated across from her and knew he would be offended if anyone offered him pity. "I'll see how

One Day at a Time

I feel about it. Why don't you talk to your nephew now, Mr. McQueen?" She passed Jerry the phone and sat stiffly as he bid his uncle bye.

Jerry frowned as soon as he hung up. "You don't have to stay if you'd rather not, Ms. McGee," Jerry offered although his chest tightened in rejection of his words. He didn't want her to leave, not yet.

"Have you changed your mind? Are you offering me the job?"

Jerry wanted to say, hell yes. But he didn't want to sound too eager, not after his earlier objections. "That depends on you, Ms. McGee. As you've probably surmised, your arrival was unexpected. I had requested a male assistant, but as usual, my uncle and my brother did as they pleased and ignored my instructions. I also hate being manipulated. So, if my, eh, reaction made you not want to stay, I'll understand."

For an apology, his sure lacked humility, thought Angela with a grimace. The man acted like he could never do wrong. And why couldn't he just give her a straight answer? How was she to investigate him if she didn't stay? "I need this job, Mr. Taylor."

"Why? Are you running away from something?"

"Of course not," Angela answered in disbelief.

"Someone perhaps?" He persisted.

Angela glared at him. "No. I just don't need the aggravation of arranging another vacation."

Jerry almost smiled at the sparkles in her eyes. She hated being doubted. But it was as clear as day that she was hiding something. *What do you want, Ms. McGee?* Was she after something from him or was she another attempt by his family to manipulate him? His family was so determined to see him involved with a woman it was pathetic. "Can you be trusted?"

Angela flushed. "No one has ever questioned my integrity, Mr. Taylor. I wouldn't insult either of us by climbing in your bed." She finished calmly.

"I didn't mean that, Ms. McGee." Why then was his mind imagining them together, her long limbs intertwined with his? "Remember you threatened to go to the tabloids if I didn't honor our agreement?"

"You know I'd never do that." She protested.

"I don't know anything of the sort. But if you're talking about the anti-disclosure papers my uncle made you sign then you must think I'm either stupid or gullible. We both know that wouldn't stop you if you were desperate."

"I'm not that desperate and I promise I'll never betray you." Her voice indicated the outrage she felt at being doubted

"Why did you say it then?"

"Your attitude pissed me off."

This time Jerry had to work hard at containing his amusement. She was very direct. Did she have a man waiting for her at home? Suddenly, he had an overwhelming urge to find out more about her. "Is there a husband at home you don't want to deal with now or a jealous lover perhaps?"

Angela almost told him that it was none of his business, but she knew that would be going too far. She curbed her tongue, ignored the intrusive question, and smiled. "Mr. Taylor, I'm a busy woman with schedules and deadlines. I can not afford to take a break whenever I feel like it. This is it for me. Besides, your family would never have suggested this arrangement if I weren't trustworthy. Believe me when I say that I was thoroughly scrutinized before this decision was made. They are very protective of you and wouldn't let just anyone near you."

"Somehow, I doubt that protection was on their minds when they employed you, Ms. McGee." He suddenly leaned forward. "So what do you know about computers?"

Her favorite subject, she thought with a smile. "A lot, I hope. I've taken PC repair classes. I can use any software in any system. I also write programs."

Although she was speaking in a matter-of-fact tone, there was a dose of pride thrown in with each sentence that he couldn't miss. "So, if I were to ask you to create a database for me, you wouldn't have any problems."

"None, whatsoever!" Angela replied without missing a beat.

Jerry leaned back and contemplated her. Intelligent, confident and very articulate! Why was she on his farm? "You said you're a busy woman, Ms. McGee. What do you do for a living?"

"I'm a nurse but I also own an Internet business—I create and maintain websites. Why are you asking me all these questions? Didn't your uncle fill you in on my credentials?"

Jerry frowned. "No. We had other concerns. Eh, does your work bring you enough revenue?"

"Why?"

Jerry smiled at her quick and defensive response. "Sorry, I know that was personal. I'm just wondering why you would want to be my assistant and vacation on my farm if your business was profitable."

"I have a laptop and a cell phone if my people need to reach me. And yes, Mr. Taylor, my business is very profitable. I just needed a break and your uncle and brother offered me this solution. I thought it was a wonderful idea. I wanted to see a part of the country I'd never visited."

Jerry's eyes narrowed as he studied her. His gut instinct told him to believe her simple explanation. But the part of him that had become wary of women and their motives questioned her reasons for wanting to be in his home. "Why don't you settle in for the night and see how you feel in the morning. After serious consideration, this holiday solution may not sound so attractive."

Angela sighed in relief when he looked away from her. Damn, the man had lethal eyes. But at least he was giving her a loop hole. She could always leave and say his display of anger was the cause. But how was that going to help her put a closure to her sister's death? No, she had to stay and finish what she started.

Why didn't that thought bring her joy? Was it worth it to accuse a man who was already suffering like Jerry was? He did lose his wife in that accident. And she was sure there was something wrong with his eyes. No, this won't do, Angela admonished herself. She was already questioning her resentment toward him. She needed to rest. Tomorrow would bring her the focus that she needed to continue her quest.

"I'll see you in the morning then, Mr. Taylor." Angela got up.

Jerry stood up, too, and walked her to the door. "Ms. McGee, don't be in a hurry to make that decision because once you commit yourself to me, I'll personally hold you to it. Today is Friday so, why don't you take the weekend to think your decision through. Be our guest for the next couple of days. If you decide you want to leave, I'll have Winston drive you to the airport first thing Monday morning." That should give him two days to show her he wasn't an arrogant, ill-mannered lout. He needed her expertise. Besides, it wouldn't hurt to have her around the farm.

Angela frowned at him. Why was he being so accommodating? She didn't want him to be nice. "Come Monday morning I'll probably be here." Angela shrugged elegantly. "And I don't mind starting work tomorrow, either."

"But I insist, Ms. McGee. Humor me." Then he smiled.

Angela stared at him in astonishment. Talk about a million dollar smile. She blinked rapidly and gathered her wits. She had to be on her guard against this man. He probably used that smile to beguile women. Well, not this woman, cowboy! The sooner she finished her investigation the faster she would leave his farm and forget he ever existed.

Angela lifted her head and smiled a slow, challenging smile. "Hmm-mm, yes, I'll take the weekend to decide whether I leave or stay." She waited for the veiled threat to sink in before she added, "I'll see you around then, Mr. Taylor."

Now why did she give him that smug smile? And did he detect a threat in her words? Jerry wondered as he watched her walk toward the kitchen. So, being charming wasn't the key to making Angela McGee amiable. Obviously, she was too smart to be easily fooled. Well, he was no fool either. He would find her weaknesses and her secrets, too. Oh, yes, it was going to be a challenge to see how long it would take to bend her to his will.

Chapter 5

Jerry cradled the phone on his shoulder and stretched his legs under the desk. "I can't believe you went along with Uncle C's scheme, Aaron. Didn't I explain why I didn't need any more female assistants?"

"That was before we found Ms. McGee. Anyway, you can thank me later, after she's straightened out your messed-up life, oh, I mean records. I heard she chewed the big guy's ears off over the deception. I would've loved to have heard that."

Aaron had a habit of ignoring things that Jerry found irritating. His brother wouldn't admit he had been wrong in collaborating with their uncle. "You should have been there because you deserved worse," Jerry growled.

Aaron laughed. "Yeah, right! Isn't she something? You should have seen the stir she caused when she came here, Jerry. We'd heard of Net Gate and how the owner was very talented and in high demand but we never expected her. You could say she impressed the hell out of us. She's very good at her stuff. You should think of asking her to create a site for Eagle's Hill, especially when you start selling or racing those horses of yours."

Jerry had already thought about it but he wasn't about to admit anything to his brother. "I don't want her to know too much about my business."

"Well, be nice to her. She maintains our website and we wouldn't want to be dropped from her A-list because of you. So, what do you think of her? Isn't she stunning?"

And then some, Jerry thought. But all he said was, "I guess she's tall for a woman."

"I don't mean that! I'm talking about the whole package."

"I haven't noticed. So, how are Sheryl and the children doing?"

Aaron laughed at Jerry's evasiveness. But instead of teasing him, he started to talk about his family. He and Sheryl had two children, a five-year old boy and a four-year-old girl, whom everyone doted on. Ever the loving father, Aaron made everything they did seem exceptional. He talked about their performance at swimming, gymnastics, and piano as if he personally coached them for these events. Jerry smiled as Aaron expounded the talents of each child, a fatherly pride in every word.

It was a while before his brother asked, "Have you seen mom lately?"

"Every other week...I go to SC Ranch for dinner every other weekend. She makes sure I don't forget—calls to remind me. She also stops to check on me although she pretends she comes to use the pool. I'll be seeing her this Sunday. You want me to pass a message?"

"Nope! Does she seem happy?" Aaron asked.

Jerry smiled as he remembered his mother's giggles during their last dinner. He'd thought she was flirting with the new foreman, Bill Skywalker. "I think so. I know she's our mom and stuff but I think she looks younger and prettier."

"I'll take your word for it. Do you think she'll ever come back to the gallery in L.A.? The kids miss her."

Jerry laughed. "To repeat Sally's words, there's no chance of that happening."

"I wish she could meet someone though. At her age, she's still young enough to start a new life with someone else," Aaron murmured.

Jerry thought his mother was sweet on Bill Skywalker but he wasn't ready to share that information with his brother until he was absolutely sure. "I feel you, bro. However, the person would have to be willing to stay with her at SC. Anyway, have you heard from Tahj?" Their brother sometimes collaborated with the FBI to apprehend criminals who'd skipped across the border into South America,

One Day at a Time

Mexico, or Canada.

"He called a week ago. He's still in Ecuador. I keep hoping he'll get tired of these dangerous assignments. One day some crazy drug dealer will blow off his head."

Their conversation stayed on Tahj before moving on to Melissa. Their baby sister had just done an exposé on a bunch of immigrant Sikhs operating a methamphetamine lab behind their temple in San Francisco. It was another ten minutes before they hung up.

Jerry loved talking to his older brother. Sure, Aaron annoyed him sometimes but he'd always been there for him. The day Jerry woke up in the hospital, blind, and without a family, Aaron had been by his side. After the funeral, Jerry had shrouded himself in a cocoon of indifference and refused to let anyone get close to him. But that hadn't stopped Aaron. His brother would drive from San Diego to Jerry's house in L.A. every weekend and talk his ears off. He had pushed and nagged until Jerry had lost his numbness. Jerry was pigheaded but Aaron took stubbornness to a different level. Nevertheless, Jerry loved his brother and would always appreciate what he had done for him.

When Jerry had decided there was much he could accomplish while blind, He'd discussed his plans with Aaron. When he'd needed to hire a physical trainer, Aaron had found Lester Wilson for him. Even when he'd decided to sell his L.A. house, it was Aaron who had handled everything. And Aaron found Angela.

A frown marred Jerry's forehead. Suddenly he wondered where she was. It was almost eleven and he hadn't seen a sign of her. Last night she had stayed in the kitchen and then disappeared into her bedroom. She had been tired and hadn't wanted dinner, Sally had told him. Well, she couldn't avoid him forever. Besides, she was a guest in his house and it was his duty as a host to check on her.

Jerry put the cell phone on the table and left the tack room. He walked to the stall where Mac and Little Joe were cleaning. He always made sure the manure was removed daily, the floor limed, and aired. The last thing his horses needed was flies. The damn bugs were a menace, whether they were stable flies, horseflies, deerflies, horn flies, or just face flies. They bit horses and were known to cause a horse with low-threshold for pain to take off in panic. Even tough horses could cause injuries to their joints and hooves by stomping their legs to rid themselves of the pestering flies.

Jerry spoke briefly to Mac before heading to the house. Whistling quietly under his breath, he pushed the kitchen door. He wasn't prepared for Angela who was on the other side of the door. He bumped into her and she lost her balance. He reached out for her.

Angela looked up in surprise. "You scared the living daylights out of me, Taylor." She sounded breathless. She stepped away from his hand. Jerry let her go but a chair was behind her and she tripped on it. Jerry reached out and wrapped his arm around her waist. Heat stole throughout her body at the intimate gesture.

Hmm, she smelled good, Jerry thought distractedly. "If you didn't try so hard to get away from me, you'd not be getting hurt. What were you doing behind the door, Angela?"

"Eh, putting away the scissors. And I'm not trying to get away from you. I just happen to have things to do." She wiggled from his hold and tried to put some distance between their bodies. He was too close. His thigh was pressing against hers and the heat from it made her dizzy. She wiggled, again. His hand tightened on her waist and didn't let go. Her mouth went dry.

"I'm sorry if I scared you." His voice had softened. His hand moved slowly from her waist to her arm.

"It's okay. Taylor? Let go of my arm, please."

"Why?" Jerry asked while his eyes searched her flushed face.

She took a deep breath and unwittingly inhaled his clean musky scent mixed with fresh air and sunshine. *Lord, give me strength.* She cleared her throat and asked, "What kind of a question is that?"

"You're shaking. Did I really scare you that much?"

Angela sucked in her breath and pulled her arm free. Her hands were trembling and she had a sudden urge to bolt. *She was not a coward, never had been, and wasn't about to become one now.* But the way she picked up the basket filled with freshly cut flowers and held it in front of her told a different story. "Well, I think I might have overdone it this morning while cutting the flowers."

Jerry's eyes moved from her face to the flowers in the basket. Slowly, he removed his glasses and smiled. It was that infuriating, totally male grin that indicated he knew how he affected her. Angela stiffened. She hated the way her body reacted to his.

He folded his arms across his chest. "You didn't wear a hat." He stated with a knowing tone. "You should never go outside without one."

She rushed into speech. "I hope you don't mind about the flowers. Sally said it was okay to cut some."

He made her nervous, he thought with amusement. "And I would never disagree with Sally. The house is her domain—whatever she says goes. So, where were you planning on putting those?"

"In different rooms, if that's okay with you. I was hoping Sally would show me where the vases are. You do have vases, don't you?"

"Yes, we do. I'll show you." He indicated that she should walk ahead of him. Smiling weakly at him, she headed toward the foyer. "You should always wear a hat when you go outside otherwise you'll get sick. The sun here is not like in California."

She stopped in the foyer. "I brought one but it is absolutely useless. I guess I'll have to go to town and buy one." When Jerry didn't say anything, she looked up. He was staring at her so intently that she blushed. "Eh, where are the vases?"

"In the basement." He pointed to a door in the inner room from the foyer. "Sally should find you a hat around here. According to her, my brother's wife, Sheryl, brings a new one every time they visit and for some reason, she always forgets to take them back." As soon as they reached the basement, Jerry touched a switch and light flooded the room.

The hand that had reached out to turn on the switch brushed against Angela's hair. She held her breath until he dropped his hand. Had it lingered there or was it just her imagination? The thought was forgotten as she turned to look at the entertainment room. It boasted a giant-size screen, comfortable chaise lounges and seats, a pool table, a dart board, and a bar. Two doors were visible from where Angela stood. "This is beautiful."

"Sheryl deserves all the credit. She did the interior decorating. Ah, here we are." He threw open a cabinet.

"The decor compliments the house, Taylor. So, she had to have something to start with." Angela's eyes lit up and her lips curled into a smile at the collection of beautiful vases perfectly displayed inside the cabinet. She walked over and reached for one. "Whoever bought these has very good taste." Angela loved fresh flowers but she collected vases. Whether they were antiques or just plain tacky, her kitchen had dozens of vases. She pulled out two, added two more and was about to reach for another pair when Jerry spoke.

"Just how many vases do you need?" Every time she reached for the vases, her top rode up and bared her mid-section. And the sounds she was making were downright erotic.

His voice sounded husky and so close that she glanced over her shoulder. His glasses were back on his nose but a tiny smile played on his lips. "You find my reaction amusing?"

"I've never seen anyone show this much enthusiasm over vases."

Angela laughed comfortably at his dry tones. "Not when you're a collector, Taylor. I can spend an afternoon scouring second hand stores for vases, and I'm not ashamed of it. Nothing lifts my spirits like flowers in the right vase."

"Then I'll make sure I ask Sheryl where she got these. I thought she'd overdone it when she bought them but she kept saying she had to stop herself before buying everything. So, how many do you need?"

"Enough for most of the rooms."

"I'll take these six, you carry the next four. If you need more, I'll get them later."

"Ah-mm! What if you, eh, slipped? I mean, one could fall and break. I know about your eyes and I don't know if you really want to carry these delicate vases...what I'm trying to say is that I can make several trips to get them." She finished lamely. Lord, she hoped she hadn't offended him. But with the sunglasses covering his eyes, she couldn't tell what he was thinking.

One Day at a Time

Jerry leaned against the counter and tried to control his amusement. "Are you saying that people with eye problems should not be allowed to do anything because they might mess up or hurt themselves?"

"I didn't say that," Angela protested.

"Or are the vases more precious than my ego, which you've just thoroughly flattened."

Had she really insulted his ego? He didn't seem annoyed. "Did I really?" He grinned wickedly at her. Rolling her eyes at his teasing, she turned and passed him two vases. She added two more. "Those are four, two more to go." She got the remaining two and pushed them into his hands. "There! Take them upstairs, Taylor."

He smiled cockily at her and said, "Please call me JT or Jerry."

She wrinkled her nose at him. "You got your six vases, Taylor. Don't let me stop you." Arrogant cowboy! She didn't put a single dent in his ego. It was too inflated for that to happen.

"What if I stumble? I wouldn't want to break these beautiful, delicate vases. After all they did put quite a hole in my bank account." He didn't move an inch but watched her struggle with embarrassment and amusement.

Angela didn't believe the vases had been that expensive. She glared at him as she fought for composure. "Taylor, I didn't mean to imply that you're...that somehow because you have a problem with your eyes that makes you..." she stopped and searched her brain. How would she explain this? She couldn't say 'less than a man' because that sounded so corny. She looked up and shrugged helplessly.

She looked so vulnerable and confused that he decided to rescue her. "I'll accept your apology on one condition."

Angela rolled her eyes and sighed. "What?"

"Stop calling me Taylor."

"Okay, Tay...Jerry, could we go upstairs before my flowers start wilting?"

He grinned at her disgruntled tone. "After you, Angela. I rather like following you."

She picked up the other four vases and marched upstairs without stopping to check on whether or not he was following her. The impossible man was toying with her and enjoying every moment of it.

She was already arranging the flowers in her vases when he swaggered into the kitchen. She ignored him.

Jerry watched her. She made an enticing picture as she chewed her lower lip and worked. Every time she leaned forward her pants stretched across her buttocks. He swallowed and controlled his desire long enough to say, "Aren't you going to help me put these down?"

"No, I'm sure you can manage just fine."

He chuckled and put the vases on the counter beside her. "You're one cruel woman, Angela McGee."

"And you're such a fraud, Jerry Taylor. Is there something wrong with yours eyes or not?"

Jerry straightened up. "What do you mean? I've already told you that there is nothing wrong with my eyes."

She snickered and took one of the vases he'd carried. Nipping the stem of a bloom, she dropped it in the vase. She pointed at his sunglasses. "Why are you wearing those?"

"It's an image thing, baby." When she shook her head, he added, "You have a very suspicious mind." Then he strutted out the kitchen door, whistling a catchy tune.

If Jerry thought he could fool her by that helpless act, he had another think coming. She would discover all his secrets. Just let him try and lie to her.

But, first things first. She was going to learn more about him and what better way to do that than by studying his home. And putting flowers in each room gave her the means to accomplish that. She smiled. Devious to the core, Nikki would say and she would agree with her. Although she had to admit that when she'd set out to cut the flowers, that thought hadn't entered her mind. She genuinely loved flowers and seeing them in perfect bloom outside had made her want to bring some indoors. Now, they would serve another purpose.

Now, where to begin? Ah, first floor. The staircase started to the left of the foyer and curved to the second floor. It divided the doors

One Day at a Time

leading to the dining room and kitchen to the left and an arch that led to the inner chamber, his den, and the living room to the right. She started with the dining room with its bi-pyramidal chandelier, ten chair elliptical dining table, wall lights, and fours niches housing wooden African candle holders. One of the dining room doors led to the kitchen while the other opened to the foyer. She left two vases on the table and walked across the foyer to the living room.

The living room was spacious and conservatively done in earthy colors. She liked the fireplace. It was done with native stones and Jerry had had the corners smoothed and curved. His heritage was reflected in the décor. There were carvings, vases, hand woven throw rugs and blankets, batiks, arrows and bows, and even a shield. Like his gallery upstairs, most of the artwork indicated he favored African and Native American art. There were also lots of family pictures. Angela picked up some and studied them. In addition to Aaron, she picked out two other brothers. There were not many family pictures of Carmen and Jerry together but the few she saw indicated that they had been happy. It was reflected in their expressions and body language. Angela left two vases of flowers in the room—one on the coffee table and the other on a side table—and went back to the foyer.

She didn't want to enter Jerry's den. That would be invading his privacy, so she ignored the closed door and headed for the doors which led to the basement, two bedrooms, and the kitchen. Sally had pointed out Lester's room, so Angela left a vase outside his door. The other bedroom was furnished but unoccupied. The hallway led her to a changing room, the steam room, the sauna, and beyond that, the gym and the gaming room. The hallway ended at a door which led directly to the pool deck. The pool was L-shaped and was screened and surrounded by a privacy wall. The gaming room had access to both the living room and the pool. She left a vase on the counter of the bar in the gaming room. Quietly, she retraced her steps back to the inner chamber.

Carrying four vases, she headed up the grand stairs to the second floor where there were several more bedrooms. She went to hers first and left a vase on her night stand. Sally had pointed out Jerry's room the previous evening as she'd escorted Angela to her room. It was to the left of hers but like Lester's, she dared not enter, and left a vase outside the door. Beside his room was the library, another room Sally had pointed out to her. She opened the door and tentatively peeked in. When she saw that it was empty, she walked in.

The room was done in brick red, from the striped wall paper to the entertainment unit at the corner. The shelves and the cabinets ran along one wall while a mocha couch was placed opposite the shelves. A coffee table was in front of it and a diamond-shaped side table with a lamp was to the right. At the corners were two black chaise lounges with floor lamps beside them. The room was so soothing. She could be inspired to compose music in this room, Angela thought and then laughed. She left two vases there.

Across the photo gallery were more bedrooms. Two of them were empty. One was done in yellow while the other in pale blue. Angela was surprised to find a crib, a dresser, and a rocking chair in the blue room. Had Jerry and Carmen been expecting a child when she died? There was a connecting door which opened into a play room, filled with children's toys. Angela walked into the room even as her eyes misted. She touched a rocking chair and watched as it moved on its elastic hinges. There were two bean bags along a wall; a small T.V. on a low level entertainment center; a double sided easel; a small, round table with two chairs, and a train set at a corner.

Lord, the wife couldn't have been pregnant. The papers never mentioned it. Or had they prepared a nursery for their future children? The constriction in Angela's chest increased. This was wrong, she thought as she left the room hurriedly.

She walked past the last door without stopping and headed straight back to her room. What had she been up to? Did she really think snooping around would produce some evidence of Jerry's guilt? What could prove that he was guilty of being an obsessive and abusive husband? What could possibly show that a man was responsible for an accident? Only Jerry could tell her what she wanted to know, not his house, his pictures, or the decor of each room. Wiping her eyes, she closed her door and fell on the bed.

One Day at a Time

After staring at the ceiling with unseeing eyes for several minutes, she reached for her cell phone. She needed to hear familiar voices to remind her that what she was doing was right. Unfortunately, Nikki was out of her office. Next she called her parents. When their answering machine started, she hung up. Finally, she placed the most important call. She called Reggie's hospital.

"Could I talk to Sheena, please," Angela asked as soon as the nurse at the front desk answered. Recognizing her voice, the woman connected her to Reggie's room.

"Angela?" Sheena asked in surprise.

"Hey, Sheena, I'm just checking in. How is he doing?"

"Okay. I just finished bathing him." Sheena answered. "Where are you calling from? I thought you were on vacation, Angela."

"I am. So, there's no change, huh?" Angela asked with resignation.

"No, though his vitals are normal—same as yesterday." Then as if she couldn't help herself, Sheena added, "You just left yesterday, Angela. Why don't you enjoy your vacation and let us worry about Reggie for the next couple of weeks?"

A sad smile crossed Angela's lips. "Can't help thinking and worrying about him, Sheena. Do you happen to know when Dr. Parker will be doing the next EEG scan? He mentioned that he would be performing one next week but he didn't give a specific date."

"Reggie is scheduled for Thursday." Sheena replied.

"Will you be on duty then? I would like to know the result." Angela added.

"I'll be in most of the day but Freda takes over after six."

"I see. I, eh, I'll try to get in touch with Dr. Parker but if I fail to catch up with him, I'll talk to whoever is on duty." Angela thanked the nurse and hung up.

Thinking about Reggie and hearing about his unimproved state made her more determined than ever to find out what happened between Jerry and his wife on the day of the accident. It also brought her anger and frustrations to the forefront.

She sniffled as a sudden rush of tears blurred her vision. *This won't do, Angela,* she told herself. She couldn't afford to become emotional, not when Reggie needed her. She owed it to him and to Sav to get to the bottom of this—to find out the truth. And nothing, not even an attraction between her and Jerry, would stop her.

She had to learn what type of a man he was. Yes, she would befriend him and hopefully, he would confide in her about his life— past and present. Having reached that conclusion, Angela pulled her recorder from its case and started playing a tune.

Chapter 6

Angela was soon engrossed in her music. Whenever she played, nothing was allowed to intrude. The feelings that arose from the lyrics she created soothed her and made her feel happy and at peace. So, she didn't hear the knock on her door or her name being called. Sally had told her lunch was at twelve but as usual, time held no meaning when she sang.

It wasn't until someone banged on her door that Angela jerked back in surprise. She raced to open it. There was Jerry leaning against the doorframe, looking unremorseful for interrupting her so rudely.

"Taylor?" Angela asked with a frown.

"I thought we agreed no more Taylor. It is lunch time and Sally sent me to fetch you." Jerry's eyes shifted from her face to the instrument then back to her face.

"Oh," Angela said as she pushed hair from her face. "I...I forgot about time."

Her eyes seemed so huge and soft, her hair more unruly, and her relaxed body so inviting that a sudden urge to pull her in his arms stole through him. "Was that the radio or you hollering?"

Angela's embarrassment disappeared. "That's so insulting." She answered indignantly. "I do not holler. I sing."

"Is that what it was? I guess it wasn't so bad. Do you perform on amateur nights in clubs in San Diego?"

Angela narrowed her eyes. She wasn't going to let him provoke her. No way. Besides, she had a plan. She smiled instead and asked, "Does that mean that you think I'm good enough to perform in front of people or that I'm so terrible I have to perform behind closed doors?"

Jerry smiled at her comeback, touched his chin in thought and then said, "I don't know for sure. I guess you'd have to play for me before I can decide."

"Dream on, cowboy." Angela turned and put the recorder on the bed.

Jerry didn't move from the doorway. When she walked back and tried to go around him, he blocked her path. "Does that mean you'd never sing for me?"

Did that question have a double meaning? Was he flirting with her? Angela frowned at him. "Hell will freeze over first, cowboy. When I sing, I do it because I want to and not because someone wants me to." She looked at him pointedly.

He leaned closer. Angela took a step back. "I bet I could make you sing."

The arrogant man was actually flirting with her, she thought as her heart skipped a beat and her stomach clenched with awareness. Could he make her sing a sonata with a touch? *Now where did that thought come from?* "Sally is waiting for us and I refuse to play betting games with you. Now move over and let me pass."

Jerry raised an arrogant eyebrow and grinned. "I'm not stopping you."

She made a face at him. "Do you know what? I bet you were a born bully. I bet you were one of those boys who cornered girls during recess and tormented them."

"Does that mean I'm tormenting you?" He laughed but moved aside for her.

She laughed. "I have a stiffer backbone, Taylor. You are just annoying."

His laughter joined hers as she headed for the stairs. "Thanks for the flowers."

"You're welcome." She started down the stairs.

Jerry leaned against the rail and watched her. "Next time, feel free to bring them in. I don't bite." He laughed when she stopped, looked up, and shook her head.

One Day at a Time

"I'll be sure to accept that invitation, when you're busy with the horses." She continued down the stairs.

"Then I'll make sure I'm there to help you cut and arrange them."

"Uh-huh." A smile tugged at the corners of her mouth.

"Oh, Angela?" He waited until she looked up before saying, "Don't hide in your room tonight. I want you to join me for dinner."

Angela smothered a laugh. Didn't he realize how arrogant he sounded? Instead of drawing his attention to it, she asked, "You do?"

"Yes. I'm going to a neighbor's ranch but I should be back by early evening." When she continued to stare at him, he added, "Well? Will you be there?"

Angela shook her head. "Try asking me next time, Taylor, instead of stating what *you* want." Then she disappeared into the kitchen.

Conversation stopped when Angela walked in. The ranch workers stared at her warily until she smiled and asked, "Is it okay if I join you for lunch? I promise not to bother you with too many questions about Montana or horses. Winston knows that I get carried away when I talk about things that interest me."

There was a chorused yes and vigorous nods. She smiled and walked toward them. Sally introduced her to everyone. There was Big Joe, a heavyset black man with massive arms and gentle manners. His teenage son, Little Joe, was a little slow and talked with a lisp. Little Joe smiled shyly at Angela and her heart melted. Sly Nunez had been on the farm for less than a month but he already got along with everyone. He was a jocular Mexican who chewed tobacco and talked nonstop about everything. Then there was Mac—a shy, Indian young man Sly called Sonny. And of course, she knew Winston, the older African American foreman with leathery skin and a slight limp. Lester, Jerry's trainer, was gone for the weekend but she had met him the day before.

She didn't know whether it was her interest in their work or because she was a woman but she was soon included in their conversation. During breakfast, Sally had filled her in on the sleeping arrangements around the ranch. The ranch hands had rooms in the old homestead that was near the barn while Sally and Winston had a self-contained unit on the south end of Jerry's house. Their place was separated from the main house by the garage. Although the ranch hands had a kitchen and a living room where they slept, they took their meals in the main house kitchen and occasionally stayed to watch T.V.

She learned the names of Jerry's horses as the men talked about their daily routine around the farms. She detected respect and admiration for Jerry when they discussed the way he ran the farm. Their sentences often started with "Jerry had said it was important to" or ended with "Jerry was right when he told us to do this or that." Apparently, Jerry knew a lot about horses and worked alongside his workers. From a few of the comments, she also figured out that he usually valued their opinions and often discussed things with them.

They were almost finished with their lunch when he joined them. She thought that the men would feel uncomfortable with the boss around, but she was wrong. The kitchen became noisier and livelier. Apparently, they held discussions during lunch time on topics ranging from chores to sports.

Angela smiled as Jerry and Big Joe started a heated debate about free agents and professional sports. Everyone had a point or two to add. Sally didn't say much, but she wore a happy expression as she watched them.

This was a happy ranch, Angela thought with amazement. And the central figure was Jerry. She could see why his workers thought highly of him; he treated them like family. The man was beginning to intrigue her, and she didn't know if that was good or bad.

She waited until the men left the kitchen, before she disappeared upstairs. She called Nikki's office again. This time she was lucky. "Hey, counselor, how is work?"

"Angela? Hey, girl, how was your flight? How is your friend doing? Is it a modern farm or one of those with outhouses and lanterns?"

Angela laughed. "My flight was okay. I was picked up in Helena by the foreman and got to enjoy the scenery as we drove to the

One Day at a Time

farm. My friend is okay and the farm...what can I say? Would you believe me if I say that it is one of those Tudor houses with a grand staircase, a pool, a gym, sauna, and steam room? The whirlpool by the pool is pure marble and defies description."

"Are you trying to make me jealous, girl? Of course, I don't believe you. No one can call such a fancy house a farm."

"Well, you better believe it. I'll even send you pictures over the Internet in the next couple of days to prove it."

"Okay. So, have you gone riding yet?" Nikki asked teasingly.

"I need to gather enough courage to go to the paddocks, let alone ride. But I doubt that I'll be doing any riding." Angela said as she left her room and headed for the library. She liked her room but the library was her favorite place.

"I told you to get back on the damn horse when you got thrown off," Nikki reminded her.

She and Nikki had decided to take riding lessons and had attended a riding school together. On the last day of their first session, Angela's horse had bolted and thrown her. Apart from a few bruises, she hadn't really been hurt. However, her pride had taken a thorough beating and her trust in horses had been destroyed. She'd refused to get back on the horse despite the instructor's urging. Since then, she steered clear of the beautiful animals. But her fascination with them had never faded.

"I'll admire them from afar. Now, what have you been up to?" Angela asked as she opened the library door and walked in, heading straight for one of the leather chaise lounges.

"You only left yesterday," Nikki retorted.

"A lot can happen in twenty-four hours. I guess my parent's are not yet back. I called but no one picked up the phone."

"No, they are not. Ooh, how could I forget? We went to Shelby's yesterday and..."

Angela interrupted with, "I thought going to clubs during week days was not your thing. What was going on at Shelby's to make you break your rule?"

"You won't know if you don't let me finish. One of the paralegals from our office got engaged and I was invited out for a drink. Anyway, you won't believe who walked in?"

"Denzel Washington and Morris Chestnut?" Angela teased her.

"Ha-ha funny! Ray Jones," Nikki added in revulsion.

Angela laughed. Ray was her ex-boyfriend. Nikki never liked him from their first meeting but had tolerated him for Angela's sake. "I'm happy he's dating."

"Who cares about that—but can you believe his nerve? Coming to our club..."

"We've no personal claim to that club, Nikki," Angela interrupted with a smile.

"We introduced his countrified-self to it. But coming to our club with some underage, Janet Jackson wanna-be hanging all over him? I felt like slapping him back to his father's share-cropping farm in Mississippi."

Angela burst out laughing. When Nikki started on a man, she got downright nasty. "I've only been gone for a day and I already miss you, girl."

"You don't know the half of it. He had the audacity to swagger up to us and act like he and I were best buddies. When I tried to snub him, he introduced himself to my colleagues—who just happened to be mostly unattached females and were already checking him out. Then he had the nerve to add that he was new in town and had recently opened his practice. As you can imagine, all their male-seeking antennas curved toward him. He would have stayed with us and they wouldn't have minded. And it was a girls-only outing to begin with."

Angle was doubled over with laughter. "How did you make him leave? Because I know you, girl, and I'm sure you didn't take his interruption lying down." Angela said between gulps.

"I swear if his clingy girlfriend hadn't pulled him away, I would have been tempted to punch his long snout of a nose—the low lying scum!"

Angela rolled back on her seat and smothered a sound. "He's not important, Nikki, not to me anyway."

But Nikki was on a roll and there was no stopping her. As she continued to vent her anger at Ray, Angela reflected on what had gone wrong between her and the man she'd thought would one day be her husband. She and Ray had met at a local charity event given by Mrs. Maitland, Sav's mother-in-law. Angela had attended the gala because Sav had begged her to accompany her. Before she knew it, Ray was pursuing her with the ardor of a man possessed. Flowers, chocolate, and love notes were sent to her office. At last she'd agreed to go on a date with him, then another, and another. Things were beginning to get serious between, when Sav died. The day Ray learned that Reggie was Angela's responsibility, the love he had professed for her dwindled away. He stopped calling her and became too busy with meetings to see her.

"Angela? Did he ever frame the painting Sav gave you?" Nikki asked.

"I don't know. I didn't have time to ask him. I'll probably get it when I get back." She didn't really want to see Ray, let alone deal with him. He was so manipulative. "Nikki, why don't you pick it up for me?"

"The pleasure will be mine. I wish I could arrive when he's giving a party...maybe when he's in the process of showing off *his* original Hanna Vas painting—hmm. I can just imagine the look on his face...the embarrassment, oh!"

"Will you quit?"

"Hmm-mm, I'm going to enjoy this, especially after what he pulled at the club last night. Revenge is best served cold, after a thorough calculation and deliberation. And you're going to miss it, too."

Revenge! That word reminded Angela of Jerry and her reasons for being in his home. Was she here for revenge? Revenge was such a nasty word. No, she was here to find out the truth. "I leave the drama to you, Nikki. Now, can we talk about something else?" Ray was the least of her worries.

They spent another ten minutes talking before hanging up. Angela looked through Jerry's book collection. He had a wide selection; from heritage and cultural books to suspense novels. But she wasn't in a mood for reading. Why not a swim? Jerry had told her to use the facilities his home offered. And she'd been longing to take a dip in that cool, blue water since she saw it.

An hour and a half later, after an invigorating swim, she was ready to face Jerry. She looked in the mirror and grinned. The outfit she chose for dinner was lethal. It hugged her body like a second skin and left her shoulders bare. Sure it was a little overdone for dinner on a farm, but a woman had to know when to cast her spell, when to enchant and seduce. She pressed her flat abs and looked at her backside in the mirror. *Hmm! Watch out, cowboy. You're not going to know what hit you!*

Would Jerry be enthralled? Did she want him to? *Oh, yes!* Wouldn't it be something to make him take notice, to make him want and need her? It would make her investigation easier because a man in love holds nothing back.

Angela sighed as she picked up her sandals. She was out of her mind. She was here for a purpose and it wasn't seduction. Besides, she had scruples. The problem was she needed everything she had to deal with Jerry and his seductive smile. And from experience, the lacy green dress always gave her that extra something to face anything or anyone. Slipping into the medium-heeled sandals and hiding the upper bodice of her outfit behind a wrap, Angela headed downstairs.

Jerry was already in the dining room when Angela walked in. She paused when she saw him. He was wearing a white shirt and black pants, and looking very urbane. The cowboy boots were replaced by loafers. He looked good—good enough to make a girl want to touch and taste, and forget her intentions. She put a stop on her wayward thoughts.

"Good evening, Jerry."

A smile played on his lips when he looked up and caught her eye. "Good evening to you, too, Ms. Angela McGee. I wasn't sure whether to send a search party or come and fetch you myself." *But the waiting was worth it because she looks sensational.* Jerry thought as he transferred the wine cooler to the table and held a chair for her. "May I?"

One Day at a Time

"Thank you." She said as she sat down. He was still standing close to her and she caught a whiff of his cologne. She scooted forward and stared fixedly ahead.

"Can I offer you some wine?" He removed the bottle from the ice, inserted the opener and deftly removed the cork. "I have one of Italy's best wines, Solare, cabernet sauvignon. But if you'd prefer something else, I'll strive to get it."

Angela smiled. "That's fine. Isn't it a rare wine?" She asked when she saw that it was the 95 vintage.

"I don't know. My brother received several bottles from a friend who owns a small vineyard near Napa Valley." He poured her a glass and filled his, too. "You see, I can be polite." He grinned and took the chair opposite hers. "Did I really sound autocratic when I asked you to join me for dinner?"

"You didn't ask, you ordered." She smiled and sipped her wine. It tasted velvety, which did not suprise her after what she had heard about it. "Your sight must be fully restored, Jerry, because there is no way you could have poured that wine without spilling it."

Jerry grinned and answered her in his unique way. "Have I complimented you on your outfit, yet? It suits you perfectly—whatever the shawl is not covering."

"Thank you."

He watched her eyes light up with suppressed mirth before directing her attention to the various dishes on the table. "Sally has outdone herself tonight so, help yourself."

The table was laden with various Mexican dishes—spicy corn and tomato soup, guacamole, grilled chicken with chile on a rice bed, spinach and mushroom enchiladas, and two side dishes—potato salad and tossed veggie salad.

As they served themselves and started eating Jerry said, "So, tell me. What did you do to Winston on your way here from the airport?"

"Why?"

"Because he sided with you yesterday. He and Sally helped raise me and had adored me since I was a baby, until your arrival."

He couldn't be disgruntled, could he? And yet his expression indicated genuine puzzlement. She grinned. "Maybe they don't think you're adorable anymore. Maybe they realized that you were being unreasonable. After all, it wasn't my fault I was here."

He grunted and said, "Well, it isn't often that a beautiful woman threatens me in my home."

She was sure all the women he knew spoiled him, when they were not tearing his clothes off his fabulous body. Jerry Taylor was a fascinating and potent man, a fact that kept playing over and over in her head. "I did apologize for that, didn't I?"

"Was that for stealing my employees' affection, or threatening to wash my mouth, sue me, and call the reporters?" Her laughter interrupted him. It was musical and sexy. "Wasn't that the right order?"

"It sounds horrible when you list them like that. Was I that awful?"

Was she? Half of the time he had been fascinated by her flashing eyes. "Very much so, but I forgive you." He waited to see how she would receive his comment. When she just laughed, he added, "Because I started it by provoking you."

She had been ready to do battle with him from the word go, Angela thought. "You are very generous," she answered with sincerity.

Appreciative gleam shone in his eyes. "I'm happy you've noticed," he teased.

She shook her head at their silly repartee. "May I ask you something? How come everyone talks about how you mastered riding Thunder and learned where everything is around the farm while blind? Even your uncle implied it during our interview."

"Uncle C hasn't been here for over two months so he doesn't know that my sight is okay. And I did learn to find my way around the farm while I was blind." He went on to explain about the Chilean doctor, Raul Rojo, and the miracle he'd performed on his eyes.

She couldn't believe he had been blind for nine months. "That's an amazing story. How did you employ your workers or choose your mares while blind?"

He chuckled. "I bought the mares before my accident. No one

One Day at a Time

can pick a good horse while blind, Angela. There are many things you have to look for before buying one. The legs, joints, teeth, the overall body structure and posture are all important to a breeder. In the last couple of years, I've spent time researching the best mares with good genetic background and talking with their owners. Over a year ago, I bought what I wanted and had Winston and Big Joe take care of them for me. As for my workers, Big Joe has been with me for over three years now. He watched over the house when it was being built and remained here to guard it while I wasn't around. He also helped me find Mac. Sly has been with us for less than a month, and Winston and Sally came from South Creek, my grandfather's ranch."

"So, you did lose your sight during, eh, when the accident happened?" *Was that too personal a question?* Angela hoped not. Still, she was dismayed when his smile disappeared and he withdrew from her. Darn it, she was moving too fast.

Jerry didn't want to think about the accident or Carmen. The memories were not for sharing with strangers, and Angela was a stranger. He stared into his plate for a few seconds before looking up with an expressionless face. He nodded briefly.

It must still be painful for him, Angela thought as she stared at her plate. She wanted to know about the child's room upstairs. Had his wife been expecting? She stared at Jerry's closed face. In a subdued tone, she said, "Tell me about your ranch. What inspired you to want to become a horse breeder?"

Jerry shrugged. "Not what, but who. First there is my grandfather, Hawkeye. You have to meet him and talk to him to appreciate his mind." He smiled and the sadness seemed to melt away. "The other person was Montana's famous black cowboy, Walter 'the kid' Jackson."

"Walter the kid? Didn't they do a documentary on him some time back?"

"I believe so. Walter was the first black baby to be born in the Montana territory. His father, George Jackson, came from the South, decided to break wild horses for some Montana ranchers, and settled

70

here." Jerry explained.

"I never knew they had black cowboys in the North." Angela interrupted with a frown. "I've heard of the Texan cowboys and I had assumed Walter was from there."

"Walter was a Montanan, which was amazing because this area had mainly whites and Indians. However, the southern black cowboys rode North with the rail herds and went back to Texas as soon as they delivered the herds and collected their wages. But one day, Walter's father—George Jackson—decided he wanted to break horses, a dangerous occupation if there ever was one. He settled here, met a black woman from the neighboring state and got married. Sadly, he died shortly before Walter was born. By thirteen, Walter knew what he wanted to do for a living, and that was corralling wild horses and breaking them. Like father like son."

Angela stopped eating as Jerry explained how Walter became a protégé of the famous Indian Joe—a college educated Indian of mixed heritage, chief of police on Flathead Reservation at one time, a gambler, and an outlaw. It was obvious that Jerry loved history. A gentle smile touched his lips as he talked and Angela found herself wishing she were free to be herself, free to enjoy his company, and to treat him as an attractive man she'd just met instead of always questioning every gesture he made and every smile he gave.

Jerry sipped his drink, noticing the interest on Angela's face. She was a good listener. "Although Walter never joined Indian Joe and his gang during a hold-up, he learned a lot about horses from him. But, it was a very strange friendship; the tough half-white and half-Indian outlaw, protective and gentle, with a young black boy in a pioneer country dominated by full-blood Indians and white men. Walter became well-known by other cowboys and ranchers for his work and perseverance but no one dared to bother him because of his relationship with Indian Joe. Stories like that inspired me to do what I love. I liked baseball and I enjoyed playing it, but I love horses."

"I love horses, too, at a distance." Angela joked as they went back to their food.

Jerry propped his chin on his knuckles and stared at her. Her smile was beckoning. Was her skin as soft as it looked? "What do you have against horses? They are the gentlest creatures God ever created."

"You mean after dogs, cats, and all domesticated birds." She laughed at his indignant expression. "One thing I can say for sure is that they are beautiful."

"So what's the problem?"

"Well, I tried riding once and the damn horse threw me; nearly broke my bones. I lost trust in them after that."

A horse's behavior depends on the rider but Jerry didn't want to tell her that. He didn't want her to leave his farm. Not if he wanted his records taken care of. Besides, he wanted to find out what made her tick. "You can't stay here without riding, Angela. I guess I'll just have to teach you." He sighed dramatically as if it were an unwelcome chore.

"No one's twisting your arm, Taylor."

"It is an insult to me and my horses. You have absolutely no say in it. We have to start as soon as possible, before the word gets around. In fact, you're going to meet them this evening. That way, you'll be prepared for tomorrow."

His arrogance was showing again, Angela thought, but all she asked was, "What's happening tomorrow?"

"You're spending the day with me. You can't learn about horses from a distance and they sure won't trust you if they don't know you."

Angela put down her fork and cupped her chin. A soft smile played on her lips as she contemplated Jerry. "I'm finally coming to a very important conclusion, Taylor."

He cupped his chin, too, and raised an eyebrow. "What?"

"You are a hopeless case. You're without a doubt the most arrogant, chauvinistic, and conceited man I've ever met."

He grinned. "Arrogant and conceited mean the same thing."

"I know. I didn't want to say doubly arrogant. Didn't your mama ever teach you to be polite and try asking for things instead of issuing orders?"

What was she talking about now? "She did. So?"

"So, why don't you ask me if I want to spend the day with you or see your horses? It's not really hard. All you have to say is, 'please, could you give me the joy of having your presence tomorrow' or 'would you mind spending some time with me tomorrow while I work around the farm'—it is very simple."

Jerry leaned back and laughed. "You're kidding, right?"

She raised an eyebrow and replied, "No, I am not."

He gave her that infuriating male smile. "First, I won't be the only one working, you'll be too. Second, does that really work with you—the politeness and the gentlemanly approach?" Angela rolled her eyes and threw her hands in defeat. "I've figured out certain things about you, too, Angela. You like twisting people around your finger, especially men. You're a very vocal, direct, and no nonsense kind of woman. You boldly tread where other people dare not go." *That would make her very loyal and tenacious about her beliefs, an admirable trait.* "And you love to twist men around your finger."

"You're beginning to repeat yourself, cowboy."

He winked. "I know. Also, I've noticed that when you're irritated with me, you call me Taylor. When I become personal, you call me cowboy. The only time you use Jerry is when you feel safe. So, do I bother you, Angela?"

Angela refused to be drawn into a flirting session with him. She got up. "Are we going to see your horses or not, cowboy?"

He laughed and stood up, too. "See what I mean?"

"I'll go change into something suitable. And, Taylor, while I'm gone, think about this—you don't know me. You may think that you do but you don't."

Jerry grinned as she glided out of the room. He was looking forward to peeling those layers back until he knew everything there was to know about Angela McGee. He grinned as he carried his wine to the foyer, sat at the foot of the stairs, and waited for her.

What made Angela tick? What were her secrets? She must have some, Jerry thought with a frown. Earlier today, he had seen her leave the playroom upstairs. What had she been doing there? Had she been

One Day at a Time

curious about his home or had she been searching for something? Just when he'd concluded that she was snooping around, she had passed the other room without entering it. But the questions still remained. Was she who she said she was or did she have a motive for being in his home?

Chapter 7

Jerry was still thinking about Angela and her motives when she came from her room.

"That is a peculiar expression you have on your face, Taylor. What are you plotting?" Angela spoke from a curve on the stair, staring at him with a teasing gleam in her eyes.

Jerry stood up and watched her as she took one step at a time. She had changed into a pair of navy blue pants and a blue and red sweater, which molded her breasts and drew attention to their fullness. He felt heat steal through his body and his stomach tightened with desire. He clamped down on those feelings. "Nothing," he mumbled distractedly.

Angela stopped in front of him, put her hands on her hips and peered into his face. "Are you okay?" She put her hand on his fore-head. "Normal. Lead the way and show off your horses, Taylor."

He ignored the warmth left by her hand and grinned. "Show off. Yeah, I like that. I may have nothing to do with their pedigree, but I take full credit for picking them out from the mangy mixed breeds. C'mon," He took hold of her elbow and led her from the foyer.

She laughed at his comments but didn't bother to point out his conceit. The man had an enormous ego, she thought to herself.

They walked past the kitchen where the ranch hands were finishing their dinner while arguing about a game they were watching on T.V. Angela nodded at them as she and Jerry headed for the kitchen door.

The night was cool and filled with night sounds. The stars were bright in the clear night sky. "You know one thing I like about this land of yours, Jerry? Everything is the way it is supposed to be. The sky is clear and the stars are bright. In cities, it is hard to see the skyline, let alone the stars. And then there are the night sounds—the birds, the crickets. It is a relief not to hear cars, loud music, and people yelling."

"That's surprising coming from someone who lives in a city," Jerry commented.

"Sometimes where we live chooses us and not the other way around." Angela replied as she followed him into the night. He opened the gate that led to the well-lit yard and turned to face her. Angela looked at him warily.

"So, have you decided you're going to stay here?" His expression was serious.

Angela relaxed. She had expected him to say something personal. "That depends," she answered.

"On what?" Jerry asked.

"How much farm work you expect me to do around here. I'm on vacation you know." She teased.

Jerry allowed a slight grin to pass his lips. He could never predict what she was going to say. "Actually I was just joking about tomorrow. I can teach you to ride without making you do chores." He indicated that they should use a side door.

Angela walked ahead of him. The pebbled yard was neat. They must clean it every day, she thought as she looked around. "But I want to know how a ranch is operated, Jerry. I won't mind helping as long as you don't ask me to do back-breaking chores.

Jerry laughed. He couldn't help it. She liked twisting him in knots. One minute she implied one thing and in the next minute she did an about face. "You're trying to turn me into a nitwit, woman. C'mon, the horses are waiting."

They entered the room which Jerry said was the grooming room. They walked through it to the central isle of the barn. Jerry turned to see Angela hovering in the doorway, her eyes staring warily at the horses. Some of them were finishing their evening feed while others held their head outside the stalls. There was nothing for her to fear. He grinned as he walked back to her.

"They can't do anything to you when they're in their stalls. Look at the stall doors—very sturdy with horse-proof bolts."

She looked over his shoulder and stared at the chestnut horse that was staring at them with a disdainful expression. Could the animal detect her wariness? "Does that mean some can break their doors?"

Jerry laughed. "It means some horses learn to open other bolts, but not these."

"Not only are they huge and beautiful, they are smart, too." Angela muttered under her breath

Jerry took her hand and almost laughed at the way she clutched onto his. He liked the idea that she needed him for something, even if it was just courage to face his horses. He'd noticed how independent she was. He gave her hand a gentle squeeze and drew her closer to his side. She pressed on his side so desperately he almost forgot she was clinging to him out of fear and nothing else.

"Never let a horse know that you're scared of it, Angela. Approach it steadily, as if you expect it to stand still and wait for you. Make sure that your movements are smooth and unhurried. Also talk softly to reassure it that you're friendly." As Jerry talked, he approached the chestnut horse.

"I think it is laughing at us," Angela whispered from his side.

"It is a she—my sorrel, Thunder. Thunder would never laugh at me. She's happy to see me. Now, quit distracting me so I can finish my explanation. You see how close we are to her now, hold out a hand so she can smell you." The sorrel licked Jerry's hand and then nudged his hand with her muzzle. "You see that? She wants more attention. But if you're a stranger, pat her neck. It also helps you bond with her." Jerry gave the horse a final rub and moved backwards until they were near the grooming room doorway.

"Well, Ms. McGee, I believe it is now your turn."

Angela slowly shook her head. "I think I'll wait until tomorrow. Things always seem possible in the day."

He stared into her eyes. He felt a stirring of his senses at their close proximity. "Now, this is a side of you I haven't seen, Angela. You, scared of something?"

One Day at a Time

"Oh, shut up, Taylor." She nudged him in the ribs good-naturedly. Then she turned to look at Thunder. She started a staring contest with the mare and didn't take notice of the way her body was intimately close to Jerry's. "You can laugh all you want, Taylor, but you weren't the one who was thrown from a horse's back at that riding school. I had never been so scared in my life. I thought the damn horse would trample me to death."

Hmm, she smelled good. Jerry thought. And he was beginning to like having her close to him. He forced himself to pay attention to what she was saying. "Actually I was thrown a lot when I was little."

Angela looked at him. Then as if she noticed their closeness, she pulled her hand from his and made a show of scratching her forehead. Why hadn't she noticed that she was practically draping herself all over the man? Her body had naturally sought his when she'd been scared. It had felt natural, too. She looked at him and caught a smug look on his face, as if he were privy to her thoughts. "Are you telling me the truth, Taylor?"

"Yep!"

"How old were you when you were first thrown?" She refused to look at Jerry now. She was concentrating on the distance between her and Thunder's stall. If the horse acted up and attacked her, Jerry should be able to rescue her.

"Three," Jerry answered though he was amused by her show of embarrassment.

She turned to look at him. "You've got to be kidding. What was it, a midget pony or a cocker spaniel? Sometimes, kids confuse childhood incidents. A dog may seem as big as a horse."

He laughed. "It was a pony. We all started riding as soon as we could walk. But maybe I was four when it happened, I can't say for sure."

"Okay, Jerry, I'm going in," Angela said as she started walking toward the stall and Thunder. She spoke softly though loud enough for Jerry to hear. "If the horse snaps my head off, I'll haunt you through centuries, Taylor. As for you, my beautiful sorrel, you better be nice to me. My opinion for the entire equine world depends on you." The horse's eyes seemed bigger and meaner the closer she got to her but she refused to be cowered. "Don't even think of intimidating me, Thunder. I have taken on people meaner than you and survived. So, Taylor named you Thunder? That's not very flattering. Such an unfitting name for such a beautiful lady"—she extended her hand as soon as she got close enough and was rewarded when the horse dropped her head and started smelling—"You're a pussy cat. And your muzzle is so smooth. Can you let me touch your coat? Oh, my! How could you name this beautiful horse Thunder, Taylor? Her skin is so soft and smooth. It reminds me of velvet. I would have called her Velvet." She continued to stroke the sorrel and she could have sworn it sighed with pleasure. "You have intelligent eyes, too." She turned to look at Jerry—her eyes sparkled and her attitude was triumphant. She winked and said, "I came, I met, I conquered."

Jerry grinned. "Good, you overcame your fears. Can we meet the other horses now?"

She saw the way he looked at her hand patting the mare. "What? You're not jealous that your horse likes me, are you?"

"Ha-ha, funny! I don't want my mare spoilt. Let's go."

Could he be jealous? Angela patted the horse's neck one last time and then moved toward Jerry. "Did you ever share your toys as a child, Jerry?"

"Of course, I did. I have an older brother and Tahj is my immediate follower."

"But Thunder is yours and special and you don't share her with anyone." She said knowingly.

She saw too much, thought Jerry. He stopped at a stall where a white horse stood proudly, her neck long and elegant. "This one here is an Arabian. Her name is Wind Dancer."

He was jealous, Angela thought but instead of teasing him about it, she turned to look at the mare he was pointing at. Wind Dancer was an all-white beauty with a long white mane. Showing off to her admiring audience, Wind Dancer swished her high-set tail.

"She is beautiful." Angela commented.

"Thank you. And the one in the next stall is her cousin, Philly."

One Day at a Time

"The mother-to-be?" She asked as they moved toward the stall of the second Arabian. Philly was dark brown. "May I?" She asked Jerry's permission but she was already moving toward the pregnant Arabian.

Jerry watched her, smiling at her nonsense chatter. She had a way of talking to the horses as if they were human. They moved down the stall and she met his two Thoroughbreds—Mystery and Rameses. Jerry explained why they were the fastest horses in the equine world. They even acquired the name "racing machines." One was gray and the other black. Like the Arabians, he intended to use the thoroughbred mares to breed racing horses. Zuri, his Saddlebred mare was as pretty and as well-behaved as her name—which meant 'good' in Swahili. Saddlebreds were show horses and Zuri's foals would mainly be for show.

Finally, they reached the stalls of the two Quarter horses. He explained that Buttercup was at a breeder but was due to be picked up any time. The other Quarter horse, Taharqa, was pure black.

"I like their names, Jerry—very creative and meaningful. Why did you pick Taharqa for this beauty?" Angela asked as she watched the mare and its owner—fascinating, imposing, and physically magnificent. They belonged together.

"Look at her. She is black, powerful, and dignified." Jerry said as he stroked his mare's neck.

"Just like her namesake, Pharaoh Taharqa, 630 B.C. He was the most famous ruler of the world's first largest empire—the combined kingdoms of Nubia and Egypt. He was also a builder—constructed temples in his two lands and numerous stelae."

Jerry took her arm and led her from the barn. "You obviously know your history."

"I try," she grinned and walked with him outside. They had barely passed the barn entrance when Jerry stopped. She stopped, too.

"I'm happy you've decided to stay, Angela. I really need your help with my records."

He was looking at her so intently that she felt a little uneasy. She

80

looked away from his all-seeing eyes and stared into the night. It was a beautiful night—a night for lovers to be gazing in each other's eyes. Unfortunately, she was standing next to a man she had every reason to hate.

Angela took a step back and crossed her arms protectively in front of her. "I think I might enjoy the experience of working in a farm, too." She looked at him and smiled uncertainly. "If we're starting early tomorrow, I better turn in now." When he continued to stare at her intensely, she added, "Oh, and thank you for showing me your horses. They are truly beautiful."

"The pleasure was mine."

She nodded briefly. "I'll bid you good night, then. See you tomorrow."

"Tomorrow, it is." He murmured, but continued to frown at her. What had just happened? One minute she was relaxed and teasing him and the next she was freezing him out. Or had he imagined the change in her attitude? What was going on here? He wondered as he slowly followed her retreating form back to the house.

***

Angela added more hay in the hay net to get the right amount. It was her first task and she wasn't doing too badly, she thought with each shove. She had slept peacefully and woken up early to bird songs and farm sounds. She had read a bit on Montanan birds and could differentiate the sounds made by a few of them.

As soon as she'd finished exchanging morning greetings with Jerry's men, Jerry assigned her her first task. Because she was a novice at farm work, she was given the chore of measuring the ration for each horse. He had shown her how to put hay in hay nets and where to weigh it. A list of each horse's portion was posted on the wall.

"I think we need a new bale, Ms. Angela."

Angela smiled at Little Joe, her partner this morning. "Let's go get one."

It was fascinating to see the chores people did on a horse ranch.

One Day at a Time

Not only did they have to measure rations for each horse but they had to wash and fill water troughs, and pick horse droppings from the stalls. Then there was grooming of the horses which went beyond brushing their coats. According to Jerry's earlier explanation, their daily routine included checking the mares' teeth, ears, eyes, mouth, nostrils, tail, and joints for diseases. They also examined the feet for injuries and loose shoes.

Angela was filling her next hay net when a whiff of feminine perfume made her look up. Staring at her was a stunning Indian woman with dark eyes, high cheek bones, and jet black hair cascading down her back. But it was the look on her face that arrested Angela's attention. It was filled with so much animosity.

"You're one of them, aren't you?" The woman asked with a sneer, critically looking at Angela's designer jeans, leather boots, and brick red shirt.

Angela raised an eyebrow and asked, "One of what?"

"The slu...the women Cyrus keep sending to Jerry." Her glance moved up and down Angela's body and then she smiled. The smile didn't reach her eyes. "What happened? Cyrus ran out of tiny women or did his interest suddenly change? You're physically different from the others."

In other words, they were the same in other aspects. Angela stared insolently back at the woman and wondered who she was. The animosity could only mean one thing. She must be Jerry's girlfriend. The hatred in her eyes had nothing to do with Angela as a person but what Angela represented—competition for Jerry's attention.

"So, what can I do for you?" Angela tried to be polite. After all, she didn't know how serious the woman's relationship with Jerry was. Besides, she had no desire to be kicked off the farm for offending Jerry's girlfriend, not before she finished what she came for.

The woman sneered. "Not a thing! So, what did Cyrus do to convince you to come here? What did he promise you? Or does he send the ones he's finished with?" The woman looked at the pile of hay Angela was measuring. "You think working around the farm will make you last longer than your predecessors?"

That was it! Angela thought with irritation. There was a time to be polite and a time to draw a line. Girlfriend just crossed it. Angela straightened up to her full length and ignored the way the woman looked her over. They were about the same height. Physically, the intruder was in great shape, but Angela placed her age to be in the late forties. She was dressed in low-hanging pants that revealed her belly button and hugged her buttocks. Her tight shirt left nothing to the imagination either. *Is she what turns Jerry on?*

"Listen here, girlfriend, twitch your,"—Angela made a play of checking her backside—"your narrow ass toward the barnyard and you'll find lover boy working with his horses. And for your information, older men like Cyrus don't turn me on."

"Bitch," the woman said under her breath as she walked away.

Angela laughed. As soon as the woman disappeared, she turned to find Little Joe grinning at her.

"She's not nice to you, Ms. Angela. She is not nice to all the ladies that come here. She says bad, mean things." Little Joe said with a pronounced lisp.

"She's not worth wasting my breath on, Little Joe. Let's get done here so you can show to me how to put a halter on a horse."

"Yes, Ms. Angela. It is not really hard."

Angela's heart had warmed to the slow but sweet young man from the first day she met him. Little Joe liked horses and like his father, was very good with them. So when she was told to work with one of the hands to prepare the hay nets, she had picked him. When she'd said that she wanted to ask his opinion about some of the horses and how to go about befriending them, the boy's eyes had sparkled with joy and pride. And indeed, he had answered all her questions about every horse on the ranch.

"Libby!"

It was Jerry's voice calling out the name, and it drew Angela's attention. She moved to the window and took a peek outside. She wasn't surprised to see the woman who'd just called her a bitch run to Jerry and gave him a tight hug then a kiss on his cheek.

But when the woman ran her hand over his arms familiarly and said, "What is this? I leave you for two weeks and you don't eat? Should I take this up with Sally or call Maya?" Angela's eyes narrowed. So, her guess had been correct. The woman was Jerry's girlfriend.

Jerry draped his arm across Libby's shoulder and used his hand to pinch her nose. "If you do that, I'll never talk to you again. So, tell me what happened. How did Peter take your news?"

"I told him I had powerful men on my side and if he wanted to take me to court, he had to go through them. By the way, I met the latest gift from Cyrus. What does he think he's doing?"

They started walking away from the yard. "You have to ask him that question." Jerry said with a laugh.

"I hate that man!" Libby said with a lot of venom.

"No, you don't." Jerry retorted playfully as they moved out of sight.

Angela remained at the window, staring at the place from which they had disappeared. So that was Jerry's girlfriend. Would she tell him that Angela had been rude to her? How could he be involved with a woman old enough to be his mother? Not that it was any of her business. She didn't care about his love-life or whom he slept with. She was only showing an interest just in case it had a direct effect on her plans. So who were Maya and Peter? "And what the hell kind of a name is Libby, anyway?"

She didn't realize she'd spoken aloud until Little Joe answered, "Her name is Liberty."

Angela smiled. "I was just curious, nothing more. So, tell me more about horses, Little Joe." She walked back toward the young man. Jerry was welcome to his girlfriend. Why then did the thought of the two of them fill her with annoyance? Did he prefer older women? And why should she care? Lord, the country air was making her act weird.

Chapter 8

A few yards away from the barn, Jerry smiled at Liberty Wilson's chatter. He opened a gate and walked with her through the paddock. Libby was his neighbor and a long time friend of his family. She had been his Uncle Cyrus' sweetheart, a woman he had loved beyond reason but who had disappointed him by marrying a man old enough to be her father—if not her grandfather.

It wasn't that Libby hadn't loved Cyrus—she still did—she had been determined to fulfill a vow she'd made to her grandfather before his death. Libby was to get back at the man who had won their ancestral land at a card game. It hadn't mattered that it was a small parcel of land and that her late husband, Jonathan Wilson, had won it fair and square from Libby's gambling grandfather. That land had been everything to Libby's family and they had wanted it back. So, she had married the old man and took care of him while his son from his first wife refused to have anything to do with him—the shame of his father marrying a full-blooded Crow Indian had been too much for Peter Wilson to stomach. Not only had Peter refused to visit the old man, he'd stopped bringing his children to see their grandfather. Yet as soon as Jonathan Wilson died and left half the land—including the homestead—to Libby and the other half to Peter, Peter had threatened to contest the will.

"Did Peter agree to back off or is he still going ahead with the suit?"

"I didn't wait around to see what he thought. I just dropped Cyrus letter's on his desk, told him where I was staying and that I'd be around for a week, and walked out. He called my hotel two days later—furious and cursing me to hell. I knew then that I had won. I decided to catch up with some girlfriends, shop, and celebrate."

"No wonder you're in such a happy mood. Is your family settling in okay then?"

"Except for my little brother who wants to finish his schooling at the reservation, we're content. My grandmother cried when we moved in. Seeing her face was worth the sacrifice." Libby said with a smile.

"Have you called Cyrus yet?"

"Why?" The smile disappeared from her face.

"To tell him that Peter is backing off," Jerry answered as he opened the next paddock.

"I'm sure Peter's lawyers will get in touch with him. So, as soon as Cyrus sends me the bill, I'll thank him and move on with my life."

"You know Uncle C will never understand why you married Wilson unless you swallow your pride and explain things to him," Jerry replied as he pulled at a weed growing in the paddock. They always checked for poisonous weeds because the horses nibbled them and got sick.

"Why should I bother? He wasn't willing to listen to me before." She touched his arm. "Tell me about your new assistant. How long has she been here?"

Jerry shook his head at her stubbornness. "Angela arrived on Friday."

"Two days and she's already helping around the farm? She's different from the others, isn't she? Even the men talk about her differently."

Jerry frowned at the change in Libby's voice. Did she think Angela was his uncle's girlfriend? "Angela likes to rise to a challenge. Can you ride with us, say, in an hour?"

"Is she coming?" Libby asked glumly.

Jerry stopped and stared at her. "What do you have against Angela? Or are you back to thinking that most of these assistants are Cyrus' girlfriends or ex-lovers?"

"I saw how physically different she was—tall just like me—and I saw red. I'm sorry I wasn't pleasant to her."

Jerry laughed. He would have loved to have seen that. "I'm sure she rose to the occasion. Angela McGee doesn't take things lying down."

"You sound like you like her," Libby said grimly.

Jerry shrugged instead of answering her. He didn't discuss people in his employ or guests in his house with anyone, including Libby. "So, can you exercise one of my horses or not?"

"Sure, just let me go and say howdy to Sally first." Libby waved to him before walking back toward the paddock gate.

Jerry shook his head and went back to hunting for poisonous weeds. Knowing how cutting Libby could be, he was sure she had been unreasonably rude to Angela. He hoped not.

A few minutes later, Jerry went to the barn and found Angela kneeling on a wooden box, her elbow on the stall door, and her eyes glued on Taharqa. She looked so at home that he smiled. Her fear for the horses was now a thing of the past. Without alerting her of his presence, he stopped behind her and waited.

Angela knew it was Jerry standing behind her. He had a distinct musky scent that was uniquely his. However, she didn't move or indicate that she knew he was there. "She is so beautiful. I could stand here forever and just watch her," She said, as much to herself as to anyone else.

"The feeling is mutual," Jerry replied from behind her. "Nothing else to do?"

She glanced at him, smiled and then said, "Nope. We finished measuring the evening meals and even weighed out concentrated feed for each horse. I guess exercising them will be next while their stalls get cleaned." Where did he leave Libby?

Jerry moved until he was standing beside her. "You're a fast learner. But you forgot the water trough in the paddocks have to be flushed and cleaned then checked and filled at least twice in the course of the day. Then there are saddles and bridles to be cleaned and oiled, fences to be mended, and horses to be checked while they eat, rest or play. Anything out of norm signifies even a bigger problem."

One Day at a Time

"Tell me again why you want to raise horses?"

He laughed softly and leaned forward to stare at her face. She stared expressionlessly back. What was going on behind her cool exterior? Why had she turned frosty on him last night?

Sighing softly, he reached for her left hand. He pulled off the gloves and checked for any welts or bruises on her palm. He did the same with the other hand. When she looked at him and then the hand he was holding, he said, "Just making sure you didn't hurt yourself. You need to use more sturdy gloves. Are you ready for more challenges?" He asked with a disarming smile—a slow seductive smile that must have beguiled women since he was old enough to walk.

Angela nodded quickly as she tried to fight her body's traitorous response to his proximity and that smile of his. *I'm not letting you get to me, Jerry Taylor,* she vowed. "Lead the way." She said calmly though she was anything but calm.

He didn't let go of her hand as he led her toward the grooming room. In fact, he tucked her arm under his and interlaced their hands. Angela took a calming breath as he played with her fingers, absently stroking the thin sensitive skin. A quiver of sensations raced up her arm. Should she pull her hand away or would that reveal how much he bothered her? No, that wouldn't do. Besides, he didn't seem aware of what he was doing.

"What are we going to do now?" As soon as she had spoken, she wished she hadn't. Her voice sounded too breathless. Did he notice?

"We aren't done with the horses. You, city slicker, will groom your first horse today." He walked into the tack room, pulled two halter ropes, and draped them over his shoulder. He still didn't let go of her hand. He picked up a plastic container filled with brushes, sponges, and soaps.

"I didn't know I would groom a horse today. Which one?"

Grinning at her doubtful expression, he wrapped her fingers around the handle of the container then he did something quite unexpected. He trailed a finger along her cheek. "Don't worry. I won't let anything happen to you." As if realizing what he was doing, he quickly turned and picked up another grooming kit. "I've chosen Zuri for you. She's sweet-tempered and likes people."

Before she could recover from that intimate touch, he had taken her arm and was leading her to the grooming room. He kept conversing as if nothing unusual had happened. He placed her kit beside his on a shelf before leading her to Zuri's stall. "Here we go. Watch how I put the halter on, just in case you might need to do it in the future."

Angela was still in shock at what Jerry had done and only paid partial attention to his words. Why had he touched her cheek? She thought with a frown. She could still feel the imprint of his fingers.

"You can lead the mare to the grooming room." Jerry said when he was finished.

Still preoccupied with her thoughts, she did as he'd taught her—walking beside the horse while talking calmly to her.

Jerry frowned as he watched her go. She was leading the horse like a professional and yet he didn't think she'd been paying much attention to his explanation. His frown intensified as he walked slowly toward Thunder's stall. What had possessed him to touch her? No, that was a silly question. He had been wondering if her skin felt as soft as it looked. Besides, she was so unapproachable that he felt he had to touch her to get her attention.

Shaking his head, he opened Thunder's stall. Using the other halter, he led the mare to the grooming room where he found Angela already brushing Zuri. She had even hooked the rope on a hook on the wall to secure the mare. He explained what brushes to use for different parts of the horse. She glanced at him occasionally and followed his lead.

"So, Angela, tell me about your computer business. What made you decide to start one?"

"I wanted to be my own boss." She said with a deadpan expression. When she looked up and caught the amusement on his face, she smiled.

"Didn't like taking orders, huh?" He teased.

She laughed. "You could say that." Then she explained how she took evening classes on computer graphics and how a website gift to her best friend, Nikki, opened doors for her. "After that, I let my work speak for me. Most of my clients contacted me after seeing those first sites."

"What about nursing? Which one is your true vocation, nursing or messing around with computers?"

"I'm a jack of all trades, although I once hoped to dazzle the world with my lyrics and vocals." A sad expression briefly flashed across her face before she covered it with a broad grin.

He didn't miss her first expression though. "What happened? I thought you sounded good. Although I'd have to hear more before I can give you my professional opinion."

Angela shook her finger at him. "And if you remember what I said yesterday, you can dream on. I'm not singing for you, Taylor."

He smiled at her ease. Had he imagined her cool attitude last night? Ever since she walked into the barn this morning and greeted his workers by their names, she had been relaxed and at ease. When her defenses were down, she was a very likeable person. "Why did you give it up? You don't look the type to give up on anything, not if it matters."

Angela shrugged as she brushed her mare's tail. "It's a long, boring story. Besides, it doesn't matter anymore. It was just a foolish girl's dream."

From her tone it didn't sound like it was a foolish girl's dream, Jerry thought. A frown marred his features as he said, "If you ever want to talk about it, feel free to bore me."

She laughed. How could she explain why she'd felt obligated to go into nursing without bringing Sav's name up? She had tried to please her parents by giving up her own dreams but in the end she'd shortchanged herself. "I'd rather hear more about the grand plans you have for your horses."

Jerry raised an eyebrow at her smooth change of topic but gladly obliged her. He was describing what was involved in raising a good show horse when Angela spotted Libby. The woman was walking toward the barn with quick steps. She didn't look happy. "It seems like your girlfriend got tired of waiting in the house."

Jerry looked up with a frown. He spotted Libby. "Libby? She's not my girlfriend." At Angela's raised eyebrow, he laughed and added, "She and Uncle C have a history that goes way back. They were sweethearts but things didn't go as they'd hoped."

Angela knew women and Libby's earlier behavior had nothing to do with Cyrus McQueen. The woman wanted Jerry and had been staking her claim from their first meeting. Before she could stop herself Angela added, "Wherever her affections were before, they have been shifted to you, Taylor."

"You're being ridiculous." Jerry added with annoyance. "She's old enough to be my mother, eh, if she had me at seventeen, that is."

Angela couldn't curb her tongue now that she'd started talking. "Girlfriend sure acted as if you're hers—signed, sealed, and delivered."

"Libby has been through a rough time and needs friends. That is all I am to her—a friend: She is a nice person. You should try being nice to her." Why did women always complicate things? Why did they imagine things that were not there and ignore things that were right under their noses?

Angela looked at Jerry's face and sighed. Men were so clueless. A woman had to literally climb on their laps and start seducing them before they realized her intentions. Not that she should care, right?

Angela looked up when Libby walked in. She could have been invisible for all the attention she received from the older woman. She headed straight for Jerry and pushed her cleavage in his face.

"Can I groom Taharqa? I want to go for the ride you promised me. And I'd like to see how rusty you've gotten since I left."

Angela smiled at the way Jerry was trying hard not to look at Libby's displayed bosom. Instead he smiled into her eyes and said, "I'll get the mare for you?"

"Thank you, Jerry. Angela and I will get to know each other while you're gone." The smile Libby gave him was sugar-coated.

Jerry looked at Angela with an I-told-you-so expression before patting Libby's arm. "Good! I think the two of you will get along very well."

One Day at a Time

As soon as Jerry disappeared, the woman walked over to Angela. She pretended to pat Zuri. "So, what's your plan, McGee? Shouldn't you be in the den working on the database he's paying you to set up instead of being out here? I've known city women like you and they come and go. The novelty of being on the ranch wears off, and it's up to us to pick up the pieces."

Angela looked at the woman and realized that she had the upper hand. Somehow, Libby felt threatened by her. She smiled. "For your information, I'm not getting paid a dime to be here. I'm on vacation. You can fill in the gaps and draw your own conclusion, Libby."

"You're not a relative, so why would you want to vacation here? What do you want with Jerry?" The woman asked belligerently.

"I don't believe I owe you any explanation, *Libby*. My arrangement is with Jerry. If you feel you're owed answers why not ask him?" She heard the sound of Jerry approaching with Taharqa and added, "In fact, here he comes. Oh, and you better remove that venomous look from your face and paste a smile quick." To her amazement, the woman did exactly that.

From then on, Libby monopolized Jerry's time. When Angela wanted someone to help her saddle her mare, she went and asked Big Joe. With Big Joe's help, she mounted Zuri. Then she followed him and Sly out of the ranch.

They were going to ride around the estate and check on the fences while exercising the horses. Although Libby and Jerry came along, too, Libby kept Jerry so occupied that he didn't talk to anyone else. They raced, and laughed over the little anecdotes she was telling him. Angela stayed with Sly and Big Joe and ignored them.

The land was beautiful, shaped by space and sky. Angela readily connected with it, absorbing its unspoiled beauty and natural landscape—the vision of timelessness in the towering mountains; the pristine waters reflecting the vast, clear sky; the gently rolling hills uncluttered by society's diversion; the vibrant wildflowers adding colorful contrast, like a painter's masterpiece. Jerry owned quite a spread because they didn't leave his land the entire time they were riding.

Big Joe and Sly kept her entertained with cowboy stories and legends. They stopped along the way as the men checked the fences. Libby ignored Angela most of the time but once or twice the woman glanced her way and Angela caught her triumphant expression. Angela ignored her.

It was over an hour later when they rode back to the homestead. Angela's buttocks hurt like hell but she didn't let anyone know. So, when Jerry and Libby decided to jump over poles erected in the southern part of the compound for training show-jumping horses, Angela forced herself to stop and watch. But when Big Joe said he was riding to the barn and wanted to talk to her about Little Joe, she sighed with relief and left with him.

As they rode toward the house, the quiet man thanked her for being kind to his son.

"Don't thank me, please. He is smart and knows a lot about horses. I enjoy talking to him."

"You're kind, Ms. Angela. Not many people have the time for people like my son. We're lucky to be working for Jerry who treats him like a man and not a child."

She had been amazed at the way Jerry handled the young man. He gave him responsibilities and expected him to perform. From the conversation she had with Little Joe, the young man adored Jerry. "He may think highly of Jerry but you are his number one hero."

A smile broke on the big guy's face as he nodded. "He is a good kid."

Big Joe helped her off her horse and offered to remove her saddle and bridle, and to turn the mare out for her. Angela sighed with relief but felt bad for not taking care of the horse assigned to her. "Thank you, Big Joe. I appreciate your help."

But when Big Joe added, "A soak in a hot tub helps the aches, Ms. Angela. Ask Sally for something to use to soothe the soreness," Angela flushed with embarrassment. He knew that her buttocks were killing her.

"I thought I had everyone fooled."

"Not me and definitely not Jerry. I didn't know what to do until he signaled me to bring you home."

Angela opened her mouth and then closed it. How thoughtful of Jerry. Was that why he had made them make several stops or insisted that they walk while he checked the fences or some weeds? Was he also responsible for the times Big Joe had been by her side to help her down or back on the horse?

"Thanks, anyway, Big Joe. I think I'll follow your advice and have that long bath." She smiled uncertainly at him and walked to the house. She paused once to look toward the Southern end of the compound and was surprised to find Jerry looking her way, too. He touched the brim of his Stetson in acknowledgement. She waved and hurried to the house. Fifteen minutes later, she was soaking in the tub.

Chapter 9

A crooning voice invaded Jerry's sleep. He turned and pulled a pillow over his head. When it didn't help, he turned toward the side table clock and almost knocked it down in his haste to shut it off. When pressing the buttons offered no reprieve, he cursed and sat up. Then he started laughing.

Angela. Her voice floated through the walls and teased his ears. The walls were too damn thin. Or maybe it was because she was in the bathroom, having a shower. He couldn't believe she had woken him up. He was thinking of going next door and smothering her when she switched to a ballad so poignant that Jerry just lay back and let her voice wash over him. She was good. She would have made it in the music business. Why hadn't she pursued it? She was intriguing him more and more.

His chest tightened and an ache started in his stomach. His body refused to obey his brain and a fierce longing sliced through him. Damn! He wanted her. Did she sound like that when making love? Jerry cursed at his thoughts. Why was he fantasizing about her? In the old days, he would have acted with the swiftness of a predator going after a kill. But Carmen had cured him of that. He was a very cautious man now. He didn't do anything without thorough delibera-tion. Besides, having anything to do with Angela—someone who would only be around for a couple weeks—was foolhardy. His thoughts shifted to the day before. Why had he acted like a jerk toward her? When Libby had told him that Angela had rebuffed her attempts to apologize for her earlier rudeness, Jerry had been irritat-ed. But when Angela continued to ignore them after they had finished with the horses and even went to seek Big Joe's help with her own mare, Jerry had decided to ignore her. A very difficult task, he had found out.

Angela wasn't the type of woman you could ignore. When they had ridden out of the homestead, he hadn't been able to help looking back and checking on her. His ears had tuned in on her voice as she'd conversed with Sly. For someone who hadn't ridden much, she wasn't a bad rider. Or so, he had thought as he'd listened to her laughter and chatter. A couple of times he had tried to include her in his conversations with Libby but for once Libby wanted to talk about her problems and needed his advice on some improvements she was making on her farm. Besides, Angela had seemed at ease talking to Sly and Big Joe. He hadn't noticed a change in her seating until they were on their way home. He had then taken a closer look at the way she rode and realized what was wrong. Her bottom was taking quite a beating with each step the mare took. To give her a rest, he had made them make several stops on the pretense of checking on some exotic plants or a landmark. But as soon as they arrived home and Libby wanted to race, he had signaled to Big Joe to take Angela back to the house and help her.

Later, he had advised Sally to let her have a lunch tray in her room. If her bottom hurt as much as he thought it did, she wouldn't want to sit down. But when he'd sent Sally to check on her, the housekeeper had informed him that Angela had fallen asleep without touching her food. Before he left for his grandfather's ranch, he, too, had stopped by her room but she had still been sleeping. He hadn't seen her since.

Deciding it was pointless to be thinking too much about Angela, Jerry rolled off his rumpled bed and stifled a yawn. Scratching his belly, he shuffled to the bathroom, smiling at the sound of her voice. Damn, she sure could sing.

As the sharp needles of the shower cleansed his body, his thoughts turned to the painting he had been trying to acquire in the last month. He had bought the first three paintings in the Seasonal Rhapsody series by Hannah Vas, but needed one more painting to make the series complete. Benjamin Goldstein, the owner of the gallery that had sold him the three paintings had promised to help him locate that last one, but so far, he hadn't heard anything from the man

So, the first thing Jerry did after the shower was place a call to San Francisco. "Mr. Goldstein, please." He didn't wait long before Goldstein was on the line. "Good morning, Ben. I'm happy to finally talk to you. You've been a difficult man to track." Jerry said in a calm voice although he was seething with anger. Goldstein had been avoiding him and using his secretary to cover for him. "What's the status of that painting you promised to acquire for me?"

Jerry spent the next thirty minutes listening to the art dealer complain and explain why he hadn't found his painting. When he hung up, he was in a crappy mood. He needed that painting, he thought in frustration. He wouldn't be satisfied until the collection was complete.

He left his room and headed straight for the den. Angela was already there. "Morning, Angela. I see you've already started."

Angela looked at him. *It was so unfair; no man had a right to be this gorgeous.* She hid her amorous thoughts behind a smile. "Morning, Jerry. I'm just trying to see what data you have on each horse." Her eyes drifted back to the notebook.

"Have you had breakfast yet?"

"Yeah, eh, I did." Angela answered distractedly. Then she remembered his thoughtful gesture of the day before. "Thanks for the ointment you left for me yesterday. It helped." She looked up and found his eyes on her legs. Her dress had ridden up. She pulled the hem down before asking, "How was dinner with your grandparents?"

He shrugged. His mother had questioned him nonstop about Angela but he wasn't about to mention that. "Okay. Did you get to eat something or did you sleep through dinner, too?"

"I woke up at four o'clock. Sally was kind enough to let me rummage through the kitchen for something to eat. Now, can you let me get back to work?" She raised an eyebrow when Jerry grinned. She was coming to recognize this particular grin. It was his *I-am-about-to-get-naughty* smile.

"Would you like for me to check your backside? It won't take

One Day at a Time

but a minute. We don't want you getting nasty bruises from your ride. Oh, which reminds me, we need to work on your riding technique."

He was flirting with her again, she thought with amusement. "I agree on taking lessons, however, I'm not allowing you to check any part of my anatomy. So, quit teasing and go play with your horses, Jerry. I need to get busy here." No matter what she told herself, she was thrilled that he was attracted to her.

"Spoilsport!" He said as left the den.

Angela shook her head as he disappeared from view. He was so silly. But he was soon forgotten as she got immersed in work.

The combination of the records from the previous owners and those from people at Eagle's Hill were amazingly detailed. From the pedigree of each mare to her behavior around other horses, nothing was left unrecorded. There was how much the horses ate, how they ate it, and the texture of their droppings; the state of their eyes; the alertness of their ears; the sheen of their tails and coats; discharge or any flaring of their nostrils, and their weight. They had even recorded each horse's behavior in the field, in the stable, and in the presence of other mares. Then there were individual characteristics like which ones bit or stamped their feet when impatient, the ones more sensitive to different things like flies or those who showed happiness easily. Like people, some horses got along with others while others were bullies. The records also indicated which mares had been through different illnesses and how the people of Eagle's Hill have dealt with them. All in all, Jerry's horses seemed relatively healthy although a lot of work was involved in caring for them.

It was almost twelve when Jerry walked back into the den and interrupted her. "Lunchtime, Angela. Sally insists everyone eats at twelve o'clock."

Angela frowned and asked, "What is cribbing?"

He doubted she had even heard his comment about lunch. "When a mare fixes her jaws on a solid object like a post and gulps in air. It is one of those habits they adopt when they are bored." He saw that she was typing as fast as he spoke. When she didn't stop, he walked behind her and peered over her shoulder. "Did you hear what

I said, Angela."

"Yeah, lunch...I just need to finish one last thing," she murmured.

Jerry reached across and clicked on save. Before he could click on the close icon, she slapped his hand. "If you don't quit messing with my work, I won't be responsible for my actions, Jerry."

"The damn machine will still be here when you get back on it tomorrow." She turned to glare at him. "Don't give me that look. I don't expect you to slave in here from morning until evening. We agreed all you had to do was put in a few hours a day."

She grabbed his hand and turned to look at him. "Jerry, how would you feel if I were to call one of your mares a damn animal?"

"You've already called them that." He grinned.

Angela rolled her eyes in exasperation. Talk about a telegraphic memory. "I don't think I was referring to your horses when I used the word damn. And I did apologize for the comparison."

He grinned at the long-suffering expression on her face. She was too serious, he thought distractedly. She needed to laugh more. He wished he knew why he wanted to see her happy. He just did. "That doesn't exonerate you, Angela McGee. So be very, very careful what you say about my work because you're already guilty of insulting my horses. I haven't fully recovered from your very low opinion of them."

She shook her head and laughed. He had knocked the wind out of her sail. "What I was going to say, you impossible man, was that you wouldn't like it if I pulled you away from your horses while you were in the middle of, say, grooming them. I, too, hate to be interrupted when I'm in the middle of something. It messes up my train of thought."

Jerry stepped back, looked at her and then the computer. "Point taken. However, calling your machine damn is not as insulting as your comments about my mares. Unlike them, that machine doesn't have feelings." He started walking away from her when he saw her pick up a piece of paper and start crumbling it. "Now if you were to say something disparaging about my horses while you're on top of one, I wouldn't interfere. Why? Because the horse is likely to hear you, get angry, and throw you. They know when someone is being insensitive to their feelings." He ducked when she threw the paper at him.

"Go away, Taylor."

He leaned against the door and asked, "Aren't you coming? I hate eating alone."

And I wouldn't like to be guilty of making you eat alone, Angela thought. "Hold on a sec while I finish this."

He smiled and walked back to stand by her side. He stared at the way she chewed her lip when she worked. She looked so serious, sexy, and unapproachable. She fascinated him though. Why? What was it about her that pulled on him? Was it the haunted look he'd glimpsed in her eyes or was it her strength? Half the time he couldn't tell what went on behind her pretty face. *But of course that didn't mean he wasn't curious.*

It wasn't long before Angela was done. When she stood up and looked at him, the look in his eyes made her a little wary. As if he knew he had been caught staring, he grinned disarmingly. She frowned. What was it he had said about eating alone? "I'm only coming because I'm hungry, Jerry. It has nothing to do with your preference. In fact, I wouldn't care if you..."

"The more you protest the more I'm convinced that you're trying to please me. I knew my charm would work on you sooner or later."

"Tell that monster to heel."

"What monster?" Jerry asked.

She poked his side. "Your enormous ego," She replied.

He laughed as he pushed the kitchen door. He waited for her to walk through before whispering, "I'm the least egotistical man alive. I just like it when a woman goes out of her way to please me."

Angela shook her head when she saw his workers already occupying the kitchen. They were seated around the kitchen table or the counter. She turned to look at him mockingly. He would have had all the company he needed without her. She mouthed, "Liar."

He grinned back at her and then led her to the two empty stools at the end of the counter. Sally smiled at them as she passed them plates of food.

After lunch, Jerry disappeared outside but not before telling Angela to stay away from computer for the rest of the day. She grinned at him agreeably, but as soon as she finished helping Sally clear the dishes, she headed right back to the den.

**

In the next several days, they settled into a routine. She worked in the den in the morning and in the afternoon she helped the men with the chores and learned more about horse rearing. The men usually welcomed her presence and didn't mind answering her questions. At times, she visited with Sally and listened to stories about life in Montana.

She and Jerry had their lunch with his men in the kitchen or in the den. Sally served dinner for the two of them in the dining room every evening. She learned a lot about Jerry's family during those meals, but to her disappointment, the subject of Carmen never came up.

When was he going to open up about his past? Angela wondered. He was a charming companion—full of funny anecdotes from his playing days and his childhood; however, his marriage and the accident were closed subjects. At times, she felt like asking him, point blank, about Carmen but she feared he would clam up on her. Worse, he would start suspecting her motives. No, she had to wait until he was ready.

Angela's mind shifted to Reggie. She had called the day before and talked with Dr. Parker. The EEG he had performed showed no change in Reggie's brain activity. Her nephew was still in a deep coma. Physically he was okay because they stimulated his muscles everyday. But, it was still frustrating to know that there was no damage to his brain and yet he was comatose. Would he ever improve? She sure hoped so.

Thinking about Reggie always reminded her of why she was

masquerading as an assistant in the middle of Montana. This week, it had been almost easy to forget—when Jerry's eyes lighted up with amusement or a lazy grin flashed across his lush lips; when sensual flames flickered in the depth of his eyes as he teased her; or like the day she found him swimming and her thoughts went into overdrive, imagining the feel, the taste, and the texture if his skin. But her calls to San Diego always served as a strong reminder of why she was where she was.

Angela walked to the window and looked outside. She loved the outdoors, and working alongside Jerry and his men was fun. Was she doing the right thing by being on this farm? What would Jerry say or think when he learned who she really was? What about his workers? They must have known Carmen. Had they liked her? How come no one talked about her? Maybe she ought to ask Jerry point blank about the accident and get it over with, because she was beginning to feel guilty and it didn't sit well with her. The fact that everyone on the farm had welcomed her wholeheartedly only made her feel worse. She felt like she was betraying their trust.

Angela sighed. Regardless of her motives or state of mind, this was also her vacation time. It was time to push aside the nagging questions and join the men. Jerry had promised to help with her riding technique when her bottom stopped hurting. Well, at last it felt better and she was ready to go riding.

Switching off the computer, she left the den. The phone started ringing as she crossed the foyer. She frowned at it, shrugged, and kept on walking toward the kitchen. It stopped ringing and started again as she left the kitchen and stepped onto the patio.

"Ms. Angela, could you pick up the phone for me, please?" Sally was coming from her house and was too far away to make it to the phone on time.

"Sure, Sally." Angela stepped back into the kitchen and picked up the phone. "Eagle's Hill."

"Who is this?" A woman asked rudely.

Angela removed the phone from her ear and looked at it with a frown. "Ma'am, this is Eagle's Hill ranch, may I help you?"

"Yes, you may start by telling me who you are?" The woman answered.

Must be one of Jerry's women, Angela thought. She saw enough of Libby around the farm—almost everyday—and had become adept at ignoring her smoldering glares. But enough was enough with these women and their animosity. She wasn't about to give out her name, not to some stranger with an attitude. "My name is not important. Do you want to speak with Taylor or Ms. Sally?"

"Are you the new girl?" The woman cut in.

Angela laughed. "I can't remember the last time someone called me a girl." Just then Sally walked through the door and Angela motioned her to the phone. "Here is someone you could..."

"I want to speak to my son." The woman interrupted.

Angela closed her eyes in mortification. "I'm sorry, eh, Mrs. Taylor. I didn't know..."

"I want to speak to my son, now, please," Jerry's mother rudely interrupted, again.

Angela made a face and passed the phone to Sally. She mouthed, "I'll get Jerry. It's his mother." She let herself out of the house and grimaced. What a rude woman! She had tried to be polite, as polite as she could under the circumstances. Oh, well, she hoped they'd never meet.

She went into the barn but there was no one there. Then she saw the three of them—Jerry, Winston, and Sly—in the arena where Sly usually trained Ellie. She headed their way.

Jerry looked up and watched Angela as she approached. Unexpectedly, an intense feeling washed over him. It was a combination of longing, helplessness, and acceptance. He couldn't help feeling that his destiny was out of his hands and was somehow intertwined with hers. How ridiculous, he thought with a frown. "Happy you could join us, Angela. Staying indoors for too long induces cabin fever."

"I had a few things to finish. Oh, your mom is on the phone. She wants to talk to you."

Jerry looked beyond her and nodded. Angela turned to see Sally

One Day at a Time

walking toward them. The phone was in her hand. Not wanting to listen to Jerry's conversation—just in case the mother decided to tell him of their brief exchange—she joined Sly and Winston.

Jerry took the phone from Sally, thanked her, and walked away from the others. "Hi, Ma," he said.

"Hi, baby. Did I catch you at a bad time?"

Jerry frowned and turned to look at the group near Ellie. Angela was laughing and he got that same feeling in his chest, again—that feeling of helplessness. It bothered him to even admit it to himself. He didn't believe in destiny. You got things because you worked hard for them not because you were fated to have them. "Oh, no, we were just checking on Ellie. Remember I told you that she had a sand crack? Well, that was a false alarm. We just found out that she has a bruised sole. I'm going to wrap it up and let it heal before she starts training, again."

"Oh, that is terrible. Is Sly a good man?"

"Very. Is everything okay, Ma?"

"Yes, dear—I just forgot to mention last weekend that I'll be traveling to San Diego to visit with your brother's family. I don't know if you'd like to take a break from the ranch for a couple of days and come with me. A change would do you some good, baby."

Jerry laughed. "Ma, we're too busy now for me to leave. Philly is due any time. I just got Mystery and Buttercup back from a stallion farm and I have to prepare the other three mares to mate with Zeus. I can't afford to leave now."

His mother sighed. "I guess it is a bad time for you to leave then. I'll stop by sometime next week to see you before I leave," she said with a resigned tone.

"When are you leaving?" Jerry asked.

"Next Saturday. Eh, baby, was that your new assistant who answered the phone?" His mother asked.

"I don't know, Ma. Sally brought me the phone." He hoped his mother wasn't going to start a tirade against his uncle and the assistants he kept sending him. He'd had enough of that last weekend.

"Sally didn't answer the phone so I assume it was that woman

104

Cyrus sent. She shouldn't answer your phone. Are you letting her run around your house, Jerry?"

"C'mon, Ma," Jerry interrupted.

"Remember, you have valuables that can easily be taken without your knowledge, son. I don't trust these women Cyrus keeps sending out here."

"Ma!" His voice was more forceful. But she ignored it as she often ignored things that she didn't want to deal with.

"Cyrus will not hear the end of this. In fact, I'm going to have a long talk with him when I get to San Diego. Is she even doing what she's being paid to do?"

Jerry sighed. He loved his mother but at times, she could drive him nuts with nagging and worrying about mundane things. "I told you she is not getting paid to be here, Ma."

"Don't you find that peculiar?"

Jerry laughed. "No. She's interested in horses and this is really a vacation for her."

"I hope you're getting your money's worth. After all, you have to feed and house her."

"I have to go now, Ma. But rest assured that she is a very seri-ous young lady. Sometimes I have to practically drag her from the den to get her to eat lunch."

"Is that so? What's wrong with her? Is she one of those women who likes to play games or is she just anti-social?"

Jerry sighed. His mother had a knack of finding problems where none existed. If Angela was too friendly, she would label her an opportunist. If she was shy and reserved, she was hiding something. "No, she is not, Ma. She's just dedicated to what she does. Believe me. She takes her work very seriously."

"We'll see, won't we?"

"I got to go, Ma. Take care and I'll see you when you get here."

"Take care too, dear. Don't be angry that I worry too much about you. You're very trusting of people, Jerry. I just don't want you to get hurt, again."

He'd heard that expression enough to last him a lifetime. "I love you, Ma and I'm hanging up now." He frowned as he switched off the phone.

His mom's comment was a hint about his relationship with Carmen. He had trusted Carmen so implicitly that when she had changed towards him, he had blamed himself. He had attributed those changes to his absences from home during baseball season and busy schedule with inner city youth baseball camps and Literacy for America meetings. He could look back now and see things clearly. Carmen had known what he did before they got married and should have been prepared to deal with it. In fact, she had not minded his trips and had often accompanied him to his seminars and games. But that was only during the first two years of their marriage. What made her change so drastically? Jerry shook his head and shrugged. Who knows, maybe the pressure of being his wife became too much for her.

"Hey?"

Jerry looked up and found Angela standing beside him. Her eyes were filled with concern. His frown intensified. Would someone like Angela crumble under pressure like Carmen did? Somehow, he doubted it.

"You were lost in thought and had a peculiar look on your face. Are you okay?"

Ah, the concern had been for him. It warmed his heart and filled his chest. "That depends. If I were to say I'm feeling downhearted, would you want to do whatever it takes to cheer me up?"

She laughed. "From that comment, I know you're okay. So, when do you want to start my lessons?"

Jerry looked toward the pasture where his horses were grazing and shrugged. His gaze turned to her and caressed her face. He wanted to touch her cheek, to hold her, and kiss her until she thought of nothing else but him. Everything about her was a turn on for him. In fact, he craved her with an intensity that surprised the hell out of him. What made it worse was the fact that he knew she wasn't indifferent to him. He had seen this in her eyes in the last week, when her guard was down. She was attracted to him, too. The question was, what was he going to do about it? "How about now?"

"Great, let me go and change." She started for the house.

"Don't take too long. I'm going to let you saddle the horse this time."

She groaned and muttered, "Slave driver!"

"Just for that, you have to get the horse from the field—another new thing to learn." When she glared at him, he grinned. "Don't say it. I might make you tame a wild mustang."

She pouted as her eyes shifted to the horses. Some were lying down while others just stood around nibbling at the grass. How the hell was she going to catch one of them?

As if Jerry read her mind, he said, "Don't worry, I'll instruct you on what to do. Now if you want to accomplish something before sundown, break a leg." Angela turned to him, wrinkled her nose, and stuck her tongue out. He laughed as she walked away. The laughter disappeared from his face as he took in the gentle sway of her hips and the way the dress caressed her legs as it swirled around her knees. He wanted to be the one caressing those legs. A grimace crossed his face. He was getting impatient in his old age.

Thirty minutes later, Jerry couldn't control his amazement as he watched Angela put the saddle and the bridle on Zuri unaided. Earlier, she had followed his instructions and gotten the horse from the field. Grinning triumphantly, she had led the horse toward him and the gate. When they had reached the barn, she had gotten the saddle and the bridle from the tack room and proudly told him she didn't need his help because Big Joe had shown her how to saddle a horse. And indeed, she had done it and done it well.

Jerry had applauded her courage. Not only had she looked scared when she'd walked into that field to get the mare, he had noticed the slight tremble in her hands as she put the metal part of the bridle in the horse's mouth. Now he was watching her as she made the mare trot round and round in the circular training arena. It had been almost an hour and she hadn't complained.

"Now, I want you to make him canter." Jerry instructed.

She brought the horse to a stop near him and looked down at him with a frown. "Are you trying to scare me, Jerry? That's a faster pace."

"I know. But after saddling that horse, I've come to realize that nothing can stop you."

Angela smiled at the compliment. "And don't ever forget it, cowboy. Okay, here goes," she murmured and used her knees and the bridle to urge the horse forward and to change the horse's gait to a trot and then finally to a canter.

Her heart was thundering as the horse picked up speed. They went round and round the arena. She glanced down once and almost lost courage. But she knew Jerry would stop the horse if it got out of control. He was watching and encouraging her with nods. But that didn't stop him from telling her what she was doing wrong every time she passed close to him.

"Feel the rhythm of the horse. Just like in a trot, make use of your thighs, Angela...that's right. Not too tight, relax...good. Now follow her rhythm, make it fun for both of you."

Angela stopped listening to him. She was enjoying herself. Laughter bubbled from her throat as she and the mare moved as one. The wind blew past her face, caressing her cheeks like a lover's breath. She saw Jerry's face as she rode past him and grinned. She had done it!

"Okay, slow her down...very good...reach down and pat her neck, praise her."

She was already talking to the mare and promising her a thorough rub-down. Her breath was coming out fast and her heart was still pounding with excitement. She stopped beside Jerry. He reached up to help her down. He was so close that her body rubbed against his as she slid down. She felt the evidence of his desire and quickly looked into his face.

She wished she hadn't. Yet, she couldn't look away either. A rush of heat stole through her body. Her heartbeat increased and a tremble shook her frame. His eyes had a warm glint in them. She knew what it meant. The man wanted her. She has been aware of it from their first meeting but had ignored it. She hadn't wanted to deal with it. Another thing she had refused to face was her growing attraction for him. She had fought against admitting it the whole week. She couldn't do it anymore.

Then his head started moving toward hers and she knew he was going to kiss her. The excitement of the ride, the sense of accomplishment, his scent, and her hormones heightened her desire. Her body swayed gently toward him and her head lifted.

"Hi, Jerry," a feminine voice called out.

Angela stiffened and the moment was lost. Jerry muttered a curse under his breath and his hand, which was still on Angela's waist, tightened briefly before dropping away. What lousy timing, he thought as he looked over his shoulder and spied the culprit. "Rosie Sanchez," he muttered under his breath.

Chapter 10

Jerry moved toward his unexpected and presently, unwanted guest. "Rosie, what are you doing here on a week day?"

"We got off early from school today. Besides, tomorrow is Saturday. Who is she?" Rosie nodded toward Angela

"Don't try to distract me, young lady. Does your dad or Juanita know that you're here?"

Rosie looked guilty for about a second then she said, "They know where to find me. Or you could call them for me."

The beatific smile Rosie gave Jerry just made him scowl more. "Not in this lifetime, young lady. Now, go on to the house and call home!"

Rosie pouted and looked beyond him at Angela who was watching their exchange with amusement. "Why are you teaching her to ride? Is she one of those weird women who keep coming here?"

"Move it before I make Mac escort you home right now!"

The tone Jerry used sent the girl scurrying toward the house. Rosie stopped once to look at Angela. The look she gave her was curious and a little peeved.

Jerry frowned as he fell in step with Angela. A perfect moment had been wasted—just when he thought he was going to hold this woman in his arms and taste those lips of hers. Damn! He wanted her so much it hurt to breathe. And being around her didn't help either. The more time he spent with her the more he wanted her. Sure, he worked hard and covered his cravings with casual banter, but that didn't stifle them. They only increased his expectations and his needs. He had never wanted a woman this urgently and this much. It hurt like hell. "Her family lets her get away with too much. She knows she shouldn't come here without telling them where she is going. Anything can happen to her along the way."

Angela looked at Jerry curiously and then away. He would make a very good father someday, she thought distractedly. "I gather she's a neighbor."

He nodded. "Yes, her father and her sister work at the Calloway's Farm."

As soon as they reached the barn, Jerry removed the saddle and the bridle and let Angela water down the horse. He disappeared into the house soon after and Angela knew he was going to check on his young guest, Rosie.

What an intriguing man, she thought as she stared thoughtfully after him. He had a way of making her wish for the impossible. Earlier, she had almost let him kiss her. Even now, her heart picked up speed at the thought of feeling those chiseled lips against hers. Somehow, she had known that she wouldn't resist him for long. *This attraction was something she had to deal with before she got in too deep.*

Angela was brushing the horse down when Rosie appeared by her side. She smiled at the Mexican girl and received a smile in return. "You've already called home?"

The girl walked further into the stall and said, "Yes. Juanita promised to tan my hide, but she does that all the time and never does it. I'm Rosie, what's your name?"

Angela saw the way the girl was checking her out—from her boots to her curly hair. She smiled. "Angela. I guess Juanita is your sister."

"Yes. She knows I often disappear here whenever school is out early or on weekends. She only acts angry. She really doesn't mind."

Angela gestured toward a brush that had fallen down and said, "Could you pass me that, please?"

Rosie gave her the brush and leaned against the doorway, checking the way Angela brushed the mare. "So, when did you get here? How long are you going to stay? Are you one of those women Jerry's uncle keeps sending or a relative? I don't mind if you're a relative.

One Day at a Time

But if you're not, I'll need to let Juanita know. I keep her informed of everything that goes on here."

"Rosie, are you being a nuisance, again?" Mac said from the doorway.

Angela looked up and was surprised to see the young girl blush. She smiled as Rosie stammered, "No, I'm not! How are you, Mac?"

The young ranch hand shook his head and muttered, "Ah-hmmm. Ms. Angela, I'll take over Zuri's care. Jerry wants you in the house."

Angela nodded and thanked him. She left the barn and was almost on the patio when Rosie appeared by her side, skipping and grinning like a well-fed cat. "Well, Rosie, looks like young Mac might be the cause of your frequent visits here."

The girl blushed, again. "Not really. So, are you a relative?"

"No," Angela answered as she stopped on the patio steps to remove her boots.

"Are you one of those...?" Rosie started but Angela raised her hand and stopped her.

Angela was getting tired of being referred to as one of those women. "Yes, I was sent by Cyrus to help Jerry with his records. Now, where did you leave Jerry?"

"In the den. He was in a grumpy mood. This time, he promised I won't use the pool for a month. Last time he'd said a week but I didn't believe him. I was very surprised when he refused me a swim after I left a note for my dad and came here. He insisted the note wasn't the same as telling."

Good for Jerry, Angela thought and chuckled. "Okay, young lady, if you promise not to ply me with too many questions, I will keep you company in the pool."

"You don't have to keep me company. This is practically my second home, you know. But I can't wait until it is my real home. Then I can use the pool all the time. I love to swim." She grinned cheekily at Angela's surprised expression.

"Well, eh, that is nice." The little imp probably had her eyes on Jerry, Angela thought with a smile.

112

"Don't you want to know why Eagle's Hill will be my home one day?" She waited for Angela to nod but when Angela shrugged indifferently, she supplied the answer. "My sister is going to marry Jerry. As soon as she's done with the shows, they'll get married."

Angela refused to let the surprise show on her face. Jerry was getting married? She shook her head in disbelief and entered the house. Rosie skipped happily behind her.

***

Jerry frowned as he opened the letter from Benjamin Goldstein, the gallery owner in San Francisco. After their last conversation, he had hinted he might commission a different gallery to get him the painting he was looking for if Goldstein couldn't deliver. Now, the man was claiming he was close to finding the painting, that he knew who owned it and was only waiting for her to come back from vacation before talking with her. Jerry was willing to pay twice what he'd paid for each of the other Hannah Vas paintings but he wasn't going to tell Goldstein that, not yet.

Angela's cell phone rang, again. It was the third time it had rung and he was tempted to pick it up. He had already sent Mac to get her. Maybe he should have mentioned the phone calls. He frowned at the phone, checked through the window, saw no one, and answered it.

"Eagle's Hill ranch—may I help you?" He asked.

"Oh," a feminine voice responded. "Is this Angela McGee's cell phone?"

"Yes, ma'am. I have sent someone to get her but since she is still not here I thought I should pick it up just in case it was an emergency." He heard the woman talk to someone in the background and heard her call him a nice young man.

"Oh, how very thoughtful of you. Well, I'm Clara, her mother. I'm returning her call. She's been calling us nearly every day but we were out of town. Where is she?"

"I'm not sure what is keeping her now, but earlier, she was brushing her horse after a ride."

There was a burst of laughter from Angela's mother. "I knew she would get back on the horse and overcome her fears. That's my baby, tenacious to the core. How is she doing—I mean, with her riding?"

"Fine, eh, actually great. She has a lot of courage, Mrs. McGee. Today, she amazed us when she went into the paddock and put a halter on one of the horses then proceeded to saddle her for a ride. It is not an easy thing to do for first timers." Jerry said with a smile.

"That's my Angela. She could be shaking in her boots but she would not give in to the fear. Do you work there on the farm? Oh, I'm sorry—I don't believe you told me your name."

The den door opened and Jerry looked up. His eyes ran over Angela's body before settling on her face. She had changed her boots and shirt for sandals and a T-shirt, but kept her Levis on. She looked good, no matter what she wore. "Your daughter is here, ma'am. And yes, I do work here on the farm. My name is Taylor."

"What a nice name. Well, it was nice talking with you, Taylor. Make sure my baby doesn't fall from a horse, you hear?"

"I understand, ma'am. She already promised to haunt me through centuries if I let anything happen to her." Jerry added with a chuckle. Angela's mother hooted with laugher, too.

Angela stared at Jerry as he finished talking to her mother. She took the phone from his hand and raised an inquiring eyebrow.

Jerry shrugged apologetically. "It kept ringing. I picked it up finally. I wasn't sure whether it was an emergency or not."

She nodded distractedly and started walking from the den. At the doorway, she turned and said, "Thank you." Taking two steps at a time as she went upstairs, she put the phone to her ear. "Mom?"

"What a nice young man Taylor seems to be. Does he live there with his wife?"

Angela laughed. "If that's your way of asking if he's married, it is pretty obvious. How are you, Ma? You guys stayed at the conference longer than I'd thought."

"Does that mean you're not going to answer my question about Taylor?"

"He works here and he's engaged to be married to a nice Mexican girl called Juanita, okay?"

"Baby, are you okay? You sound funny." Concern laced her mother's words.

Angela shook her head and groaned. Her mother could read her moods no matter how well she tried to hide them. Angela entered her room and closed the door. She had to admit it bothered her to hear that Jerry was engaged. In fact, she was disappointed and peeved—*Lord knows why*—that he was to be married and he never told her. Maybe her anger stemmed from the fact that she was beginning to see him differently and starting to like him. No, it was more than that. She'd taken to imagining what it would be like to kiss him.

"Angela? Are you still there, Hon?"

Angela leaned back against the pillow and sighed. "Yes, Ma, I'm still here. So, how was your trip?"

"The meetings were long and boring. Tell me about Montana. Is it vast and hot?"

Angela was happy that her mother had stopped questioning her about Jerry. "It is really beautiful up here. But we are closer to the mountains than the prairies."

"Well, I'm happy you're taking it easy, dear and that Marjorie finally took in my complaints and insisted that you take a break."

So it was her mother who had talked to Mrs. Maitland about her, Angela thought with a smile. No matter how involved she was with the children at her school, her mother always looked out for her and Sav. She had obviously gotten tired of Angela's excuses about taking a break from nursing Reggie and had gone straight to Marjorie Maitland. Knowing her mother's lack of subtlety, she probably lectured Marjorie on taking advantage of Angela and not giving her the break that she needed.

"Thanks for insisting I take a break, Mom. It is fun here and I'm already feeling the difference."

Her mother chuckled. "That's what mothers are for—to look out for their children. I was scared you'd make yourself sick, baby. You give too much of yourself to others and neglect yourself."

Angela laughed. "No, I don't. Besides, Reggie needs me and that is more important."

One Day at a Time

"I know, child, I know. So, tell me more about the ranch and about your friend, Melissa. Your note mentioned that it is her family that owns the ranch." Her mother added.

Angela spent the next fifteen minutes talking to her mother about Montana, the men on the ranch, horses and rearing them. She didn't mention Melissa except to say that she was in California on an assignment. Then the conversation moved to her parents' recent conference and her mother's students. Finally, they discussed Reggie and his condition.

Angela's eyes filled with tears when her mother talked about seeing Reggie that morning. "Maybe I need to come home, Ma."

"No, no, child, you stay there and relax. You were pushing yourself too hard with Reggie and your business. I've already lost Savannah and have no intention of losing you, too. Get over the pain and anger, Angela."

Angela sucked her breath. What did her mother know? "What are you talking about, Mom?"

"Just because I don't nag doesn't mean I'm blind, child. You are my child and no one can dare say that I don't know my own. I knew you blamed yourself for not saving Savannah. You cried for weeks after she was gone and my heart ached for you. Your mourning wasn't natural. I saw the self-blame in your eyes whenever you looked at Reggie or talked about him. Get over her death, baby. The good Lord saw fit to take our Savannah and we won't question Him. We have Reggie and he, too, will come back when the Lord wishes it. None of this is your fault. You did your best for Savannah during those few hours she was in and out of consciousness and gave her the peace of mind she needed before her journey. Didn't you reassure her that you would take care of Reggie? And haven't you taken care of Reggie since? Our Savannah knows that because she's an angel watching over us now." Her mother paused to sniffle before continuing, "Reggie hears your voice everyday, you know. And if anything can bring him back, it's that voice of yours. He always liked your singing and listening to your voice on these tapes is just as good as having you here."

116

Angela wiped tears from her face. Talking to her mom always helped. She had a knack for saying the right things and easing one's worries. "I love you, Ma. And thank you. I feel much better now that we've talked. How is Dad? Can I talk to him?"

"Of course, dear, just a second," Her mother murmured.

Angela didn't wait long before her dad was on the line. "How's my angel?"

Her eyes watered afresh. She loved her mother but she was a daddy's girl. "Fine, Daddy? How are you doing?"

"Fine, fine, baby. How is Montana? They say it gets hot there. Are you drinking enough water and staying out of the sun?"

How like her dad to worry about her health. "They have a good air conditioning system and a pool, so, don't worry about me. How is the team?" Her dad was the head coach of his high school.

"Okay. We have some amazing freshmen this year, very talented young men. But as usual, their home situation is a different story." Her father went into a discussion about how sports was 80% mental and 20% physical and all the things he needed to do with the young ballplayers to turn them into champions. They talked for another ten minutes before she hung up.

Feeling better after talking with her family, Angela pulled out her swimsuit and headed downstairs. She decided to check the pool before changing but she found it empty. Where was Rosie? A lot of shouting, whistling, and clapping from outside drew her attention.

The sight that caught her eye was too awesome for words. A rider was galloping from the southern end of the compound at full speed. Angela couldn't see whether it was a man or a woman because a helmet covered the head. But whoever the rider was, he or she knew how to handle a horse. Angela's breath stuck in her throat when the rider smoothly slid off the horse—while it was still galloping at full speed—pulled something from the ground and swung back onto the horse's back in another perfect motion.

A loud cheer greeted the performance. The rider turned the horse, waved the scarf he or she had picked from the ground and brought it to Jerry. The hand that had been holding the scarf pulled

117

off the helmet and long, brown hair was released. Angela's eyes widened. The rider was a woman.

Just when understanding dawned on her that the woman had to be Jerry's fiancée, Juanita, Rosie ran up to the patio where Angela was standing and shouted, "Isn't she great? That is my sister, Juanita. One day, I'll ride just like her."

No wonder Jerry wanted to marry her. Angela thought enviously. The woman rode like the wind was on her tail. She was tiny enough to be a jockey and obviously knew enough about horses to help Jerry around his ranch. In fact, with her around, Jerry wouldn't need to hire anyone to race his horses.

Angela was startled when she looked up and found Jerry and the beaming Juanita by her side. "Angela, I want you to meet Juanita Sanchez, Rosie's famous older sister. Juanita, Angela McGee, a friend. She is visiting us from San Diego."

Angela looked at Jerry questioningly but didn't refute his introduction. "Hi, Juanita. I've never seen anyone pull that stunt so flawlessly. That was amazing."

The woman let go of Jerry's arm and reached over to shake Angela's hand. "Thank you. That was a nice compliment." Her eyes traveled up and down Angela's form, not missing a thing. But when it settled on Angela's face, there was surprisingly no animosity. "I've trained long and hard and I intend to be the best at it. I'm also not ashamed to say I want to win as much money as I can. So, how long have you been at Eagle's Hill?"

Angela looked at Jerry who was staring at Juanita with an expression she couldn't define. He probably loved her very much, she thought. Her chest squeezed painfully at the thought and a deflated feeling washed over her. What was wrong with her? She turned to Juanita and interrupted an understanding look in her eyes. *The woman had seen the look on her face.* Angela stiffened. "Oh, I've been here a week."

When Juanita nodded and said, "Then you and I are going to be friends," Angela almost laughed. She doubted that they would ever be friends. And why was Juanita being so cordial? What woman in her proper mind would befriend a single woman living in the same house as her fiancée? Juanita was speaking again and Angela forced herself to pay attention.

"I'll show you around the area and introduce you to the real Montanan life. Jerry is too boring. He never does anything but work, work, and work."

"Well, that would be nice." Angela looked at Jerry and wondered how he liked hearing his future wife call him boring. He was staring at the fields, not even paying attention to them. What was wrong with him?

"Hey, where is the wine you promised me, marble man? If I remember correctly, it was a bottle for every event I won." Juanita stuck her hand in her pocket and pulled out five ribbons. "Five of your best and most expensive bottles is what I want. Deliver now, *por favor*, or forever forfeit your lands." She finished dramatically.

Jerry shook his head and entered the house. He muttered, "Women," under his breath but Juanita just laughed.

As soon as he had disappeared, Juanita turned to Angela and stared at her curiously. "That is the first time I've heard Jerry introduce one of the women Cyrus sent him as a friend. I knew as soon as I heard about you that you were different."

Intrigued and surprised by the woman's comment, Angela asked, "Heard about me?"

"Word spreads fast around here. But this time the guilty person is Liberty Wilson. She wants Jerry for herself and any woman that dares look at him becomes her enemy. So pathetic! Isn't it sad what becomes of us when we age? We start behaving like Libby—running after men young enough to be our sons."

Angela laughed. She couldn't help liking this tiny woman and her sharp wit. "I guess her interest doesn't bother you then, huh?"

Juanita raised a perfectly trimmed eyebrow. "Should it?"

Angela looked at her with a frown and then beyond her to Rosie. "Well, I just thought that since you and Jerry are engaged that you would mind..." Juanita's laughter stopped her. Then she stared at the hand the Mexican woman was holding up.

119

One Day at a Time

"You don't see a ring here, do you? Believe me when I say that if he asks, I'd not be engaged for a month, let alone a week. I'd rush him fast to the altar before some gorgeous woman,"—she looked pointedly at Angela—"changed his mind."

Did that mean they were lovers but he hadn't asked? Angela thought distractedly. Or was it a case of she was interested and he wasn't?

"My sister has been talking to you." Juanita turned and shouted, "Maria Rosita Sanchez! Get your fanny over here before I tan it!" When her sister hid behind the horse, she added, "Let me not catch you getting into the pool either, Rosita. Get your horse ready. We're leaving!" At Angela's bewildered expression, Juanita sighed. "My sister is a fibber. She somehow got it into her head that Jerry and I should marry and she tells everyone about it. Silly girl. Anyway, she has an overactive imagination. Take everything she says with a grain of salt." The woman winked and indicated that they should go in.

Angela looked at her in amazement and then turned to look at Rosie. How could she have believed her lies? She shook her head.

Jerry was putting a box of wine on the table when they walked in. Juanita hurried beside him and checked inside the box. When Jerry looked down at her, she made a face and said, "Just making sure you don't stiff me." She took the box and closed the flaps, crisscrossing them so they didn't stick out. "I'll visit longer next time. I've got to take that naughty sister of mine home before someone kills her. Thanks for the wine." She reached up and gave Jerry a brief kiss on the cheek.

"I'll carry that for you, Juanita." Jerry offered and took the box from the petite woman's hands. He walked out ahead of them.

Juanita turned to Angela and smiled. "Isn't he such a gentle-man? Anyway, I'll come and show you around soon. Don't let Jerry work you too hard, Angela."

Angela nodded and waved at her. She liked Juanita. She didn't care that Jerry might feel something for her—no, that was a lie. It bothered the hell out of her, and she couldn't explain her reaction. And she refused to examine why she was beginning to think more and more of Jerry the man and not Jerry the possible murderer. All she knew was that it had upset her to think of him with Juanita.

Shaking her head, she started walking across the kitchen. She had intended to swim and that was what she was going to do. And yet, she found herself walking to the kitchen window first. She held her breath when she saw Jerry and Juanita.

The Mexican woman was on her horse and Jerry was standing beside her. What were they talking about? Did Jerry like her or just admire her horsemanship? Angela shook her head and turned away. She'd better go swimming before she started acting even more weird.

Chapter 11

Jerry walked to the pool deck and headed straight for the bar. After mixing himself a Martini, he leaned against one of the stools and turned to watch Angela. She was a smooth swimmer, he thought distractedly as her figure swayed under the water. He picked up his drink and moved closer to the edge of the pool.

Exhausted, Angela stopped at the shallow end of the pool and pushed her hair from her face. A pair of loafers at the edge of the pool caught her eyes. She looked up. "Hey, Jerry, want to join me?"

He stared into her eyes and shook his head. He put his glass down, picked a robe from the lounge, and held it out for her. "Are you coming out?"

"Thanks," she said as she hoisted herself to the side of the pool.

Jerry's body hardened as the water flowed off her body a few inches at a time, caressing her skin. He held his breath when she stood at the edge of the pool in her full glory. Her body was fabulous. Then his eyes shifted to her face, free of make up, wet, and so perfect. "You're so beautiful."

She smiled and her eyes shifted. "Thank you. May I?" She indicated the robe.

The expression on her face held his attention. There was vulnerability in it that surprised him. But what amazed him the most was that he'd never wanted her as much as he wanted her now. "Can I get you something?"

"What are you having?"

"Martini," Jerry answered

"I'll have the same, with lots of ice," she answered as she tied the sash of her robe. Actually, it was one of Jerry's guest robes—one of those fluffy soft numbers that enveloped its wearer like a lover's embrace. She looked up and found Jerry standing close to her. She smiled weakly at him and took the drink. "So, did you see your girl-friend off?"

Jerry followed her to the bar. "Who?"

"Juanita."

He laughed. "You must be confusing me with someone else. First Libby and now Juanita—what do you think I am?"

She looked over her shoulder at him and grinned. "Hey, I'm just drawing conclusions from the evidence."

"Don't you know you should never take things at face value?" He took a seat across from her and a sad expression crossed his face. "I learned early in life to question everything—everything I read, see, or I am told."

Angela's heart picked up a beat. Was he talking about what the papers had written about him? Could he be opening up about his past? "Like what?"

"Like why you're so eager to saddle me with two girlfriends when I don't have any."

Angela looked away from his eyes. He wasn't playing games now. Before, his eyes would sparkle with a devilish light and his lips would curl with amusement. Now they were serious. He was gen-uinely seeking an answer. Could she bluff her way through this? "What a ridiculous idea. I'm not eager to saddle you with anything."

"That's a lie." Angela opened her mouth to protest but Jerry got up and moved closer to her. "Don't! Don't lie to me, Angela. I know and you know that there is something between us. We can tap dance around it but we'll have to deal with it sometime." He reached over and pushed wet hair from her cheek. His fingers shook with the inten-sity of his feelings. Lord, he'd never needed this so much—with every breath he took and every inch of his body. "I want you. Unfortunately, you're scared."

Angela moved her face until his hand fell away. She'd been tempted to lean against it or trap it between her cheek and her shoul-der. "Where do you get this idea that I'm scared?"

One Day at a Time

"I know you are. You're scared of your feelings or where they might lead you. You know that you can trust me, Angela. I'd never hurt you."

If only it were that easy, Angela thought wistfully. If only she could forget Sav and Reggie and the accident and the stories in the magazines. She looked into his eyes and sighed. She wanted to forget about the past and live in the present. Lord knows how much she wanted to. And in Jerry's trusting eyes she saw that possibility. She remembered his kindness, understanding, and generosity with everyone around him. There was the way he helped her with the horses, the way he treated Little Joe, the way his workers looked up to him, and the way he valued their opinion. And she couldn't ignore the way he watched over a neighbor's child as if she were his own flesh and blood.

How could this man be the same one the papers had written about? How she wished that for once she wasn't burdened with the past. But how could she let go? "I'm not scared of anything. Don't you remember what I said to you earlier? I can handle anything..."

His thumb touched her lips as if to keep the words from coming out. "Can you handle this?" Then his mouth hovered above hers.

"No, Jerry, don't!" She protested.

The protest died when his lips covered hers. Whatever breath Angela had left was sucked out of her. Hot and burning, their lips molded together, tasting, nibbling, and leaving her wanting more. Her knees buckled as her arms reached for him and landed on his waist. He snapped her body up and against his. His arousal was at the tilt and she felt it pushing, pulsating, and demanding to be released. She responded instinctively, pressing closer, and seeking more contact. Was this passion or lunacy? The thought fleetingly passed through her mind before his tongue invaded her mouth. Then she was lost in sensations.

The kiss that had started as a lesson backfired on Jerry as he moaned his need. He wanted much more than a mere kiss from this woman. He wanted to devour her, brand her and make her his. "Angela. Oh, Angela," he groaned as his lips searched, drank, and

124

craved for more.

She tightened her hold on his back as she rubbed and kneaded his muscles. She never knew a kiss could be this consuming, this devastating to the senses, and so satisfying. Pressing pressed herself closer and tighter to his hot body; she wanted to absorb him, seeking satisfaction that only he could bring.

"Yes, Baby. Closer." He breathed. His lips moved from their hot dueling mouths and traveled along her jaws while moaning her name. His tongue seared the satiny skin of her neck. He savored the texture and tasted the sweet sexy scent that was pure Angela. One hand pressed her closer while the other moved to caress the swellings on her chest.

The whole week, he'd wondered if she could fill his palms. He was now confirming it in the most intimate way. He sighed in contentment as he played with a tight nipple. A satisfied sound escaped his lips when she moaned and lifted her body higher, giving him better access.

The barrier of the robe didn't stop his fingers from tormenting her senses, teasing her nipples until the buds became a pool of sensations. Waves of spiked heat rushed through her and settled on her belly. It made her body hot and tingly. It needed fulfillment. She needed validation for her womanhood.

When his hand pushed the robe down, she helped him shrug it off, wanting to feel his hands on her skin. The feel of cool air on her shoulder was soon replaced with heat of his palm as he sought her collarbone, touched her with reverence and passion. She arched her back as his fingers caressed the mounds on her chest, as he pulled the fabric across the sensitized buds and shamelessly used it to heighten the sensations. She cried out.

Somehow her cry of passion fanned his. He wanted her, now! He could not wait. His hands moved lower and caressed her flat, hard stomach. He felt the muscles contract and groaned. He wanted to devour her, right here next to the pool. He didn't care that he could not make her any promises or that tomorrow, he could let her leave if she wanted. All he cared about right now was to assuage his hunger for her body, thirst for her heat, and ache for a piece of heaven. His knee pushed hers apart.

When his knee brushed hers apart, she willingly welcomed him, until she was riding his thigh. The position aroused her senses to a higher level. The swim suit offered no barrier to his jean-clad leg. It felt like he was already touching her in the most intimate way possible.

His breath caught and held. Oh, Lord, he could feel her heat. It seared through their clothing and reached his sensitive skin. The muscles on his body tensed painfully. He imagined himself getting lost in her moist interior, her muscles squeezing and caressing him, the moans of her passion filling his ears while he found total absolution. He groaned and moved his hands to her rounded backside. He pulled her higher until her knee grazed his arousal. He gasped.

Angela tensed. Is this what she wanted? Her body was crying for fulfillment. The ache in her tummy intensified as his scent overwhelmed her nostrils and his body leaped at her touch. But her mind argued with her body. Could she have an affair with a man who could be responsible for her sister's death? But could she walk away, knowing she'd finally met someone who could mean something to her?

"I need you, Angela," Jerry growled in a heated voice.

"No, please, stop! Please, stop!" She begged and yet her body seemed to become more pliant and to fold more intimately on his.

"Oh, baby. You have no idea how I've longed to touch you, to kiss every inch of you and hear your sighs." Each word was punctuated with hot caresses on her face and stamped by the rough hands kneading her flesh. "I want you so much," he groaned.

"Please…" she begged as convulsions raked her body. Her hands held him tight even as her mouth was denying them.

He groaned in response, moved his lips to hers, and gave her a hard kiss as if to convince her that what he wanted was right. He rocked their body together, showing her what tune they could be dancing to. "Lord, you're exquisite. I need you, baby."

She drew a deep breath and prayed for strength. "We must stop, please," she begged with a trembling voice.

He paused and looked into her eyes. He saw vulnerability mixed with desire. She was right. They had to stop, he thought with regret. He withdrew and felt the effect all the way to his toes. She shifted and he let her ago.

Angela leaned back on her stool. Her world had changed. That one kiss had touched her all the way to her core. She would never be the same again. After what seemed like an eternity, she whispered, "I guess, it wasn't a great idea, huh?"

Jerry shook his head. "Except for not finishing what I started, I find absolutely nothing to regret about it."

She shook her head at him. "Jerry..."

"Don't say anything, not unless you want me to kiss you, again, Angela." Jerry warned with a determined look. Lord, he ached! He ached so much he felt like crying.

She glanced at him. "There will be no more kissing, Jerry."

He looked at her and saw the way her chin was sticking out stubbornly. There were other ways to get to her without kissing her. "Okay."

Angela frowned at him. He surrendered too easily and too fast. "What do you mean, okay?"

"I accept your terms." Then he added, "For now."

Her eyes widened. "No, Taylor. This is not negotiable. No more kissing. I came here for a job and that is all I intend to do."

"What if you decide to kiss me? I won't have qualms taking you up to it," he promised and grinned at her astonished face. Smiling cockily, he moved away from the bar. "Now, I need a very cold shower. Would you like to join me—in the shower, I mean."

Angela opened her mouth and then closed it. He wasn't getting a response from her, she vowed.

"Don't worry, there will be no kissing, just touching. I'll scrub your back and you do mine, although I wouldn't mind my front being scrubbed, too."

His words created images in her mind that were downright sinful. "Go away, Taylor." When he grinned cockily at her, she turned her back to him.

One Day at a Time

Jerry felt bad for baiting her but damn it, that was the first time a woman had told him that kissing him was a bad idea. It had rankled, especially when the kiss had been hot, sizzling, and toe-curling. *Next time, there would be no stopping, not if he could help it,* he vowed to himself as he entered the house.

Angela left the pool deck as soon as he was gone. Using the living room door, she went past the foyer, ran up the stairs and disappeared into her room. Fifteen minutes later, after a near-cold shower, she was pacing back and forth. What was she going to do about Jerry? And how was she going to forget the kiss they'd just shared? Even now, thinking about it made her skin tingle and most of her sensitive spots throb with need. She wanted to be in his arms again, to feel alive and desirable. But he was Jerry Tyrell Taylor, the man who had killed her sister. Damn, damn, damn!

She pulled out her recorder and started playing a tune. Music always gave her peace of mind but after that kiss, she had to work extra hard to be absorbed by it. And it was his fault.

An hour later, Sally came to get her. Angela was still singing and recording a song for her nephew when the older woman knocked on her door. "Come in, Sally."

Sally found her seated cross-legged on her bed, the recorder still in her arms. "Was that you playing, Ms. Angela?"

She nodded. "I was trying to record something for my nephew. He likes to hear my version of popular tunes. Is it dinner time?" She scooted to the edge of the bed but Sally was still staring at her instrument with fascination.

"You have a very beautiful voice. Do you know some of the oldies—the kind country folks like?"

"Some, I guess. But if you start a song I can pick it up and string something for it." She put the instrument down and got up.

"Oh, no, don't leave it behind. Please, play something for us tonight, after dinner. The boys would sure love that—beats all the arguments and the sports they watch most evenings."

Angela frowned. That should give her the excuse to finish her dinner fast and disappear into the kitchen. Now that Lester was back, he and Jerry could keep each other company. "Why don't I bring it down after dinner?"

Sally looked at her with shiny eyes. "I knew there would be changes around here as a soon as I set my eyes on you. There is nothing cowboys like more than to sing, and although my Winston used to string a Banjo, his arthritis won't let him do it anymore."

"Then it will be my honor to accompany their singing, Sally."

As they discussed songs and other entertainments cowboys liked, they walked down the stairs. Sally left her at the dining room door and disappeared in the kitchen. Angela had changed into a casual summer dress and sandals.

Jerry stood up as soon as she entered. The look he gave her was possessive. Angela glared at him before turning toward Lester who had also gotten up. Jerry had better behave in front of Lester or she would box his ear.

"You look and smell great," Jerry whispered as he helped her in her chair. He had intentionally leaned closer to her as he spoke. His cheek grazed her hair. "I'm happy you could join us, Angela." This time he spoke loud enough for Lester to hear. She glared at him and he grinned back, unrepentant.

"I got caught up with my music and forgot about the time." She directed the comment at Lester and did her best to ignore Jerry.

Jerry chuckled and cut in, "Angela has a very beautiful voice. I was hoping she would play something for m...us some time so we could appreciate her talents."

Not for you, cowboy! "Actually, Sally invited me to join the men after dinner and sing something. She asked so nicely I gladly accepted."

"May I come and listen, too?" Lester asked.

"Sure, Lester. So, how was your trip to Helena?" She asked, pointedly ignoring Jerry.

Lester talked about his fiancée and the trainer's exam he was due to take in a couple of weeks. After that she listened as he and Jerry discussed sports. Then the conversation became general, though Angela only contributed when a question was directed at her. In no time, she was done with her dinner. She happily excused herself from the table.

She joined the workers who had finished their dinner and were seated on the patio. Sly was smoking a cigarette while the others were either drinking coffee or finishing their desserts. As soon as she walked outside, everyone started asking her about the songs she knew and offering her a place to sit. Big Joe pulled out a harmonica and showed it off. He was ready when she was, he said.

Angela smiled at their enthusiasm, sat next to Little Joe, and started an old cowboy tune that was popular in the south. The men soon joined in. Some clapped while others stamped their feet. Sally came out and started dancing. She was soon joined by Lester, who seemed to have deserted Jerry. Angela laughed as the dancers kicked their heels and the others yowled at their performance. Not wanting to miss the fun, she pressed a button to make the tune repeat itself, put the recorder down, and jumped up. She bowed before Little Joe and requested a dance. The teenager grinned and jumped up. Soon she was kicking her feet, shaking her body, and having a ball. That was how Jerry found them when he opened the door and joined the boisterous group outside.

Angela didn't stop. She may have faltered a bit but she continued dancing and doing her thing. She thought the others might feel uneasy with Jerry around but they just offered him a place to sit and continued their singing and clapping. He stood and watched them. She was aware of him and knew exactly when he left.

***

For the next week, Jerry's attitude changed toward her. He became very courteous. He seemed to find reasons to hold her arm or her hand, push her hair from her forehead, or remove something from her cheek. The first time he'd held her hand longer than necessary, she'd laughed and said she wasn't delicate.

But he'd just laughed and said, "Humor me."

She found herself enjoying his company more and more. They rode together. He joined her during lunch and spent time with her in

130

the den, discussing her work or his. They also swam together in the evenings or worked out in the gym. The kiss they'd exchanged was never mentioned but neither was it forgotten. Her senses were more attuned to his. And she had caught him watching her with smoldering eyes on too many occasions.

Juanita and hers sister stopped by for a visit. They spent a fun afternoon together. The two sisters even stayed for dinner. Two days Juanita took her to Twin Ridges, the nearest town to the farm. They had lunch and did a little shopping before driving back to Eagles Hill.

Angela left her desk and walked to the window when she heard raised voices coming from outside. She shook her head when she saw Libby talking animatedly to Jerry. What did Libby want now? She was always coming to the ranch with one problem or another. In fact, the woman was beginning to irritate her.

Angela's eyes shifted to Jerry when he shouted something to Winston and then started for the house. What was going on?

"Angela?" Jerry called as soon as he walked into the house.

Angela met him in the foyer. "Is something wrong, Jerry?"

"I need to go to Libby's for something. I should be back within the hour."

She frowned. "But weren't you expecting the vet today?"

He rubbed his nape and smothered a curse. "Ned Vogel! He was supposed to have been here yesterday. His office called and said he had an emergency delivery but would be here today. Well, half the day is gone and I have no idea where he is." His hand reached for hers. "Do me a favor, baby. Could you look out for him? Mac and Sly took two of the mares out and Big Joe and Little Joe are mending fences. I need Winston with me at Libby's. So, please, keep an eye out for Ned's truck—dark green with his name and trade on it. If he gets here before we do, take him to see Wind Dancer. She's in the northern paddock."

Angela saw how frustrated Jerry was and she was tempted to ask what Libby wanted. Instead, she squeezed his hand in understanding. "You go on ahead. I'll look out for him. I'm done for the day anyway and could use some fresh air."

One Day at a Time

He smiled and said, "Thanks, baby," and then unexpectedly, dropped a kiss on her forehead.

She frowned as she watched him go. She would bet he hadn't realized that he'd kissed her or called her baby—twice. What was he up to now? Angela shook her head and sighed at her foolishness. It was obvious he was preoccupied with other matters and hadn't planned his actions or words. She laughed at herself and went outside.

Jerry was riding away with Libby and Winston when Angela stepped on the patio. As she stared after them, the patio door opened behind her and Sally joined her. "Do you know what's going on at Libby's, Sally?"

The older woman sighed and sat beside her. "I hear that old Wilson's son, Peter, has come home and is trying to evict Libby and her family from the house. That boy is pure evil. Libby got that land fair and square from Wilson but Peter refuses to believe it."

"Why can't she call the police?" Angela asked. Why call Jerry? What if he got hurt?

"Because quite a number of people around here still believe that the Indians should only live in the reservation. They forget about the ones who marry outside their race and inherit properties, like Libby, or children from such unions, like Jerry's grandpa. No, the police aren't likely to be on her side." Sally finished with a sigh.

Just like they won't be on Jerry's if they found him there. "But what can Jerry do? He could get hurt," Angela added worriedly.

Sally looked at her and smiled. "Libby said that Peter was drunk and was throwing their belongings outside. Now if that's true, then Jerry or Winston could restrain him until he calmed down. Maybe they could reason with Peter or be a witness to his deeds. They are more liable to believe someone of Jerry's stature than three Crow Indian women." Sally shook her head before continuing. "It is interesting that he picked a day when Libby's brothers are gone and she's alone with her mother and grandmother. Young Peter is a big man, too. The women are no match for him. It is a good thing Libby has us to turn to for help."

Angela bit her tongue to stop blurting out that Libby's problems weren't Jerry's. He had enough to deal with without running at her beck and call. What if the man turned on Jerry and his eyes got injured again? Angela bit her lip and sat on the patio. Sally sat down beside her.

None of the women spoke for a while as they waited for the men to come back. For once, Angela didn't question why she was worried for Jerry. She just was. *Please, let him be okay*, she thought with a frown.

Chapter 12

It was over an hour later when Jerry and Winston rode back from Libby's farm. Angela found herself following Sally to meet them as they neared the barn. "How did it go?"

"We calmed Peter and convinced him to leave before the police could be called. Did Ned show up?" Jerry asked as he started rubbing his temple.

He looked tired, Angela thought. Were his eyes bothering him? "No. Would you like for me to check with his office?"

He shook his head and got off his horse. "We've already started treating the mare. I might just drive to Butte and consult with a different vet if Ned doesn't come today. Is Sly home yet?"

"Yes. He's in the barn." She answered as she followed. "Do you do this sort of thing a lot?"

"What thing?"

"Run to your neighbor's aid, rescue damsels in distress kind of thing," She added.

He smiled and stopped. "Now I know why you're dogging my steps while chewing your lip. You were worried about me." She was scowling but didn't deny his statement. His grin broadened.

Angela berated herself for that telling remark. She looked toward the house and said, "Of course I was worried. However, it was purely for selfish reasons. If he'd hurt you, I would've been forced to cut my vacation short."

He chuckled as he turned her face toward him. He ignored her explanation and gently caressed her chin. "Thanks for caring, Angela. Peter was drunk and making a fool of himself. He knows that that piece of land is legally Libby's and that the old man was of sound mind when he made his will. It is just hard for him to accept that his father married an Indian and then dared to leave part of his land to her. Peter forgets that Libby cared for the old man when he wouldn't have anything to do with him." A screeching of tires made him look up. "Ned! Do me a favor, baby. Take Thunder in and give her some water. Ned and I have a few things to discuss."

Did he realize he'd called her baby, again? That was the third time. She didn't know whether to call his attention to it or just ignore it. Then he surprised her again by giving her brief hug before passing her the reins. "Thanks for caring, Angela."

Angela hesitated. She turned to look at the man Jerry was about to confront. Ned Vogel had just jumped down from the truck. He had a receding hairline, a protruding belly, and a shaggy blondish beard. He didn't look remorseful for being a day and half late for his appointment. In fact, his beady eyes seemed to scan the farm greedily. Angela shook her head, shrugged, and walked the mare into the barn.

Jerry cleared his expression as he approached the vet. This was the last time he was asking for Ned's services. In fact he had already begun investigating other veterinary possibilities.

"Howdy, Jerry," Ned said though his eyes were on the barn entrance where Angela had disappeared.

"Nice of you to come, Ned," Jerry said as he shook his hand. "I heard about the foaling at Randal's."

"Yes, one of his mares had some difficulties—a breach birth. Anyway, we saved both mare and foal. How is Wind Dancer?"

"She needs a pelvic exam to confirm that the infection is gone." He indicated that the older man walk ahead of him to a corral on the north side of the farm.

"Did you follow the instructions I gave you over the telephone?" The vet asked.

"Yes, we used one of the tubes and placed the saline solution of the antibiotics into her uterus. I think she is okay now but I need confirmation—another culture, if possible, before I can take her for breeding." Jerry explained.

One Day at a Time

"Are you breeding all of them at Circle K?"

Jerry stopped at the fence. "Just some of them, Ned. As soon as Wind Dancer is well, I'm sending her with two other mares to Duncan's farm in the North. You've heard of Zeus, of course."

"Who hasn't? Duncan is as cantankerous as they come and expensive, but Zeus has good pedigree. He is the best Thoroughbred stallion in this area. Was he accommodating about the stallion?"

Duncan Parker ran a stallion farm in the north and had some of the best Arabian and Thoroughbred stallions in the state. His prized stallion was Zeus, a thoroughbred with impeccable lineage. Jerry wanted to try and breed three mares with him. "Yes. I booked everything well in advance. He's expecting the mares soon."

They stopped and watched as Wind Dancer grazed comfortably in the paddock. "You're Hawk's boy, and I'm sure that made a big difference to Duncan."

Jerry didn't let the vet's comment about his grandfather rankle him. It was going to take a while before the people around here believed he was a good horseman in his own right and not just because his grandfather was wealthy and well-known. He hadn't used grandfather's name to get the booking with Duncan. The fact was that when he was younger, he and his brothers visited Duncan's farm often. During those visits, he learned a lot about stallions and breeding. The old man came to like him, too. He'd often said Jerry was like a sponge, so eager to learn about horses and always asking questions. "My grandfather is too busy with his own farm to meddle in mine."

The older man brushed his thinning blonde hair and stared curiously at Jerry. "I thought I saw a pretty, young woman when I drove up. Is Cyrus still sending you assistants?"

Jerry squinted as he looked beyond the paddocks to his house. He had made the mistake of explaining to Ned the presence of the different women in his home. Unfortunately, Ned loved to gossip. That was how word got spread around the local farms—through Ned's network. "No, she is a personal friend—visiting for a couple of weeks."

Ned reached over and slapped Jerry on the shoulder. "Now,

that's the way things should be. Your sight is okay and girls are coming in doves. Do you think you'll go back to playing ball? You were at the height of your career when you lost your sight and you should be a welcomed addition to any team. Why should you try your hand at horse breeding when you could earn millions playing?"

Jerry let the insults pass. Like most old geezers around southwest Montana, Ned thought that Jerry—a young black male—had no business farming or breeding horses. They were all waiting for him to fold up and go back to California or to the ball park. White men like Ned were more comfortable seeing young black men like Jerry play ball, where he didn't threaten the good-old-boy neatly set system. But like Jerry's grandpa always said, one didn't do things to show off or prove any thing to anybody, but only because it was the right thing to do and because it was what you wanted to do. Well, Jerry loved horses and was damn good with them. It was what he loved to do. Some people may be reluctant to offer him their services but he'd learned from a very tender age that money talks—especially with hypocritical people like Ned. Jerry knew that if he couldn't get what he wanted from Ned, he could get it elsewhere, at a price. "I'm a horse breeder, Ned. My playing days are over."

"Yes, well, if Michael Jordan can go back two or three times, so can you. We'll just have to wait and see. Have you checked to confirm the mares' heat cycles?"

Jerry gave a humorless laugh. He resented it when Ned talked to him in a condescending way. But he didn't let him get to him. If it weren't for the damn cultures, the man wouldn't be on his farm. "Yes. They should be ready to breed in a week or two. But like I said over the phone, I need to know if Wind Dancer needs more medication before delivering her to Duncan's ranch."

The two men followed Sly and Wind Dancer back to the grooming room. They discussed the work Jerry was doing, the health of his mares, and Philly. They stopped by Philly's stall and watched the expecting mother.

"Her udder is enlarged, that's a good sign."

Jerry smiled. Ned wasn't sounding patronizing now. "I don't

know Ned, that's not the first time it has swollen. Philly has been swelling on and off throughout her pregnancy."

The vet nodded his head while checking the horse's swollen stomach and her flanks. "She's a first timer, so that's expected. Just make sure you record everything; when the udder fills and how long she carries the foal. She will be ready to foal when her flanks are sunken in. If she's still rounded, that may spell trouble so, call me."

Jerry wasn't going to call Ned for anything. Winston had had enough experience with difficult foaling. Between him and Jerry, Philly should be fine. The only reason Ned was on his farm now was because of Wind Dancer's infection. Otherwise, he didn't welcome the vet's unsolicited advice on horse breeding, his smirking expression, or derision.

Ned spent hours getting samples for a culture and then checking on the other horses. It was going on to four when he left Eagle's Hill. Jerry made sure the check he gave him covered all his services. He was happy to see him go.

***

What a morning, Jerry thought as he wrote in Wind Dancer's journal. First it was Libby and her problems then Ned and his innuendos. He had a headache. In fact, his head was pounding relentlessly. Finishing the final entry, he left the tack room and headed for the house and Angela. Talking to her often relaxed him. He enjoyed her company a lot—when he wasn't thinking about making love to her.

She was in the den, working. "I thought we agreed you'd only work in the mornings," He commented as he stared down at her bent head. He stilled the urge to touch the baby hair at her nape and instead, braced himself on the back of her chair. Her fingers stopped typing and she looked up at him.

A sudden wave of longing washed through him. It was desire mixed with a need to just hold her in his arms. He straightened his body and moved away from the temptation she offered. "You shouldn't work too hard on this, Angela. Take time to relax and enjoy yourself."

Angela stared at Jerry's retreating back. It wasn't what he'd just said that made her pause but the tone he'd used. He sounded drained and a little sad. "Is he gone?"

"Ned? Yes, at last." He flopped on the leather chair across from his desk. His back was to her and so, he allowed his eyes to close in relief.

"Does that mean you won't be calling his office again?" She asked as she left her chair and approached him. She swallowed as she watched him stretch his body on the seat. When he started rubbing his temple she frowned. His head must still be aching. She could ease his headache by massaging his shoulders and neck.

"You got that right! I'm going to take an Internet course in basic veterinary. I'd rather do things by myself than depend on people like Ned." He murmured softly to himself.

"Good for you, Jerry. Sally filled me in on that man's attitude and I think you're dong the right thing. I just can't stand people with attitudes like that. Wait and see if he doesn't come begging to take care of your mares when you ditch him. People like that love to act smug until you don't need their services any more." She came to stand behind his chair.

He looked up at her and smiled. "You're a tiger when you defend people you care about, aren't you?"

She grinned back and quipped, "Don't let it go to your head, cowboy. I'd defend my people any day against racist pigs." Then she reached for his glasses and pulled them off. "How are your eyes?"

"Give those back!" He reached out as if to grab them then sank back in his seat. "My eyes are fine."

She ignored his growled words. "What about the headache?"

"Who said I had a headache?" Jerry asked defensively. How the hell did she know he had a headache? "Can I have my glasses back, please?"

Angela sighed. "Very politely put but I can't give them back to you, yet. I'm going to give you a massage first, to ease that headache. I guess you're one of those men who'd be on his death bed before admitting he's not feeling well."

His head felt like a saw was splitting his head in two but he was not about to let her touch him. No way! The way he reacted to her nearness, he was likely to throw her on the floor and have his way with her. "I don't need a massage, just my damn…"

"Hush! Close your eyes and let me take over," she whispered and covered his temples with her hands. With her heart beating double time, she leaned against his chair and gently pulled his head backward until it was resting on the back. "Just relax. Breathe in and out, slowly and deeply. Think of somewhere you'd rather be or something you'd rather be doing than sitting here. Let me perform my magic." She finished in a whisper.

Didn't she realize what she was doing? Jerry thought and let out a rugged breath. Somewhere he would rather be was with her upstairs in his huge bed, getting lost in her sweetness. Her breath grazed his face and he nearly groaned out aloud.

It was one thing to bait and flirt with each other across a table but another thing all together to have her hands all over him. When was the last time a woman showered him with such attention? To borrow her expression, he could be as grumpy as a bear with buckshot on his rear end but like Winston and Maria, she still wouldn't back away from him. She was so stubborn, smart, and yet, compassionate and caring. And now she was breathing down his neck, her sweet scent washing over him and his body refusing to obey his brain, again. He tried to control his body. It didn't work. He had to do something soon about this attraction between them. "Okay, have your way with me, tigress."

"You must really be tired because your jokes are beginning to sound lame." He tried to say something but she laid her finger across his lips and added. "Hush, now. Stop distracting me."

Ten minutes later, Jerry sighed in contentment. Her hands were truly magical. For a woman, her hands were strong. Her fingers and palm worked on his taut neck muscles and then moved to his face and head. Places he never imagined could be massaged were receiving careful attention. He sighed deeply and wished he were leaning on her. He needed softness in his life. Except for his mother and sister, Jerry hasn't welcomed a woman's presence since the accident. But Angela was different. She stirred his senses and challenged him in every way, and yet she was the one he wanted. She didn't give in to him or pander to his ego, and yet he sought her approval. She seemed oblivious to his torment, and yet, he fantasized about her.

Actually, Angela wasn't oblivious to his needs. She knew he wanted her. And that she wanted him. Sure, she fought the feelings he evoked in her and tried hard not to be overwhelmed by his charms, but Jerry wasn't a man one could easily ignore. He exuded an aura of raw sensuality. Well-toned muscles rippled whenever he moved. To put it plainly—he was beautiful. Then he had a quiet, confident way of doing things that fascinated her.

And now for the first time, she was enjoying touching the velvet smoothness of his skin. She kneaded and stroked it, loving the roughness around the chin, the smooth sculptured muscles on his shoulders and the soft skin behind his ears. She messaged the temples and leaned closer to inhale more of his musky essence. He smelled nice. It was a mixture of soap, after shave, and natural male scent that called to something in her. She sighed and leaned even closer, unconsciously answering a call from him.

"That's enough!" Jerry muttered hoarsely. Then with a stronger voice added, "I feel better, thank you. You were right, you do have magical fingers."

"Thanks. Feel free to ask for them when it gets unbearable." She offered.

He knew where they would end up if she touched him again; trapped underneath his body, being kissed senseless, or asked to go beyond that. Now he watched as she moved beside him and stretched. Her breasts pushed forward so enticingly he swallowed.

Oblivious to his thoughts, she picked his glasses from her desk and brought them back to him. "Here you go,"—she slipped the glasses back on his face.

She didn't guess his intentions until his hand closed over hers. She squealed in shock as he pulled her on to his lap. Then she looked

141

into his eyes and her mouth went dry. His eyes were hot. "What do you think you are doing, Jerry?"

"Holding you and getting ready to kiss you." He murmured just before his mouth closed over hers.

Thoughts disappeared from Angela's head and sensations took over. His lips were so hot she felt their effect all the way down to her toes. One hand held her head in place while the other went around her waist.

When Angela didn't pull away, Jerry groaned in satisfaction. Lord, he had wanted this. No, he had needed to taste her. Like a starved man, he drank from her lips. When her hands wrapped around him, he pulled her legs over the armchair and held her even closer. The chair was uncomfortable but he could put up with anything just to have her in his arms.

When their lips separated, both of them were gasping. Her lips were wet and swollen. She looked so beautiful and wild and so damn desirable he wanted more. His hand closed around her nape and pulled her head toward him. There were caresses, sighs and sounds of hungry lips as they strained to get closer and assuage their hunger.

It was a while before they stopped. Jerry tucked her head under his chin and leaned backward. He was holding her like he never wanted to let her go.

Reality hit Angela when she heard Jerry's thundering heart in her ears. Or was it the blood pounding in her head? She didn't know whether to curl against him and absorb his heat or bolt upstairs to analyze what she had let happen. She couldn't dare deny that she had enjoyed every minute of it. She closed her eyes and decided she didn't want to think. She was staying.

It was a long time before she said, "I thought I'd said there would be no more kissing."

Jerry chuckled. "I decided I didn't like your rules."

She smiled at his arrogance. "Don't I have a say in it?"

"No. We've played by your rules so far. Now we are following mine."

She tried to sit up but his arm tightened around her. His hand was creeping slowly down her thigh. The dress was no barrier to the heat from his hand. He reached the hem of her dress and touched her skin. She sucked in her breath. Her hand closed over his. "I need to finish my work."

"The computer can wait." Jerry murmured as he caressed her neck.

She shivered. "Jerry, someone might catch us in here."

"I don't care." He replied. His other hand moved toward her breast.

"But I do." She said it so forcefully that he stopped.

He removed his hand from underneath hers and said, "Can we go upstairs?" She shook her head. "Why?"

Angela jumped up from his lap and put some distance between them. "I need to take care of a few things, excuse me."

"Angela? You can't keep fighting this." She refused to look at him. He sighed. How could she kiss him like that and walk away? Couldn't she taste his need in his mouth, his hands, or in every breath he took? He couldn't figure her out. He knew she wanted him. What was making her hesitate? "Could you do me a favor?"

Angela turned to look at him warily. *Please, don't ask me any more questions that I can't answer,* she begged him with her eyes.

Jerry looked at her vulnerable eyes and he knew he couldn't continue to push her. "Do you think you could get me a glass or a pitcher of water from the kitchen, please?"

Angela sighed in relief at his request. "Sure," she said and hurried from the den.

As she walked from the den, her eyes fell on a middle aged, medium height, slender woman who was crossing the foyer. The woman was dressed in jeans, boots, and a crisp white shirt. She had been heading toward the kitchen when she saw Angela and stopped.

The woman checked her thoroughly then said expressionlessly, "You must be Jerry's new assistant."

Angela nodded. "Yes, I'm Angela McGee." She didn't extend her hand because the woman didn't seem ready to close the gap between them. Then she recognized her as Jerry's mother. She could-

One Day at a Time

n't forget those eyes—so much like Jerry's.

This morning, Jerry casually mentioned that his mother would be visiting and Angela had known that the harmony they'd enjoyed the entire week would end with her arrival. After their telephone conversation, Angela had concluded that his mother either didn't like her or distrusted any woman who got close to her precious son. Well, here she was, and from her tone, she had not forgotten their telephone conversation.

Ignoring the look the woman gave her, Angela smiled. "How are you, Mrs. Taylor?"

The woman moved closer and tilted her head sideways—a habit Angela had seen Jerry do often. She stared pointedly at Angela's unruly hair and shoeless feet. Angela liked to fiddle with her hair when she was working or kick off her sandals when indoors. But the censoring way Jerry's mother was looking at her almost made her feel guilty about those innocent habits. Or could the woman tell she'd been messing around with her son in the den?

"I'm fine. Thanks for asking. Where is my son?" Jerry's mother said in a toneless voice. "He's in the den."

"What is he doing there in the middle of the afternoon?" She looked at the den door and back at Angela. Her glance touched Angela's hair and bare feet again.

Angela flushed. "Resting. It's been rather an eventful day. I was going to get him a drink of water."

The woman frowned. "Is that right? Where is Sally?"

Angela stiffened. The way she worded it indicated that she was censoring Angela for doing Sally's job. *Take it easy*, Angela told herself. She was very close to losing it with this woman and her rudeness. This might be her son's house but there was a limit to what Angela could take from anyone. "I don't know. I was working and haven't seen her since early afternoon."

"I see. I'll go see my son now, Ms. McGee. It was nice to talk with you."

Angela waited until Jerry's mother reached the den door before she started for the kitchen. Why should that woman hold a grudge against her? She wasn't the one who had been rude over the phone. Or did she treat every woman who came near her son that way?

Angela stayed in the kitchen, holding an empty pitcher. Should she ignore Jerry's request and let him catch up with his mother? Or should she find Sally and let her deal with the situation? She didn't think she could go on being polite if Jerry's mother continued to bait her. She was still debating on what to do when Sally walked into the room from outside.

"I saw Maya's truck outside. Have you seen her?" Sally asked as soon as she saw Angela.

Ah, so that was the Maya Libby had been talking about on her first day here. It didn't surprise Angela now that Jerry's mother and Libby knew each other. They both were possessive of Jerry and were unreasonably rude toward her. "Yes. She's in the den. Is she always so protective of Jerry or is it just my imagination?" She regretted the question when Sally turned to contemplate her. "Never mind I asked."

Sally twisted her lips in thought. "Maya loves her children very much, Ms. Angela. However, you have to know what Jerry went through with his wife to understand her attitude. If she was short with you, she didn't mean it. It is just her way of protecting her son." She nodded at her and smiled. Then she mumbled. "It is a wonder that boy is back to being the young man we knew before that woman Carmen did her number on him. Oh, well, I better go and see if Maya wants something to drink. But you never mind her now, you hear. When you get to know her, you'll find that she's a very nice and loving woman," Sally added as she started for the foyer.

Angela was still in shock at Sally's revelation. Jerry's marriage hadn't been a happy one? The sudden opening of the door leading to the foyer reminded her of the pitcher she was holding. "Ah, Sally? Jerry wanted water. I was, eh, coming to get him some when I met his mother."

"Oh, Ned must have left then," Sally mumbled as she took the pitcher from her.

"Yes, he's gone," Angela murmured. She was still distracted by the information Sally had casually given her. So, Jerry and Carmen had a difficult marriage. Why then were there pictures of him and Carmen in the living room?

Angela shook her head and started for the foyer. Sally said something to her but she didn't hear her. She was too absorbed with her thoughts. If Jerry's marriage had been an unhappy one then the arrangements of the bedrooms upstairs made sense. She had peeked inside all of them and discovered a lavender-colored, feminine bedroom next to the child's room but across the divide from the master bedroom. Jerry and Carmen must have been sleeping in separate rooms.

Did they have separate rooms in L.A., too? Was Jerry really obsessed with his wife as the papers had insinuated? Was that why he had been following her around town? Angela couldn't imagine Jerry as an obsessive man. He was way too proud to stoop to that. Then who had wanted separate bedrooms—he or she?

Angela shook her head as questions she had pushed aside came back to haunt her. Should she ask Sally for more details or wait until Jerry was ready to confide in her? Damn, now she was beginning to have a headache. She had pushed aside the issue of Jerry and the accident, but now doubts were clouding her mind again. Should she check to see if the spare bedroom had Carmen's things? Other than confirming that they had separate rooms, she had no proof of Jerry's guilt or innocence.

No, she was done with snooping around. She would wait until Jerry trusted her enough to talk about his past. But for now, she'd at least learned something new—Jerry's marriage had not been a happy one.

Angela dragged her feet upstairs. Her sandals were in the den but she wouldn't dare step in there, not when she could hear Jerry's and his mother's voices emanating from it. What were they talking about? Not about her, she hoped. She needed Tylenol and a rest. There were too many things on her mind now.

Chapter 13

Jerry smiled at something his mother said. Earlier, he had heard her footsteps and assumed she was Angela. When he'd mistakenly called her 'baby' she had twisted her lips in disapproval. Now she was recounting the events that had taken place at SC ranch the day before while trying to convince him to travel with her to California.

"I told your grandfather that you're pushing yourself too hard and needed a break, too. Are you sure you don't want to come with me to San Diego?"

Jerry chuckled. "You didn't come here to try and change my mind, Ma. And grandpa would agree with me that I'm needed here." He leaned against his desk and contemplated her. After their conversation a few days ago, he would bet his entire farm that his mother's visit had something to do with Angela. However, he was not going to help her by bringing up Angela's name. "So, have you packed everything for your trip?" He grinned when she glared at him.

"I didn't come here to exchange small talk, Jerry."

"And I thought you came to see me for one last time before you left for Aaron's. How else would you convince him that I'm doing fine?" He teased.

She shook her head and chuckled. "Okay, smart mouth, what's been happening around here—aside from the fact that you have a new assistant."

Jerry grinned at her comment but refused to be drawn into another argument over Angela. "You should have come earlier. Libby's step son visited her farm and decided to help her and her family relocate."

His mother raised an eyebrow. "Silly woman, she should have

married Cyrus. He would have made her happier, and her family would have had a home, too."

"C'mon, Mom, you know this land means a lot to Libby's family. Owning SC would not have been the same."

She waved her hand in dismissal. "I want to know everything that happened."

Jerry explained how he and Winston had gone to Libby's farm and the talk he had with Peter Wilson. He mother shook her head when he told her about helping the women put back some of the things Peter had thrown out and their brief conversation with the local sheriff. "When I got home, Ned was just arriving to help me with Wind Dancer."

His mother interrupted. "What's wrong with Wind Dancer?"

"Nothing serious...just a bothersome yeast infection that needed treatment. Ned was supposed to have been here days ago. He promised he would be here yesterday, but unfortunately, he had to stop by Randal's for a difficult foaling. He arrived this afternoon a little drunk, and talking a mile a minute."

"Why don't you use our vet, baby? Ned is a fool, and I fear his drinking will only get worse. What if he harmed one of your mares? Our Graham may be old but he knows a lot about horses. And he would never disrespect you by postponing a visit he had scheduled. He's a very principled vet."

"Actually, I had already decided to stop using Ned, Ma. But I don't know if I want to call on old Graham either. In fact, I'm thinking of taking veterinary classes through the Internet."

"Oh? But what about your eyes? you can't strain them. Isn't that why you've hired Ms. McGee to help with your records?"

"I'll manage, Ma. Quit worrying. Now, can I get you something to drink?"

"Your Ms. McGee seemed to be way too comfortable around here, Jerry. Does she make a habit of walking around half clothed?"

He'd known that somehow his mother would bring the conversation back to Angela. "Half clothed, Ma? C'mon," Jerry teased her.

"I just met her and she was wearing a very short dress and walking around bare footed."

"She was? I hadn't noticed," Jerry answered with a grin.

"Hmm! And that hair of hers, can't she do something with it? I even heard she helps you with the horses."

Jerry leaned forward and tweaked his mother's nose. "She's on vacation and can do whatever she likes. You see that?"—he pointed at the computer—"She works on it every day. Notice that it is still on. She was on it instead of out in the pool or resting upstairs or out riding.

"Humph! Where is she, anyway? She told me she was fetching you water. Isn't that one of Sally's duties?"

"Will you let up, Ma?"

"I just don't know about her, Jerry. She's a little too accommodating. Fetching things for you, helping you take care of the horses—what will she offer you next?"

"Believe me when I tell you that usually Angela would tell me to fetch my own damn drink if I wanted it. I just happened to catch her in an accommodating mood today."

"There is no need to swear, Jerry. But don't you think it is strange that she owns her own company and yet she's vacationing here? She could go anywhere and write it off as company expense. And how do you know if she even owns a company? And what do you mean she would tell you to fetch things yourself? You're doing her a favor by letting her stay here. She should be appreciative."

"I'm not discussing this, Mother."

"I think you need to confirm everything she's said. I don't trust her."

"That is your right, Ma. Let's talk about something else."

"But..."

"She is a guest in this house and I'm not discussing her, mother. Tell me about your new foreman, Bill. Libby mentioned that she'd met him a few days ago. She wondered if he was married." He smiled as his mother's eyes widened. Thank goodness he'd hit on a topic that was sure to get her riled up and her mind off Angela. She worried too much about him. One would think he wasn't a grown man with full faculties.

"Liberty Wilson should better watch out where she hunts for her next husband. Dad would throw a fit if Bill left us."

Jerry smiled as he listened to her extol the virtues of Bill Skywalker and how he would never be interested in Libby. He smiled. He just got his confirmation that his mother was interested in their new foreman. Did she realize how transparent she was?

***

When Angela came downstairs for dinner, she prayed that Jerry's mother would be gone. Then she heard her voice in the dining room and knew she was in for a dreadful dinner. As she stepped off the stairs, she saw Lester leave his room and waited for him.

"How is the studying, Lester?" He was planning on taking a physical trainer's exam.

The younger man grimaced. "Don't ask. But I'll be ready for it."

"What are your plans after passing the exam?"

Lester joined her by the stairs and leaned against the wall. "I've already started checking for openings at various gyms in California. I shouldn't have a problem finding something after I'm certified."

"Good for you." Angela looked toward the dining room where Jerry's laughter mingled with his mom's. She grimaced. "Shall we?"

Lester nodded in understanding. "You've met the indomitable Maya Taylor."

"Hmm-mm," Angela murmured.

"She scared the hell out of me when we first met. Now we're best buddies," he grinned as he offered Angela his arm.

Angela slid her arm through his with relief. It didn't matter that she topped him by at least a foot. She was just happy she wasn't about to face that woman alone. "Good for you. I doubt that such camaraderie will ever be possible between Mrs. Taylor and me."

As soon as they entered the dining room, Jerry stood up. His mother remained seated. Jerry raised an eyebrow when he saw Angela and Lester linking arms. Angela ignored him. Her eyes were on his mother whose eyes seemed glued to their linked arms, too.

"Good evening, Ms. McGee." The woman didn't bother to wait for Angela to answer before she turned to Lester. "Where have you been hiding, Lester? Every time I come here you're either visiting your fiancée or in your room."

"Busy with the books, Maya. I'll be taking my exams soon." Lester answered as he helped Angela to a seat and took one beside her.

"Oh, good! Are you and Janice intending to marry soon?" She turned to Angela. "Lester is engaged to a wonderful girl who works at a bank in Helena. Janice is one of those few women who restore one's faith in humanity. She's not only beautiful; she has character."

That must mean that she, Angela, had none of those qualities, Angela thought with amusement. Did the woman think she didn't know about Janice? Angela smiled at her thoughts, looked up and found Jerry's eyes on her. Her grin broadened when he winked. He must know his mother was being insufferable. Lester laughed and drew their attention.

"I couldn't afford to take care of her, yet. I intend to find a job first, and once I'm settled, she can move in with me."

Jerry's mother turned to her son and intercepted a look he had been giving Angela. She frowned. "I didn't know Lester would be leaving so soon, Jerry."

"I promise to keep you informed from now on, Ma. More wine?" He asked. After he filled her glass and Angela's, he passed the bottle to Lester.

"Don't you know people in L.A. you could call for him, Jerry?" His mother asked.

Jerry looked past his mother's inquiring face to grin at Lester. His mother was such a busybody—she stuck her nose in everyone's business. "Lester and I have already discussed that, Mom. How is the steak?"

"Sally always knows just how I like mine. Do you like your steak, Ms. McGee?"

"Yes, ma'am, it is very tender and juicy," Angela replied polite-

One Day at a Time

ly. Ten minutes later, she didn't know whether to leave the table or tell the woman to go to hell. Mrs. Taylor spent the better part of dinner grilling her. She asked her about her work, her family, her life, how she met Cyrus and why she decided to vacation on Jerry's ranch. Several times, Jerry tried to steer the conversation to other areas but his mother always managed to bring it back to Angela. So, Angela did her best to keep her cool and answer the inquisitive questions as politely as possible.

Then the woman asked her for the third time the name of her company and Angela knew that she'd reached her limit. Her eyes narrowed as she prepared to tell her to get a pen and write the damn name down. But Jerry saved the day by reaching under the table and grasping her hand.

"No more grilling Angela like she's a criminal, mother. Have you decided to spend the night or should I escort you home?"

His mother sighed. "I'll spend the night. There is no point in making you or someone follow me all the way back to the ranch, which you'd insist on doing. I'm not helpless, you know. Well, I hope you all will excuse me. I promised to visit with Sally for a little while," she added as she pushed her chair from the table. Jerry and Lester got up. Angela ignored her.

Angela excused herself as soon as the door closed behind Jerry's mother. "I think I'll also go upstairs. I've a few things I need to accomplish."

Jerry frowned at her but nodded. Lester wished her goodnight. She wished both of them goodnight and left the room. Within thirty minutes, she was fast asleep.

***

The next day Jerry drove his mother back to SC ranch. He tried to talk to her about her attitude toward Angela, but she just grimaced and shook her head. In the end he gave up and changed the subject. It was almost nine when they arrived at the ranch.

Jerry parked his truck in front of the sprawling house. It held fond childhood memories for him, he thought with a smile. As usual,

152

it was bustling with activities. There were cowhands everywhere, cleaning, branding, or rounding up newborn calves. Hawk was a beef man—he raised beef cattle and a few horses. He had five permanent cowboys working for him, a foreman—Bill Skywalker, and then there was his Grandma Martha.

His grandma counted for two men, mused Jerry. She was time-less and tireless, and could also talk a person's ears off. At five-feet-four, she was like a bundle of energy, always on the move, giving orders, asking questions, and not waiting for answers. Most of the cowboys at SC were in awe of her. He smiled when she started toward him.

"Jerry, what are you doing here so early in the morning? Weren't you here a couple of days ago? Are things okay with you? Did Philly have her foal? Ah, you brought Maya home." She squinted at him then turned toward the corral where three cowhands were waving and shouting at calves. They were trying to make them go into a cattle chute to be counted and then branded. "C'mon, child, I have break-fast ready. I hope you have an appetite. Now where is Hawk? Bill, there are a couple of calves grazing among the cows and the bulls yonder," she informed the foreman.

Jerry smothered a laugh. Grandma Martha was a no nonsense woman who ruled SC with an iron hand. The employees respected her, and his grandchildren adored her. His grandpa had met her when he was attending a rodeo in Helena—she, an African American woman who'd come North with her father as his cook and stayed on after he died, while he was the half Crow who didn't fit with his moth-er's people on the reservation or his Irish father's cronies in Butte. Being outsiders had drawn them together, but it was their love and total devotion to one another that had made them a formidable team and one of the wealthiest cattle owners in Southwest Montana.

"I'll take care of them, ma'am," Bill responded to Jerry's grand-mother's comment.

"It's okay, Bill. I'll round them up," Jerry's mother walked from her car. Her eyes were on Bill who was branding the calves with the other cowboys.

One Day at a Time

Jerry's grandmother walked toward him and asked, "Have you had breakfast yet, child?"

Jerry gave her a hug and a kiss on each cheek. "Point the way, grandma, I'm starving."

They started for the house. "Now, how are you, Jerry? Are your eyes okay? Why do you need an assistant if your eyes are better? There is really no point in wasting good money, you know."

"I don't pay Angela anything, grandma."

"Hmm, is that so? Is she pretty?"

"I guess so," Jerry replied with a grin.

His grandma stopped and looked him in the eye. "What do you mean you guess so? She is either pretty or she's not. Is she nice? Does she like living out there on the farm?"

Jerry leaned forward and dropped a kiss on her creased forehead. "She's just my assistant, grandma."

"Ah! You young people never take anything seriously."

"Woman, leave the boy alone." Hawk's voice called from the kitchen.

"Oh, there you are. When did you slip in here?"—she turned toward Jerry—"I heard his voice outside but when I followed it, he'd disappeared." She passed by his grandfather and touched his shoulder reassuringly. He patted her hand.

"That's my Martha, always worrying about me."

"Why are you wearing a robe and having breakfast at nine in the morning, Grandpa?" A sniffle made Jerry turn toward his grandmother. She was standing near the stove but wiping her eyes with her apron. Jerry got up. "Grandma? What's wrong?"

She waved him back to his chair. "Tell him, Hawk."—a sniffle then—"Sure-foot threw Hawk yesterday—almost broke his back. If I hadn't been out there helping round up stray calves, he would've been out there forever, unattended." His grandmother sniffled again.

"There you go again, Martha, making a knocked toe into a big accident. I tripped when walking my horse home. I'm fine except for a little soreness."

"I had to use my special salve to ease his aches." His Grandma was wringing her hands now. "And he refused to see a doctor, Jerry."

"Young Dobbs already checked me and said I'd be fine," his grandfather added just before he dug into his breakfast.

"Who's Dobbs?" Jerry asked as he got up to get his plate from his grandmother.

"Young Dobbs is the new apprentice of old Dr. Graham," she answered him as she handed him a mouth watering steak omelet.

"A vet?" Jerry asked her and received a nod in return. "Grandpa, a vet checked your back?"

"The boy knows a thing or two about aches," Hawk grumbled.

"See...see, he's as stubborn as a mule," his grandmother muttered. She was back to wringing her hands.

Jerry looked at her and knew she had a reason to worry. Hawk was not young. At seventy-five, he was likely to break more than a few bones if he fell from a horse. Jerry sat by his grandpa, leaned closer, and whispered, "You know she won't stop worrying until you go in and see a proper doctor, grandpa."

Hawk lifted his head and smiled at his wife. "Okay, dumplings. How about we visit Butte on Monday? We'll go see one of those fancy doctors at the hospital. We could stay at one of the fancy hotels—spend an evening in town, just you and I, huh?"

"Oh, Hawk! What a wonderful idea!" Then she paused before commenting, "But what about the food for the hands? All the branding going on here and the rounding up of strays need to be checked. And Maya will be gone. Oh, Connie is here now. She can take care of that. Oh, I better go talk to her now." And she disappeared from the kitchen. Connie was the wife of one of the permanent cowboys in the ranch and also the ranch's cook.

Jerry turned to his grandfather and smiled. "She worries a lot, doesn't she?"

"That's love, my boy. You can never truly know if a woman loves you until she feels your pain. And my Martha may be as tough as a hide when it comes to work around the farm but when it concerns me, she's a softie." He stopped then said, "I don't know if this farm would have prospered without her. Do you know she still rides out

155

with Maya and the men to round up strays? She scares the heck out of them, too. Nothing ever escapes her eyes. Now, what's happening at Eagle's Hill?"

"Everything is okay, Grandpa. I came to pick up the truck but if you're going to need it for your trip then..."

His grandfather waved his hand and dismissed his worries. "Bill's already fixed mine. How are the mares doing?"

"Fine," Jerry answered as he munched on the delicious omelet.

"Now what is this I hear about your assistant?"

"Does anything happen in my home without your knowing? I swear I'll send them packing as soon as I get home."

"That would break Sally's heart. And Winston doesn't need to be bothered with another move. Besides, Bill has the foreman's cabin now." His grandfather started to get up. "Cow's teeth, that hurts!"

"You need to take it easy, Grandpa." Jerry said as he got up to help him.

"There is still life left in these old bones, my boy. C'mon, help me with this coat."

The crafty old man had gotten dressed but wore the housecoat to placate his wife. Jerry laughed as he hung the coat behind the door. "You're still as crafty as ever."

"You better believe it, my boy. Now, let's head behind the house before Martha comes clucking after me. The truck is in one of the sheds. You can tell me about this new assistant of yours and why Maya dislikes her."

Jerry smiled. He could always talk to his grandfather about anything. He would like to hear the old man's take on Angela and what he now knew were his growing feelings for her.

Chapter 14

Angela switched off the cell phone and threw it on her bed. She had just finished conversing with Reggie's doctor. There was still no change. Would anything or anyone ever reach that boy? What had he seen before he lost consciousness? Maybe this was his way of dealing with that. She had to admit she had tried everything she could to bring him back—talking to him, singing, and reminding him of his favorite things. His grandparents had done their best, too, giving him all the comfort money could buy and bringing in one specialist after another. Maybe her mother was right, the good Lord was letting Reggie heal and he would join them when he was ready.

Angela was on her way downstairs when the doorbell rang. Knowing that Maria and Winston were at church and Jerry had gone to drop off his mother, she answered it.

A delivery man grinned at her when she opened the door. "We have three paintings for Eagle's Hill ranch. Is this the right address?" Behind him was a delivery truck with a California license plate. One of the men was already opening the back of the truck.

Angela nodded. "Yes it is. But I'm not sure I should sign for them. I'm just a guest here."

"Ma'am, we've been on the road for days. You can either sign for them or we'll just leave them out here. You've confirmed that this is the right address."

Angela glared at him. He grinned back. "Okay?"

She decided she had no choice but to step aside to let the men bring in the three, huge, rectangular boxes. When they were done, the man who had talked to her gave her the clipboard without smiling. Angela signed it.

One Day at a Time

Then he had the audacity to salute her and smile cockily. "Thank you, ma'am."

Angela watched them drive off before she closed the door. Her glance fell on the boxes. Paintings, the man had said. Although she was curious about them, she couldn't open them without Jerry.

A smile touched her lips as she thought about Jerry. He had been gone most of the morning and she missed him. She was used to having breakfast with him or seeing him on and off throughout the day. When would he be back? Was his mother poisoning his mind against her? A sigh escaped her lips. She didn't want to think about that insufferable woman, although she found her protectiveness a little amusing. It was much more pleasant to think about Jerry and how it had felt to be in his arms yesterday.

As she went to get her gloves, shears, and a basket for flowers, Angela wondered what she was going to do about the situation she was in. The last week had been the hardest she had ever experienced. She'd had to struggle with her undeniable attraction for Jerry and the fact that she had no proof of his innocence. The more she got to be around him and know him, the more she realized that she might have misjudged him. Her heart told her the man she'd come to know couldn't have done the things the papers had reported. But even though she had accepted that she was more than attracted to him, she couldn't stop doubts from clouding her mind. Was she betraying her sister by admitting her attraction to Jerry? Would it be wrong to get involved with him?

And what had she been thinking of when she'd thought she could resist him? In fact, she now knew that fighting the attraction she felt for him was futile. She had never felt drawn to a man the way she was drawn to him. He was easy to like or love. So where did the love come from? Of course she couldn't love Jerry. She had only known him for two weeks but she knew that she liked him. He had character. She admired his dedication to his work, his workers, and his horses. Then there was his courage and tenacity when faced with a life-threatening incident like his blindness, and his loyalty to his family.

She smiled as images of Jerry flashed through her mind—Jerry doing chores around the farm, teasing her, or his eyes lighting up when he saw her. Sometimes while working, something he had said or done would suddenly cross her mind and make her laugh, like a fool.

The sound of a truck made her look up. Pleasure washed through her being when she recognized him behind the wheel. Her heart pounded as he drove into the courtyard. She waited expectantly as his lithe body uncoiled from the truck and he strutted toward her.

"Hey, cowboy," she hailed him.

Jerry enjoyed the picture Angela made and smiled. She seemed very much at home with the basket filled with flowers on the crock of her elbow, gloves covering her hands, and a pair of shears on one hand. She was wearing a dull yellow shirt and a denim skirt. She looked good, he thought, as he stopped beside her.

"Hey, baby." Then as if he couldn't help it, he reached out and caressed her cheek. He wanted to kiss her. "You look absolutely gorgeous."

"Keep talking," she replied playfully.

He grinned at her reply. Then as if he couldn't control himself, he dropped a kiss on her lips. When she didn't pull away or stiffen, he wrapped his arms around her and kissed her deeply.

"Hmm, I missed you." He grinned at her dewy eyes. He loved the way she responded to him. "May I carry that basket for you?" He asked while removing the basket from her arm.

"What?" Her brain was so muddled by the kiss that she stared at him stupidly.

He smiled and put his arm around her shoulder. Knowing that she would be embarrassed by her behavior, he changed the subject. "I see you're wearing one of Sally's hats"—it was a little small for her but she didn't seem to care—"Is it blocking any sun at all?"

Angela poked his ribs. "Why don't you give me yours instead?"

"Sure, why not?" He pulled Sally's hat off her head and replaced it with his Stetson. He made sure he pulled her hair from her forehead and arranged it on her shoulders. His hand lingered on her warm skin. He frowned. "You're hot. Always wear a decent hat, Angela. I'd hate to have you suffer from heat stroke." He caressed her chin. "I like my Stetson on you though. Make sure you take good care of it. It is my best and favorite hat."

She nodded her head and said, "How come I need it and you don't?"

"I'm a man." She kicked his shin. "Ouch!"

"That is what you get for being arrogant. Now, give me back my basket. You had a delivery today—huge boxes that might need your attention."

"The paintings! Finally—I've been waiting for them forever. I knew they'd be arriving but not this soon." He took her arm and started leading her away from the flower beds. "You'll love them, Angela."

"Love what? What about my flowers?" She protested feebly as she went along with him.

"The paintings beat sweating out here in the sun, cutting the flowers."

She knew she ought to object to his arrogance but she wanted to see what made him this excited. He was like a child in a candy store. She slipped her hand through his.

He led her through the door, took the shears from her hand and started cutting the boxes. Meanwhile he explained the paintings. "My mom has a very good eye for art. I had to depend on her when it came to these paintings. They capture your imagination and hold it."

Angela was smiling at his boyish enthusiasm when he exposed the first painting. Shock sucked the breath out of her. A shiver ran through her frame. No, it couldn't be Sav's painting.

The last time she had seen that painting, it was being crated for an exhibition in San Francisco. What did the man say when he approached her parents with the proposal to show her paintings? Oh, a collector wanted to buy some of Sav's work but insisted on seeing everything. Angela had balked at the thought of strangers critiquing Sav's work. It had been too soon after her death and she had resented their intrusion. Her parents did not have the power of attorney to make any decision regarding the paintings because they were not the executors of Sav's will; Angela was. So, she had refused. It had taken weeks of endless phone calls and beseeching messages from the art gallery before she agreed to meet with them. They had flown her to San Francisco, shown her around the gallery, introduced her to the key people there, wined, and dined her. But she had already checked their reputation and had known they were legitimate and respectable. At last, she had given the go-ahead to have Sav's work exhibited.

But she hadn't attended the exhibition. She just couldn't. Her parents had attended though. They were the ones who'd told her that the person who'd insisted on the exhibition had bought the three paintings in the Seasonal Rhapsody series. Paying a couple of thousand dollars for each painting, he'd bench marked the price for the rest of the paintings. Those three paintings were now lying on the floor of Jerry's foyer.

She reached out a trembling hand and touched the frame as if touching one of her sister's masterpieces would make the pain go away and clarify things. What were the paintings doing here?

"Breathtaking, aren't they?" Jerry misunderstood her silence and emotional connection to the paintings.

"Yes," Angela whispered.

"Can you believe this is the first time I'm seeing them? I've seen their photographs but they don't come close to the real things. Look at the blend of colors, the boldness of the strokes, the details. Doesn't it make you imagine you're there, caught in the same scene season after season?"

Sav had painted four pictures of the same scenery by the pond. Like the leaves, the grass and the water level, the people changed with each season. Jerry possessed only three of the paintings in the series. Was he the person who'd originally bought them or had he acquired them through another person?

"I'm still waiting for Goldstein to find the last one in the series." Jerry said, oblivious to the tormenting thoughts going through Angela's head. "You have to help me decide where to hang them. We'll need to make sure we leave a space for the last one."

One Day at a Time

The last one, Autumn Splendor, was the only painting Sav ever gave to Angela. It was also the missing painting in Jerry's series. "Jerry, I want to hear the story behind these paintings," Angela whispered.

Jerry had been walking around his foyer, trying to find the best position to display his paintings when Angela spoke. He walked back to her and wrapped his arms around her waist. "The long or the short version?"

"The long version," she whispered, her eyes still glued on the paintings.

"That would take a while," he replied as he nuzzled her neck.

She didn't respond to his ministration. Her mind was consumed with conflicting emotions—guilt, doubt, and sorrow. If Jerry was the one who had bought these paintings then she had misjudged him terribly. "Please, I need to know."

Jerry frowned while his arms tightened about her. "My drunkard wife drove her car through an intersection and smashed into Hanna Vas's Camry before an oil tanker ran both cars down."

At last he was talking about Carmen! Angela thought. She felt the pounding of his heart and the stillness of his taut body. This wasn't easy for him, either. She wanted to ask him what happened next, how it happened, and why. But her voice failed her. And yet she needed to know the whole story. It could be the beginning or the end of everything between them but she had to know.

Jerry pried loose Angela's grip. Her fingers had been digging into his skin. "I know it sounds gruesome. But they said death was instantaneous for her, and for Hannah and her husband."

They lied, Angela thought. Sav had died in her arms and Reggie was still in a coma. Why didn't he mention Reggie? Wasn't he aware that the boy had been in the car with his parents? But Jerry was talking and Angela forced herself to listen.

"However, I still felt guilty about what happened. Carmen had been acting strange and drinking heavily. If I had done something—I don't know what—I might have prevented their deaths. So, I decided to do something to compensate Hannah's family for their loss—not

162

that what I did could ever bring Hannah or her husband back. When I heard that Hannah was a painter and that she was just beginning to make a name for herself in the industry, I had mother convince a friend of hers in San Francisco to exhibit her work. The gallery was a bit wary, but I've been known to be persuasive. One of the conditions was that I would buy the first couple of paintings. My mother saw this series, liked them, and bought them on my behalf. After that, word got around. According to my mom, people loved her work."

By the time Jerry finished his explanation, Angela had tears running down her face. She couldn't believe she had ever thought this man was a spoilt celebrity. He had cared enough to do something about the victims of his wife's carelessness. And he didn't seem to know anything about Reggie. Could his family have failed to mention her nephew? Why?

"Oh, Jerry, that is the most beautiful story I've ever heard. And to think,"—should she tell him about Sav and that she was her sister or about Reggie and his condition?—"You have a heart of gold." Could she dare tell him her secrets now?

"Now that is a compliment," he teased when he realized how moved she was by the story. He wiped her tears and kissed her eyes.

Tell him, a voice insisted in her mind. Angela shivered. "I'm not joking, Jerry. It takes more than good character to think of doing something like that." She looked up at him, her feelings overwhelming her and making her feel guiltier. Could she dare disillusion him? Would he understand her reasons? She knew he would not like her confession and might even tell her to leave. Maybe she was being a coward but she just couldn't do it, not yet.

"I guess you could say I felt partially responsible. Maybe there is something I could have done," Jerry said with a scowl. "Lord knows I tried to stop her from driving that night. Sometimes I think about it and I can't see myself doing anything differently. And yet, I felt I wasn't blameless."

"It is ludicrous to blame yourself. How could you be responsible for someone else's actions, Jerry?" What a hypocrite she was turning out to be? . Didn't she blame him for Carmen's actions, too?

One Day at a Time

Could he have been partly responsible? What if he were? Could she handle it? No, she had to know if he was totally blameless. "Tell me about Carmen, Jerry. What happened that day? What makes you think you could have helped her?"

Jerry looked at her face. It was taut with tension. Her eyes were bright with tears and curiosity. He caressed her cheeks and nodded. "Let's go into the living room. This will take a long time."

He waited until he was lying on the couch with Angela wrapped in his arms before he started talking. His past often depressed him but talking about it to Angela was somehow liberating.

When he'd first met Carmen, she had seemed to be everything he wanted in a wife. Her personality had seemed to compliment his. While he was masculine, stubborn, cautious and an introvert, she had been utterly feminine, flexible, spontaneous, and outgoing. At twenty-eight, he had been convinced he knew what he wanted out of life and that had included a wife and family. And Carmen, two years his junior, had been willing to be the kind of wife he'd wanted. With ease, he'd slipped into the role of the head of the family while she had been content to be his supporter, taking care of their home. She hadn't minded letting him make most decisions either and her attitude had suited him.

But that changed. He started seeking her advice. He tried to convince her that her input in any major decision affecting their lives was as important as his. He sought her opinion on all important issues. However, she always deferred to him. Whether it was what they needed in their house or their investments, she hadn't wanted to be bothered. But that didn't stop him from asking her. Of course, she would listen as he talked and then say, "Whatever you pick is okay with me, love" or "I like your idea better, baby." Needless to say, when major things like his retirement from baseball or building the house in Montana had come up, Carmen had readily supported him.

Then she changed. She became shrewish and suffered from mood-swings. She began to drink heavily. Their home was plagued with mistrust, jealousy, and temper tantrums. She began to accuse him of having affairs or using his work to avoid being with her. She questioned his whereabouts while he was at home and yet she would forget when and where he was having a game. At times, she'd refuse to travel with him but then fly in the day after the game. Their love started crumbling. When he finished building the ranch house and tried talking to her about his retirement from baseball, she refused to consider moving from L.A.

Finally, she told him why she was drinking herself into a stupor every night. She was pregnant. When he told her that she needed to think about their unborn baby and stop drinking, she'd laughed and said it was her body and she could do whatever she wanted with it.

Angela's heart broke as she listened. He spoke in a flat tone but she heard the pain behind the words. Why would Carmen reject his child? Why had she hated him? She heard the questions although he didn't voice them. The frustration of not knowing the answers was evident in the way he had narrated the story. As he talked of how he jumped in Carmen's car and tried to calm her down, buckling her belt and forgetting his, being thrown from the car when Carmen's car hit Sav's Camry and watching the oil tanker crush Carmen's car before bursting into flames, Angela knew she was finally hearing the proof that exonerated Jerry of all wrong doing. He had not been stalking his wife as the papers had insinuated. Neither was he a possessive man who had caught his wife with another man and become enraged. From his story, he still had no idea who she was meeting in the diner that day. All he did was follow a distraught wife and try to calm her down.

Everything he was telling her came from his heart and she knew it was the truth. She was elated by the proof of his innocence but was also caught up in his pain—pain of not having all the answers and being haunted by the past. Would Jerry ever know what Carmen was up to? Could he be emotionally available to any woman when he still had unfinished past business?

When he had finished his explanation, Angela turned and wrapped her arms around him. She pressed her cheek on his shoulder. "I have only known you for a couple of weeks, Jerry, but I know you'd never harm anyone. There was no way you would not have helped Carmen. You tried to make her stop and let you drive but she wasn't listening. It wasn't your fault she drove that car into the highway without looking. Neither did you pour alcohol down her throat and make her drunk and reckless. The demons chasing her were from within and there was nothing anyone, including you, could have done." She fought back tears and bit her lower lip.

Jerry squeezed her gently. Her faith in him touched him deeply. "You don't know what it means to hear you say that you believe in me." He laced her hand with his and then kissed the back of her hand.

Angela did something she could never have done a couple of days ago, she kissed his lips softly. The euphoria of knowing she had been wrong about him combined with the acceptance of her growing attraction for him was like an aphrodisiac. He had filled her dreams, even when she had denied her attraction to him. Now, she wanted to touch and be touched, to blend his hardness with her softness, and to see if the thoughts that had made her tremble with intense feelings could become a reality. She wanted to feel—freely and without restrains.

Was she going crazy? Probably, but she didn't care. She had suppressed her feelings for far too long but now that they were coming out, she didn't want to control them. "You're an easy man to believe in, cowboy. Now, let's find a place to hang those paintings of yours."

That evening, she could barely contain her feelings as he walked her to her bedroom door. They had just finished a wonderful dinner followed by a challenging board game. She was wired. Should she let him know that she wanted him? She was a twenty-first century woman, for crying out loud! She should be able to show a man that she wanted him without feeling embarrassed. She smiled at something he said and decided not to rush things with this man.

Before she could decide on what to do or say to him, they were stopping outside her door. He leaned toward her and her heart almost stopped. *Was he going to initiate a kiss?* She wondered as her heart beat hard and her body throbbed with need. Instead, he pulled her in his arms and held her tightly. She could feel his erection as it pressed against her.

What was he going to do next? Angela wondered, and sighed with disappointment when he caressed her cheek and pulled away.

"Goodnight, baby. Tomorrow, I have a wonderful surprise for you." Then he opened her door and waited for her to go in before he walked down the hallway to his room.

Was he aching with need like she was? She grinned at her thoughts then laughed. She was acting crazy, very unlike her usual self. Well, there was a time to be rational and a time to let your heart lead the way. She was thinking with her heart now and it was very liberating. What did tomorrow have in store for her? The thought slipped through her mind just before sleep claimed her.

Chapter 15

The surprise Jerry had promised her turned out to be his canyon —his favorite place in the world. It was absolutely beautiful—nature at its best. Wild flowers grew all around the area in a continuous blend of colors. Jerry explained that it was part of his land but he was preserving it from man and domesticated animals. Angela refused to walk through the flowers for fear of stepping on them but he dragged her all over the area and to her chagrin, picked some for her.

"What? I can't give you flowers?" he asked teasingly.

"Not when you're trying to preserve them, Jerry."

He gave her a brief kiss and swung her around. "A woman after my heart! I was trying to be a romantic but I apologize. C'mon, you have to see my cave."

The cave was well lit by a single beam of light coming from a crack on the roof. It was clean and had a rolled up blanket trapped by some stones on one side and a heap of sticks at another corner. "I always make sure there is a dry blanket for cover, clothes, matches and firewood, and some dried food. Just in case someone stops by and needs help."

They left after exploring the cave and went to the pond, which was further up the canyon. He challenged her to a swim. Angela shuddered in revulsion at the murky water. She was a city person through and through. If she couldn't see the bottom, she wasn't stepping in it. She squealed when he grabbed her and pretended to throw her in.

"Where is your sense of adventure, woman?" He complained.

His arms were wrapped around her but her grips on his arms were like pincers. "Right here, Jerry, but I'm not getting in that water without a swimsuit." She eyed the water with a dubious expression. Did she see something move in it? Even if she had a swim suit, she wouldn't dare get into that dark water. "Next time, okay? I promise."

"I'll hold you to it." He took her hand and started walking along the pond, pointing out different plants. He explained how his grandpa Hawk used them for different ailments. "He learned from his mother when he lived at the reservation, before great grandpa McQueen decided to adopt him and make him his heir."

"You have an interesting family history," Angela commented as she fingered a plant that he'd said cured stomach ache.

"Most black people have interesting history."

They spent the rest of the time exploring the canyon. He helped her over rocks, carried her over a brook, and used every opportunity to kiss or hug her. It was close to lunchtime when they went back home.

After lunch, Angela disappeared in the library to read, but she found herself staring at the words and not seeing a thing. Finally, she got her tape recorder and started recording things for Reggie.

"What are you doing?" Jerry asked from the doorway.

Angela's eyes lit up when she saw him. How long had he been standing there? "Just making a recording of what I saw and did the last couple of days for my nephew." Now why did she mention Reggie?

Jerry raised an eyebrow. "Nephew? I didn't know you had siblings. You've told me about your mom, dad, and best friend, Nikki but nothing about siblings or a nephew. Is he from your brother or sister?"

Wrong topic! Angela thought regretfully. But she'd brought it up and she now had to deal with it. "Reggie is my sister's son. She died awhile back and left him in my care."

Jerry thought she sounded funny. Maybe she still missed her sister. "No brothers?"

Angela stared at her hands and shook her head. "No."

"Count yourself lucky. I have three who are total nightmares. So, you must be a doting aunt then," he quizzed, trying to read her face.

Angela looked up and smiled. It was time to change the subject or blurt everything out. "I try. So, where have you been, cowboy?"

"Here and there," he commented then beckoned her with his finger. "Come here."

She'd missed him but she refused to pander to his ego by jumping at his every command. She shook her head and motioned him to her side.

He smiled. Stubborn to the core but that didn't stop him from wanting her. "If you won't come to me, I'll come to you—it is as simple as that. So, have you missed me?"

Her eyes twinkled as she said, "Not really. I've kept myself so busy in here that I—oh, what are you doing?" He had pulled her up and brought her body against his.

"Don't lie to me. Say you've missed me," he said looking at her lips. Last night he had wanted to make love to her. And this morning at the canyon, he had been tempted to make use of secluded areas including the cave. But, there was a time for everything and with Angela, he'd come to realize that she could not be rushed unless she was ready. She was ready now.

Angela looked in Jerry's eyes and knew what he was thinking. It was the same thing that had been in her mind since last night. The same thing she wanted and needed but never like this. The intensity scared her. "I've missed you."

"Hmm-mm, that's an improvement. Now, put your arms around me because I'm going to kiss you and make up for the last two weeks—ever since you promised to wash my mouth out for cursing." She opened her mouth but he put a finger across it. "No reprimands. I'm through listening to you. Like I said yesterday, we're going to do things my way."

"We are?" she asked with a raised eyebrow and a soft smile.

"Hmm-mm, and don't give me that look either because it is not going to work. If you have any complaining to do, take it up with the higher powers. Some things were meant to happen," he whispered and touched the corner of her lips with his thumb. Her lips were velvet soft, delicate, and moist, and he felt an urge to capture the sweet air rushing from them with his mouth. He took a fortifying breath and said, "So beautiful...and so exquisite..."

"You don't think I'm too tall?" Angela asked.

"With your body fitting mine perfectly like this? I don't think so, baby. You're perfect." Then he lifted her chin and studied her face. How could she ever doubt that she was exquisite? The look in her eyes made his chest constrict. Whoever told her that her height was a problem was a fool. He pressed her closer.

Angela sucked her breath at his arousal. They did fit perfectly, right to the V between her legs, she thought in amazement. "You're the perfect one," she whispered as her hands lifted to his face. Her fingers ran over the planes of his face, his ears and then they came to rest on his lips. She caressed them gently, appreciating his beauty.

"I want you so very much, Angela, I ache." Jerry whispered and licked her finger.

Angela gasped at the heat from his mouth. The nerves tingled where his wet tongue had grazed. Then his lips closed on hers.

Touching her lips was like tasting a live wire. They sizzled. They trembled. They burned. The kiss was hotter and better than before. He welcomed her heat and reveled in having her in his arms, again. Every touch he gave, she returned with equal measure. Every stroke from her fingers awakened sensations that made his body tremble. He wanted and needed her and the kiss wasn't enough. As his frame shook, he found the strength to control his raging senses and enjoy the feel of her without rushing her. This woman who trembled in his arms and yet was so strong in every aspect humbled him and made him want to be the best at everything, including loving her. He touched her with tenderness mixed with passion, pouring all his feelings in each caress.

Angela found herself enveloped in a swirl of heat that she couldn't escape—she didn't want to escape. A cloud of sensations pulled her and made her long to be part of him. Every touch from him went straight to her core. She couldn't get enough. She had been a fool to deny him, to deny herself, and to deny them.

171

One Day at a Time

His touch made her sing a special symphony that welcomed them and made them part of it. She felt herself falling, floating away as he lifted her and pulled her closer to his hard body. He touched every part of her reverently and the sensations pooled in her belly, making a ball of fire in her that only he could put out.

As they hummed under their passion, touching and stroking, Jerry moved and fell back on the couch, taking her with him. She was on top now, their legs intertwined.

"I need you, baby." Jerry growled in a heated voice.

"Yes!" Her position made her the aggressor and she welcomed the challenge. Her hand slid between his waist and the couch while her lips welcomed his. She loved the heat of his mouth, the way it tormented and excited her. Her hands moved lower, caressing each sinew of muscle and appreciating the perfect planes of his body. She didn't know a man's skin could respond as Jerry's responded to her fingers. She got bolder, wanting to make him need her as much as she needed him.

But in one smooth motion, Jerry turned around and swept her in his arms. "What are you doing, Jerry?"

"Carrying you to bed," he murmured and kissed her lips.

"I'm too big to be carried anywhere. I can walk."

He'd find the bastard who did this to her and beat the hell out of him. "Don't ever insult my masculinity by telling me I can't carry you. Nothing gives me greater pleasure than cradling you against my chest. Now, stop talking and kiss me, woman?"

With abandonment, she kissed him. Reveling in being able to express her feelings, she kissed his neck, licked the saltiness of his skin and inhaled his tantalizing male scent. She nibbled his lips greedily and boldly caressed his tongue with hers. When their lips parted, she hid her face on the crook of his neck and hung on tight to his broad shoulders. Lord, how she wanted to please him. This man who treated her like she was a precious gem was already erasing her past pains. Her height wasn't a problem with him. He didn't complain about her stubbornness. He listened to her opinion and valued her as a person. And she wanted to love him until she erased the pain

172

and hurt from his past life.

He asked, "Yours or mine?"

Angela didn't care but the thought of inhaling his scent after he was gone made her say, "Mine."

In no time, Jerry was in her room and the door was closed behind them. He lowered her to the bed and then cupped her face. He stared at her as if memorizing every feature. "I've ached for you for so long, baby." Before she could respond, he closed the gap between their lips, tongues caressed, and hands sought heated skin. He quickly removed her dress and dispensed with her panties and bra.

"My God, you're gorgeous!" He muttered reverently. His finger traced a line from her neck to her nipple. They puckered at his touch. Angela sucked in her breath.

"Please?" She begged and reached for his shirt. While she fumbled with the buttons, he explored her body, murmuring how long he had imagined her in his arms, how gorgeous she was, how soft her skin was, and what he was going to do to her.

He pulled her against his bare chest. He lay there with her in his arms for a moment, then he released her, quickly stood up and just stared at her lying there and exposed. She didn't flinch or try to hide any part of her body from his gaze. But when he jerked his belt off and pulled down his pants and underwear, her eyes widened. His chest puffed at her reaction before he slid beside her and reached for her with eager hands.

When Jerry's entire length pressed against Angela, she wrapped her arms around him, loving the feel of his chiseled form, the unleashed power in his muscles, and the smoothness of his chest. She hadn't known it was possible to feel like she did in his arms. He knew just where to touch, kiss, or nibble to elicit maximum response from her. With each moan, he encouraged her, verbally and by action.

"That's it, love. Don't hold back...give in to me...let me make you feel good..."

And when his hot mouth closed on her nipples, Angela's body jerked in reaction and she cried out. Sensations radiated to every region of her body, making her twist in need and ecstasy. She tried to

One Day at a Time

kiss him but the impossible man wouldn't let her.

"I need to taste you first, baby. If you touch me, I'll be lost," he murmured as his lips continued on their southern journey.

Angela tried to sit up and reach for him but all she got was his shoulder. His lips were moving lower. She fell backwards with a moan and gripped the bedspread. He had reached her thighs. Her hips lifted upward, seeking his warmth. But when his mouth reached closer to where her legs joined, she jerked up and protested. "No, please."

"Oh, yes!" He countered just as his finger teased her folds and found her.

"Please, Jerry. No one..."

"Their loss," he replied as he his mouth closed over her.

Angela was lost as sensation after sensation assaulted her senses. The pressure increased as he used his teeth to ignite more nerve endings, his tongue to fan them, and his lips to take her to a different sensual level. Moans filled her room but she wasn't aware she was the one making them. Her hands gripped the bedspread then moved to his head to hold him closer. He lifted her higher until nothing else mattered but his mouth and the sensations cascading through her. When she peaked and shattered into tiny pieces, he was there to hold her and cushion her fall, to reassure her it had been okay to let go and fly.

While her body trembled, he pulled a protective sheath from the pocket of his pants, put it on with trembling fingers, and boldly entered her. She was wet, hot, and tight. It was more than a joining of bodies. He felt one with her—soul to soul. He heard her gasp then jerkily release her breath. He deepened the kiss as he started their ritual dance. Her inner muscles were still contracting and he caught her waves and rode them. With each moan, she showed her appreciation. With each gasp, she made him feel invincible. Lord, she was responsive! He slowed his strokes when he could have welcomed a release. He wanted to pleasure her and create new memories for her—their memories.

It had never been like this. The thought slipped in her passion-dazed mind as he boldly stroked her fires and reduced her to a ball of sensations. He did things to her. He awakened senses that had become dormant. She arched her back and matched his rhythm, meeting him and enhancing each stroke. Her hands roamed his sweat-drenched back and kneaded the sculptured muscles. Her lips were locked with his, loving his heat, his moistness. Then he capped her buttocks and increased tempo.

She wrapped her long legs around his flank, urging him on with the sounds she emitted. He was taking them higher now, past sanity to the gray area where pleasure and pain crossed lines. But he was there with her, urging her on, a willing partner in this journey into the realm of energy and sensual waves. He groaned and cried out her name just as another orgasmic wave claimed her. She clutched him closer as they weathered the storm together.

Angela couldn't speak. Her body was limp. Was this the way it was meant to be—this soul shattering experience that made her feel reborn and yet in perfect harmony with another? She floated peacefully back to the present and heard his heart beat, so strong and in perfect rhythm with hers. She felt at home in his arms—loved and appreciated.

She didn't even know that tears were running down her face until he kissed them and pulled her closer to his form. He rolled on his back, his arms around her, and not ready to let her go. They were still joined—their souls were one and their heart beat as one. She draped herself on top of his body and fell asleep.

Jerry cradled her in his arms and listened to her breathing. He pulled another pillow behind his head and held her while she slept. What had just happened? He'd had his share of women but what he'd just shared with Angela was different.

How could he tell her what he had felt? How could he begin to explain the feelings that had gripped him when she gave herself totally to him and held nothing back? He had never wanted to give a woman mindless pleasure as he had done with her. And that had been his intention, right from when he'd slipped the box of condoms in the pocket of his pants and gone searching for her or when he'd opened her like a flower and tasted her. The way she responded and accommodated him had surprised and thrilled him. But the way she had affected him mentally and emotionally had released something in his soul. There had been unique bonding and liberation, vulnerability and absolute invincibility. How could he explain that to her when he couldn't understand it himself?

Jerry didn't know how long he was lost in thought. But it was a while before he sighed and felt his body harden in need. He wanted her again. He shifted and tried to ease out from under her but her thighs tightened. He kissed her forehead. "Are you awake, baby?"

"Very much so," she whispered. "Am I too heavy for you?" She teased and wiggled her hips.

Jerry groaned. "Just right. Don't start that unless you're willing to finish it."

She sat up and looked at the evidence of his desire for her. "Hmm, I love a man who knows what he wants. And I intend to finish this, cowboy." She slid her palm up his chest until she was lying on him and her legs were straddling his hips. "It's my turn now, so just lie back and enjoy."

She didn't give him a chance to respond because she was already kissing him. When he tried to reach for her, she stalled him. "I touch, you don't!"—and pushed his arms above his head. Then she moved lower and reached his sensitive nipples and played with them, using her teeth as effectively as he'd used his. She tormented and he groaned. Every sound he made was arousing. He made her feel powerful.

Jerry knew he wouldn't last long, not when she was causing havoc with his senses. Her fingers, tongue, mouth, and teeth were everywhere. He groaned and jerked upward when she moved even lower and started caressing his abs. Then her hands slid under his firm buttocks to squeeze them and he barely controlled the moan that slipped from his lips

"Do you know how I admired these the first day I walked into your house? I wondered if they felt as good as they looked," she whispered.

Her hot breath seemed to sear his skin straight to his muscles. They contracted. Now he was rock hard and he prayed she wouldn't touch him. He would fall apart and embarrass both of them. Her breasts grazed his erection and caused him to groan. No, he couldn't take it.

He reached down and pulled her up and simultaneously, rolled them so she was underneath him. "I'm going to love you, again. You, sassy lady, are bent on driving me insane."

"But it's so unfair. Why can't I take charge?"

She pouted so prettily that he couldn't help kissing her lips. "You do that with every look, every touch, and ...oh!" Her hand closed around him. He closed his eyes in ecstasy.

"It is my turn, cowboy. I'll be accommodating and take your preferences in consideration but I'm still in charge." She whispered in his ears and bit his lobe. Jerry groaned and Angela smiled with satisfaction. "Where are they?"

"Huh?" He asked with a dazed expression. Her hands were driving him crazy and her mouth—she was intentionally pushing him to the brink.

"Protection, baby—where are they?"

He picked the box from where it had fallen on the floor. Angela took it from him and removed one silver-wrapped condom. Then she proceeded to prepare him. He stared at her. He loved the look in her eyes, bold but a little uncertain. The soft glow of her skin under the moonlight pouring through the window mesmerized him. The smug smile on her soft lips called to him. Her hands trembled slightly and she bit her lower lip in concentration. Then her eyes connected with his and she paused.

He reached forward and wrapped his hands around hers. Without breaking eye-contact, he guided her hand then leaned back on the pillows to see what she would do next.

But just because she was inept at preparing him didn't mean she didn't know anything about loving. With a glitter in her eyes and a saucy smile on her lips, she crawled on all fours until he was positioned right where she wanted him. Then she proceeded to kiss his chest and neck. Then while staring deep into his eyes, she boldly claimed him. Jerry caught his breath.

"Ride with me," she whispered as she guided his hands to her hips and initiated their next sensual dance.

By the time she lay on his chest, panting and exhausted, Jerry was so satiated he grinned like a fool. "I don't think I will ever move again, love. You've sucked the life out of me."

But move he did, again and again—in the middle of the night and in the early hours of morning. In between, he must have fed her—she just couldn't remember. When she woke up in the morning, she was one satiated lady. Her body ached in all the right places, too. She didn't appear downstairs until way after nine o'clock.

The next two days were blissful. Angela and Jerry spent a lot of time together. Evenings were spent either in the basement playing pool, darts, or board games. Jerry was naturally competitive but in Angela, he found a worthy opponent. She didn't spare him when they played scrabble or monopoly. But neither did he spare her when they played chess or pool. But that was not all they did together. They took advantage of any privacy they would get and made love—night or day, it didn't matter.

The turn in their relationship didn't escape anyone on the farm, either. Everyone noticed that they couldn't keep away from each other. Angela's eye glowed whenever she was around Jerry and he always seemed to know where she was. Then there was the way they talked to each other, the arguments, the shared laughter, and kisses that they exchanged and thought no one noticed.

Maybe it was too good to be true or too perfect to last because on Monday evening, things changed. Jerry and Angela were upstairs in the library, resting before dinner, when Winston came to tell Jerry that Philly was showing signs of an early labor. Jerry hurried after the foreman. Ten minutes later, he was heading back to the house. Philly's condition turned out to be colic.

"Angela?" He called as soon as he reached the foyer.

"Upstairs," Angela called from the library.

He started upstairs, taking two steps at a time. The door opened behind him but he ignored it. He was intent on getting to the library and playing hooky before dinner.

"Jerry? Oh, there you are, dear. Look at the surprise I brought you." His mother called from the foyer.

Jerry paused, cursed under his breath, and turned to look at his mother. He stared at her just as a vision in a white jumpsuit, a frothy duster, and a white hat floated into the room.

"Hi, darling Jerry. Am I not a wonderful surprise?" The woman in white asked while flashing pearly-white teeth. Her face was beautifully striking. Her petite figure was displayed to its best advantage in the white outfit. Could it be Tatiana? No, that wasn't possible. Tatiana was a movie star now and had no time for high school friends. Jerry looked at the library door longingly before starting down the stairs.

Angela heard him walk away and left the library to see what was going on.

"Tatiana? Tatiana Sloan?" Jerry asked in amazement when he recognized the actress.

Angela's eyes narrowed. Tatiana Sloan, the actress, was here? She stepped closer and looked below. Tatiana moved toward Jerry like a lover who'd found her long, lost love. Her arms were stretched forward, her eyes shining, and her lips parted. Angela stiffened.

"Oh, darling, how wonderful you recognized me. That must mean I haven't changed since high school." She purred in a sultry voice and floated into his arms.

Angela glowered as Tatiana wrapped her arms around him and looked up as if she was expecting a kiss. *Don't you dare, Jerry Taylor,* Angela thought resentfully. Anger replaced jealousy when Jerry picked up Tatiana and swung her around. *Oh, that must be easy for him*, Angela thought. Tatiana Sloan was about five feet two, the type of woman who often made Angela feel like a giant. It annoyed her to see Jerry pick her up like she was a doll he could tuck in his pocket.

Should she go back into the library? Angela thought. No, she

One Day at a Time

wasn't running away and she definitely wasn't going into hiding because Ms. Thing was down there as well as Jerry's mother. She started downstairs just as Jerry gave his mother a hug.

Chapter 16

"This is a wonderful surprise. How long has it been, Tatiana? Fourteen years? I remember the day you promised us that you'd one day be a Hollywood star."

With her hands on his arms, she looked into his eyes and grinned. "The night, darling—it was on the prom night when you were the king and I, your queen. We made such a perfect couple, didn't we—the future diva and future baseball legend. We promised to achieve our dreams through thick and thin, and we did."

Angela's eyes narrowed. High school sweethearts, were they? Well, that was fourteen years ago and let girlfriend not think she could pick up where they left off, Angela thought as she walked down the stairs.

Jerry smiled at Tatiana and added, "We didn't believe you would do it until you landed the role in *The Bold and the Beautiful*. But how did you two meet, Mom?"

"By accident, in San Diego. But when Tatiana told me she was recovering from an illness, I had to bring her with me." His mother moved to hug the petite actress. "Of course, she wouldn't have come if I hadn't told her she would be seeing you. I guess she's been trying to get in touch with you for a while."

Tatiana looked up at Jerry. Her hand reached up to caress his cheek. "I know I get busy with filming but I still heard about your tragedy, Jerry dear. I tried to get in touch but I just couldn't reach you." Her eyes watered. "Poor baby, I felt terrible for your loss. I really tried to find you."

And the award for the best actress in a dramatic role goes to...Tatiana Sloan! Angela could not believe how convincing the actress was. Both Jerry and his mother were buying her act. Jerry's mother looked at her with shiny eyes while Jerry—*poor darling Jerry*—was looking at her as if she were the answer to all his dreams. Was it the same look she had seen in his eyes when they were together? Couldn't he see how phony Tatiana was? Angela cleared her throat delicately to get their attention. The sound made the three people below look up.

"Oh, and who is this?" Tatiana asked, her eyes moving from Angela's hair to her sandaled feet and back up again to her face.

Angela ignored this and focused on Jerry who was looking at her—Angela—with hot eyes and a possessiveness that thrilled her to her toes. Despite his delight in seeing his long-lost, high school friend, it was she—Angela—that he still wanted. It was there in his eyes.

Tatiana had noticed the look that had passed between them.

"Darling Jerry, I didn't know you had a guest." She gushed as she scrutinized Angela who walked toward them.

"I'm hardly a guest, Ms. Sloan—I'm Angela McGee, Jerry's assistant. Good evening, Mrs. Taylor."

Jerry's mother nodded at her then turned to her son. "Jerry, let me find Sally while you and Tatiana got reacquainted," with that she disappeared into the kitchen.

Tatiana slipped her hand possessively through Jerry's. "An employee, baby? She is so, eh, strikingly large, or maybe it's my size." She squeezed Jerry's arm and drew his attention back to her. He had been looking at Angela, again. "Anyone taller than I always seems so giant-like, even you baby." She nudged him playfully.

So it was going to be like that, Angela thought without dropping the smile from her face. If Tatiana wanted to trade insults and sugar coat them as compliments, then she would oblige her. Angela didn't take attacks lying down—never had and never would.

Jerry looked up from Tatiana's eyes and smiled at Angela. He didn't think Angela was giant-like or large. She was gorgeous and perfect—for him. As if Angela understood what he was thinking, her eyes softened. Jerry was tempted to let his mother entertain Tatiana while he and Angela disappeared upstairs but he knew that would be rude.

"You carry your weight well, Angela—may I call you Angela? So, you recognized me."

"I've seen your pictures in the magazines, Ms. Sloan." Her face had been in the tabloids more often than Angela cared to count. Somebody must have told her that publicity—negative or positive— was good for her because Ms. Thing was often involved in one scandal after another. But while it reduced her popularity with black audiences, glitzy Hollywood seemed to love her bad-girl image. She got parts in more mainstream movies than more worthy sisters.

"Oh, how wonderful! I love to meet new fans." Then she turned to Jerry and completely ignored Angela. "Darling, I'd love to see this fabulous house of yours but I simply must sit down. I've been horribly sick and haven't completely recovered, you know. Will you help me to a seat?" Tatiana asked while clinging to Jerry's arm.

Jerry took most of Tatiana's weight and started for the living room. Where was Angela? He wondered and looked over his shoulder at her.

Angela was glowering at the woman and wondering how long she could stand seeing her drape herself all over Jerry. And why was Jerry allowing it? Then he looked at her with beseeching eyes and her anger disappeared.

As if Tatiana realized why Jerry had paused, she turned to Angela. "Do join us, Angela. I would really love to know you better. I think you and I are going to become great friends—you know, a sister-friend kind of thing"

Yeah, like a lion and an antelope. Who did the woman think she was fooling? And where had Jerry's mother disappeared to? She should be enjoying this, even encouraging it. Angela thought with amusement. It was obvious why the woman had come back from California with Jerry's ex-girlfriend in tow. She was willing to do anything to spoil her budding relationship with Jerry.

"Just what do you need an assistant for, baby?" Tatiana asked as they entered the living room and interrupted Angela's thoughts.

One Day at a Time

"Computer stuff—Angela is very good with computers." Jerry said with pride.

"Is that so? I often thought that was a masculine domain. But I guess everyone has to find a niche where his or her talent is appreciated. Isn't that right, Angela?"

"Of course, Tatiana," Angela answered politely when she would have loved to add a thing or two about Tatiana's talents or lack thereof.

Tatiana sat down and patted the couch beside her for Jerry to sit. As soon as he sat down, she had the nerve to put her hand on his thigh. *She better take her hand off my man!* Angela thought when she saw the uncomfortable look on Jerry's face.

Tatiana seemed oblivious to his discomfort as she said, "I once employed some computer geek to design a website for me and the man didn't know anything beyond copying what others had already done. People who don't know how to be creative with the state-of-the-art computer software shouldn't call themselves experts. So, what is your field, Angela?"

"Website design," Jerry replied before Angela could speak. "In fact she is quite well-known on the west coast. She created one for my uncle's company—do you remember Uncle C?"

"Of course, baby, I do," Tatiana replied, staring adoringly into his eyes.

"They loved her work. I would like for her to design one for my ranch, too. She is very creative." Jerry looked at Angela and smiled.

That's my hero. Angela thought as she listened to Jerry expound her talents.

"Really? I don't think I've heard her name. But then, the west coast is pretty large. Tell me more about your farm and what you're planning for your horses, darling Jerry. Your mom told me you raised some."

"Can I get you something to drink first?" Jerry asked.

Tatiana smiled. "Champagne is my drink of choice but I'll have..."

"Then champagne it is." Jerry interrupted as he started to get up.

"Don't leave, baby. We have a lot of catching up to do, and I don't want to be separated from you for even a second. Don't you have servants here?"

Jerry grinned charmingly. "I do but they are all busy. Besides, for such a beautiful and unexpected guest, I don't mind offering my services."

Tatiana giggled. "You were always such a flatterer." Then she looked over at Angela. "Have I told you that Jerry was my high school sweetheart? He always said such sweet things to me. I was once convinced that he and I would marry. I remember planning our marriage down to the names of the two children we were going to have. Do you know my mom often tells me that I was a fool to let you go?" Her eye watered.

Angela could barely contain her amusement. Tatiana was good, she thought. Jerry, on the other hand, was bewildered. He didn't know what to do with her.

"Why don't I show you to your room, Tatiana? You've been ill and need rest. We can always talk later." He suggested desperately.

Tatiana gripped both his hands and stopped him from moving away. "No, I need to let this out, baby. My therapist insisted. You were the best thing that ever happened to me. I was such a fool, and look what I keep finding—men who treat me so abominably."

Jerry looked over at Angela as if to ask for help. But since Angela knew that Tatiana was acting the part of the helpless and mis-understood diva, she just lifted an eyebrow and shrugged. Jerry glared at her. She grinned and turned to look at the charming heroine who was busy wiping her pretty eyes.

Tatiana patted Jerry's hand. "Don't look so distraught, baby. I'm okay now. It is just that I tend to get emotional ever since my ill-ness. Talk to me, Jerry. Make me laugh like you used to. What hap-pened to the gang we used to hang with every Friday night—Bobby, Clay, Desiree, and Lauren. Did you keep in touch with anyone?"

"Yes, I did. Let me get us all drinks, okay? Then I'll fill you in." He patted her shoulder then looked at Angela, asking her with his expression to stay with Tatiana.

One Day at a Time

He frowned when Angela saluted him and mouthed, "Aye, aye, sir."

Tatiana waited until Jerry was gone before she jumped from her chair. She looked healthy as a fiddle, thought Angela. In fact, the actress' eyes roamed the room curiously. She moved to a slanted top Chippendale desk and touched its smooth surface. Her hand reached for a priceless vase on the mantle and examined it. She put it down and turned to face Angela.

Angela stared right back. *Time for the truth,* Angela thought with amusement. She couldn't wait to hear what the woman had to say.

"You know why I'm here, don't you?" Tatiana asked.

Angela leaned back on her seat and raised an eyebrow. "To recuperate?"

The woman sneered and the ugly expression marred the perfection of her face. "Jerry's mother brought me here because she knows Jerry needs me. He's been through so much and I'm the only one who can help him."

Angela swallowed a smile. "Oh, that's nice. I'm sure you have a lot in common. But why are you telling me this? It is none of my business what your plans are."

"Let's not be coy now, Angela. I saw the look you and Jerry exchanged. You've been sleeping with him. But now that I am here, it has to stop."

Angela stared at the woman in amazement. "Let me see if I get this straight. Within a space of fifteen minutes, you've concluded that Jerry and I are lovers and you've decided you are here to replace me."

Tatiana smiled. "I knew you would understand, darling. Step aside because I don't share my men."

Angela leaned forward. "When did you decide he was your man, Tatiana? Could it be when the producers of *The Bold and the Beautiful* fired you or when your latest beau dropped you because he caught you with another man, or was it when you saw this *fabulous* house? Let me tell you something, Ms. Thing. Jerry is his own man. You can't dictate to him what he should or should not do."

Tatiana looked at Angela with loathing. "I hate women like you. With your common looks and common jobs, you wish for a handsome, rich, man to come and rescue you from your dreary lives. Well, it's pathetic. You can't have Jerry. He is mine."

Angela got up and moved closer to the shorter woman. "Let me make something clear, Tatiana. I have a very lucrative business which I started without sleeping with anyone, just my sweat, labor and talent—something you wouldn't know about. And second, I don't run after men nor wait around for them. If Jerry wants me, he knows where to find me. If it is you he wants then he's welcome to you. But don't ever come in my face and accuse me of being less than what I am just because it applies to you—and you know the word I'm dying to say." Angela left Tatiana sputtering and walked from the living room. She almost bumped into Jerry who was carrying three glasses and a wine cooler.

"Hey! Where are you going?" He asked.

"I think I'll go get some fresh air. Why don't you catch up with your *old* friend in there? I'll see you later." She answered calmly but inside, she was seething.

"Are you okay, Angela?" Jerry asked as he peered into her eyes.

Angela held herself stiffly. "Of course, I am. I promised to help Little Joe with the feeds this evening. I'll see you at dinner."

Jerry frowned as he watched her walk away. Women! He didn't understand them. It was obvious something was wrong and yet Angela was denying it. He shrugged and carried the drinks into the living room.

Angela spent the next thirty minutes pouring water in the horses' troughs. Occasionally, she stopped to kick at something and imagined it was Tatiana's head. Common, huh! She had been called exotic, never common.

She didn't think things could get worse. Throughout dinner, Tatiana monopolized Jerry's attention. His mother encouraged her by bringing up childhood incidents or friends. If Lester hadn't been at the table, Angela would have gotten up and left. She barely ate her food but every time she forked something she imagined it to be a part of Jerry's anatomy. She was royally pissed at him. She'd seen women make fools out of men but this was too much. Tatiana was an actress and expert at making everything she said and did look real. She had Jerry and his mother supplying her with tissue wipes every time she started her crying routine. That was when she wasn't asking Jerry to get her more of this and that. The woman had nearly finished a whole bottle of champagne and was still asking for more. A lush in the making, Angela thought.

They were talking about another childhood incident when Angela put her fork down. "Excuse me. I promised to help Sally with something in the kitchen. I'll see you all later."

She had promised to play for the guys but she had to drag her feet upstairs to get her recorder. She wasn't in the mood for an evening of singing and dancing but she would rather hang with the men in the kitchen than listen to Jerry and Tatiana as they went down memory lane.

In a little while, she was absorbed in her music. The ranch hands joined in, clapping and singing. Forgotten were Jerry and Tatiana—not really forgotten, just pushed aside. But at least she was having fun. She didn't know when Jerry's mother joined them. Angela was teasing Big Joe about his favorite bawdy song and didn't notice the woman until she turned to ask Sally a question. Her glance collided with Maya's. She ignored the speculation and surprise in her eyes and started a tune for Big Joe's song.

***

Jerry could hear the music coming from outside but determinedly ignored it as he looked at Tatiana with concern. She had been drinking steadily and her words were beginning to slur. "Why don't I show you to your room, Tatiana? You can take a rest and we'll talk some more tomorrow."

"But darling, there is delightful music coming from outside that I would like to listen to. Sounds like your men are having fun. I like to have fun, too. Maybe we should join them." She got up and took Jerry's arm. "Besides, you haven't introduced me."

They walked outside just when Angela had gotten up to dance with Sly. She had the recorder in a prerecorded mode. The men were cheering and whistling. Even Jerry's mother was smiling at them.

Jerry watched as Angela picked her dress and swished it with the beat. She twisted her waist enticingly, throwing back her head as she and Sly danced closer. Sly started clapping his hands while going around her as she turned, twisted and shook her body to the beat. That was his Angela, he thought with amusement. She knew how to make their evenings special.

"Your assistant is full of surprises, isn't she?" Tatiana asked as she leaned on his arm.

Jerry looked down at her bent head and smiled. "She is a multi-talented young lady."

Tatiana stared at Angela with envy. "Why don't you ask them to play something more urbane?"

Jerry looked at the grinning faces on the patio and knew it would be wrong to stop them. "We could return to the house. I have some really good CDs in my collection."

"No, darling, I want to be with everyone." She moved from his side and nudged Winston—who was closest to her feet. "Can you stop that music? We want to hear something different." Her voice made everyone stop what they were doing. They turned toward her.

She looked ethereal in her white outfit, especially with her hair flowing behind her, her eyes glazed from too much champagne, and her smile flashy. "Hi, everyone. I am Tatiana—a very good friend of Mr. Taylor."

"Is she an angel?" Little Joe whispered but it was loud enough for everyone to hear.

Tatiana looked down at him. "No, darling, I'm an actress. I'm taking a rest after filming my latest movie?"

Jerry moved to her side. "Tatiana?"

She smiled at him and put her hand on his chest. "I'm almost done, darling. I just loved hearing you sing. Could you play something for me, something modern so I can dance with this handsome boss of yours?" She giggled.

One Day at a Time

Everyone turned to look at Angela. She had been glaring at Jerry and Tatiana but when the workers turned to look helplessly at her, she smiled. "Of course, Tatiana. What would you like? We can offer classics like Mozart, soulful sounds of Aretha or just hip hop renditions of Destiny's Child. Or we could do some country westerns. The cowboys love to sing them around a camp fire." The men smiled uneasily.

"You're so funny, Angela. I was talking to the men."

"But I do the playing and most of the singing. Unfortunately, I love to do what they like—good old, bawdy western numbers like this one." She started a tune. Slowly, her voice rose above the instrument. The men nodded their heads in rhythm but the cheerful and lively atmosphere had been destroyed.

A brief silence followed her performance. Then Tatiana said with feigned enthusiasm, "You are so talented, Angela. Thank you for the entertainment. Baby, I think I'm ready for bed now." She said to Jerry.

As soon as they were gone, the men thanked Angela and went to their quarters. Sally and Jerry's mom left, too. Angela picked up her instrument and walked upstairs. Luckily, she met neither Tatiana or Jerry on the way.

She had changed into her nightdress when a knock sounded at her door. When she opened it, she wasn't surprised to see that it was Jerry. "What do you want, Taylor?"

"Sorry for spoiling this evening's entertainment," he said regretfully.

Angela wished she had something to throw at him. Did he think she was pissed over that? "Take that up with your workers. Is there anything else?"

His eyes narrowed. "You're angry with me. Why?"

If he didn't know, she wasn't going to help him. How could he ignore her the entire evening and now act so clueless? And she wasn't falling for that lost puppy look either. "I'm tired, Taylor. If you have nothing else to add, I would like to go to bed."

"I tried to make her come upstairs but she couldn't move. I'm terribly sorry she interfered with our evening, Angela."

Angela shook her head. "But she's so tiny, baby. You could've just picked up her up and thrown her up here."

Jerry tilted his head sideways as a realization hit him. "You're jealous of her?"

"Me? Puh-lease! I have better things to do with my energy than being jealous of *her.*" Jerry smiled—a smug grin that infuriated her even more. She started to close the door. He blocked it with his foot.

"Baby, you know there is no woman for me but you." He reached out and touched her cheek. "I know I spent this evening with Tatiana but she's a guest in my house. Besides, I hadn't seen her in a while."

She glared at him. If he didn't remove his fingers from her face, she would bite them off. She thought irrationally. "Goodnight, Taylor."

In one smooth motion, Jerry pushed the door and pulled her in his arms. "Hush! The whole time I was with her all I thought about was you—when I'd be alone with you, how you feel in my arms, and when I'd kiss you, again." Then his mouth closed over hers.

Angela tried to stay indifferent. She wasn't giving in to him, she vowed. He had ignored her since Tatiana arrived, pushed her aside as if she meant nothing to him. She'd show him that she wasn't easily conquered.

But Jerry knew how to make her respond. He used his teeth to torment and his tongue to soothe. His hands sought her sensitive spots and created swirls of sensations. Before she knew it, the warmth from his lips was spreading over her being. She found herself wanting to hold him.

When her arms went around his neck, he groaned and pulled her closer. Her response was instantaneous and he welcomed it. No matter how much she fought him, Angela belonged to him, Jerry thought with satisfaction. She was soft and yet firm, vulnerable but with an underlying strength. And he wanted it all. He showed her with his mouth, his hand, and his body that it was she he wanted.

When they came apart, he wrapped his arms around her and held her tight. "I'm sorry for ignoring you this evening. Will you forgive me?"

Angela stared at his handsome face and then slowly nodded. "She's an actress, Jerry. Don't believe everything she says."

"She's a helpless woman who's been through rough times. She needs understanding and compassion." He countered back.

She shook her head in resignation. "Another Libby, Jerry? What do you do? Collect wounded women like trophies? Or is it your ego that has to be fed?"

He frowned. "I never thought you'd be this cruel, Angela. Just because you've never been in such a helpless position doesn't mean you can't understand someone's plight."

She pushed his arms away. "I know the genuine thing and I know acting, Jerry. I don't know what her story is, but if you need to nurse her then you're welcome to it."

"Don't be like this, baby. We all need help sometimes." He stared at her, at the way her silk nightdress clung to her curves and the way the light shining from behind her revealed her contours. "I want you tonight, baby." He reached for her. She took a step backward and moved out of his reach.

Angela shook her head. "I don't think so. Besides, Tatiana needs her darling Jerry, now." When he turned to look toward the hallway with a frown, she added, "I rest my case."

"Angela?"

"Go, please. The last thing I need is for your mom to see me entertaining you in my nightdress—another mark against me."

Jerry walked toward the door, his body rigid with unfulfilled desire and frustration. He paused at the entrance and turned to look at her. "My mother, Tatiana, Libby—you've got a problem with every woman in my life, don't you, Angela? You mean more to me than a passing fancy, but you still refuse to see that."

"I see possibilities, Jerry. The problem is not me. It is you and your inability to be firm with women. Where do you draw the line? When is enough going to be enough? I don't share my man with anyone, Jerry. Call me greedy or juvenile but I have to be first *and* enough for my man—no girlfriends, ex-girlfriends or widowed neighbors."

His eyes took in her rigid, beautiful form. She was wonderful and yet so difficult to please. What did she want from him? He was who he was and if she couldn't accept that, there was no future for them. A constriction in his chest stopped his thoughts. No, there had to be a way, he vowed. "I hope you feel better tomorrow, baby. Maybe then we can talk." He closed the door gently behind him.

Angela crawled into her bed. Her eyelids ached and sleep eluded her. Why couldn't he see that he couldn't put her on the shelf when it suited him? She wasn't a toy to be picked up for play and then ignored the rest of the time. She wanted a man who was willing to let the world know that she was his woman. And that included telling off a disapproving mother and a glamorous ex-girlfriend.

Chapter 17

If Angela thought the evening before was bad, the next several days were worse. Jerry's mom got up early the day after their arrival, and left. Tatiana didn't appear downstairs until ten o'clock. Then she insisted that Jerry show her around the house and the horses. They were coming back from the stables when Tatiana suddenly fell against Jerry and screamed that she'd twisted her ankle.

Angela, who had seen the whole incident from the balcony of her bedroom, felt like applauding until the significance of the twisted ankle became clear. Tatiana didn't want to leave. Her smile turned into a grimace as she watched Jerry lift the woman and carry her indoors.

For the next two days, she watched as Tatiana whined and demanded every comfort she could possibly get. Sally became her personal servant. Tatiana asked for eggs and then complained about the way Sally cooked them. She liked her steak medium rare with no traces of fat. But did she specify that before they were cooked? No! At every meal, Tatiana instructed Sally on what she wanted cooked or redone.

Angela waited for Jerry to do something about the situation but he seemed oblivious to the woman's behavior. In fact, he did not seem to mind carrying her everywhere—the dining room, living room, upstairs, downstairs, patio. When was he going to realize that she was a spoilt bitch who was stringing him by his balls?

During dinners, Angela and Lester pretended Tatiana didn't exist—a perfect solution really since she ignored the two of them and concentrated all her attention on Jerry. She regaled him with stories of her life, Hollywood, and filming locations. She cried over minor

194

incidents and made herself the focus of his attention. The talk he'd had with Angela two nights back was all but forgotten.

During those two days, there were occasions when Angela hoped Jerry would complain or tell Tatiana off. She even heard him smother a curse several times before he hurried to the house to see what the actress wanted. He even brought her with him to the barn. The tack room had a couch and she sat there and watched him work at the table located in the center of the room. When Jerry was out of the tack room, one of his men had to suffer through her nonstop chatter. But never, not once, did Tatiana show interest in the horses or Jerry's work.

Angela kept her distance from Jerry. He must have realized how angry she was because he stopped trying to engage her in any discussion. Once, he tried to tell her that she was being juvenile, but the look she gave him cut him short. Since then, he had kept his distance.

Thursday evening before dinner, Angela found him lying down in the library lounge. He looked so tired and dispirited. She shook her head and smiled. When was he going to learn? "You can stop pretending. I know you aren't asleep."

He had peeked at her and grimaced. "I was sleeping."

"Ah-huh! So, why are you hiding here? Tatiana needs something downstairs." She waited for his response.

"Sally can see to it. I'm tired." Jerry growled. He didn't want to think of Tatiana. He waited until Angela was close to him then he reached out and grabbed her. She fell on him, face down. While she was still tongue tied with shock, he pressed her head on his chest and wrapped his arms around her. "I need to hold you now, baby. Please, don't complain or push me away," he begged and closed his eyes.

Angela tried to relax. But she was too aware of every breath he took and the hard plane of his body. She wanted to touch him and kiss him until there was no breath left in her.

"Keep still, woman! How am I supposed to sleep when you keep wiggling? I'm trying hard not to start kissing you. If I do, I won't be able to stop." He promised with a strained voice.

Poor man, the last couple of days had taken a toll on him, she thought. Luckily for him, she knew the remedy. She smiled as she let her fingers dance across his chest.

He wiggled. "Stop that, you tease," he murmured.

"Why, Jerry Tyrell Taylor, you are ticklish," she said as her fingers became bolder.

"No, I'm not," he replied as he tried to stop squirming and laughing.

Angela laughed and zoomed in on his armpit, the base of his neck, his sides and stomach. He tried to evade her questing fingers, but she was faster. At last, he pinned her hands above her head and stared into her luminous eyes. "You want a duel, my lovely beauty?"

She giggled and screeched, "No!"

"Too late," he muttered as he swiftly flipped her onto her back. He looked into her laughing eyes, then her heaving breasts, and then he grinned. He held her wrists with one hand and tickled her with the other. She kicked and promised retribution, but he didn't stop. He restrained her with his hips and worked on her until tears ran down her face.

"So, unfair," she mumbled weak with laughter and happiness. "You're stronger."

They switched positions again, as he wrapped his arms around her. "And you are wonderful—I needed that."

"And so did I," she replied and kissed his chin. She looked at his brown face with longing and affection. This wonderful man brought out the best in her, she thought. She lost her inhibitions when she was with him—she wanted to dance in the rain, swims nude, make love in broad daylight at his pond in the canyon. She smiled at her thoughts. Then there were other intimate things she wanted to do to him— smother his broad chest with ice cream and lick it...

She must have fallen asleep because when she woke up, she was lying on the couch and Jerry was lying sideways, staring at her.

"How long did I sleep?" She asked, blushing from her head to her toes.

He traced her nose and shrugged indifferently. "It doesn't matter. I fell asleep, too. I woke up when Sally came in here looking for us."

Angela frowned. "What time is it?"

"Nine O'clock." He still wasn't smiling. "You mean a lot to me, Angela. You know that, don't you?"

She grinned. "Keep talking."

A brief smile touched his lips. "I have never met a woman like you."

"Good! I wouldn't like you to confuse me with another."

He touched her lips and silenced her. He knew the last couple of days had been rough on her. He had caught her staring at him on occasions with anger, but she never complained. Neither had she been rude to Tatiana. Sure, she went out of her way to ignore her but that hadn't bothered him. Unfortunately, Tatiana wasn't used to being ignored, and she had complained to Jerry about Angela's attitude. But he had neither explained Angela's position in his house nor apologized for her attitude. If the two women wanted to be difficult then they should go ahead, as long as he was left out of it. That was what he'd thought. Now he wasn't too sure about his judgment.

He reached down and gave her a gentle kiss. She tasted so sweet and soft. He lifted his head and stared into her eyes. They were teary. "Baby, what's wrong?"

Angela shook her head. How could she start explaining that the kiss he had just given her had been so sweet and yet soul shattering? It had been gentle and reverent. The memory of it could keep her warm on cold, dreary days. She touched his cheek tentatively. "Nothing. I've missed spending time with you."

He frowned. "Let's slip away tomorrow and go to the canyon for a picnic."

She grinned. "That would be fun."

He draped a leg over her hip. "But now, I need sustenance."

"Me, too. I'm famished." She pulled his head and kissed him.

He laughed. "I like it when we think alike."

It was another hour before they walked downstairs. Everyone had retired for the night. They grinned naughtily as they warmed some food and then slipped outside on the patio to eat. After their meal, they walked over to the horses which were being kept in the fields at night and in the barn during the day because of the heat. They talked as they walked and occasionally stopped to gaze up at the sky. They even tried to outdo each other naming different constellations. After a while, they went back into the house.

***

The next day was sunny, or maybe it was Angela's disposition that made it seem perfect. She was in the den finishing the final touches on Jerry's database, when the door opened. She looked up expectantly, thinking it was Jerry. It wasn't.

"May I interrupt, Angela?" Tatiana asked tentatively.

Angela sighed. "Make it a fast one, Tatiana. I have things to do."

"I saw you last night with Jerry," the woman stated quietly.

"And?" Angela turned to face her.

The woman looked her over. "What is it about you, anyway? I'm prettier and sexier than you. I am also famous—a movie star. I'm perfect for Jerry while you...you're nothing. There is nothing special about you. You're also so big. He can't carry you the way he does me."

Angela smiled sadly at the woman. "Are you done?" Tatiana's eyes watered. "Please, don't. I won't fall for that act anymore than I can be fooled by the hopping around you've been doing. There is really nothing wrong with your ankle, Tatiana." Angela leaned back in her chair and smiled smugly at Tatiana. "Don't you know that most men are repulsed by clingy women? Some might like the novelty for a while, but it soon wears off. As for your looks, they will fade with time. And you won't always be a movie star. What then will you have to offer, Tatiana? A man needs a woman who is willing to work with him, a woman who is interested in his dreams. All you do is talk about yourself."

"So that's why you break your back working out there with those stinking horses?"

Angela laughed. "I love horses, Tatiana. And they don't stink.

But they have nothing to do with my interest in Jerry. With or without his horses, rich or poor, Jerry would always interest me. What about you? Would you be interested in him if he weren't wealthy?"

The woman looked at her with hatred. "Why are you being mean to me? I was only trying to be your friend. But you hate me. You're jealous because I was Jerry's girlfriend, because I'm famous." Then she leaned forward as if she were in pain. "I don't like being ill. Why do you I insist that I'm faking my illness?"

Angela watched Tatiana's performance with amazement. That piece of drama would have won her an Oscar, she thought with amusement.

"Angela? What's going on here?" Jerry asked from the doorway. He sounded so angry that Angela stood up.

No wonder the woman's acting had become more dramatic. She must have known Jerry was within hearing distance. "I was just enjoying Tatiana's..."

Tatiana interrupted. "She was at it again, Jerry. She said I'm faking my injury and that I'm a terrible actress."

Angela's jaw dropped in disbelief. How could Tatiana lie like that? And how dare Jerry condemn her without hearing her side of it? She crossed her arms across her chest and glared at him. She was not bringing herself to Tatiana's level by explaining anything to him. "Carry her away before she faints, Jerry. She is very fragile, you know."

When Jerry helped Tatiana out of the room, Angela moved to the computer and switched it off with shaking hands. She was angry and hurt. How dare he act like that toward her? Had he forgotten what they had shared before Tatiana's arrival? What about last night? Didn't their time together mean anything to him? Tears burned her eyelids. *I will not cry over you, Jerry Taylor*, she thought angrily as she hurried through the house and onto the patio. She was breathing hard and fighting back tears. Damn it, she wasn't going to cry over him, she vowed.

Why then did it feel like someone had punched her in the gut? Why did it hurt so bad to see him take Tatiana's side? Why? *I love him*. She thought and closed her eyes tight. Yes, she did. She loved Jerry with all his arrogance and sweetness. How did she let this happen? She wasn't supposed to get emotionally involved to this extent.

A sob escaped her and she crossed her arms across her stomach as if to block the pain. Then a sound made her look up. It was Sally. She was limping while walking slowly toward the patio. Angela wiped her tears and got up. Her anguish was forgotten as she rushed to the housekeeper. "Sally, what's wrong?"

Sally tried to smile bravely at her but it still came out wobbly. "My leg is acting up a little. I just need to sit down for a few seconds before I can get Ms. Sloan her drink.

"Her drink can wait," Angela said as she led the housekeeper to the patio. She made sure she was seated comfortably before kneeling in front of her. "What is it?"

"Ms. Angela..."

"I'm a nurse. Now, show me where the problem is."

The housekeeper pulled up her pants and exposed a swollen leg. Angela tried not to show horror. Instead, she lifted the leg and rested it on her lap. "What happened?"

"I got stung by something but I expected the swelling to disappear. I didn't want Jerry's movie star friend to stay unattended."

Angela smothered a curse. "When did it happen?"

"Two days ago. But, why does it keep swelling? I thought that if I put cold packs on it, the swelling would disappear."

Angela smiled reassuringly at her. "I think you might have been bitten by a poisonous spider. You see the swelling is spread from this point onwards. Right here is more swollen and red." She put Sally's leg down and smiled at her. "Do you see a local doctor, Sally?"

"I'm too old to be running back and forth to some doctor's office, Ms. Angela. If I need to see one, I go to the hospital at Twin Ridges."

"I think you need to see a doctor." Angela tried to be calm but Sally's leg looked really terrible. It needed immediate medical attention.

The housekeeper frowned. "You think it really needs a doctor's attention, Ms. Angela? I don't want Jerry to have to take care of Ms. Sloan."

"Maybe it is time he dealt with her, Sally. You can't work while sick. I won't let you." Sally was looking behind her with tears in her eyes. Angela wasn't surprised when she turned around and found every ranch hand, including Winston, standing there. They were worried about her. "Winston, if it is okay with you, I'll drive her into town and take her to the hospital."

"I have the keys to the truck." The cowboy said with a concerned voice.

"That won't do, Winston. I need a car that is comfortable enough for her to elevate her leg. She needs to release pressure from it. What about the pathfinder?"

"I'll get the keys." Winston started walking away. He paused once to look at his wife, shook his head, and continued to the house.

"But what will you eat while I'm gone? I haven't started lunch and Ms. Sloan needs me to make her special chicken dish and then there is..."

Angela patted Sally's arm. "She can get anything she needs by herself, Sally. There is nothing wrong with that woman's ankle. If she wants to continue faking her injury, let Jerry deal with her. I'm going to get my wallet. I'll be back shortly."

When she got up, the others were still lingering around. Nobody wanted to go back to their chores. She went in the kitchen, came out with a cushion and propped Sally's leg. "Don't move."

She hurried through the house and almost bumped into Winston. She explained what she suspected the problem was and told him what she needed packed for Sally. She then ran upstairs for her wallet and a book. She also threw in overnight things just in case.

Jerry was pacing the foyer when she came downstairs. He looked up when she stepped off the stairs. "Angela, what's going on?"

"I'm taking Sally to the hospital. She has a leg injury infection that requires medical attention. And running up and down pandering to our needs only made it worse."

One Day at a Time

"Oh, where is she now?" He asked with a frown.

"Outside," Angela answered as she walked toward the kitchen.

"Why the hell didn't she say something? Angela, about Tatiana..."

Angela stopped him with a raised hand. "Not now, Jerry. Tatiana is such a liar but you believe in her so much you can't see beyond her pretty face." She looked hard at him and wondered why he had the power to make her happy and at the same time, make her so angry. How could he care for her or look at her with so much tenderness and yet believe the things Tatiana had said about her? "You can believe whatever you like, Jerry. I'm tired of being the villain in Tatiana's stories. I have to go. Sally needs me. I'm taking her to the hospital now." She walked toward the patio as she talked. She pushed the door and saw Winston standing with a black bag, a worried look on his face. "Ready to go?" Winston nodded.

Sally saw Jerry and sighed. "Jerry, I'm terribly sorry. I didn't want to leave your guest, but Ms. Angela insists that we have to go to the hospital."

Jerry squatted next to her and put his arm around her shoulders. "Don't worry about us, Sally. We'll manage. Can you put weight on it?" He asked as he helped her up. Sally tried but winced so visibly that Jerry smothered a curse. "Don't ever put your health in danger because of me, Sally Briscoe. I don't care if I have the President of this country visiting. When you're sick, you come first." Then he picked up the housekeeper and carried her to the truck.

"Jerry, you mustn't." Sally protested while sniffling.

"I can't believe you were in this much pain and didn't say anything, Sally. Look how swollen your leg is. What do you think would happen to me if you were to become ill? Who would nag and scold me when I need it." Winston opened the back seat and Jerry settled the housekeeper in gently. Sally sniffled. Jerry patted her hand. "You'll be okay. Make sure you listen to Angela. She may be the most pig headed woman I know but she's usually right."

"Okay," Sally said with a nod.

Jerry squeezed her hand and closed the door. He moved to the driver's side of the truck where Angela waited with the window rolled down. Her arm was draped over the steering wheel and her eyes stared ahead. She was angry with him again, Jerry thought ruefully. He reached in and gently squeezed her arm. She turned to look at him with an unreadable expression. "I didn't know. Take good care of her, okay? Let me give you my cell phone number. We'll be in the barn and it is easier to reach it than the main house phone." He wrote his number on a piece of paper and gave it to her. Then as if he couldn't help himself, he touched her cheek. "Call me as soon as you talk with the doctors."

Chapter 18

Jerry watched the truck until it disappeared. He felt bereft and abandoned. What was he going to do about Angela? Why was she angry now? He really hadn't known about Sally's leg. "I will never understand women," he muttered under his breath.

Winston who was beside him added, "Neither can I. I asked Sally about her leg but she kept saying it was fine. I should have insisted on seeing it."

Jerry chuckled. "Insisting! Does it ever work?"

"Not really. But at least I could say I tried."

They smiled. Winston headed for the barn while Jerry went to the house to get his cell phone. For the next hour, they worked together in the tack room and kept their ears tuned to the ringing of the phone. It usually took one hour to get to Twin Ridges, but Angela might be driving slowly because of Sally's leg.

Fifteen minutes later, the men started getting worried. Winston sat down on the couch and just stared at the phone. Jerry continued to work at the bench and occasionally glanced at his foreman with a frown.

"Jerry?"

"What?" He snapped with annoyance. Tatiana stood on the doorway. "Sorry, I didn't know it was you, Tatiana. What is it?"

"I'm sorry to disturb you, but I've been calling for your house-keeper to help me and she is not answering." Tatiana pouted as she leaned against the door frame.

"Sally is not well, Tatiana. Angela had to take her to the hospital. What did you want?" Jerry glanced briefly at the woman.

"I wanted her to get me a drink."

Jerry stared at her as if she had gone crazy. Before he could say anything, Winston spoke.

"If you can walk all that way to the barn, surely you should be able to get yourself a drink." Winston said with a growl.

Tatiana gasped. "Jerry! He's being rude to me."

Jerry sighed in irritation. He didn't understand how some women were so strong and dependable while others, like Tatiana, were absolutely useless. "His wife is very sick so, please, try to understand his reaction. But he does have a point. Since you can walk, why not help us out, Tatiana."

"Help? Doing what?" She screeched.

"Fix us lunch. We're busy now but the men could do with a meal in an hour."

"Cook?" Tatiana asked in disbelief.

Jerry continued to clean the saddle as he said, "There are cans of foods in the pantry and leftover meals in the refrigerator that you could fix up. I would appreciate it if you could try, okay?"

Tatiana blinked rapidly and then nodded. Limping, she walked from the tack room. Winston chuckled. Jerry grinned.

"You're a brave man to trust that woman anywhere near a kitchen. She might..." The telephone interrupted Winston but it was Jerry who picked it up.

It was Angela. Jerry listened to her without interrupting and then said, "I'll tell him. He might want to come and stay with her...okay." Jerry looked up with a frown. "Winston, they want to keep Sally overnight and observe her. Angela couldn't talk for long, but she promised to call again as soon as she's done with the paperwork and Sally has been assigned a room."

"Tell her I'll be there in an hour or less," Winston said as he rushed from the room.

Jerry relayed his message to Angela. He would have loved to talk with her a little longer, but she sounded so preoccupied and worried that he hung up when she said she had to go.

Jerry left the barn and went to tell the others the news. He knew they were worried about Sally, too. He was talking to Sly when the fire alarm went off. They both looked up.

"I hope it's not the barn." Sly said.

"The horses!" Jerry shouted and broke into a run. Sly was right behind him. Big Joe and Mac were also running toward the barn from a different direction.

They were almost there when they realized the alarm was coming from the house. In fact, smoke was coming from the kitchen window. Jerry ran faster. He broke through the kitchen door to find Tatiana splashing water on a burning pan. He cursed as he ran to the pantry, got the fire extinguisher, and extinguished the burning pan.

"I'm sorry, Jerry. I was trying to warm up the steak. I just sat down for a few minutes and then it started burning." Tatiana was crying as she spoke.

Jerry couldn't look at her. He knew if he did, he would say something that he might regret. So, he kept his eyes on the charred slices of steak in the pan and the filthy stove top.

"I'm sorry," she said pitifully.

Jerry nodded briefly and walked away from her. He couldn't talk. He walked past his men who were staring at the kitchen in disbelief. He left the house and headed for the barn.

"C'mon, Ms. Sloan, let Big Joe clean up this mess for you. You go sit down and rest your ankle."

Tatiana looked at the big man and beyond him, at the others. "I just wanted to please him. I don't know how to cook."

"Now, now, don't worry your pretty head, little lady. We'll clean up in here real good and make you a mouth watering meal, too," Big Joe said as he led her into the foyer.

Mac and Sly looked at each other and burst into laughter. Little Joe joined them. "That woman is absolutely useless." Mac said with disgust.

"I'll cook us lunch, but I'm not cleaning that mess," Sly said with a grin.

"Okay, Sly. Little Joe and I will clean this up and then we'll let you take over the kitchen." The braying of a horse drew Big Joe's attention to the window. "I guess Jerry won't be around for lunch."

Everyone ran to the window. Jerry was mounted on Thunder. "Where is he going?" Sly asked with a frown.

"The canyon—if it's any of your business. He has a lot on his mind." Big Joe said. "C'mon, break a leg. I want Sally to find this kitchen the way she left it." The mention of Sally's name galvanized everyone.

***

By the pond, Jerry sat and stared into the cool water. Since he brought Angela here, the place didn't seem like his place anymore— it was their place now. He remembered her laughter and how she had screamed when he'd chased her along the path. Even the flowers reminded him of her scent. He missed her. He knew what she was doing was important but he wished she was here with him.

Did he love her? When he wasn't with her, he thought about her. When he was in her presence, he wanted to touch her or see her smile or laugh. What was it about her that made her different from the women he'd known in his life? She was beautiful, smart, witty, tenacious, and stubborn to the core. But then he'd known women with such qualities. Was it her strength that drew him to her? Was that what made her so different from other women? Yeah, others like Tatiana and Carmen.

Tatiana was beginning to irritate him. He couldn't explain it. She needed him. He had been taught at a young age that people in need had to be taken care of, even tolerated. And yet, Tatiana was becoming bothersome. In fact, when he was with her, all he thought about was Angela. He was forever comparing them and finding Tatiana lacking. There were times, in the last two days, when he'd wished she would leave. But he couldn't ask her to leave. It was not in his nature to be rude to his visitors, especially someone as helpless as Tatiana was.

Jerry rubbed his temples. His head was beginning to hurt from the conflicting emotions gripping him. He shook his head and got up as his cell phone dropped from his pocket. He frowned as he picked it up. Should he call Angela and see how Sally was doing?

One Day at a Time

***

Angela was talking to Sally when her cell phone rang. She frowned as she pulled it from her purse. "Hello?"

"Angela, Jerry here. How are you two doing?"

She smiled when she heard his voice. "We're okay, Jerry. We are waiting for the doctor. Is everything okay? Is Winston on his way?"

"Everything is fine and yes, he's on his way. He should be there any time now. How is Sally doing? Do you need me there, too?" What he wanted to tell her was that he missed her and that it was wonderful to hear her voice.

"Who would take care of your precious Tatiana if you came?" Angela regretted the words as soon as they left her mouth.

"Why are you so consumed with Tatiana, Angela? I've already told you that you have no reason to resent her. How can you be jealous of her?"

Angela looked at Sally who was listening to her side of the conversation. She walked to the windows and looked outside with unseeing eyes. "I'm not jealous of that woman, Taylor. I'm just incensed by the way she twists you around her fingers and the way you keep taking her side."

Jerry groaned. "Take her side? I haven't taken her side. You didn't give me a chance to say anything, Angela."

Angela sucked her teeth. "It was your attitude, Jerry. Anyway, Tatiana is faking her injuries. She only acts ill when you're around. And you make matters worse when you buy into her act."

Jerry sighed. "I didn't call you to exchange words over Tatiana. I thought...never mind. Tell Sally that Winston is on his way. I'm sorry I bothered you."

She heard the weariness in his voice and felt terrible for starting a fight over the phone. "Oh, Jerry..."

He interrupted with, "I got to go," And then he hung up.

Angela looked away with haunted eyes. What was she doing? What did she want? Why was she letting Tatiana drive them apart?

She wasn't insecure because of Tatiana. It just seemed like history was repeating itself. In high school, she had lost her boyfriend to some petite cheerleader with no brains and big breasts. The few men she'd ever dated had often had problems with her height. Then when they separated, they would always hook up with some tiny woman. Every time that happened she'd vow to steer clear of men with big egos and small brains. Yet she knew Jerry wasn't like that. Why then was she was letting Tatiana come between them? Was she letting her past influence her behavior now? She shook her head as she walked back to her chair.

"Why do you two fight, Ms. Angela? I have never met two people who are more suited for each other and yet work so hard at being apart." Sally commented quietly from her bed.

Angela looked at the woman whom she'd come to like and respect the last couple of weeks. She shook her head as she thought of a reply. "Why does he have to have a harem of woman always hanging around him, Sally? Why can't he ever say no to them?"

"But isn't it his caring nature that makes him so wonderful and easy to love?" When Angela frowned at the woman, Sally added, "You see, Jerry sees women like Libby, Tatiana, and even Juanita and her sister as his responsibility because they are in situations they can't cope with. He gives himself selflessly, just like he does with his mares or the people who work for him. Like his grandfather, he is a healer. While Hawk uses herbs, Jerry heals by putting his faith in people, by infusing confidence in them and making them believe in themselves. Do you think anyone would employ Big Joe and his son? Little Joe is a security risk. He has made enough mistakes at the ranch to drive a man insane and yet, Jerry is very patient with him. Because of Jerry, Little Joe is not the same boy who first came to Eagle's Hill. He's a very confident young man now. Mac is an orphan who's been mistreated all his life but he's very good with horses. Jerry took his chances with him. My husband is old and has an old injury that sometimes makes riding difficult and yet he is the foreman at Eagle's Hill. So, the way Jerry believes in his people and works with them is the same way he treats these women—he makes no distinction. The only one he treats differently is you." The housekeeper reached for Angela's hand and gave it a squeeze. "See him for what he is and not what you think he is."

Angela covered Sally's hand with hers. "I'll try, Sally. It is just hard to know what to do sometimes." She wanted to explain why she'd come to his home but thought better of it. Things weren't working between them as she'd expected.

"Follow your heart, Ms. Angela. It never fails you." Sally told her with a smile. She patted Angela's arm for the last time and said, "And here is my number one man."

Angela turned to see Winston standing in the doorway. She smiled and moved aside for the two of them to talk. Sally had given her much to think about. Later when Winston called Eagle's Hill to talk to Jerry, he heard about Tatiana and the burnt lunch. He chuckled as he shared that bit of news with Sally and her.

Sally wasn't amused. She turned to Angela with a worried expression. "Please, could you go home and take care of my boy, Ms. Angela? I won't have peace of mind until I know he's in capable hands."

"I told Jerry not to trust that woman in the kitchen. She doesn't use the brain the good Lord gave her." Winston shook his head as he settled on the seat, picked up the remote control, and changed the TV channel.

"I would leave right now if the doctors said it was okay." Sally added, looking at Angela with beseeching eyes.

Angela touched Sally's arm reassuringly. "Don't worry about a thing, Sally. I'll go. I had booked a room at the Best Western across the street from here but Winston can have it. I'll stop by and explain everything to them before I leave town."

After exchanging hugs, Angela left, stopping by the hotel before she headed toward Eagles' Hill. It was getting dark when she arrived at the ranch. Little Joe opened the gate for her and she gave him a ride to the house. Slowly, she followed him round back where a barbecue was going on.

Jerry looked up from turning a piece of chicken when he saw

Angela. A grin broke on his face as he put the tongs down. Oh, it felt good to see her. Another realization hit him as he walked toward her—he loved her. Yes, he did with all his heart. "You made it back," he said as his hand came to rest on her arm.

"Sally was worried about you but it seems like she didn't need to be. The food smells good." She looked into his eyes and smiled. She was sorry for being mean to him over the phone.

When she looked at him with a mixture of contrition and pleasure, he pulled her closer. "I do what I can. But I'm happy you made it back." Then he reached for her chin, held her head still, and kissed her.

"What are you doing, Jerry?" She whispered, very conscious of the people on the patio.

"Just doing something I should have done a long time ago. By the way, I forgive you," he added and kissed her again.

Angela licked her lip and frowned. "Forgive me for what?"

"For being so unreasonable and mean to me over the phone," he explained. "I called to hear your voice and you lit into me like a virago." He started leading her toward the others.

Angela laughed. "I'm the one who should apologize."

"Absolutely!" He wrapped his arm possessively around her.

She poked him and then turned to look at the people on the patio. They had curious expressions on their face. Angela flushed in embarrassment. "I'm going to kill you for this, Jerry. And I'm sorry for starting a fight over the phone. It was juvenile." She finished in a whisper.

"You're forgiven." He whispered in her ear, "Why don't you grab a seat, baby, while I distribute this meal?" Then he added in a loud voice, "The first piece of chicken goes to Joe Junior for helping me with the grill."

As everyone got up and went to the grill, Angela noticed Tatiana. She had been so absorbed with Jerry when she arrived that she hadn't realized that the woman was also seated on the patio. She nodded at her but only received a glare in return. Angela shrugged indifferently and turned to find Jerry watching her. *I didn't do anything,* she thought as she waited for his reaction, and then grinned when he winked at her.

Beside her was cold potato salad and mashed potatoes with gravy beside it and a bowl of tossed salad. She was wondering who made the side dishes when Little Joe spoke.

"My pops made the mashed potatoes and potato salad. I made the gravy and the lettuce," he supplied.

Angela grinned at him and then whispered. "What did Sly and Mac do?"

Little Joe whispered back. "They made lunch. Ms. Sloan tried but she burnt everything." Little Joe chuckled. "Sly and Mac cooked after that."

Angela looked up and caught Tatiana's scowl. Jerry was giving her a plate.

"I'll be leaving tomorrow." Tatiana announced.

Thank goodness, Angela thought. Everyone paused for about a second and then continued eating and talking.

Jerry was the only one who bothered to respond. "I thought you would be staying longer, Tatiana."

This time, everyone stopped eating to stare at him in amazement. Angela hid her grin as Jerry brought her a plate and made Lester move so he could sit beside her. He added mashed potatoes and tossed salad to both their plates and gave her a fork.

"I called your mother and she'll be picking me up tomorrow afternoon." Tatiana explained.

"I could drop you at the SC if you want," Jerry offered like a good host.

"Take it up with your mother, Jerry. I'm leaving tomorrow." She added petulantly.

Good riddance, Angela thought. Jerry nudged her and she turned to look at him. "What?"

"Wipe that silly grin off your face. Someone might think you're happy to see her go." He nodded toward the sullen actress.

"I'm not known for my acting talents." She told him with a grin.

The meal was over too soon. After helping Jerry collect the

plates and clean the patio, Angela disappeared upstairs and jumped into the shower. She changed into a dress and followed Jerry's voice to the poolside. He was talking to Lester, who was leaving the next day.

Angela gave him a hug and wished him the best of luck. As Jerry walked from the pool to add his well wishes to hers, she walked to the poolside bar and poured herself a drink. Jerry was right behind her when she turned around.

He had a robe on but she could still see droplets on his chest. She felt an urge to touch and taste. "Hi, cowboy," she offered weakly.

"Hi, gorgeous," he countered and took the drink from her hand. He liked it when her eyes became soft and her body trembled just for him. He put the drink aside and pulled her into his arms. "I've been dying to hold you in my arms. This afternoon when I called, I'm sorry..."

"Hush!" She interrupted and placed a finger on his lips. When he kissed it, she removed it and palmed his jaw. "I'm the one who should be sorry. I've been thinking a lot about things and I've come to the realization that I was being foolish and inconsiderate. Tatiana is a guest in your home and I was wrong to try and make you choose sides." Lord, how she loved and wanted this man. Being held so gently and close to him only reminded her of what she'd missed with her ex-boyfriend. Ray was never demonstrative and had often acted like Angela didn't need to be coddled. Her arms went around his shoulders. "Have I told you how much I love being in your arms? It makes me feel nice inside."

"Nice? We need to work on your vocabulary, baby." Jerry whispered as he lifted her chin. He stared at her beautiful face and trembling lips. It humbled him that he affected her this much and that she was not afraid to let him see it. "You're magnificent and special."

"Show me," Angela urged. She didn't want to talk. She wanted to be loved until she didn't know where he began and she ended. She leaned forward and their lips mated briefly then parted company. They exchanged breaths and joined back again, mouth-to-mouth, hip-to-hip, and chest-to-chest. They explored each other's inner cheeks, sucked and caressed tongues as their hands worked their own magic, caressing and carousing.

Lord, she tasted good, thought Jerry as he pulled her closer. The problem was it made him greedy. He wanted to taste more and have more. Whenever she'd touched him before, he'd wanted to explode with need. Now he felt like he was drowning.

Angela welcomed his embrace and his caresses like a starving woman. He was kissing her differently, with more passion but also tenderness. Goosebumps covered her skin and yet she was burning on the inside. Emotions churned through her. Her heart was bursting. Somehow, her feelings abducted her mind and she couldn't think. She didn't care about anything except him. She pressed closer to his hard form. Her hand slipped underneath his robe and found his well-tone sinews. She touched. She squeezed. She wanted to taste.

His hand traced the shape of her breast then zeroed in on her nipples. Angela moaned and pressed against his hand. Her nipples hardened and demanded his attention. He teased them until she whimpered. Then he undid the buttons and closed his mouth over one tight bud. It didn't matter that it was covered by a silky bra. He knew how to make her ache—his teeth grazed the sensitive nerve endings and his tongue soothed them. Then his lips moved up and closed on hers.

Angela gasped at the renewed heat in his kiss. He clasped her backside and pulled her up. Her dress rode up and his hand closed on one smooth satiny thigh, caressing, and seeking more flesh, more heat. His lips closed on her collar bone, her shoulders, and her neck. Anywhere his mouth could reach, he left a sensual trail. "I want you."

"Yes, yes, Jerry," Angela sighed and slid a thigh against his. He groaned.

He scooped her up. "I like a woman who knows her mind."

"And I like a man who knows when to listen. Kiss me, cowboy," Angela commanded as she clung to his shoulders.

He laughed and complied. It wasn't easy doing her bidding while carrying her upstairs, but he managed just fine.

Chapter 19

As soon as Jerry got back from dropping off Tatiana, he went in search of Angela. She wasn't upstairs or in the den. On top of his desk was a hard copy of the database she had been working on. He smiled as he flipped through it. She had completed it and from the looks of it, she'd done a darn good job, too. He thought in admiration.

Putting the papers aside, he saw a stack of bills and letters that he knew needed his attention. A brown package from his brother caught his attention. He was reaching for it when a sound from the doorway distracted him. It was Big Joe.

"Yes, Joe?"

"Do you want me to prepare Philly for delivery?"

"No, I'll do it. Has the bedding been changed in the birthing stall?" Jerry asked as he followed him outside.

Big Joe chuckled. "Ms. Angela is taking care of it."

"What?" Jerry asked.

"She asked me if there were any chores that she could do this morning, and I mentioned that the birthing stall needed to be cleaned. I didn't intend for her to start on it," Big Joe added apologetically.

"Not your fault, Big Joe. I'm sure she's already wishing she hadn't offered. That stall is twice the size of the others"—he paused to stare at Philly—"Have Philly brought inside."

"Do we inform Ned?"

"No!" Jerry's response was fast. He didn't want the vet anywhere near his farm. "We don't need Ned looking over our shoulder." He headed for the barn as Big Joe walked toward Philly's paddock.

Did Angela really think she could muck that stall by herself?

One Day at a Time

Jerry paused to watch her as she scooped the dirty bedding and dumped it in a wheelbarrow. He grinned at the determined look in her eyes. "Hey."

Angela smiled when she saw him. Scenes from last night's love-making played in her head, making her blush. "Hey. I, eh, think I might have underestimated the work involved here." She indicated the stall with her hand.

He chuckled at her expression. "Don't worry, we'll all pitch in. But to do it right, the first thing you need to do is change those slacks and get yourself decent gloves. Don't you have a pair of old jeans you could use?"

"No," she replied, glancing down at her tan pants.

"Borrow a pair of mine from upstairs. You'll find them in the closest on the right side of the bed and the belts are hanging on a rack. I'll get you a pair of heavy duty gloves." When she frowned at the pair she was wearing, he added, "Philly won't wait forever so break a leg." He smacked her backside as she passed him. She gave him a saucy smile and ran from the barn.

Angela's heart was pounding as she entered his room. Expecting to find clothes thrown haphazardly around the room, she was surprised to find the room in perfect order. It was done in beige and gold. French doors led to the balcony and overlooked the paddocks. Angela peeked outside and then walked back into the room. She touched the golden duvet and caught herself just before she sat on it. Philly was waiting.

She had to open several closets before she found the huge walk-in closet with rows of pants, shirts, casuals and everything a man could wear. She was completely caught up looking around when she heard a sound filtering through the window. Philly! She grabbed a pair of worn-out jeans, jumped into them, and belted them. As if she couldn't help herself she pulled on a T-shirt, too. It had Rio written on it. She was soon racing down the stairs and then toward the barn.

When she walked back into the barn, Jerry was tying Philly's tail while the ranch workers watched. He was preparing the mare for birthing. She walked into the stall and picked up her shovel.

When Jerry finished with the mare, he walked across the aisle to where Angela was busy shoveling. The pants she'd borrowed from him stretched across her rounded buttocks as she bent to scoop more dirty sod. He felt a stirring of his senses. Would he ever get used to wanting her?

Angela caught the lustful look in his eyes and smiled. "Aren't you going to help?"

"I'm trying to decide whether to get the others or not," he answered, still admiring the way she filled his pants. "Are your arms beginning to ache yet?"

"Mm-hmm," she nodded sheepishly.

"Take a break. You're not used to farm work."

Soon the stall was filled with sounds of metal scraping rubber floor. The two of them were shoveling while Joe and his son hauled the wet beddings outside to a truck for disposal. While they worked, Jerry told her that he had stopped by the hospital to check on Sally. She was doing fine and would be discharged that evening or the next morning.

The work seemed to go on forever. Angela rested while the men limed the floor. They left it to dry during lunch. Soon after, they were back at work, replacing the old sod.

Hours later, Angela left the men in the barn and disappeared into the kitchen to make dinner. Jerry had asked her to help while Sally was in the hospital. She was singing while finishing the final touches on the meal when they started piling in.

"Something smells good," Sly commented as he swaggered through the door.

"Better than yesterday," Mac added in a whisper.

Jerry walked in and saw the men peering at the various dishes Angela had prepared. And she looked tired. He watched as she leaned against the counter and rubbed her brow. He walked forward. "I think we all need to sit down, including the chef." He walked behind her and put his arms around her waist.

"Thanks." She put her hand on his arm and looked into his face. "I hope the men will like my cooking."

One Day at a Time

"If it tastes as good as it smells, they will. Why don't you sit down? I'll get the plates and the drinks." He led her to the couch. The fact that she went without arguing indicated just how tired she was.

As he was about to walk away, she held on to his arm. "Could you put the covered casserole dishes in the fridge for me?"

He caressed her cheek and nodded. He dished out disposable plates and cups. Then he pulled a twelve pack from the fridge and put it on the table. Everyone served themselves. There was a spicy sauce to go with the spaghetti, meat loaf, buttered corn, steamed broccoli, and collard greens. There was also the left over potato salad.

Jerry prepared a plate for her. She had made enough food for two meals but the men obviously liked it because they kept going for more helpings until the bowls were empty.

"This is really good, baby," Jerry commented as he licked his fingers. "I could live on this sauce."

"Could you make a trough of it so we'd have it everyday?" Sly added. The others nodded.

Angela covered a yawn and smiled. "Wouldn't you be bored eating the same thing everyday?" There was a chorus of no from everyone. "I'll see what I can do." She yawned again as she pushed her food around the plate. She was losing a fight against exhaustion. She watched Jerry as he explained a point. She wasn't listening to his words, just staring at his lips and wondering if they would spend this night together. Tonight, she just wanted to be held until she fell asleep.

Jerry was aware of her drooping eyelids. The occasional stretches indicated she was also sore. Well, there was only one cure for that and he was good at giving it. "Excuse me. I'll be back in a sec," Jerry said. He grazed her arm reassuringly before disappearing from the kitchen.

When Jerry left the kitchen, he headed straight for the bar by the pool and fetched a bottle of chilled champagne, and two glasses. Then he headed upstairs, taking two steps at a time. He went straight to his bathroom and set the temperature for the water and turned on

218

the faucet. He spent the next ten minutes readying everything until the bathroom was the way he wanted it. He closed the door and rushed back downstairs.

He arrived at the kitchen to find Angela trying to clean up. He shook his head as he walked to her side. "You have done enough for tonight, love. Let the men take over." He turned to them. "Philly needs to be watched tonight. Who is taking the first watch? Big Joe? Okay, the rest of you guys can help Ms. Angela by taking care of the kitchen. She made us a wonderful meal after mucking the stall, and now needs her rest. After you're done in here, make sure the door is locked, Mac. Thank you, guys, and goodnight."

Angela looked up uneasily at the men but they seemed not to mind their new assignments. They were already throwing their paper plates in the garbage and putting the bowls in the dish washer. "Good night, guys. And thanks for cleaning up after me." Every one wished her goodnight. As soon as they left the kitchen, Angela added, "That was very nice of them."

Jerry smiled. "My men are good people. They know you did us a favor by preparing that meal tonight. C'mon, baby." He took her hand.

She paused. "Jerry, were you thinking of, eh, you know, tonight?"

Jerry laughed and gave her a brief kiss on her lips. "Does that *you know* mean ravishing and worshiping your body up close and per-sonal?"

Angela pinched him. "Behave yourself. I'm too tired to think of a rebuttal."

"Who said I want to think when I'm with you?" he asked before scooping her in his arms.

"Put me down, you impossible man," she complained but still clung to him.

He kissed her forehead and grinned into her sparkling eyes. "Still not used to being carried, love?"

She hid her face on his neck and murmured, "No."

He kissed her again and commanded, "Then quit pouting and

enjoy it."

She enjoyed it, way too much. In fact, she was coming to expect it from him. The man was clearly spoiling her for other men. "Have you always been this arrogant?"

"Me? I'm the most unassuming man ever born." He replied as he paused near his doorway.

Angela noted the lighted bedroom with its huge King-size bed and smiled uneasily. How was she going to tell him that she was too physically drained for love making? Would he take it as a rejection? Her body felt like a truck had run over it. She looked into his proud face and tried to smile. "Jerry, about tonight—I don't think...hmm...I mean...would you mind if we don't do anything tonight?"

"Yes, I would. In fact, I would be so offended,"—he carried her past the bed—"and insulted if all my efforts have been wasted." He walked through the bathroom door. "Maybe I should drain the tub, put the champagne away, and let you crawl in bed with that achy body."

Angela's eyes were wide as they darted around the large bathroom. Bubbles were churning in a huge oval marble tub. Aromatic salt and other soothing scents filled the room. "Oh, Jerry, this is...this is great."

"Hey, the best for my girl," Jerry said with a cocky grin.

Angela gave him a soft kiss. When they pulled apart, she said, "You're wonderful. How did you know this was what I needed?"

"You worked very hard this afternoon, love. Hell, you've been such a trooper the whole week—with Tatiana and her whining, with Sally, finishing my database, working with the men in the barn, cooking." Still listing all the wonderful things she'd done, he put her down and started undressing her.

His gentleness warmed her. The way his eyes ran down her body wasn't even sexual. She sensed pride and appreciation in his eyes and touch. After she was totally naked, he took her hand and helped her into the tub. "Why don't you slide in there and relax. I'll get the champagne and the glasses."

She turned luminous eyes in his direction, again. Her glance kissed his face lovingly. Lord, how she loved this man. Bemusedly, she glanced around the bathroom then nodded. "Thanks, baby. I needed this."

"Hey, my intentions aren't honorable. I want you enamored with me so much that when I make any indecent proposal,"—he leered playfully—"you'd have no choice but to agree."

He was so silly, Angela thought as she laughed. She didn't expect to be laughing at all this evening, but the bath, combined with Jerry's magic, was already working on her. "Consider myself charmed." She blew him a kiss before he left the room.

A sigh escaped her lips. This was much better than the steam room or the whirlpool downstairs. The sweet scent of wild orchids teased her nostrils. The aromatic salts soothed her aches and her tired senses. She slid lower into the tub and positioned her back on a water outlet. The water massaged her achy lower back. She fitted the bath pillow for comfort and closed her eyes. She could fall asleep in here, she thought with a sigh.

Everyday Jerry did something that made her love him more. He was thoughtful, caring, and kind. How could she have believed the things the papers had said about him? Now that she was away from home, away from Reggie, and everything that reminded her of her sister, she was able to see things much more clearly. She had been very angry at her sister's sudden death and had needed someone to blame. Jerry had been the perfect scapegoat. Usually she wasn't easily swayed by the media, especially when it came to articles about black people. She should have known the stories were just malicious rumors or an attempt by the media to bring another black man down. Well, they tried to break Jerry but he showed them.

"Ready for a drink?" Jerry asked from the doorway.

She looked up at his strong, brown face and smiled. "Yes. But I might fall asleep in here. This was very thoughtful of you, baby. Thank you."

He sat on the edge of the tub and uncorked the bottle. "I'm happy that you approve." He turned to give her a glass. He stared at her wet face with spirals of damp hair hanging enticingly around it.

One Day at a Time

"Don't ever doubt that I want or care about you. But I'm not too self-ish to recognize that you're tired. Do you know your eyes were drooping during dinner?"

She eyed him as she sipped the champagne. It tickled her nose. "I guess I'm not used to such hard work. But you were right beside me, cowboy. Aren't you tired?"

Jerry eyed her. "Does that mean you think I should have a relaxing bath, too?"

Angela grinned. "I guess I'm little a lonely in here."

"Why didn't you say so?" Jerry said as he jumped up and started removing his shirt.

Suddenly she wished she was the one removing his shirt. She would kiss the exposed skin as each button was undone. He looked good. Muscles rippled as he threw the shirt aside. He was pure poetry in motion, each muscle defined and yet part of the whole landscape.

"Quit looking at me like that, woman! I may not be responsible for what happens next," he growled.

She flushed but refused to look away. "You shouldn't be displaying your stuff if you don't want me to watch."

"By all means, watch," he teased as his fingers pulled at his belt. Damn, he was already hard. When Angela's eyes moved from his face and settled below his belt, he smothered another curse. Bold and shameless, that was what he was. He refused to turn around. Instead, he pulled down both his pants and underwear together. When he was totally nude, he stood up and grinned at her. She had averted her eyes but had turned to take a peek when he took a step toward the tub. He laughed. "You're a shameless hussy," he mocked as he stepped into the water.

"Look who's talking. You could've changed in the bedroom, you know."

"And miss that adoring look on your face?" He teased as he sat opposite her. He laughed as she ducked her head. "I saw you peeking."

"Got a right to check out my man," Angela replied sassily.

"Like I said, shameless—come on, scoot over here so I can take care of those muscles."

Angela scooted towards him and settled between his legs. She felt the sleek muscles of his chest—now wet with soapy water—and a quiver shook her frame. This wasn't going to work she thought and started scooting away.

"Don't even think about it," Jerry said in a low voice. "If I can handle it so can you. Just don't wiggle. Here"—he pressed her glass into her hand—"drink, relax, and let me get to work."

Angela took a sip of her drink, put the glass beside the tub, and leaned back against him. Pure heaven and hell! She closed her eyes and prayed for mercy. It came in the form of Jerry Taylor. As he worked on her muscles he talked about his days as a baseball player. Soon, Angela forgot about everything and just relaxed. She asked appropriate questions, laughed over the jokes, and teased him when he made conceited comments. The effect of the wine, the massage, and the bath soon became too much for her. Her eyes started closing.

Jerry was the first to get out of the tub. He put on a robe before holding out one for Angela. She stumbled a bit getting out of the tub but his arms went around her. It wasn't easy putting the robe on her. She kept thrusting her arms in the wrong places. Finally, after he had her snuggly wrapped, he lifted her up and carried her to his room.

"My bed," Angela whispered drowsily as Jerry finished drying her off.

"No, mine—I want to hold you tonight, baby. We're both tired and need to rest. Will you let me?"

"Oh, okay. What about my nightdress?" Angela mumbled as she snuggled deeper into the fluffy robe.

Jerry slept nude and there was nothing he would like better than to feel Angela's skin against his. In fact, every time they'd slept together, they had slept nude. He removed her robe, helped her under the covers, and kissed her forehead. "You don't need one."

She giggled. "Hmm, I guess, I don't. Thanks for being so sweet," she whispered haltingly.

"I'm investing, baby. I'm in this for the long haul," he said in a serious tone.

He doubted that she had heard because she was already asleep. As he crawled in after her and pulled her in his arms, a smile played on his lips. Yes, he was in this for a long time. No man could be as lucky as he was, he thought. He was getting a second chance at love and life.

Chapter 20

The next several days were blissful. Sally and Winston returned home. Sally followed the doctor's instructions and kept her weight off her leg. Angela became the ranch's designated cook. Despite being busy, she still called home and talked to both her mother and Nikki. There was no change in Reggie's condition but his doctor still sounded optimistic. Angela was now praying for a miracle.

It was Friday evening when Philly went into labor. The sun was dipping over the horizon and Angela was putting the final touches on their dinner when Little Joe stopped by the kitchen to inform her that the mare was in labor. She ran to the barn.

The men were seated around the table in the tack room. Their eyes were glued to the screen, watching and waiting. Jerry had installed close-circuit T.V cameras in his foaling stalls to monitor the mares during foaling. Philly was pawing the ground, pacing the stall, and curling her lip.

"She's close," Winston commented from beside Jerry.

"Yes she is," Jerry answered in a preoccupied tone.

Angela sat on the couch and waited with everyone. It was fifteen minutes later when Philly started having contractions. The mare settled down and made a bed for herself. Jerry pushed a button and changed the angle of the camera and zoomed in on the mare. The contractions were strong now. All eyes stayed on the screen.

Ten minutes later the mare was still struggling to deliver. Jerry got up. The grim set of his profile indicated the seriousness of the situation. He had made the choice not to call the vet. If he lost his mare or the foal, he would always blame himself. He glanced briefly in Angela's direction. His skin was drawn. His eyes were bloodshot but sharp. And his lips were taut with tension. Angela let her eyes convey to him her support. He must have read her thoughts because he nodded briefly.

"There is something wrong. I'm going to help Philly." He'd barely finished speaking when there was flurry of activity in the tack room.

Angela wanted to ask what she could do to help. But instead, she let the men take care of things. Her eyes stayed on Jerry though. She watched as he washed and disinfected his hands. Winston was standing beside him, carrying a load of clean towels. This was about the most important step toward accomplishing his dream as a horse breeder. If his first foal died—especially after what she had heard about the negative attitude of people around the area—Jerry might think he wasn't cut out to be a breeder. He must succeed, Angela thought. He'd worked hard to get the farm going without a failed foaling messing it up. She moved closer to the desk and the screen as Jerry and Winston left the tack room.

Jerry walked into the foaling stall and knelt beside the mare. He talked calmly as he moved to her flank. He tried not to think about failure because it wasn't an option. Philly and the foal would be okay. They must be okay. He repeated this as a litany as he worked his hand gently into the mare. The mare tensed.

"I need her to be calm. She might be less inclined to push if she were calmer." Jerry said just as he encountered a leg.

"The contractions are very strong," Winston whispered.

"I know. But she can control the pushing. I need her to be calm," Jerry whispered.

Across the stall, in the tack room, the occupants heard Jerry's words. Angela didn't wait for a second before she started singing. Her singing always drew the mare's attention and she prayed it would calm her today. Her feet carried her through the door to the stall where the mare was fighting for her unborn foal's survival.

"I have the foal's legs," Jerry informed Winston. His hand was following one leg when he heard Angela's voice. The effect on the mare was startling. As she got closer, the mare's movements stilled.

Philly was listening to her soothing words.

Jerry didn't look up as Angela got close to the mare's head and continued to sing softly. He was busy trying to determine whether he held front or back legs. His hand grazed a tail. Back legs would mean the foal was breach. Breach he could handle, he thought in relief. He grasped the foal's hind legs and gently pulled them downwards towards the mare's heel.

As he pulled, beads of sweat stood on his forehead while some trickled down his cheek. Angela wiped the sweat away with a cool towel. She didn't stop singing though she alternated her time between wiping his brows and patting the mare. Listening to her voice also calmed him. He knew he would not fail Philly. He would deliver the foal.

Slowly, he worked with Philly's contraction, pulling when she strained and allowing the mare to help deliver her foal. Finally with one push, the foal was out, alive and breathing.

With soulful but grateful eyes, Philly turned to stare at Jerry who sat back on his heel and sighed in relief. "We did it, guys," he muttered under his breath. Winston touched his shoulder and then left the stall.

Jerry rolled on his heels for a few minutes before he looked up and straight into Angela's wet face. His eyes shimmered with tears of relief as well. "I couldn't have done it without you, baby. Thank you."

Angela shook her head. "You were wonderful. You never hesitated, not once." She moved closer to him, her eyes shiny with admiration and love. Then as if embarrassed by her open display of affection she turned to look at the foal. It was struggling to get up. They watched breathlessly as she finally stood on all fours. Then Angela and Jerry grinned at each other.

"She's beautiful, isn't she?" Angela asked.

"Yes, she is." Jerry replied as he pulled Angela in his arms. They hugged tightly. Fresh tears started falling from her eyes.

Jerry walked with her to the door. Winston and the others were waiting for them. Winston's hand rested briefly on Jerry's shoulder before he gave him a bear hug. "I knew you had it in you, Jerry." The others added their congratulations, too.

Angela watched the camaraderie and the well-wishers from afar. Her shirt was smeared with blood from Jerry's hands, her pants smelled of horse urine and yet, she'd never been happier. She'd just witnessed the start of a new life. Without Jerry that life would have been taken.

"What the hell is going on here?" A booming voice called out from the barn entrance. Everyone froze.

No one said a thing but their eyes shifted and stayed riveted on a tall, old, white man with long, grey hair held in a pony tail. He swaggered toward them. Jerry stared at him with an expressionless face. Angela frowned.

Since he was using the entrance closest to Angela, he reached her first. Instead of passing her, he stopped and stared insolently at her. "I asked you a question, boy. Aren't you tired of this horse breeding nonsense? Doesn't the smell of horse manure make you wish for the good old days when you played ball? Aren't you ready to quit yet? I didn't think you had it in you to be a breeder and from the looks of things, I still don't."

Although the attack was directed at Jerry, the man's hazel eyes were locked on Angela. She'd stopped breathing as soon as the man started attacking Jerry. But when he finished that last sentence, Angela was ready to take him on and all the Montanan ranchers who thought Jerry was only qualified to be a ballplayer and not a horse breeder.

"Of all the—I cannot believe the nerve—who the hell do you think you are to come in here and talk to Jerry Taylor like that?"

The man glared at her. She glared back. They were about the same height but Angela refused to be intimidated, not by this arrogant racist.

The old man's hazel gaze checked her—from her hair to her filthy shoes. He didn't miss a smudge in between. Then he turned to Jerry. "Who is this? If this is the best you can do, you're slipping, my boy,"—his eyes took in her murderous expression before he continued—"She can't even complete a decent sentence. Do you have a speech problem, girl? She's not much to look at either, is she?" He took a step back and his eyes zeroed in on the blood and dirt on her shirt. "She's filthy,"—then he sniffed the air before adding—"and she smells, too. Go back to playing ball, my boy, and get yourself a decent woman. Yeah, you did much better as a ball player." He finished as he gave Angela another look.

Before the old man could walk away, Angela recovered from that blatant attack and blocked his path. "I don't know who you think you are to come here and talk to Jerry like that. He's busted his ass to make this farm work and the last thing he needs is some illiterate,"—she pointed a finger at his chest—"redneck from some tiny, hick town in Montana telling him that he's not fit to be a horse breeder." Then to emphasize her next point, she pushed at his chest, "And I'll have you know that he just saved both his prized mare and her foal from death by delivering a breach birth. I bet even your precious vet, Ned, couldn't have done it with such confidence." She stopped when she realized that the old man was staring at her in shock.

"Didn't think I had it in me—a smelling, dirty, not much to look at, black woman? For your information, I'm a very eloquent speaker. And slavery days are over, mister. We're stepping on anyone—and I mean anyone—who dares to stand in our way."

Angela felt a hand on her shoulder and turned to find Jerry behind her. She relaxed and let him support her weight. She was confused by Jerry's attitude. Why didn't he stand up for himself? Why didn't he say a word to this man who dared to insult him in his home? Angela turned to question Jerry but the old man was speaking again.

"She's too mouthy, Jerry. This one will talk you to an early grave. Now, woman, move aside so I can see this new foal." He waited as if he expected Angela and Jerry to accommodate his demands.

"If you don't throw him out, Jerry, I swear I will," Angela muttered under her breath.

"Grandpa, please stop the act and be nice," Jerry implored the old man.

As Jerry spoke, Angela noticed the woman standing at the barn door. It was Jerry's grandmother. Angela turned horrified eyes on the old man and saw what she hadn't noticed in her anger. The twinkling eyes, the same nose that he had passed down, through his daughter, to his grandson, and the very distinct high cheekbones.

"Got you going there, didn't I?" The old man asked gleefully.

Angela's eyes filled with tears. Anger and humiliation vied for dominance. She turned to look at Jerry. How could he let her humiliate herself like that? Her eyes accused. "Your grandfather, Taylor?"

"I'm sorry to claim him but yes, he's my grandfather." Jerry sounded genuinely contrite.

His lost puppy look didn't work on her. "Why?" Angela asked with a shaking voice.

She didn't have to elaborate for him to understand. "I know, I should have said something. But you were defending me so faithfully that I couldn't interfere." He tried to put his arms around her.

"Don't!" Angela whispered, tears blocking her throat.

"Angela, please. Grandpa Hawk is a practical joker and he was only..."

"Picking me as his guinea pig for the evening? Excuse me." She stepped away from them.

"Angela!" Jerry called out.

Go to hell, Taylor! She thought but lifted her hand in dismissal. She felt like running but she knew her legs would fail her. So, she lifted up her head, squared her shoulders and without a backward glance, strolled out of the aisle. She disappeared through the grooming room and headed for the house.

Jerry started going after her but his grandfather's words stopped him. "That one is a keeper, son. If you let her get away then you're a fool."

Jerry turned toward the old man in surprise but he was already walking toward the new foal. Before he could think of a reply, his grandmother was touching his arm. "Don't just stand there, child, go after her. And I'm in total agreement with Hawk—don't let her get away."

Jerry ran after Angela. Hearing his grandparents voice what he'd been telling himself the last couple of days made it all so plausible. He was not letting Angela go.

***

Angela ran to the house and went straight to her room. Stripping her clothes with jerky movements, she threw them on the bed. She started for the bathroom then stopped. Picking up the clothes, she smelled them and grimaced. They stank. She threw them on the floor. Then as if the situation was too comical for anger, she started laughing.

Did she actually call Jerry's grandfather an illiterate, redneck? She laughed even harder when she looked at herself in the mirror. There was straw on her hair, mud on her cheeks, and she was sure that combined with the stinking clothes, she must have looked a sight. Damn, that old man had her going. And he was Jerry's grandfather? No wonder Jerry was the way he was. He probably got it from his grandfather.

Angela was still chuckling when she got in the shower. She was humming a tune while letting the hot water wash away the emotions of the last couple of hours when Jerry arrived.

"Angela?"

"Bathroom," she shouted back.

The opening of her bathroom door alerted her of his presence. "Baby, I'm sorry I let Hawk tease you like that. He's so unpredictable. He's always doing something to test a person but that's still no excuse for his behavior or mine."

Angela smiled at Jerry's reconciliatory tone. "If you take a step in here Jerry Tyrell Taylor, I'll maim you. How could you let me humiliate myself like that in front of your family?"

"But you didn't. You were magnificent. Grandpa fell in love with you as soon as you opened your mouth."

"That's a crock of crap and you know it!"

"I didn't have the heart to interfere, baby. You were standing up for me and saying such wonderful things." Then he stuck his head behind the shower curtain. "Am I forgiven?"

One Day at a Time

She checked the repentant expression. Reaching forward, she pinched his nose. "If you rub my back, I might reconsider." She released his nose and Jerry gave a whooping sound. Laughing, he started removing his dirty clothes. "And don't put those clothes anywhere near my bed. They stink as bad as mine—as your grandfather gleefully pointed out."

Jerry threw the clothes on the bathroom floor, got in the shower and wrapped his arms around her waist. Then he proceeded to kiss her. "Isn't he something?"

"He's a menace," she breathed out huskily.

"He already adores you," Jerry replied as he turned her around and proceeded to scrub her back.

"I highly doubt that. So, what are you going to name your first foal?" Angela asked.

"Hmm, I was hoping you would do the honors, considering the special bond between you and her mother."

"Oh, Jerry, I'd love to. I already know what I will call her." She turned her head and kissed him. "Thank you for the honor. Are you sure you don't mind?"

He ignored her question and continued to wash her back. His touch became less impersonal and more intimate. Soon, he had her aching for more. Despite her protest that his grandparents were waiting for them downstairs, he continued to make sweet love to her.

Angela was still trying to catch her breath when he left the shower. She smiled with wicked contentment as she finished and got dressed. A few minutes later, she was heading downstairs while rehearsing what she would say to Jerry's grandfather. How was she supposed to have behaved when faced with such provocation? After the battle Jerry had had saving Philly and her baby, Angela hadn't cared about being sensible. Her instinct to protect had kicked in.

She was halfway down the stairs when she realized Hawk McQueen was watching her, nursing a drink. Her feet faltered. What was she going to say to him?

"Now, now, Princess, we have to face one another soon. Don't run away." The impossible old man teased.

Angela smothered a smile and walked forward until she was two steps from where he stood. She stopped and looked down at him. He was a tall man but standing on that step gave her some advantage. "I'm sorry for my earlier rudeness, Mr. McQueen. I didn't know..."

"No, no, don't apologize. I rather liked 'slavery days are over and you're stepping on anyone who dares to stand in your way'."

Blood rushed to Angela's face as she fought embarrassment. "Don't remind me," she whispered apologetically.

"You were magnificent. And it is I who should be apologizing. I had no business talking to you like that. My only excuse is I'm too old to mince words. You could call it my preservation act."

Angela shook her head at the old man. He had an adorable twinkle in his eye that reminded her too much of Jerry. "Preservation act?" She asked, genuinely puzzled.

"I needed to know if you had what it takes to be by my grandson's side, that you understood what it means to be a horse breeder, and that you believed in what he was doing, or if you were one those young women who couldn't wait for him to go back to playing ball."

What had Jerry told his grandfather about their relationship? The old man was talking as if she and Jerry were getting hitched. "Mr. McQueen, I don't know what Jerry has told you because..."

He lifted a hand and interrupted her. "Hawk, please. And my grandson told me what a wonderful assistant you've been, that's all. Now will you get down from there and take my arm? I'm beginning to get a crick in my neck." Casually he walked her toward the kitchen. "Please, tell me you've forgiven me," he implored.

"Only if you promise not to mind the things I said."

"So, I'm not an illiterate redneck anymore?" Hawk asked as he pushed opened the kitchen door. Three pairs of eyes looked up but Angela was staring at Hawk and didn't notice.

"Not with that irresistible twinkle in your eyes and that booming laughter. You're just Jerry's nightmare of a grandfather."

He threw his head back and laughed. He was joined by his wife, his grandson, and Sally. Angela flushed painfully as she realized that once again, she had been caught unaware. She and her big mouth!

One Day at a Time

"Well-said, child...well said." The older, short woman moved to their side. "He needed to hear that. Not everyone falls for your charms, Hawk. Now, my dear, I'm Martha McQueen—Jerry's grandmother. I was just telling Sally what a wonderful cook you are. What did you put in this sauce?"

Angela was bemused by the woman's friendly attitude. After meeting Jerry's mother, she had thought all his relatives were naturally protective of him and suspicious of any woman who got close to him. "Sun-dried tomatoes, roasted garlic, fresh parsley, and..."

"Grandma, it is her secret recipe. If you want to taste the sauce, you'll have to visit us more often." Jerry took Angela's arm and led her to sit by his side.

Angela frowned at him. She had only one more week to go before she left his home and yet he was talking as if she were going to be around forever.

"Can I have a taste of this sauce everyone is talking about?" Jerry's grandpa added.

Angela started getting up but Jerry stopped her and offered to get it. She was amazed by how friendly Jerry's grandparents were. And she was touched by the loving bickering between them. Even Sally joined in occasionally.

It wasn't long before Jerry's grandmother looked at her husband and said, "Hawk, we should be heading home now."

"Are you sure you don't want to spend the night, grandma?" Jerry asked.

"Not tonight, dear," his grandmother said. "Besides, we came with one of the ranch hands. He'll see us home. Jerry, will you bring Angela to dinner tomorrow?"

"What a wonderful idea! It is not often I have a beautiful woman grace my table—other than my wife and daughter, of course." His grandfather added.

Jerry nodded and took Angela's hand. "She is taken grandpa, so hands off."

Angela was so surprised by Jerry's open display of possessiveness that she didn't say anything until after they saw his grandparents off. As they walked toward the kitchen she said, "Jerry? You know I have only a week before my vacation is over."

A lot could happen in a week, he thought. "Yes, I know. Now, can we make use of the little time we have left, starting now?"

Angela's throat closed with unshed tears. Didn't he care that she would be leaving soon? And how could he act nonchalantly when earlier he'd talked as if she were going to be staying in his ranch forever? "I have to a foal to name and you have your ranch hands to feed."

"But it is your duty to cook and serve..."

"Don't finish that sentence if you know what is good for you, Taylor." She pushed opened the kitchen door, and there was everyone talking excitedly about the new foal. Sally was on her feet, passing them plates. Angela went to the older woman. "Doctor's orders, Sally—no weight on that leg for awhile. Let someone else take over." She said as she led her back to the couch. The fact that Sally didn't complain indicated that her leg was still hurting.

While Mac and Little Joe took over for Sally, Jerry and Angela went to the barn to visit the foal. "She is beautiful, Jerry. Do you think she will look like her mother?"

"From the coloring, I'd say her sire." He wrapped his arms around her waist and pulled her closer. "So what are you going to name her?"

She inhaled his scent and smiled. "Majesty—she looks beautiful and majestic." She rubbed the foal's neck as it turned and sniffed her hand.

They stayed in the barn for awhile before heading back to the house

Chapter 21

Sunday dawned with a slight drizzle. Jerry woke up first. Careful not to wake Angela, he removed his arm from under her neck. His glance filled with warmth as he took in her soft golden-brown skin. She was such a bed hoarder. She was sleeping on her tummy, her head to one side, her arms and legs extended like a spider's legs across the bed. If he were in bed with her, one of her legs would be over his hips and her arm across his chest.

Jerry knelt beside the bed and tried to wake her up by tickling her nose. She murmured something and pressed her face into the pillow. He smiled. It still amazed him that she was his—this stubborn, strong, and wonderful woman. He dropped a kiss on her forehead and walked to the bathroom.

After a quick shower, he put on a pair of old jeans and a gray UCLA T-shirt. Since Angela was still asleep, he headed downstairs. Someone had fixed eggs, sausages, and toast for breakfast. He picked a piece of toast and headed to his den. He had ignored his mail for the last three days and he needed to catch up.

It wasn't long before he was opening the brown package from his brother. Inside were another package and a brief note from him. Apparently, the package had been sent to their office. It contained Carmen's diary but according to Aaron, the sender wished to remain anonymous.

Why would anyone have Carmen's diary in their possession? He hadn't known Carmen kept a diary, Jerry thought with a frown. Leaning back in his chair, he flipped through the pages until he reached the final entry.

Bella McFarland

DEAR DIARY,

I AM OFF TO SEE PETE FOR THE LAST TIME. IF HE REFUSES TO UNDERSTAND MY POSITION THEN THAT IS JUST TOO BAD BECAUSE I'VE REACHED MY LIMIT. I AM TIRED AND DEPRESSED. I REFUSE TO LIVE LIKE THIS ANY MORE. I KNOW I HAVE DESTROYED THE LOVE JERRY HAD FOR ME BUT THE LEAST I CAN DO NOW IS TELL HIM THE TRUTH. I HOPE THAT HE FORGIVES ME, ABOUT THE BABY AND PETE.

Jerry rubbed his temple in confusion. Who the hell was Pete? Carmen's lover? Jerry flipped through the pages until he found where the name Pete first appeared. Anger flashed through him as he read what Carmen had written. Having an affair with Pete, her high school sweetheart, and then transferring her guilt onto Jerry by accusing him of cheating on her barely covered what she did. She had refused to accompany Jerry on trips because of her lover and used Jerry's hard-earned money not only to pay her lover's bills but to feed his drug habit. To add insult to injury, she used to bring the man to their home while he was on trips.

After fifteen minutes of reading the detailed diary, his anger slowly changed to disgust at what Carmen had allowed Pete to do to her—the depraved lifestyle, the drugs and alcohol. By the time Jerry finished reading the rest of the diary, all he felt was relief—relief that finally he understood why she had been drinking herself into a stupor every night. Pete had been blackmailing her into giving him more money because he had made her pregnant.

Jerry threw the diary in his drawer and got up. It was wonderful to finally know the truth. It wasn't his child Carmen had been trying to destroy but her lover's baby. And he wasn't responsible for the changes in her, either. He would have forgiven her unfaithfulness but not her excessive drinking while pregnant. The thought that she had hated him enough to want to destroy his offspring had haunted him for a very long time. Now all he felt was pity for the poor, unborn child. It didn't deserve the abuse Carmen had subjected it to by her excessive drinking and drug addiction.

With springs in his gait, Jerry left the house and headed for the barn. Twenty minutes later, he was on Thunder, taking off for their morning ride. He did his best thinking on the back of his horse and he had a lot of things to sort through. His thoughts shifted to Angela and he smiled. Yeah, he had a lot to be happy about today

***

When Angela finally woke up there was an indentation on the pillow where Jerry had slept. She inhaled his scent and sighed. It was time she started thinking about the future—the future that included a boy in a coma and possibly Jerry. She couldn't afford to live one day at a time, not now, and definitely not when she knew she loved Jerry and wanted more than just an affair with him.

How was she going to approach the subject of Sav? How would Jerry take her confession? When they'd become intimate she hadn't envisioned that she would fall in love with the man. She'd thought she could easily handle an affair. But things changed. No man had ever treated her with such tenderness, such loving care, and thoughtfulness as Jerry had. Everything he'd done since and even before they became intimate should have warned her. Jerry was not a man you could get involved with and remain emotionally detached.

Why had she thought that their relationship would end as soon as her contract was over? She should have known from his first touch that this wasn't a passing fascination, not for her anyway. So, now she was in love with a man who hadn't resolved his past, a man who probably wasn't ready for any type of commitment and even if he were, it wasn't going to be with a woman who was hiding things from him.

Angela squinted against the glare of the sun and wished she could reverse the clock. Should she have told him who she was on their first encounter? She didn't think so. The question that now remained was whether Jerry would understand her reasons for coming to his ranch. He loved his family as much she loved hers. Surely, he would understand that she had no choice but to find the truth behind the accident that had devastated them all.

She'd had time to accept Sav's death, especially since Jerry explained what had happened the day she died. It hadn't been his fault. She knew that now and accepted it. It was still hard to accept that Reggie might stay in a coma for a long time or that he might never come out of it, but she didn't blame Jerry for that either. That only thing she had left to deal with was explaining to Jerry her connection to Sav and why she had been forced to hide it.

She had to confess everything today, she vowed. Tonight when they got back from his grandparent's home, she would confess and then deal with the consequences. She couldn't live with the guilt anymore.

***

Angela didn't see Jerry until a couple of hours later. She was in her room trying to decide what to wear to his grandparent's farm when he appeared. "Hey, baby. I can't seem to decide on what to wear tonight." She pulled out a dress and held it in front of her. When Jerry didn't say anything, she glanced at him through the mirror. The expression on his face stopped her. "What's wrong, baby?"

Jerry's eyes were focused totally on her. Not her lovely figure or her beautiful face, but everything that made her so special. Angela would never do what Carmen did. She was strong, dependable, and honest to her core. He would trust her with his life and it was time he let her know it. "I love you."

Angela gasped and turned toward him. All thoughts flew from her mind as the words reverberated around the room. Her hand moved from her waist to her chest. No, he didn't mean it. He couldn't. She must have imagined it. Then he started walking toward her, each step measured and sure.

"I love you, Angela McGee. It may seem like a short time to fall for someone but I did—I do."

Oh, please, not now. What was she supposed to tell him? She wasn't ready to confess her love or her sins. "Oh, Jerry, I love you, too," Angela heard herself whisper achingly. She couldn't stop her words. *Oh, God, what am I doing? Help me here, please.*

He stopped in front of her and pulled her in his arms. She felt safe and needed as she listened to his heart slam against his chest. Leaning backward, she looked into his eyes—those sincere eyes that now shone with love and acceptance. How would they look when he finds out about her deception? She reached out and touched his cheek. "Jerry, there are so many things about me that you don't know—things that could destroy what you feel for me or make you doubt my love for you."

He caressed her cheek. "I love what I know about you, baby. I love your essence. I love the way you fill my arms and the way I feel when I hold you. I love kissing you and making love with you. I love the way you laugh and the way you make me laugh. I love your zest for life. I love working by your side. I love the way you care about people around you and make them happy. I even love it when you scold me for being such an arrogant fool." He dropped a kiss on her forehead. "Nothing could ever make me doubt your love. In fact, it humbles me that you love me."

A sad smile touched Angela's lips. What a coward she was turning out to be, she thought sadly. Even at this crucial time in their relationship she couldn't bring herself to come clean. "How can I not love you? You're wonderful in every way."

Jerry's heart slammed hard against his chest. It felt wonderful to hear her words. They filled his insides and made him complete. His chest tightened as the past flashed briefly through his mind. He pushed the thoughts away, keeping them where they belonged. The present had nothing to do with the past and he meant to keep it that way. In Angela, he was starting afresh. With her, he could be himself and not worry about a thing. She didn't have to tell him that he could always count on her love, total devotion, or honesty. He just knew it.

Pulling her tighter in his arms, he bent his head and grazed her shoulder with his lips. Her scent filled his nostrils and he knew he wanted to make love to her, to possess her, and seal their commitment to each other. "I want you now, baby." Jerry whispered hoarsely.

When his hand slipped underneath her pants and squeezed her buttocks, her body responded. There was a wildness in him that she found exciting. Was it her confession that produced this fierceness in him? Angela wondered as a shiver ran through her. She kissed him and murmured, "What about your grandparents?"

"We have more than enough time," He said as he scooped her up and laid her on her bed. Reaching around her, he deftly removed her bra. He pulled off his shirt and lay beside her. Then his mouth possessively covered her puckered nipple. When she arched her back and welcomed his passion, he groaned in satisfaction.

Angela welcomed him with eager hands. Forgotten was her confession or the guilt of not coming clean. She was totally enthralled by him. His eyes glistened with the force of his feelings. Then his mouth closed over hers, mesmerizing her with his boldness and driving her crazy with its heat. His hands turned her body into a musical instrument. Everywhere he touched her nerves sent sensual tunes cascading down her body. He was branding her with every cell in his body, every stroke from his fingers and every kiss from his sculptured lips.

A primitive sound came from deep inside Jerry as he moved down Angela's body. A satisfied grunt escaped his lips when she moaned and trembled. His Angela was a match for him, he thought as he picked the edge of her panties with his teeth and pulled them down her thighs. His chest expanded as he inhaled her scent. When she lay naked and panting, he started nibbling and caressing her. From her toes to her inner thighs, he didn't miss a spot. While she writhed and begged for him to stop, his kisses grew bolder. He was going insane with the feel and the taste and the scent of her but he wasn't done.

His head was pounding, his muscles straining, and his heart bursting. He wrapped her legs around his flank and claimed her. Her passionate scream fueled his desire. He was lost in her heat but he showed her with his hands, his mouth, with each stroke and groan that she was his only way out, his anchor, his everything. His hand moved over her body until he found her hands. He trapped them under his.

One Day at a Time

He heard her gasp as she started to peak. Her eyes rolled in their sockets as she whimpered with passion. Only then did he allow himself to join her. He shouted his love for her as he rode the sensual wave with her.

"I'm sorry, baby." Jerry whispered a little while later. He was lying on his back, cradling her in his arms.

"Why?" Her arms were still wrapped around him. She caressed his sweaty chest.

"I don't know what came over me. I didn't mean to be rough with you."

She pinched his nipple. "I once told you there was nothing you could dish out that I couldn't handle, cowboy." He laughed. She smiled.

***

The drive to Jerry's grandparents' ranch was fun. Jerry talked about the history of the area, pointing out landmarks where the famous explorers, Lewis and Clark, either rested or marked. They stopped by a few ghost towns and did a little exploration before continuing on their way. So, it was nearly four o'clock when they passed the gate with the sign *South Creek Ranch*.

As they got closer to the homestead, they passed herds of cows under the watch of cowboys on horsebacks. Jerry waved to the men and told Angela that they worked for his grandfather.

"You made it, how wonderful." Jerry's grandmother greeted them as soon as the truck stopped outside the sprawling ranch house. She gave them each a warm hug. Then she took Angela's arm and led her away from Jerry.

"I want to introduce you around, child. Bill?" Jerry's grandmother hailed a tough looking, handsome, black cowboy who had to be in his mid-fifties but had the lithe body of a much younger man. "This is our foreman, Bill Skywalker. Bill, this is Jerry's girl, Angela McGee."

Angela flushed to her toes. He had a firm handshake and direct, intelligent eyes. "I'm not Jerry's girl as she put it, just his assistant.

It is nice to meet you, Mr. Skywalker."

"The pleasure is mine, ma'am." He tilted his Stetson politely. "Please, call me Bill."

"And I am Angela." She smiled at him.

Jerry's grandmother introduced her to the three other cowboys who were branding the calves. She explained that the others were out on the range with the cows and would not be back until sundown. Angela tried to pay attention as she explained what the men were doing and why. She had a way of asking and answering her own questions that was endearing and Angela enjoyed listening to her talk about cattle rearing.

They were walking back to the house when they met Jerry's mother. "Hello Mrs. Taylor."

"Hi, Ms. McGee—I hope mom showed you everything around the ranch."

"Please, no formality between the two of you. Maya, her name is Angela. Is dinner ready?"

"Yes, Ma. I was going to ask Bill to join us."

Jerry's grandmother nodded. "You do that." Then she turned to Angela. "C'mon, child. Don't mind my Maya. Now, tell me how you like living on a ranch." She asked as she led her to the house.

Lunch was fun and long. There was so much food of all kinds, from traditional fried chicken, macaroni and cheese, collard greens, and corn bread to cowboy favorites like steaks, meat stew, corn, mashed potatoes, gravy, and pies. The conversation was so stimulating that even Jerry's mother let her guard down. Angela watched as the woman lost her inhibitions and laughed at her father's antics. Angela noticed that she and Bill Skywalker made eye contact several times during the meal and she wondered if there was something going on between them. Bill was intelligent and articulate. He'd been a cowboy all his life and knew a lot about ranching. He and Jerry's grandfather got into an argument over government grazing lands. But from everyone's amused expression, it had to be their favorite dinner topic. In fact, everyone was hooting with laughter as the two men became downright nasty.

One Day at a Time

Later, Angela and Jerry joined his grandparents on the patio. The couple had fond memories of their youth and talked at length about growing up in Montana, their meeting, and falling in love. They laughed over incidents that happened when they met and when they moved to SC to live with Jerry's great grandfather. They seemed perfectly in tune with each other, even finishing one another's sentences.

It was a while later that Jerry and Angela left them napping on the patio and joined the men branding calves in the corral. Angela didn't have the stomach for branding and kept wincing every time a man grabbed a calf. So, she walked a little distance away and sat under a tree. She was trying hard not to watch the men but her eyes kept straying to Jerry who seemed to be having so much fun.

It still amazed her that he loved her. This strong, wonderful man who filled her life with happiness with just a smile could be her mate for life. All she had to do was talk to him. The slate needed to be clean. Surely he would understand her reasons. He, too, loved his family as much as she did hers and would probably do the same if the situations were reversed. *Please, Lord, make him understand. Let him have enough love for me to see that I didn't mean him harm.*

A sound behind the barn got Angela's attention. She watched as Bill Skywalker stalked away from the building, then pause to mutter something before continuing toward her. She didn't think he had spotted her yet. Just before she hailed him, she saw Jerry's mother come from the same direction as the foreman but instead of following him, she disappeared inside the barn.

"Hi, Bill," Angela called out when he would have walked past her without stopping.

The foreman paused and touched his hat. "Howdy, Angela. I see you have no stomach for branding?"

"I can't say I do. I keep imagining their pain every time I see that hot iron approach their skins."

Bill leaned against the tree and pushed his hands in his pocket. "It is necessary. Otherwise we'd lose our cattle to our neighbors." There was silence then the foreman blurted out. "Jerry is a good man."

Angela turned to look at him then she smiled. "I know."

"Then you and he...no, it's none of my business." When Angela kept staring at him with a smile, he added, "Hawk...well, Hawk thinks that you and he could have something good."

"I hope so, Bill. What about you and Maya?" Bill scowled at her. She grinned. "Well, you asked about me and Jerry. That gives me license to ask about you and his mother, right? I noticed things during lunch that suggested you might have a good thing there, too."

The foreman shook his head. "No, Maya is too pig-headed, too independent, and too arrogant. I'd hoped...well, that was wishful thinking."

"You know there are some things I've noticed about this family—Jerry and Cyrus included—they are all stubborn, arrogant and think their word is law."

They laughed comfortably together before Bill said, "And isn't that true. They all take after the old man. Hawk is fair but very vocal about lots of things."

"Sounds like you admire him," Angela said with a gentle smile.

"Oh, yes. He's very wise. I've never heard him predict something that didn't come true. Then he has the healing ways that he learned from his mother. It is not easy to live in both worlds and keep everything in balance. He has done it."

"You're needed in the corral, Bill." Jerry's mother interrupted them. Both Angela and Bill looked up with varied expressions. They had not seen her approach.

"Are you talking to me, Ma'am?" Bill asked her politely.

Angela looked from one to the other. Their eyes were on each other. Maya's expression was angry and condemning. Bill's eyes were blazing with love mixed with frustration.

"Yes. A calf is down and they need to know what to do. I'm sure Ms. McGee can survive without your company for a few minutes."

Bill took a step toward the woman, paused and passed a palm on his nape before turning away. "It was nice to visit with you, Angela." He touched the brim of his hat and walked away.

Angela stared after him, feeling sorry him. It must be hard living with a woman you wanted and yet couldn't have. She turned to look at Jerry's mother but her eyes were on the foreman's retreating back. The look in Maya's eyes indicated that Bill's feelings were returned. What was keeping them apart?

"Isn't one man enough for you? Or do you collect men like trophies?"

The attack was so unexpected that Angela blinked in confusion. "I beg your pardon. I'm not sure I understand what you're implying." Why was Jerry's mother attacking her? Why was she doing it here, in front of her family? "Excuse me," Angela tried to diffuse the situation by walking away.

Maya grabbed her arm. "Don't you walk away from me when I'm talking to you!"

Angela turned to look at her in shock. She could put up with a rude tone but to physically grab her like that was inexcusable. "Get your hands off me, Mrs. Taylor." When the woman let her arm go, she added, "Don't do this, okay? It is totally unnecessary."

"You think so? Jerry is a few feet away and you're making a play at another man."

Angela looked toward the house where the older couple was still resting, then the corral where the men were busy working before staring at the woman blocking her path. "I wasn't making a play at Bill, Mrs. Taylor. We were just conversing, like two normal adults."

"Don't try that wide-eyed, innocent look on me. Bill may be many things, but he can see through you like that,"—she clicked her fingers for emphasis.

Angela lost it then. "Maybe if you'd get off your high horse for a minute and stop bossing him around, you'd see him as he sees you—someone who needs to be loved."

Jerry's mother sputtered in disbelief. "How dare you! I'm not like you, pretending to be something I'm not!"

Fear clutched Angela's chest. What did the woman mean? Did she know that she was Sav's sister? "At least I'd know when to give a man a chance. Men like Bill need to be needed. They don't want a woman ordering them around like they were her minions. You need to stop seeing him as an employee of your father's or yours, for that matter, and start seeing him as the man that he is—a strong, black man who happens to be crazy about you."

There was silence and Angela wondered if she'd gone too far. Jerry's mother was staring toward the corral with a haunted look in her eyes. Didn't the woman know that their foreman was crazy about her?

"Are you . . .? Oh, you think you're so clever, don't you? You think you know the answers to everything. Well, we'll just have to see about that, won't we? As soon as my son is done investigating you, we'll know exactly what you want from Jerry."

Angela tensed. "Investigating me? Who is investigating me?"

"Tahj. I asked him to do it as soon as he came back from Central America. Did you think I didn't know what you were up to from the first day I talked to you? How dare you come to my son's ranch on the pretense of being his assistant and then seduce him? Was that your intention all along? I know women like you, pretending to be what they are not just to get a man."

As she talked, Angela could only stare at her in amazement and anger. She wasn't listening to her words anymore. Her mind was going in circles. What if Jerry got to know who she was from his brother or mother? Oh, my God! He would feel betrayed. Where was Jerry? She turned and bumped into a solid body. She looked up and encountered his blazing eyes. *Oh, Lord, he knows*!

Jerry put his arm around Angela's shoulder and turned to his mother. "Mother, this has to stop. I'm tired of the way you keep treating Angela. You grilled her in my house and I tolerated it to be polite. But to do this here in front of grandpa, grandma, and the workers? What's wrong with you?"

Angela looked up and saw that they had attracted everyone's interest. Even Jerry's grandparents were standing on the patio, looking their way with worried expressions. Just how much had they heard? "Jerry, please, there is no need to do this." Angela begged.

"Yes, there is. I should have taken care of this from the very first day." He turned to his mother. "Why do you keep treating me like an imbecile? I can make my own decisions, good or bad. I'm the one who has to live with them. I can also choose who to date or to love. I happen to care very deeply about Angela, but I'm very disappointed at the way you keep insulting her."

Jerry's mother shook her head. "Baby, I wasn't trying to imply that you couldn't make your own decisions. We just don't know anything about her? We don't know who her people are. How do we even know if..."

"Enough, mother. What Angela and I do is our business. It is up to me to find out or know everything about her."

"I'm just trying to protect you, baby." His mother added. When she tried to touch his arm, he moved it.

"I can protect myself. I know things weren't perfect between Carmen and me but you can't keep acting like every woman is deceitful and sneaky or out to use me. Angela is nothing like Carmen. When you are ready to meet us halfway, call me. But right now, I'm so angry over the way you've behaved that I think it is best that you don't visit us for awhile."

"Jerry, please," Angela tried to stop him. She refused to be the cause of the quarrel between him and his mother.

His mother pointed at her. "You see, she's already causing problems between us. I just don't want you to be hurt again, Jerry."

"Getting hurt is part of life, mother. If I get hurt then at least I'll know it was of my own choosing. I've made my decision. Goodbye, mother. Let's go home, Angela."

Angela felt terrible. What could she do? She looked at Jerry and sighed. His eyes were hard and determined. His mother seemed ready to cry. "Jerry, don't leave her like this."

"Let her deal with it. She was wrong and she knows it. Let's go."

Angela glanced back once and saw Bill approach Jerry's mother. At least she had Bill to turn to now. She and Jerry finished saying their goodbyes to his grandparents and were driving away when she saw Bill and Jerry's mother ride away from the homestead, too. Angela didn't feel like talking to Jerry. Instead, she stared at the passing scenery with unseeing eyes.

It was her fault. If she hadn't come into their lives, everything would be okay. She glanced at Jerry's set expression and guilt overwhelmed her. His mother might have her suspicions, but Angela knew they were justified. *Was finding the truth about her sister's death worth all this?*

Jerry reached for her hand. He was so incensed by his mother's attitude he wanted to rant and rave. Angela didn't deserve the treatment Maya had dished out today. How could she be so mean and petty? Angela meant a lot to him and his mother had better get used to it. "I feel terrible about all this, Angela."

"I'm sure she didn't mean half the things she said." Angela whispered.

"My mother? Huh! She can be as stubborn as a mule, but so can I."

She lifted his hand and pressed it against her cheek. She kissed his knuckles. "She loves you and wants to protect you. I would do the same for a child of mine."

"Well, you're more understanding than I am. There is protecting children and there is interfering in their lives. What mom does is interfere. We're almost home."

Angela smiled and nodded. Eagle's Hill was like a home to her and her heart lifted as the gate came into view. "Call her when you feel a little better, Jerry. Don't let this fester."

He parked the car in front of the house and leaned forward to kiss her. "You've got a soft heart, love." He kissed her lips.

She caressed his cheek and smiled. But the smile disappeared from her lips at the thought of her impending confession. "Can you come with me upstairs, baby? I have something I'd like to share with you."

"Sounds serious," Jerry said as he left the driver's side of the truck to open her door.

Angela nodded. "It is important to me."

They walked in the house, their hands linked together. The first person Angela saw was Tatiana Sloan. What was the actress doing here? She wondered just as a man moved from the opposite side of the foyer where he had been studying Sav's paintings. When Angela saw his face, something clutched at her stomach. Except for the long hair, he could pass for Jerry's twin.

"Tahj?" Jerry asked then laughed. He let go of Angela's hand as he said, "Damn! Every time I see you, you look more and more like a savage." Then he enveloped his younger brother in a big hug.

"And you look more like a farmer. It's good to see you, J.T. I see you're putting on weight!" Tahj teased as he hugged him again. "Must come from seeing again and wanting to eat everything you see."

Jerry looked at his brother's long hair. "Don't let me start on that hair. You look like a caveman."

"Don't be jealous. Women love to run their fingers through it, bro." Jerry threw a punch in his mid-section. Tahj ducked. They hugged, again.

"It's good to see you. When did you get back? Are you going to stay at home this time and quit worrying mom?" Jerry asked teasingly as he led his brother toward Angela.

"I leave that to you, bro." Tahj stopped and beckoned Tatiana forward. "Tatiana told me she was visiting you last week but still had a couple of days on her vacation so, I brought her along."

"That's fine with me." Jerry nodded at the actress. "How are you doing, Tatiana?" He waited for the actress to acknowledge his greeting before turning to his brother. "Tahj, I want you to meet someone, Angela McGee. Angela, this is my globe trotting brother, Tahj."

Angela's heart fell. From the look in Tahj's eyes, he already knew about her. What was she going to do? Oh, why had she waited until now to tell Jerry everything?

Chapter 22

Angela squared her shoulders, pasted a smile on her lips, and extended her hand. "Nice to meet you, Tahj," she said with a weak smile while her eyes begged him not to say anything.

"I believe that you and I almost met once, Angela. I was taking care of some business for Jerry in San Francisco." When Jerry looked at him inquiringly, he pointed at the painting he had been staring at. "It was at the gallery."

"There must be a mistake. I wasn't there when that work was exhibited." Angela said then turned to Jerry. "We need to talk, Jerry, now."

"But it wasn't that day, Angela. I believe it was the day you agreed to have your sister's paintings exhibited there. In fact, we passed each other at the entrance. I didn't know who you were but the secretary told me you were Savannah's sister."

Angela glared at Tahj briefly before she turned toward Jerry who had a bewildered expression on his face. "Jerry, I need to talk to you, please."

He nodded and put his arms around her shoulders. Smiling, he turned to his brother. "I didn't know you knew Angela's sister, Tahj. It's a small world, isn't it? Anyway, why don't you entertain Tatiana for a few minutes? We'll join you shortly."

Angela turned to glance at Tahj. He had an uncertain smile on his face. *Please, don't blurt this out, her eyes begged him. Don't hurt him just to expose me.* But she didn't take into account family loyalty.

Tahj blocked their path. "Jerry, I didn't know Angela's sister. I came to know her after she passed away, when you bribed that gallery in San Francisco to show her work." When Jerry raised his eyebrow in confusion, Tahj added. "Savannah Maitland, Angela's sister, was Hannah Vas. She often used her first name spelled backward as a pseudonym. Didn't Angela tell you that?"

Jerry stared blankly at his brother. Then the words started sinking in. Angela was Hannah's sister? How was that possible? Angela couldn't be Hannah Vas's sister. Angela's sister died awhile back. Besides, Angela would have told him if she were Hannah's sister.

Jerry looked at her and saw the stricken look in her eyes. Could Tahj be telling the truth? He felt his chest tighten and his stomach clench in rejection. His hand tightened briefly on Angela's shoulder. No, it couldn't be true, he thought as his eyes stayed riveted on her face. And yet there was guilt written all over it. Had she lied to him? Why?

Angela wished she could deck Tahj for blurting out that information. "Jerry..."

"I even met some of your friends at a club in San Diego— Shelby's I believe it is called. They said you'd sworn to get back at Jerry, the man you believed was responsible for your sister's death. But things worked perfectly for you when your high school friend, Janine Forster—who works for Uncle C and Aaron—told you about Jerry needing an assistant."

Angela stopped listening to Tahj and turned to look at Jerry. *Forgive me, baby.* She begged silently. He was looking at her with probing eyes that shone with feelings that went beyond disbelief. There was anger and disappointment. Then as if he didn't want her to know his feelings, he smiled.

He turned to his brother and grimaced. "Tahj, I knew about Angela's sister. It's just been awhile since we discussed her. Anyway, why don't we move to the living room? I have a bottle of my best Dom Perignon that I've been saving just for you,"—His brother stared at him with concern but Jerry ignored the look—"Champagne, Tatiana?" The actress nodded. "Angela, why don't you help me with the drinks?" His fingers dug deep into her shoulder and propelled her away from the foyer.

As soon as Tahj and Tatiana were out of sight, Angela started, "Jerry? I was going..."

"Don't!" He ground out then removed his arm from her shoulder as if repulsed by her nearness. He walked ahead of her.

How could she keep such a thing from him? What had she hoped to gain? She must have read the articles in the papers and believed them. He looked back on her past behavior and everything made sense. When she had been snooping around his house, she must have been looking for evidence. When she tried to encourage him to talk about Carmen, was it out of concern for him or for her own agenda? Everything she did during the three and a half weeks she had stayed in his ranch was now suspect. Her attitude when she'd first arrived, insisting on staying in his house despite his protest, even spending time with him and working along side him all had new meaning. She must have been waiting for him to say something she could use. That had to be it. She knew he was innocent when her sister's paintings were delivered and he opened up and talked about his past. She didn't mention then that she was Hannah's sister. What about when he asked her about her sister, when they were talking about her nephew? She had the opportunity to tell him then. She never did. She must have suspected him still.

They reached the basement. Jerry waited for her to pass then closed the door and leaned on it. He turned to look at her with loathing. Had she slept with him and pretended she loved him just to hurt him? What did that say about her? Was everything he thought he knew about her a lie?

"I'm sorry, Jerry. I was going to tell you everything tonight but Tahj's arrival..."

He shook his head and stopped her explanation with a look. "You had your chance, Angela. Anything else you have to say now is just an excuse."

She looked beseechingly at his rigid form. "At least hear me out, Jerry."

"No! I'm tired of being manipulated by women—by you. I want you off my property first thing tomorrow morning, Angela. If

253

there was still daylight left, I would have insisted you leave immediately. Unfortunately, I have discovered who you really are and your real intentions a little too late for that." He paused and looked away from her. Looking at her made the pain in his chest more intense. How could she betray him? He loved her. He had wanted to spend the rest of his life with her. "Isn't it amazing what people can do in the name of revenge? You wanted to pay me back for your sister's death and you just did."

Angela's heart broke with each word from his mouth. His tone was flat and yet she felt his pain. It was there in every word, every glance, and his rigid body. His eyes were empty. It was almost like he hadn't told her that he loved her this morning, like he hadn't defended her against his mother, or loved her like he couldn't get enough of her. "Don't you want to hear my explanation, Jerry? I am not the same person I was when I first came here."

He interrupted her, calmly and indifferently. "There is nothing you have to say that I would be interested in, Angela. You had many chances to tell me the truth but you didn't." He opened the door leading to the wine room.

"My nephew has been in a coma since the accident, Jerry. Watching him everyday and seeing how unreachable he is, made it hard for me to let go. I had to know." Angela whispered

Jerry stiffened then slowly turned toward her. "What are you trying to say, Angela? What has your nephew got to do with what we are discussing?"

"He was in the car with his parents the night of the accident."

His eyes narrowed dangerously. "That's a lie! No one told me anything about a child being in the car. What are trying to do to me? Haven't you gotten your revenge by making a fool out of me? How much do I have to suffer to satisfy you?"

"I don't want you to suffer for something you didn't do, Jerry. Reggie was really in the car with his parents and yes, he's been in a coma since. I'm not lying about this. How can I lie about it when I talk to the hospital every week and I tape songs and stories for him so he can hear my voice while I'm away?" Angela looked away from

Jerry's eyes, blazing with distrust. She sighed in resignation. She had lost him. "Ask your brother. With all the research he did on me, I'm sure he would tell you about Reggie."

Could she be lying again? How could he ever again believe anything she said after her lies? Then Jerry recalled that she was now her nephew's legal guardian. "What do you want from me, Angela? Are the medical bills overwhelming? Is it money you're after? How much will it take to make you happy, Angela?"

Angela's eyes narrowed in anger. "I don't want your money, Jerry. I never did. I just want a chance to explain why I needed to know that you weren't responsible for the suffering my family has been through. Wouldn't you do the same if someone hurt a member of your family? Wouldn't you want to know the truth?"

"I wouldn't stoop so low as to sleep with my enemy for the sake of revenge." He replied bitterly.

"I never slept with you for revenge. I knew way before Sav's pictures arrived that you weren't the monster the papers painted." Angela looked at her trembling hands and frowned. She clutched them tighter and put them behind her. "Perhaps one day you'll forgive my deception. When you do, remember this; I didn't sleep with you for revenge but because of my feelings for you. I love you." He turned to glare at her. The hatred that blazed in his eyes chilled her.

"Don't take me for a fool, Angela. There was never any love and we both know it. Anyway, it doesn't matter anymore. You're not the person I thought you were. The feelings I had were for someone I wanted you to be, not the real you. There is nothing lovable about a liar and a deceiver. Just like Carmen..."

"Don't, please!" Angela felt the pressure increase in her chest. Her eyes stung with tears. "Don't try to hurt me by comparing me with her, Jerry. You're not a cruel person by nature so don't try to be now."

Jerry laughed derisively. "Don't delude yourself about me. Everyone has a cruel streak." He took a step away from her then stopped. With his back to her, he added, "I'll have a ticket waiting for you at Delta Airlines' counter tomorrow morning. One of the ranch hands will drive you to Helena. Goodbye, Angela. I'll think up an excuse for your sudden departure." When he turned toward her, she was looking his way with a sad and pitying expression. Jerry stiffened.

What right did she have to pity him? As the door closed behind her, he roughly pulled a bottle from the racks and smothered a curse. Good riddance! He wasn't going to miss her or ever think about her again.

Angela was grateful that she didn't meet anyone as she walked up the stairs. An hour later, Sally stopped by her room to talk to her. The housekeeper explained that Jerry had told her and Winston that her nephew was ill and she had to go home. Winston was to drive her to the airport early the next morning. A ticket for an eight o'clock flight was waiting for her at the Delta counter in Helena, Sally explained. Angela nodded as the woman spoke. She didn't disagree with the explanation Jerry had given his people.

She spent the rest of the night staring at the ceiling. It was going on two o'clock in the morning when she heard movements in Jerry's room. She pressed her hand against the wall and wished she were there with him. *Goodbye, my love. I'm sorry for hurting you.*

***

Jerry had gotten drunk the night before. And yet, he heard Angela leave her room the next morning. He walked to the furthest bedroom, stood on the balcony as she was driven away. It hurt to know that she was leaving. But he also accepted that it was for the best. She and he were never meant to be.

Instead of going back to bed, Jerry went to the kitchen and made himself coffee. After drinking three cups, he went to the barn and took Thunder for a morning ride. He didn't realize he was following the car carrying Angela away until he reached the entrance to his property. He turned around and rode home.

For the next two days, he kept himself busy with work. Work kept the pain at bay. Work made him stop thinking or analyzing things. He pretended things were normal. He worked, ate, slept, and spent time with his brother. But his insides hurt. It felt like someone shot had him in the chest but left him alive. The pain was there, unrelenting, and throbbing. He functioned like an automaton, getting the horse and the trailers ready for his trip but he was filled with anger and self-loathing. Knowing that his mother had been right about Angela only added to his anger. Now he wished he had listened to her.

His brother's presence helped things. But Tahj was too intelligent to buy the explanation Jerry had given for Angela's sudden departure. Although he once tried to bring her name up, Jerry stopped his words with a look. After that, her name was never mentioned between them.

But that didn't mean Jerry wasn't reminded of her absence. His workers mentioned her whenever they talked about things she'd liked or disliked. Juanita stopped by to see her. He was even surprised when Libby also asked about her.

How was he to forget her when everyone and everything reminded him of her? When they went riding, he thought about her. When he worked in the barn he remembered something she had done there. When they ate, he missed hearing her laughter or her easy camaraderie with his men. The nights were worse. He had gotten used to sleeping with her, holding her in his arms, or having her there in the mornings when he woke up. There was only one solution—find another woman to replace her.

***

Angela didn't let anyone know she was back in town. For two days, she hid in her house and nursed her heart. She cleaned her house, did her laundry, and rearranged everything in her living room, kitchen, and bedroom. The only place she called was the hospital to check on Reggie. But the activity didn't stop the heartache, the pain, and the regrets. Jerry filled her every thought. What was he doing now? She knew he was taking three of his mares to mate with Zeus. Then on Sunday, he was to fly to California.

What if she wrote him a letter and explained everything?

Maybe, he might call her after reading it. They could even get together when he was in California and talk things over. Or he could always throw it away without reading it. Oh, it still didn't hurt to try.

When her own company became unbearable, Angela called Nikki. "Hey, girl, I'm back."

"Why didn't you let me know? I would have picked you up from the airport." Nikki said.

"I wanted to surprise everyone. Listen, I'm off to see Reggie now but could we do lunch today?"

"Sure. Pick me up at twelve thirty. I want to know everything, Angela. Did you meet someone? Your mom said she talked to some hunk when she called."

Angela closed her eyes as pain sliced through her. "Don't believe everything you hear, Nikki. I got to go, girl—see you at lunch."

First, Angela stopped by her nephew's hospital and spent an hour with him. She had a chance to talk with his doctor but he didn't tell her anything she hadn't heard before. Later, she stopped by her office and caught up with her correspondence. She had offers from five companies needing her services. Three of them were casinos in Vegas. She had created a site for a casino there earlier and word must have gotten around. The other two companies were in California— one in San Francisco and the other in San Jose.

She didn't feel the rush that usually accompanied receiving such letters. She called the Vegas people first and made arrangements for telephone conferences. The San Jose people wanted a quote and a meeting at her earliest convenience. She agreed to meet them that Friday. The San Francisco people also asked for a quote and then promised to get back with her.

Nikki was full of energy when Angela picked her up. They drove to their favorite Italian restaurant. They had barely sat down before Nikki started probing her mind. Angela didn't try to be evasive. She talked about the ranch, the people, and the surrounding area. Nikki was impressed when she mentioned meeting Tatiana Sloan.

She had hardly finished talking when Nikki asked, "Then what's wrong, Angela? You talk like you had fun and yet your eyes tell a different story. What else happened?

Angela tried to avoid discussing Jerry. The waitress brought their food and she used hers as an excuse not to discuss anything serious. But Nikki kept pushing. "Okay, nosey, I met someone I really liked. Things worked out for awhile but it just wasn't meant to be."

Nikki perked up. "What? He couldn't deal with a strong, black woman? Or was it fear of commitment?"

Angela smiled at Nikki's indignation. "We just saw things differently."

Nikki squinted and looked at her thoughtfully. "It's his loss. If he didn't appreciate your worth then he didn't deserve you." She continued on about men who had no appreciation for strong sisters or were scared of commitment.

Lunch was over too soon. Angela drove Nikki back to work but her mind was still on what Nikki had said about Jerry not appreciating her. Jerry had appreciated her. And he hadn't been scared of commitment, either. It was she who hadn't appreciated him and who hadn't been committed to him. If she had, she would have been honest with him much earlier, like when he'd received his paintings.

The paintings! What if she used the one she had as a peace offering? Surely Jerry would understand the significance? "Did you get my painting from Ray, Nikki?"

"Yep! And I enjoyed doing it, too. The party wasn't big—just he and his latest woman. But it was still nice to have him pull it from his living room wall. It is in the closet in your spare bedroom."

Angela smiled weakly and said, "Thanks, Nikki. I owe you one."

Her friend got out of the car and gave her shoulder a squeeze. "I'll collect, with interest. Want to do dinner tonight—my place, Chinese?"

Angela nodded. "Sure. See you later."

She went back to her apartment and picked up the painting. Remembering the name of the store that had framed Jerry's three paintings wasn't hard. But convincing them to do a rush framing job and having it delivered to Jerry's farm turned out to be a lot harder.

After she put a dent in her savings account and promised them more work—she had the paintings she had kept for Reggie from his mother's collections that needed framing—they agreed to accommodate her wishes. Luckily for her, they still had the same materials they had ordered for Jerry's paintings. She made sure they understood that the painting had to be in Eagle's Hill by Saturday. She wanted Jerry to find the painting waiting for him when he came back from delivering his mares.

For the next two days, Angela kept herself busy. Between the times she spent at the hospital with Reggie, she managed to send the letter to Jerry and call the framing store to make sure they had also finished with the painting and mailed it. Later, she drove to San Jose and had a successful talk with the company there. She came back with a contract.

Saturday evening, she waited and hoped Jerry would call. She refused to go dancing with Nikki for fear of missing his call. It never came.

On Sunday, she was surprised to hear that Reggie had had a visitor—Jerry Taylor. The staff on the entire floor talked of nothing else. As she visited with Reggie, Angela kept hoping Jerry would walk in the room. But he never did. And he never called, either.

Hoping work would make the pain bearable Angela flew to Las Vegas on Monday and spent two days there conducting business. Her cell phone never rang and her voice mail was empty when she checked it. On Wednesday, she flew back to San Diego and went through the motion of discussing the new accounts with Khalid. Finally, she stopped by the hospital and spent the afternoon by her nephew's side.

It was going on six when the thread holding Angela's emotions broke. She was trying to be cheerful as she told Reggie about the things she'd seen in Vegas when a sob escaped. "I'm sorry, baby. I wish you were here and not so far from me. It would make everything bearable. Why can't you"—sniffle—"wake up. I miss you. I'm miserable and heartbroken. And you know what? It is my fault." When it became too much for her, she gripped his hand, buried her head in his blanket, and sobbed.

She was beginning to calm down when she felt a slight pressure from Reggie's fingers. At first she thought it was her imagination. Then she felt it again. Frantically, her eyes searched his face. His eyes were still closed, his face serene. "Reggie? Baby, can you hear me? If you can hear me, squeeze my hand." The boy's fingers moved in an attempt to squeeze hers. "Oh, Reggie, oh, baby—nurse! Where is everyone?" She pressed the button for assistance. "I knew you'd come back. Can you hear me?" The boy's fingers moved again, just as a nurse walked into his room. "He moved...his fingers moved." When the nurse looked at her skeptically, she added, "Here, take his hand."

The woman held Reggie's hand and waited. "Okay, baby. It is Aunty Angela talking to you. If you can hear me, squeeze my hand." There was no motion. The nurse shook her head. "C'mon, baby. Squeeze my hand, I mean, the nurse's hand. Just give us a slight motion, any indication that you can hear me, Reggie." She touched his cheek as she spoke but her eyes were on his hand. She saw the slight movement. "Did you see that? Did you feel it? It moved. I saw it. You must have felt it."

"Angela, I felt it. I'll call the doctor."

After that, things moved fast. She laughed and cried as she talked to him. Someone called his grandparents and Angela's parents. Before long, everyone was waiting as the doctors worked with him. Reggie was coming back.

The next two days brought wonderful changes. He regained consciousness and Angela found herself spending a lot of time with him. He still had to go through physical therapy and counseling but he was on his way to getting better. He talked about hearing their voices and her music. By Sunday, he was starting to sound like the old Reggie.

Seeing her nephew's improved state made it easier for Angela to reach an important decision, too. She had to see Jerry. Before she could change her mind, she bought herself a ticket for Montana. After telling her family that she was off on a business trip, she flew to Helena.

She rented a car and set off for the farm. Along the way, she formulated a plan—what she would tell him, how she would go about doing it, and what she hoped to achieve. Without a doubt, she wanted him back. She wanted what they had, even if it meant begging him to listen to her side of the story.

Little Joe met her at the gate. She gave the boy a hug, her eyes brimming with tears. It was nice to be back and she prayed she wouldn't leave without getting what she wanted. As Little Joe filled her in on what had been happening since she left—which wasn't much—they walked toward the kitchen.

Sally was on the patio, peeling potatoes. The housekeeper let out a loud scream and rushed to give her a hug and scolded her for not calling them. "I was beginning to worry about you. Ms. Angela."

Angela laughed as she wiped tears from her eyes. "I knew I'd be seeing you soon, Sally. Where is..."

Sally interrupted. "He's in the den. He's missed you, child. He's been very...well, you'll see for yourself." Sally finished mysteriously as she ushered her into the house.

Angela walked toward the partially opened door with trepidation. Would Jerry be happy to see her? Why hadn't he replied to the letter she'd sent him? And how could he have kept quiet about the painting she'd sent him? It wasn't hung on the wall in the foyer but she knew he had received it. She had a delivery-confirmation from the framing company.

She pushed the door. There he was—his head was bent over a book, his frame so familiar and so beloved. She felt like reaching out and touching his hair, caressing his shoulder. Her hand shook as she pressed it against her side. She had lost the right to touch him two weeks ago, but she wanted it back.

"I'm very busy right now, Tatiana. Could we go riding later?" Jerry said without looking up.

Tatiana was here? Had Tatiana replaced her? Angela thought

with pain and anguish.

When there was no reply, Jerry looked up with frown. A wild surge of joy rushed though him when he saw her. She was back. His Angela was back. He searched her face. Lord, how he had missed her.

While he stared at her, she stared back. He had lost weight. He looked overworked and tired, too. And lord, how she had missed him. What was he thinking? His eyes didn't reveal much. She smiled tentatively and said, "Hello, Jerry."

"Hello, Angela." He answered in his deep voice and then leaned back in his chair. He continued to contemplate her. She looked good. Her smile was more radiant, and her skin glowed. Why should she look so good while he felt crappy? Obviously, she had not missed him. She hadn't gone through the same pain and torture that he had. But then why should she? "What are you doing here?"

His voice was so cold she shivered. "Why didn't you reply to my letter, Jerry?" She asked.

Jerry blinked. Her voice held traces of emotion that found an echo deep in him. He had buried them but not deep enough. She only had to look at him to bring them back. Slowly, he put his pen down and raised an eyebrow. "I don't know what you're talking about. I haven't received a letter from you, Angela."

She shifted her stance. "It has been over a week since I sent a letter explaining everything, Jerry. In fact, I sent it express mail. I know it was delivered here. What about the painting?"

"What painting?"

Anger stirred in her. "The Autumn Splendor—the last one in the series of Seasonal Rhapsody. I owned it, but I decided to give it to you." *To show you how sorry I am and how much I love you*, she thought when her voice failed. She waited until she'd regained control of her emotions before asking, "Did you not get it, too?"

"No, I didn't. Maybe it went to a wrong address." He shrugged. "I guess you made the trip for nothing, Angela. Will you be leaving now?"

Angela looked at his closed face and swallowed a sob. He was indifferent to her. He didn't care that she had come back or that she had sent him an expensive painting with a lot of sentimental value to her.

Did he hate her now? Did he want her to leave? No, she wasn't choosing the coward's way out by running back to San Diego. She came here to convince him of her love and she wasn't leaving until she did. "I need to find out what happened to my painting and letter."

Jerry got up and nodded. He didn't know if she was lying about the letter or the painting. Whatever her reasons were for coming back, he was elated that she was staying. However, there were other emotions running through him. Why did he really want her to stay? Was it for more punishment? To have her close and not touch her would be pure hell. No, he didn't need her anymore. He would show her that another woman could replace her and that he could live without her.

Smiling with satisfaction, Jerry walked past her. "You can use your old room. Excuse me. I have an appointment with a lady."

Angela turned to watch him walk away. It was too late for them. Jerry had obviously moved on. Tatiana's presence here was a clear proof of that. Well, Angela wasn't a person to give up without a fight. She would find the letter and make Jerry read it. If that didn't change his mind, she would force him to listen to her

Chapter 23

Angela thought being away from Jerry was painful. But to be this close to him and be completely ignored was downright heartbreaking. He was completely indifferent toward her and spent his time with Tatiana. She had watched them go into the barn and ride off together. Later, she had seen them ride back, laughing and talking like they were best friends.

According to Sally, Tatiana had taken a sudden interest in the farm. She worked alongside Jerry now, had learned every worker's name, and was even taking cooking lessons. That could only mean one thing, Tatiana was here to stay. And from the looks of things, Jerry was very happy to have her.

Angela walked down the stairs. Other than visiting a few minutes in the kitchen with Sally, she had spent the better part of the afternoon in her room. Sally had said that some packages had been delivered while Angela had been away but she couldn't confirm who received them. Since Jerry never made it home until after nightfall on Saturday and had left the next day for California, he couldn't have been around to sign for her painting. That left Tahj and Tatiana.

"You? What the hell are you doing here?"

Tahj's voice made Angela pause in the middle of the staircase. She looked at him and decided not to answer him. In the first place, she hated rudeness. Secondly, Tahj had done enough damage to her relationship with Jerry for her to care about being polite to him. She continued down the stairs.

"Haven't you done enough harm? Or did you think that your deceit would go unnoticed? Does Jerry know you are back?" Tahj blocked her path at the foot of the stairs.

One Day at a Time

Angela stared at the face that was so much like Jerry's and felt like slapping it. "Yes, he does. So?"

"So what sob story did you give him? You had amnesia and couldn't remember that Savannah Maitland was your sister? Damn, my brother is so trusting! I know you for what you are, lady. But I'm not like Jerry. I will not let you humiliate and hurt him. Do you understand?"

Angela just glared at him. She had nothing to tell this arrogant man. And she was happy Jerry was nothing like him. A smile touched her lips.

"You think this is a joke? You play with a man's feelings and you think it's amusing?" Tahj moved menacingly closer.

He was as tall as Jerry but the steps gave Angela the advantage. She looked down her nose at him. Her insides clenched with pain and regret at what she had done to Jerry, but Tahj had no business getting involved in their relationship. "You may find this hard to believe, Tahj Taylor, but I happen to love your brother very much."

He grabbed her arm. "You wouldn't know what love is if it came and bit you in the ass, you lying bitch!"

She tried to pull her arm free but he was stronger. "Let go of my arm!"

"Let her go, Tahj!" Jerry's voice interrupted them.

But he only tightened his grip. "Jerry, how can you allow her . . .?"

"I said get your hand off her, now!" Jerry was angry enough to deck his brother, if need be. *How dare he touch Angela!*

Tahj muttered something and stepped away. "You're a fool to let this bitch walk all over you, Jerry."

Jerry barely controlled himself. "Whatever problems Angela and I have are between us. And if I were you, I'd watch my language, brother."

Tahj held Jerry's eyes for a second, then turned and marched through the front door, banging it shut behind him. Jerry walked to Angela's side. "Did he hurt you?"

She looked at him with shimmering eyes. How she loved him.

He was gallant and wonderful. Despite being angry with her, he still wanted to protect her. Tears threatened to fall. "No, Jerry. I'm fine."

Despite her words, Jerry reached for her arm and checked the dents his brother had left. He rubbed them absentmindedly. Seeing the vulnerable look in her eyes made him wish he could take her in his arms and offer her comfort. Did she mean the words she told Tahj? Could he ever believe anything she said? She had hurt and disappointed him. That was hard to forget. He let go of her arm and stepped back. "If he bothers you again, let me know."

Angela nodded. Then she watched helplessly as he turned and walked away. What could she say to hold him back? As he disappeared into the kitchen, Angela sat down at the foot of the stairs. She wiped her eyes and stared dismally into space. Then a sound to her left got her attention. It was Tatiana.

Angela went on the offensive. "Where is my letter, Tatiana?"

"What letter?" The woman asked with indifference.

"You know what I'm talking about. I bet you were the one who received my package, too. What are you trying to do? You can't get a man through trickery, Tatiana."

"Shouldn't you be telling yourself that, Angela? Don't you see you are not wanted here? You've only been back half a day, and already you're causing problems between brothers. Are you so desperate that you'd humiliate yourself by crawling back in here after having been thrown out? Have you no shame or pride?"

She had neither shame nor pride when it came to Jerry but this smug woman had no business telling her that. "What is really bothering you, Tatiana? You know he still loves me otherwise he wouldn't have taken on his brother in my behalf. He may be angry with me now but he and I belong together."

The woman stepped closer and smiled. "We'll just have to see about that, won't we?"

Angela glared at her. "Where is my painting, Tatiana, and my letter?"

Tatiana moved back. "I have no idea what you're talking about, Angela. This imaginary letter and painting is just the latest ruse you're using to stay here. It won't work." She laughed derisively as she walked away.

Angela went back upstairs and started making calls. It wasn't hard to confirm who had signed for the painting. They said a woman had done it. Unless Jerry's mother had been visiting and received the painting, Tatiana was lying. The mailman who had delivered the letter was unavailable but the post office people promised to have him give her a call first thing the next day.

"Has Jerry's mother visited since I left?" Angela asked Sally at her first opportunity.

"The Sunday after you left. She didn't spend the night, just talked to Jerry and then went on her way."

That eliminated Jerry's mother. Tatiana was lying. Now she had only two days to find her painting and convince Jerry of her love. She was flying home on Thursday.

That night, Angela didn't think she could sit through dinner with Jerry, his brother and Tatiana. So, she ate in the kitchen with Sally and the ranch hands. Everyone wanted to know how her nephew was doing. Sly discussed Ellie's training and how great the mare was doing. Winston talked about Majesty—the foal that Angela had helped deliver. Big Joe filled her in on the other expecting mares and Mac made sure that he mentioned Philly's good health. Little Joe had hurt his toe and wanted her to check it. She told him not to worry about it because it was healing fine. Tears choked her at their show of concern and affection.

She was crossing the foyer on her way to her room when Jerry walked from the dining room. "Angela? Eh, why didn't you join us for dinner?"

She stared at his black slacks and maroon shirt. He had dressed for dinner and looked good. But his eyes were distant. "The men had a few things to share with me so, I decided to join them."

"I see. I would appreciate it if you'd join us for lunch and dinner tomorrow."

Angela stared at his hard face. One minute he showed her that he cared and the next he acted like she was just a passing acquaintance. Why couldn't he give them a chance? And how could she make him understand how sorry she was and how much she loved him when he was so aloof?

Just as she started toward him, Tatiana walked from the dining room and stood beside Jerry, her hand possessively on his arm. Angela's eyes followed Jerry's hand as it covered Tatiana's. When she looked up, he was staring at her with an unreadable expression.

Pain sliced through her when she saw how comfortable he and Tatiana were. Her chest constricted and her heart fell. She couldn't stay here and watch this.

"If I get my letter and my painting by tomorrow, I will not be around for lunch or dinner. Excuse me." Her voice broke. Without waiting for comment, she turned and went up the stairs. Had she looked back, she would have seen the ferocious frown on Jerry's face as he watched her walk away.

What was he doing? Jerry asked himself. Angela might be gone tomorrow. What if there was some truth to this letter and painting she kept talking about? But she had lied before. What if this was just another lie?

That night, sleep eluded Jerry. He raked his mind. Why had she sent him a painting? Was he making a mistake by keeping her at a distance? He loved her. Even though he was angry with her and disappointed at her behavior, he still loved her. But could he ever trust her again? What if she had other secrets? What guarantee did he have she would never lie to him again?

***

The next morning, Angela didn't make it downstairs until after ten. She had spent the morning making calls. At last she had her confirmation. Tatiana was the one who had received and signed for both her painting and her letter. The UPS offices in Butte promised to fax to her a copy of the signed form. That was all she needed to expose the actress for the liar that she was. But first things first! She and Miss Actress needed to have a little chat.

Angela needed to find out which room Tatiana was in. "Sally

269

would know," she thought and headed for her house when she saw Jerry's mother. Please, no. Not another person who hated her. She turned away.

"Angela?" Jerry's mother caught up with her on the patio.

Angela sighed and turned to face the woman. *What now?* "Good morning, Mrs. Taylor."

"Maya, please. No more Mrs. Taylor." The woman smiled as she came to stand at the foot of the patio steps. "I'm happy you came back. It gives me a chance to apologize for the way I treated you. Jerry was right. I had no business talking to you the way I did. He's an adult and can decide whom to be involved with. Now, can we start over?"

Angela's eyes widened. Obviously, Jerry had not told his mother about Sav and Reggie. "Maybe you had reasons to be suspicious, Mrs. Taylor."

"No, it is time I stopped meddling in my children's lives. Bill told me—which brings me to another thing. Thank you for opening my eyes about Bill. Both of us would like to thank you for pointing out what I was doing wrong. Because of you I now have a wonderful man in my life and I'm very happy." She turned to look toward the barn. "He will probably want to thank you in person as soon as he's done talking with Winston."

"Well, I'm happy for you." Angela murmured distantly. She hoped the woman would take the hint and leave her alone now.

"How is your nephew? I was told you had to go to him because he was very ill." She leaned against the patio rail and stared at Angela.

I can't need to deal with this now, Angela thought wearily. "Who told you that my nephew was ill?"

Jerry's mother smiled. "Jerry, of course. I had stopped by to visit with you, but he informed me that you had to leave because of your nephew's illness. How is he doing?"

Angela stared at this person who'd resented her from the first time they talked and who was now being so charming. She didn't know whether to cry or laugh. "My nephew recently came out of a coma. He had been in a coma since he lost his parents a year ago."

Maya frowned. "But I was made to understand that this was a sudden illness."

"That was your son being kind and generous, Mrs. Taylor. My nephew is the only son of my sister, Savannah Maitland. Does the name ring a bell?" When Maya just frowned at her, Angela continued. "Savannah was the painter who was killed along with her husband when Carmen drove her car into the highway. Yes, Mrs. Taylor, it was my sister whom Carmen killed and my nephew whom she put in a coma. I came here under false pretense, just as you'd suspected. I wanted to see if Jerry was the man the papers said he was—the monster who drove his wife to killing my only sister and her husband, and the man who was responsible for putting my five-year old nephew in a coma. I wanted to find out everything I could about him and if possible, bring him to justice."

Angela didn't know tears were running down her face. She glared at Maya and wished she would say something. When she continued to look at her without rancor, she added, "There! You were right to be suspicious of me. I did mean your son harm, Mrs. Taylor. I hated him before meeting him and wanted him to pay for my suffering." Angela looked away. Her hands were shaking. But most of all, she was emotionally drained. "I know it sounds absurd, but I was hurting and angry. I wanted someone to pay for my loss and my pain."

Then Jerry's mother did something unexpected. She reached for Angela's arm and pulled her down on the patio step. Gently, she squeezed her hand. "But what did you find when you arrived here? Was there a monster here—a guilty man?"

Angela shook her head. A tear dropped on Maya's hand. Angela realized then that she was crying. "No. I found Jerry and he is this...this hard-working, wonderful, and caring person. He has principles. People gravitate toward him and he helps them."

"And you found yourself falling in love," Jerry's mother whispered. When Angela just stared at her, she asked. "You love my son, don't you?"

One Day at a Time

Angela glanced away and nodded. What was the point of bringing that up? There was no hope for them. "I couldn't reconcile the man I'd read about and the one I was seeing. I had my doubts as soon as I met him, but as the days passed by, I knew I was seeing the real Jerry Taylor. By the time the paintings arrived, I had already made up my mind. I didn't need any more proof. I knew in my heart that he was innocent." Angela looked toward the barn and remembered what happened when Tahj arrived. "I was going to tell him everything the evening we came from your home. But Tahj arrived and everything changed."

"I'm terribly sorry I interfered. If I hadn't, Tahj wouldn't have known. I'm one of those people who could never shut up about things. Unfortunately, my son Tahj takes after me."

Angela grimaced. "I think I've talked enough, Mrs. Taylor. I have a few things to sort out before I leave tomorrow." She started to get up. Jerry's mother's hand gripped hers in understanding but Angela didn't want any sympathy. She needed to find her painting and letter so she could leave. She was tired of being ignored by Jerry. It hurt too much.

"I want to help. I want my son to be happy and I believe your going away won't achieve it. Tell me what's been happening here? What do you need to sort?" When Angela stared at her dubiously, the woman smiled. "I know. I was completely horrid to you. I always act and ask questions later—a deplorable trait, I must confess. You, on the other hand, are a very patient person." The woman leaned closer to her and whispered, "I admire your patience, my dear. Now, what can I do to help?"

***

Jerry arrived home from his morning ride to find his workers standing idly near the patio. "What is going on, Winston? Isn't there enough work to keep people busy around here?"

"I think you'd better go inside, Jerry." Winston told Jerry as soon as he slid down from his horse.

Jerry passed him the reigns. "What's going on?"

"I'm sorry, Jerry. But the people inside will give you a better explanation than I," his foreman answered and led his horse away.

Jerry ran to the house. Raised voices led him to the living room where Angela and Tatiana were facing each other. Angela was waving a piece of paper in front of Tatiana's face while the actress kept saying, "I don't know where that came from."

"What's going on here? Angela, Tatiana?" His mother and brother were also in the room, watching the drama and saying very little—a very surprising thing since the two of them usually talked a mile a minute.

"Why don't you tell him, Tatiana?"

Tatiana ran to Jerry's side and caught his arm. "She went through my things, Jerry. My room is a mess. Now she says I stole her letter. I've never seen that letter in my life."

Jerry removed Tatiana's hands from his arm and stepped away from her. He turned to Angela. "Is this the letter you said you'd sent me?"

"Yes." Angela spared him a brief glance but it warmed her heart that he wasn't paying much attention to what Tatiana was saying. "It was found in Tatiana's suitcase."

"She had no right to go through my things, Jerry. She probably planted it there because she was becoming desperate."

Jerry's mother interrupted the conversation with, "Sorry to disappoint you, Tatiana, but it was I who searched your room. You had no business hiding Angela's letter or opening it."

"And my painting Tatiana? How did it wind up in a closet in your room?"

Jerry turned to look at the painting Tahj was holding. He sucked in his breath. Slowly, he walked toward his brother. It was the missing painting in the Seasonal Rhapsody. He touched the frame. What had she said about it yesterday? Why hadn't he paid attention? "How did you get it, Angela?"

"It was the only painting of my sister's that I owned. She painted it first and gave it to me way before she did the other three."

My God! And she was willing to part with it? He turned to look at her. She had never looked more beautiful and more vulnerable as she did now. She was also angry. And her hand was still clutching the letter—the letter she had written to him. Before he could ask to see it, his mother spoke, again.

"Since you still insist on denying that you hid Angela's painting, how can you account for the fact that your signature is on the UPS delivery form, Tatiana?"

"What form? I didn't sign for anything." No one believed her denials. She looked at Jerry but his eyes were on Angela. Tahj looked amused by the turn of events but he wasn't coming to her aid either. She started moaning. "I'm not feeling well. I need to lie down."

Angela went to Jerry's mother, took the form from her and thrust it under the actress' chin. "Here is the copy of the form you signed. It was faxed a few minutes ago. And the mailman who delivered my letter said he gave the letter to you."

Tatiana looked at the form and moved away from it. "Jerry?"

"Why would you do this, Tatiana? How could you?" Jerry countered back. He couldn't believe she was this dubious.

Angela watched as the actress cringed and started weeping. Jerry was staring at her in shock. Oh, let him make up his mind who he wanted, Angela thought as she turned and left the room. She loved him too much to stay around while he decided. She had recovered the letter and the painting for him.

Jerry stared at Angela's retreating back. He started after her but his mother pressed a hand on his arm and stopped him. She pushed the thick letter in his hand. "Read it, son. You need to know what she wrote before talking to her."

Jerry frowned at his mother who turned to follow Angela. Then he looked at Tatiana briefly and finally turned to his brother. "Get her out of here."

For the next thirty minutes, Jerry read and reread Angela's letter. It was detailed and so revealing. She had explained her relationship with her sister and how she'd felt holding her in her arms when she died. Then she wrote of her nephew's coma. Jerry felt her pain in every word. He had to stop several times to compose himself. How had she kept going after meeting him? As he read how she felt when she read about him and Carmen, he understood just how much it must have cost her to keep quiet the first week she was in his home. But his heart warmed as he read about her feelings for him. How and when she fell in love with him, the list of reasons why she loved him, and how heartbroken she was when she left his ranch. Now he knew that giving him the painting wasn't her way of asking to be forgiven. It was a proof of her love.

A wide grin split Jerry's face. Angela really loved him. How could he have doubted her? With her nephew in a coma and his name linked to her sister's death, she wouldn't have let him touch her unless she had forgiven him. And right from the beginning, she had given him the benefit of the doubt.

His steps were lighter as he left the den. He was eager to see Angela and ask her to forgive him for being mean to her yesterday. He had been unnecessarily vindictive. But she wasn't in her room. In fact, her room was cleaned out. He started panicking as he ran downstairs. "Have you seen Angela?" He asked Tahj who was coming in from outside.

"She and mom left,"—he checked his watch—"twenty minutes ago."

"What? And you didn't think of stopping them?" Jerry asked his brother in disbelief.

"Hey, you told me to keep out of your business." Tahj replied.

Jerry glared at him, but couldn't deny that he was right. He went into the den and dialed his grandfather's ranch. His grandmother told him that his mother had called and yes, she was bringing Angela with her.

Jerry drove like a maniac to his grandfather's ranch. Unfortunately, he got a flat tire, and just after he replaced it and took off, the police pulled him over for speeding. When he arrived at the ranch, he was out of sorts. But the presence of Angela's rental car lifted his spirit. Then he saw her. She was on the patio with his grandparents and his mother. Bill's truck was parked beside Angela's car so the foreman must have left his ranch at the same time as Angela and his mother.

Jerry got out of his truck and viewed the people seated on the patio. No one was smiling except his grandfather. The old man was grinning like a cat that had eaten a whole bowl of cream. Oh, so, it was going to be like that. Jerry thought as he approached them.

He walked straight to Angela and extended his hand. "Come home with me, baby. We need to talk. I was a jerk two weeks ago and my behavior since you came back has been inexcusable. I love you and I want you to come with me."

"I told you we did a good job of raising the boy," his grandmother muttered to his mother. "Now what are your intentions, son?"

"Leave the boy alone," his grandfather interrupted, ushering the two older women into the house.

Jerry was too busy enjoying the soft, warm glow in Angela's eyes to pay attention to his grandparents. Extending his hand, he said, "C'mon, love."

Angela put her hand in his. He helped her up and pulled her in his arms. Looking at his family, he grinned triumphantly. "I'm not proposing to her in front of you bunch of old busybodies," he informed them as he and Angela started for car.

***

"No more secrets, okay?" Jerry made a pact with Angela several hours later. They had arrived home, ignored curious workers—including his nosey brother—and closeted themselves in the library. They had talked and talked for hours. Now Angela lay in his arms.

"No more secrets." She vowed.

"Sorry I proposed without a ring. But I promise to get you one as soon as I can."

Angela caressed his cheek and blocked his mouth with her finger. "I don't need a ring to know that you're committed to me. We're in this together. I love you so much, baby. I don't know what I would have done if you hadn't come after me."

"Hey, a man can only be a fool once." He kissed her palm and wrist.

She smiled dreamily. "Now, what do you think I should do about my business?"

Damn, he hadn't thought about that, Jerry thought. "If we spend half of the year here and the other half in San Diego, would that work for you?"

She laughed. "Very noble of you, sweetie, but that won't do. You are a horse breeder now and you can't do that in California. Besides, what would you be doing there those six months?"

"I don't want us to lead two separate lives, Angela. No way!" He said vehemently.

"Neither do I, but I have my lap top and my cell phone. I can work from the ranch. If I have to travel to San Diego, I'll try to be gone for only a few days. If that doesn't work, I'll get a partner."

"Don't do this because of me, love. You've worked hard to start this company and to develop a reputation. I don't want you to throw it away."

Jerry looked so sincere when he said it that Angela scooted up and gave him a brief kiss. "I won't. Can you travel with me to San Diego tomorrow? I need to talk to my parents."

"Tomorrow? Let's go on Friday." His hand moved lower as he spoke.

"Why? Is one of the mares ill?" Angela asked with concern.

He stood up, still cradling her close to his heart. "I need to make up for the two weeks you've been gone." He proceeded to kiss her thoroughly. When they came up for air, he added hoarsely, "Just one day is all I ask for and then you can keep me in San Diego as long as you want."

"Let's make it two days. Saturday sounds as good as Friday. Besides, my parents aren't going anywhere." She kissed his chin.

Jerry laughed. His Angela would always want to win their arguments and he would probably let her win some of them, especially when he totally agreed with her. He laughed again and then proceeded to demonstrate how they would spend the next two days.

The End

At Last

Lisa G. Riley

CHAPTER 1

Caroline Singleton slammed her car door, hurried across the parking garage and through the downtown Chicago early afternoon pedestrian traffic. Struggling to hold onto her large black portfolio as she juggled her purse, she sighed and tapped her foot as she waited impatiently for the light to turn green. If she were late for her job interview, she'd scream. She couldn't believe that she was cutting it so close, but as usual, it was all her fault. She'd had an idea for a painting when she'd awakened that morning, and hadn't been able to tear herself away from her easel until it was almost too late.

As it was, she barely had enough time to jump in the shower, change her clothes and push, prod, and force her thick hair into the heavy bun currently resting at the back of her neck. Surprising for May in Chicago, it was incredibly hot. With her lightweight white suit sticking to her, she didn't feel like she'd only gotten out of the shower less than an hour ago. The little miniskirt of the suit show-cased long, shapely brown legs resting atop slender ankles. Her 5'9" slender frame garnered looks to begin with, but to put that same frame atop three-inch heels and in a white suit that contrasted beautifully with her chocolate brown skin was akin to stopping traffic.

Caroline didn't notice the looks people gave her; she didn't care about them. She'd been told she was beautiful, but she knew that looks weren't important. As her mother had fondly told her practi-cally every day of her life: at the end of the day, if you didn't have brains to go with them, the most good looks could get you was a free cup of coffee, and possibly a stale doughnut. Having brains and using them were what guaranteed one success in life.

Her wide, smooth brow creased into a frown as her snapping brown eyes peeked at her watch. Eleven lousy minutes, the light was taking far too long. When the light finally changed, her long strides ate up the distance of the street and she rushed through the lobby of the 48-story building where her interview was being held. While she waited for the elevator that would take her to the 18th floor, she tried to get into the right mindset for the meeting by consciously relaxing her face, closing her eyes to better clear her mind of annoyance, and smiling. Her eyes popped open as the bell signaling the car's arrival gave a discreet "bing".

Smiling again, she moved to enter the car and was unceremoniously pushed back, causing her to lose her precarious hold on her portfolio and her purse.

"Excuse me." A deep voice rumbled while Caroline bent to pick up her things. "Allow me," the man said as he took her elbow to bring her to a standing position.

Caroline stood frowning in impatience and wondered why Murphy's Law seemed to be following her around that day. She looked down at the man's lavishly black hair as he bent to pick up her portfolio. "Oh damn, damn and double damn!" she said when she heard the elevator leave without her. Worrying and biting her bottom lip, she didn't look at the man as he stood. Absently thanking him when he handed her the case, she didn't take her eyes off of the panel of numbers above the elevator. When the number 15 was highlighted, she turned away.

ORDER FORM

Mail to: Genesis Press, Inc.
315 3rd Avenue North
Columbus, MS 39701

Name _____

Address _____

City/State _____ Zip _____

Telephone _____

Ship to (if different from above)

Name _____

Address _____

City/State _____ Zip _____

Telephone _____

Qty.	Author	Title	Price	Total

Use this order form, or call 1-888-INDIGO-1

Total for books	_____
Shipping and handling: $5 first two books, $1 each additional book	_____
Total S & H	_____
Total amount enclosed	_____

Mississippi residents add 7% sales tax